AN AMISH
HOMECOMING

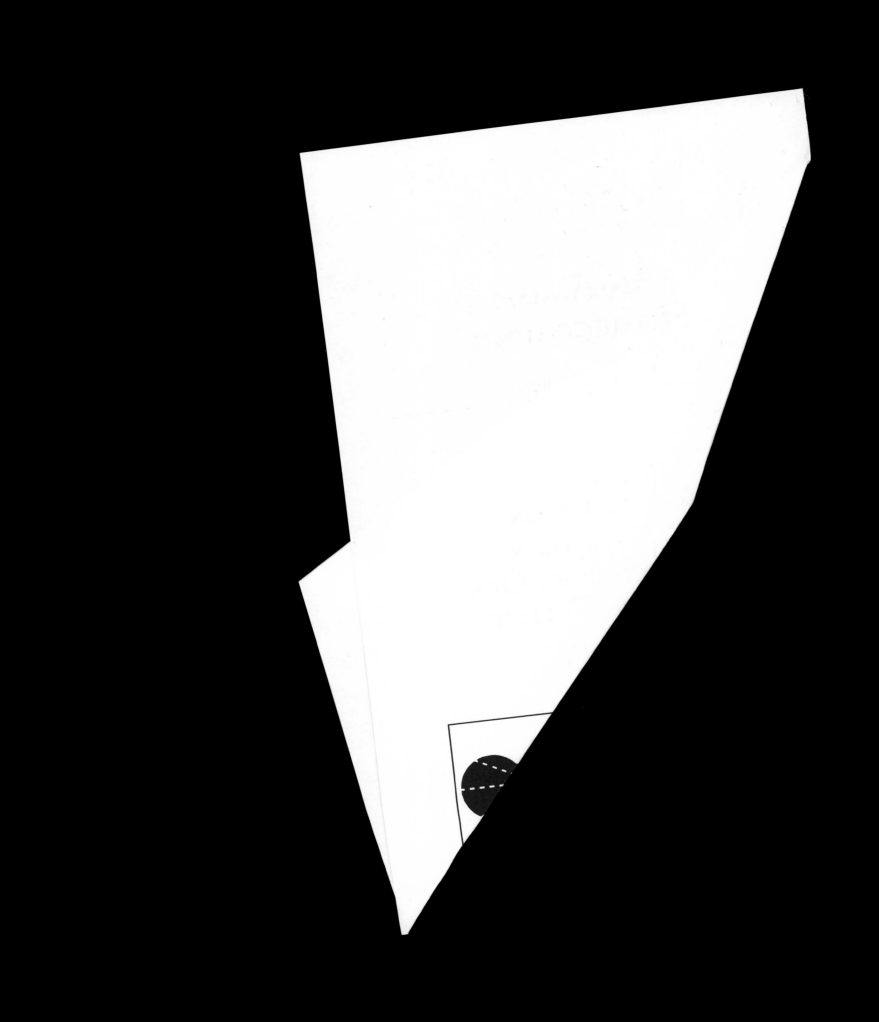

AN AMISH HOMECOMING

FOUR STORIES

AMY CLIPSTON
BETH WISEMAN
SHELLEY SHEPARD GRAY
KATHLEEN FULLER

THORNDIKE PRESS
A part of Gale, a Cengage Company

GALE
A Cengage Company

Farmington Hills, Mich • San Francisco • New York • Waterville, Maine
Meriden, Conn • Mason, Ohio • Chicago

LIBRARY OF CONGRESS CIP DATA ON FILE.
CATALOGUING IN PUBLICATION FOR THIS BOOK
IS AVAILABLE FROM THE LIBRARY OF CONGRESS

ISBN-13: 978-1-4328-6024-0 (hardcover)

Published in 2019 by arrangement with The Zondervan Corporation LLC, a subsidiary of HarperCollins Christian Publishing, Inc.

Printed in the United States of America
1 2 3 4 5 6 7 23 22 21 20 19

CONTENTS

GLOSSARY

ach (also *ack*): oh
aenti: aunt
appeditlich: delicious
bedauerlich: sad
boppli: baby
brot: bread
bruder, bruders: brother, brothers
bruderskinner: nieces and nephews
bu, buwe: boy, boys
Budget, The: a weekly newspaper serving Amish and Mennonite communities everywhere
daadi: grandfather
daadihaus (also *daadi haus, dawdi haus*): grandparents' house, usually a smaller dwelling on the same property
danki: thank you
daed (also *dat*): dad
Die Botschaft: a weekly correspondent newspaper that includes reports from scribes in many Amish settlements across

the nation
dochder: daughter
English, Englisher (also *Englisch, Englischer*): non-Amish
familye, familyes: family, families
fraa (also *frau*): wife
freind, freinden: friend, friends
froh: happy
gegisch: silly
geh: go
gern gschehne: you're welcome
Gott: God
grossmutter: grandmother
Gude mariye: Good morning
gut: good
Gut nacht (also *Gute nacht*): Good night
haus: house
Ich liebe dich: I love you
jah: yes
kaffi (also *kaffee*): coffee
kapp: prayer covering or cap
kichli, kichlin: cookie, cookies
kind, kinner: child, children
lieb: love
liewe: love, a term of endearment
maedel, maed: young woman or girl, young women or girls
mamm: mom
mammi: grandmother
mann: husband or man

mei: my
mudder: mother
naut: night
nee: no
nix: nothing
nohma: name
onkel: uncle
Ordnung: the written and unwritten rules of the Amish; the understood behavior by which the Amish are expected to live, passed down from generation to generation. Most Amish know the rules by heart.
Pennsylvania Deutsch: the language most commonly used by the Amish. Although widely known as Pennsylvania Dutch, the language is actually a form of German (Deutsch).
Plain: the Amish way of life
rumschpringe (also *rumspringa*): running-around period when a teenager turns sixteen years old
schee: pretty
schmaert: smart
schtupp: family room
schwester: sister
sohn: son
vatter: father
Was iss letz?: What's wrong?
wunderbaar: wonderful

ya: yes
yer, yerself: your, yourself

■ ■ ■ ■

No Place Like Home

AMY CLIPSTON

■ ■ ■ ■

For my amazing, handsome, super-cool
sons, Zac and Matt, with love

FEATURED AMISH
HOMESTEAD SERIES
CHARACTERS

Mary m. Harvey Bender
Eva Bender Dienner

Marilyn m.Willie Dienner
Simeon (deceased)
Kayla Dienner Riehl
Nathan

Eva m. Simeon (deceased) Dienner
Simeon Jr. ("Junior")

Miriam Faye m. Joel Stoltzfoos
Hannah

Kayla m. James ("Jamie") Riehl

15

CHAPTER 1

Eva Dienner sniffed as she stared at the letter in her trembling hands. Grief, hot and unexpected, poured from her eyes in the form of tears as she studied her mother's beautiful handwriting. She missed her parents as memories of them pricked her heart.

She glanced around the small apartment she once shared with her beloved husband. Six years ago, she left her parents in Western Pennsylvania to marry Simeon Dienner and live with him and his family here in Ronks, Lancaster County, Pennsylvania, nearly a five-hour bus ride away. Then Simeon died while on duty as a volunteer firefighter more than four years ago, leaving her and their unborn child behind. Heaviness settled in the center of her chest. Oh, how she missed him.

"Mamm?" Simeon Jr. entered the apartment from the main house where her in-

laws and brother-in-law lived. "Are you crying?"

"I'm fine." She shook her head and wiped her eyes.

"Don't cry." He crawled up on the sofa beside her and took her hand in his. At almost four years old, he resembled his handsome father with his shock of blond hair and cornflower-blue eyes. "I'm here."

"Danki." She smiled down at him. He also had his father's kind heart.

"Why are you *bedauerlich*?"

"I was just thinking about *mei mamm* and *dat.*" She held up the letter, the first she'd received from her mother in nearly four months. "*Mei mamm* wrote a letter and told me my best *freind,* Miriam Faye, stopped by the other day and asked about me." She sniffed again as memories of her old friends tumbled through her mind.

"Your *mamm*?" He tilted his head.

"Right. She's your other *mammi.*"

He pointed toward the door leading to her mother-in-law's kitchen. "I have another *mammi*?"

"Ya." Eva cleared her throat. "You have another *mammi* and *daadi* who live in New Wilmington, where I grew up."

"Can we go there so I can meet them?" His eyes sparkled.

18

Stunned by the question, she swallowed.

"Please?" he begged.

"I-I don't know." Her heart raced at the thought of seeing her parents again. Would they even *want* to see her? Her mother's letters always seemed so . . . reserved.

He folded his hands as if praying. "Plee-ease?"

How could she say no?

"Let me write *mei mamm* and ask her."

"I'm going to tell *Mammi* and *Daadi* we're going on a trip!" As Junior jumped off the sofa and ran to the door, Eva wondered if her parents would be as excited to meet him.

A barrage of new memories nearly overcame Eva as she prepared to get off the bus two weeks later. She wiped at the wetness forming under her eyes and worked to control her emotions. Before she left six years ago, she'd had a terrible argument with her mother. Was coming back now a mistake, even though her mother had readily agreed to this visit? Could she and her mother ever recover from the rift between them?

Apprehension chewed on her stomach as she swung her purse over one shoulder and took Junior's hand in hers.

"*Mamm,* your hand is wet."

"Just go." She nodded toward the bus exit.

They climbed off the bus, and she retrieved their duffel bag from the luggage compartment. After hefting it onto her other shoulder, they made their way through the knot of people in the terminal.

A familiar face emerged.

"Ian. Hi." Eva's throat tightened as she looked up at Ian Miller — a man she'd known for half her life. She hadn't expected to see him, at least not here.

"It's nice to see you again." Ian's smile was warm as his brown eyes flickered to Junior. "You must be Simeon. I'm Ian. It's *wunderbaar* to meet you." He held out his hand for a shake.

"Hi." Junior grinned as he shook Ian's hand. "I'm Junior."

"Junior." Ian reached for the strap of the heavy duffel bag digging into Eva's shoulder. "Let me take that for you."

"Danki." Eva swiveled slightly, allowing Ian to take the bag as she searched the crowd behind him. "Are my parents outside?"

"No." Ian hefted the bag onto his broad shoulder and then pulled on the brim of the straw hat sitting atop his dark hair. "They should be home by the time we get there."

"I thought they'd meet us at the bus station." She felt her brow furrow as she met his gaze. "They've known we were arriving this afternoon for over a week."

"They had an appointment." He nodded toward the exit. "The van is waiting. We should get on the road." He started toward the door.

Anxiety twisted a tight knot in her stomach. "Wait." She grabbed his hand and pulled him back. She felt a fluttering in her chest at the touch of his warm skin against hers. She swallowed a gasp. Where had that come from . . . after all these years?

He raised his eyebrows. "Did you forget something?"

"No." She cleared her throat as her cheeks heated with embarrassment. "What kind of appointment did my parents have?"

"Your *dat* had a doctor's appointment that's been scheduled for a month."

Alarm filled Eva as she swallowed another gasp. "Is he okay?"

Ian nodded. "*Ya*. He's fine."

Eva studied his face. Was he telling her the truth? She took a trembling breath as various illnesses came to her mind. Did her father have cancer? Or maybe heart trouble? Why didn't she know he was ill? Her mother never mentioned it in her letters. Did *Mamm* assume she wouldn't care?

"*Mamm?*" Junior tugged on her hand. "*Was iss letz?*"

Eva swallowed her fears as she looked down into her son's blue eyes. She couldn't allow herself to get upset in front of Junior.

"Really. Your *dat* is fine." Ian's voice was warm. "It was just a follow-up appointment. Your *mamm* wanted to be sure he asked the right questions, so she went with him."

"Oh." Her shoulders loosened, but doubt continued to poke at her, as well as regret at the thought that her mother might think she wouldn't care about their health.

"Your parents felt terrible about not being here to pick you up," Ian continued, "but I insisted on taking care of it for them so they wouldn't miss that appointment. You know how hard it is to reschedule them."

"Are we going to see *Mammi* and *Daadi* now?" Excitement bubbled in Junior's voice.

Eva forced her lips into a smile. *"Ya."*

"I can't wait to meet them," Junior said as they started toward the exit. "It's been so long since you said we could come to their *haus.*"

Eva bit her lower lip to conceal her amusement. When she glanced at Ian beside her, his lips twitched.

"How old are you, Junior?" Ian held open the door. "Ten?"

"No, I'm almost four." Junior's smile widened as he started outside.

"Really?" Ian grinned at Eva, and she looked down at the worn cement floor to avoid his eyes. "I thought for certain you were ten."

"I'm not." Junior turned and puffed out his chest, reminding her of the peacocks they'd seen during a recent trip to a farm near their house.

"You could've fooled me."

"*Mei mammi* back in Ronks says I'm tall for my age," Junior continued as they made their way to the parking lot.

"Don't brag," Eva cautioned as the warm June afternoon sun kissed her cheeks. "Wait!" She grabbed his hand before he reached the edge of the sidewalk. "Don't step into the street."

Ian pointed. "The van is over there. Ted is waiting for us."

"Ted Jenkins?" she asked, and Ian nodded. "He's still driving for my parents?"

"That's right."

Eva smiled as she approached another man she'd known for many years. While Ted's dark hair had turned gray, his warm smile and brown eyes were the same. "How are you?" She shook his hand.

"Eva. It's so good to see you." He looked down at Junior. "You must be Simeon Jr. Your grandparents can't wait to meet you."

Now a knot of guilt formed in her belly as Junior's face lit up with a wide grin. "I can't wait to meet them too."

Maybe she'd been wrong not to make this trip earlier.

A door slammed, and Eva jumped. As she turned toward the back of the van where Ian had loaded her bag, he met her gaze. Unnerved, she turned her attention back to Junior and Ted. She wrenched open one of the rear doors, climbed into the van, and sat down on the other side of the car seat that drivers for the Amish carried for passengers Junior's size. Ian helped Junior hop into it, and Eva buckled him in.

"*Danki,*" she muttered before Ian closed the door, and then he settled in the front passenger seat.

"How have you been?" Ted glanced at her in the rearview mirror before steering the van out of the parking lot.

"Fine, thank you." Eva folded her hands in her lap. "How's your family?"

"They're great. I have five grandchildren now."

As Ted talked about his grandchildren, Eva glanced out the window from time to time. Familiar sights rushed by in a blur, and a fresh tangle of emotions washed over her all at once — guilt, regret, anxiety, and melancholy, but excitement too.

"Eva?"

"What?" She turned to face Ian, who eyed her with suspicion as he looked back at her from the front seat. "I'm sorry. I was lost in thought."

"I can see that." Ian's intelligent dark eyes seemed to assess her, causing her to shift in her seat. "Ted asked you how long you were going to stay."

"Oh. I haven't decided that yet."

Ian tilted his head to the side. "Don't your in-laws need your help at their restaurant?"

"No. I've been working at home doing quilting and sewing ever since Junior got too big to go to the restaurant with me. My in-laws hired a couple of young women from our community to wait tables."

"Oh," Ian said. An awkward silence wafted over the car for a few moments. Then Ian cleared his throat before turning back toward Ted. "Looks like it's going to be another dry weekend."

"Yeah, that's what I heard on the news this morning," Ted said, his eyes trained on the road ahead.

Eva settled into her seat as the men discussed the threat of an unusually hot summer in New Wilmington. After several minutes, she turned toward her son and was

25

greeted by the back of his blond head. He seemed mesmerized as he stared out his window.

Swallowing a shuddering breath, Eva silently asked God to help her parents love and cherish Junior despite their differences with her — the way grandparents should.

CHAPTER 2

"Thank you, Ted." Ian handed Ted a couple of bills after he brought the van to a stop in the Bender driveway. "Are you still available to take Harvey and Mary out to run a few errands next Thursday?"

"Yeah, of course. Just give me a call if something changes." Ted stuck the bills into his pocket.

Eva felt confused. Why was Ian paying Ted and setting up rides for her parents?

Ted caught Eva's gaze in the rearview mirror. "It was nice seeing you, Eva. I hope to see you and Junior again before you leave."

"Thank you. I hope so too." Eva gathered her purse and then nodded toward the door as she turned toward her son. "Carefully climb out," she said after unbuckling him.

"I'll help him out." Ian jumped out of the van and opened Junior's door. "Go ahead. I'll make sure the door doesn't hit you."

"*Danki.*" Junior slipped out of the van and

bounded up the rock drive.

Eva climbed out and walked to the front of the van, where she stopped short as if cemented in place. Her heart hammered as she looked up at the two-story brick home where she had been born and raised. Suddenly, the last conversation she had with her mother on the wraparound porch echoed through her mind.

"I don't understand why you have to go all the way to Ronks. Why can't Simeon come out here and work on your dat's *dairy farm?"*

"I've already told you. His parents own a restaurant. Plus he volunteers at the local fire station. It only makes sense that we would work for his parents and build a life there."

"But we need you here." Mamm's *eyes glimmered in the morning light as she pointed to the porch floor. "You're our only* kind. *Simeon has siblings. Why can't they help with the restaurant and he move here?"*

Eva pinched the bridge of her nose, where a migraine brewed. "We've been through this. He's the oldest sohn, *and his* dat *needs him at the restaurant. Besides, he likes working there, and I think I will too. He also enjoys volunteering at the fire station with his* freinden. *I need you to support me in this."*

Mamm *wiped away a tear. "I can't."*

And she didn't.

Eva couldn't take her mother's disappointed sighs, disapproving frowns, and manipulative weeping any longer. At the age of twenty-two, putting a traditional wedding in her parents' home aside, she fled to Ronks. It wasn't the first time she'd left to gain some breathing room away from her mother's stifling interference. She'd interfered before Eva met Simeon, and she was interfering still.

She did invite *Mamm* and *Dat* to her wedding, but they didn't attend, making their relationship even more strained. Then instead of expecting any support from them when Simeon died, Eva turned to her inlaws, who had fast become her surrogate parents.

Now Eva would face her parents for the first time in six years. How was she going to navigate this painful visit when they had become more like strangers than family to her?

But she owed this to her son, didn't she?

"Mamm?"

Junior's voice yanked Eva from her thoughts. She forced a pleasant expression onto her face as she looked at him.

"Are you coming?" Standing on the porch steps, Junior pointed to the front door.

"Was iss letz?" Ian's voice was low in her

ear, sending an unexpected shiver shimmying up her spine. He stood beside her with the duffel bag slung over his shoulder.

"Nothing." She stepped away from him and tried to ignore the way his voice had affected her.

His eyes seemed to watch her for a moment. Then he nodded toward the house. "They should be back by now. I asked my parents' driver to take them since Ted had already agreed to pick you up."

"Let's go, *Mamm*!" Junior yelled before rushing to wrench open the screen door and knock.

She took a deep breath to gather all her courage and then touched her prayer covering to make sure it was straight.

"You look fine."

Startled, Eva looked up at Ian. She hadn't realized he was still standing so close to her.

"They're excited to see you and Junior. It's all your parents have talked about since you wrote about coming." He gestured toward the house. "Go inside. You'll see what I mean."

Eva nodded as she walked beside Ian.

Junior knocked on the door again and then turned toward Eva and Ian. "Where are *Mammi* and *Daadi*?"

"I'm sure they're on their way," Ian responded.

Eva's hands trembled as she held on to the handrail and climbed the steps. When she reached the top, the door swung open. Her mother stepped outside, letting the screen door close behind her.

Junior approached her, his whole body shaking with what Eva knew was hope and excitement. "Are you *mei mammi?*"

Mamm gasped as she crouched in front of him. "*Ya,* I am." She opened her arms, and Junior walked into her hug. *Mamm* held him close, her hazel eyes glassy with unshed tears. "It's so nice to meet you, Junior." Her voice sounded thin and shaky.

Eva gripped the handrail as emotion clogged her throat.

When Junior stepped out of the hug, *Mamm* touched his cheek. "We're so *froh* you're here."

"Me too," Junior said. "I asked *mei mamm* to bring me here to meet you and *Daadi.* Where's *Daadi?*"

"He's inside, and he can't wait to meet you." She gestured toward the door. "You can go in and find him."

Junior rushed inside.

As the screen door clicked closed, *Mamm* turned her gaze to Eva. Despite her approaching her midfifties, the light-brown hair peeking out from under *Mamm*'s prayer covering showed no threads of gray, and her skin was still smooth and youthful. Tiny wrinkles around her eyes were the only hint that six years had passed.

"Eva," *Mamm* said, her voice still shaky. "It's *gut* to see you." *Mamm* reached for her, but Eva instinctively took a step back, away from her touch. Something that looked like hurt and disappointment flashed across her mother's face.

"Danki." Eva fought back threatening tears. "You look well." Her voice sounded as strained as her mother's. When had their relationship become so formal, so dysfunctional?

Then the answer rang loud and clear in Eva's head: *When* Mamm *refused to bless my marriage to Simeon Dienner because it meant my moving away.*

"Did you have a *gut* trip?" *Mamm* asked.

"*Ya,* we did."

"I made your favorite for supper, roast beef and potatoes. It's almost ready." *Mamm* pointed toward the door. "Let's go inside."

As Eva followed her mother into her childhood home, unexpected nostalgia rolled over her. The family room hadn't changed. The two brown sofas her parents purchased before she was born still sat in the middle of the room, surrounded by her father's favorite tan wing chair, the same two propane lamps, and the same matching oak end tables and coffee table.

"Eva, I'm sorry we didn't pick you up at the bus station, but I couldn't change my doctor's appointment."

She spun as her father crossed the room with Junior in tow. Although his honey-brown eyes and warm smile were the same, his dark-brown hair and beard were threaded with gray, and his handsome face was lined with wrinkles.

"Dat." She breathed the word as he pulled her into his arms. He smelled just as she remembered — a mixture of earth, soap, and hay. In an instant, she felt like a little girl again, and the tears she'd tried to hold at bay slipped from her eyes. Their relationship had been strained as well, but not like it was between her and *Mamm.*

"Why were you at the doctor's office?" Her voice sounded small, as if she truly were a little girl again.

"It was just a follow-up. My blood pressure had been too high, but the doctor prescribed medicine to bring it down. Everything is fine."

When she stepped out of his embrace, she wiped the tears from her cheeks with the back of her hand and cleared her throat. Out of the corner of one eye, she spotted Ian focusing his attention on her.

"I've met Junior." *Dat* smiled down at her. "He reminds me of you at that age — a real chatterbox."

"*Daadi* has chickens! He says they're in a coop, like the ones at *Aenti* Kayla's *haus.*" Junior made this announcement from the doorway leading to the kitchen. "Can I go see them?"

"After supper you can help with chores." *Mamm* turned to Eva, and her eyes widened. "If that's all right with you."

Eva nodded. "*Ya,* it's fine."

"I'm sure you want to get settled before we sit down to eat," *Mamm* said.

"Right." Eva looked toward the stairs that led to her former bedroom, the sewing room, a spare bedroom, and the second bathroom. "Is there a room for us upstairs?"

"*Ya,*" *Dat* said. "There's a room for each of you."

"*Danki.*" Eva walked over to Junior and held out her hand. "Let's go upstairs and get cleaned up."

"I'll carry your bag," Ian offered.

Junior held on to Eva's hand as they made their way up the steep steps she'd climbed at least twice a day until she moved away.

When she reached the landing, she gazed into her old bedroom and froze. Everything was exactly the way she left it. Her double bed was still against the middle of the nearest wall, and her dresser, bookshelf, and desk lined the far wall.

The trinkets she'd left on her dresser sat there as if patiently awaiting her return, including the heart-shaped wooden box and a framed photo of a beach sunset Ian had given her on her last birthday before she left for Ronks. Beside it was the ceramic tray she used to keep her bobby pins, sitting on top of the white lace doily her grandmother made her when she was a little girl.

The books she'd left behind also remained on her bookshelf, and the quilt her grandmother made for her when she was ten still adorned the bed. Why hadn't her mother redecorated her room?

"Would you like me to put your bag in here?" Ian's question pulled her from her confusion.

She forced a smile onto her lips. *"Ya. Danki."*

Ian went inside and set it on the floor.

She followed him to the stairs, where he turned toward her, his expression warming.

"I want to tell you I'm sorry for your loss."

Her heart twisted. *"Danki."*

"Gern gschehne." He nodded toward the stairs. "I'll let you get settled."

"Whose room is this?" Junior tugged on her arm as Ian's footsteps echoed down the stairwell.

"It's been mine since I was a *boppli.*" She turned toward the spare room her mother used when relatives occasionally came to visit. "I think *Mammi* made up this room for you."

Eva guided Junior inside and scanned the room with surprise. The double bed was made up with a beautiful log cabin–patterned quilt, hand-stitched in gorgeous shades of blue, gray, and white. Eva crossed the room and moved her hand over the quilt, marveling at the love and skill poured into it. Had *Mamm* made it to sell and then decided to keep it? Or had she made the quilt for Junior? Her eyes burned with more threatening tears as the thought settled into her battered soul.

"*Mamm!* Look!"

Junior's squeal caused Eva to turn toward a wooden shelf full of toys, and she tilted her head as she studied the variety of metal tractors, cars, and trains. That shelf had always been packed with her parents' favorite books.

"Wow!" Junior rushed over to the shelf

and picked up a tractor. "Look!" He put it back on the shelf and picked up two toy cars. "Do you think *Mammi* bought these for me?"

"I guess so."

He ran the cars on the floor while making motor noises.

As Eva watched him play, confusion plagued her once again. Her parents had stayed out of her life for the past six years, which meant they stayed out of their grandson's life too. Yet her mother had welcomed Junior with open arms and made up a room just for him. Perhaps they did accept him, just as she'd prayed they would.

But would that acceptance extend to their daughter?

CHAPTER 3

"Supper is ready!" *Mamm* called from downstairs as Eva finished putting Junior's clothes in the spare room dresser.

"May I take the tractor to the kitchen with me?" Junior sat down on the floor and began playing with the toy.

"You may take it with you, but you have to leave it in the *schtupp* while we eat." Eva closed the last drawer. "Let's go downstairs before supper gets cold."

"Okay." Junior rushed ahead toward the staircase.

"Slow down!" she called after him. "You could fall."

When she and Junior reached the kitchen, she found her father sitting at his usual spot at the head of the table. Ian was sitting to his right. She had assumed he would go home after dropping her off, but maybe her parents had asked him to stay for supper as a thank-you for arranging their rides.

Junior rushed over to the table and hopped up on the chair beside Ian. "I want to sit by you."

Ian grinned. *"Wunderbaar."*

Eva sidled up to her mother as she scraped mashed potatoes from a pot into a serving dish. "May I help you?"

Mamm paused for a fraction of a moment, as if surprised by the offer. "That would be great." She pointed to a bowl of salad. "Would you please take that to the table? The bottles of dressing are in the refrigerator."

Eva helped carry all the food to the table and then sat down across from Ian. Her mother sat down across from her father, and after a silent prayer, they all began filling their plates with salad, roast beef, mashed potatoes, and green beans.

After Eva ate a bite of roast beef, she looked at *Mamm*. "It's *appeditlich.*"

"I'm glad you like it." *Mamm* smiled, but the smile didn't quite reach her eyes.

"Did you have a nice trip?" *Dat* asked.

"*Ya,* it was *gut.* The hours went by quickly, but I'm sure Junior thinks it's been too long since we ate our lunch on the bus." Eva took a roll from the basket in the center of the table and then pushed the basket toward Junior. "Do you want *brot*?"

"Ya." Junior swiped a roll from the basket.

"Ian," Eva began, and his eyes snapped to hers. "Would you please cut it open and butter it for him?"

"Of course." Ian reached for the roll. "Let me help you with that, buddy."

As Ian sliced open the roll and buttered it, Eva watched him, truly taking him in for the first time since seeing him at the bus station. He was the same Ian she remembered from their childhood and early years as adults, but maturity had made his chiseled cheekbones, strong jaw, and long, thin nose somehow more defined.

Then it hit her that he was clean-shaven. He was thirty years old and still unmarried. Why hadn't he settled down and married one of the young women in the community?

"Eva?"

"Ya?" She spun toward her father.

"How is everyone doing since you lost Simeon?" *Dat's* expression was warm.

"Oh." She paused, caught off guard by the question. "We're all managing."

Mamm nodded, her expression solemn.

"But the restaurant keeps everyone busy." Eva finished cutting her slice of roast beef.

"What kind of food do they serve there?" *Mamm* asked.

"They have a variety, and then a daily

special."

Her parents and Ian asked questions about her life in Ronks throughout the meal and as they ate dessert — her mother's homemade cherry pie and coffee. Then Eva stood and began gathering plates and utensils, amazed they had all seemed so interested.

"Well, we'd better get started on the chores." *Dat* stood and turned to Junior. "Do you still want to help close up the chicken coop?"

"Ya." Junior looked up at Eva. "Is that okay, *Mamm*?"

"Of course it is." Eva carried the stack of dishes and utensils to the counter and turned on the faucet at the sink.

"Let's go." Ian pushed his chair back and stood. "It will be dark before we know it." Then he followed *Dat* and Junior through the mudroom and out the back door.

As Eva put dishwashing liquid in the filled sink, she thought it seemed strange that Ian not only had stayed for supper but was now helping her father with evening chores. He must still be helping them part-time. But even so, why would he be working in the evening? He never did before.

"Are you and Junior settled upstairs?"

Eva turned toward the counter as her

mother lifted the first dish Eva put in the drying rack. "*Ya, danki.* We'll be very comfortable." She washed another plate as questions from earlier swirled through her mind. "Did you set up the extra room just for Junior?"

Mamm nodded as she set the plate she'd just dried in a cabinet. "I did."

"Did you buy those toys for him?"

"*Ya.* I thought he might like to have a few to play with while he's here."

"A few?" Eva gave a little laugh. "I saw at least two dozen."

Mamm shrugged. "I spotted them at a yard sale and couldn't resist. I wanted to be ready for him in case you ever decided to bring him for a visit."

Eva spun toward her mother. "You mean you've had them for a while?"

"I picked up some of them last year and then found a few more about a month ago."

"Did you make that quilt?"

Mamm hesitated and then nodded. "I made it for Junior when he was born. I was going to mail it to you, but I decided to save it for a visit. I'm just grateful he can have it now." Her eyes sparkled. Were they wet with tears, just as they were when she and Junior first arrived?

Eva's jaw worked as her mother's words

marinated in her mind. *Mamm* had been preparing for this visit for a long time. Then why had she never invited them to come home? Why had she kept her distance other than writing a few skimpy letters every year?

Pushing the questions away, Eva turned back to the sink. She and her mother continued to wash and dry dishes in an amicable silence, and then *Mamm* wiped down the table as Eva swept the floor.

After draping her dishrag on one side of the sink, *Mamm* held up the kettle. "Would you like to have a cup of tea on the back porch like we used to?"

"*Ya,* that would be nice," Eva said as she finished sweeping the crumbs into the dustpan.

Mamm filled the kettle and set it on the propane stove before taking tea bags from a cabinet.

Eva decided to ask her most burning question as she set the dustpan and broom back in the pantry. "I assume Ian is still helping *Dat* part-time. But why is he helping with the evening chores?"

Mamm seemed to hesitate for a moment.

"Well, because he helps your *dat* run the farm full-time now. I know I never mentioned it in my letters, but Ian lives in the *daadihaus* too. I just thought —"

"What?" Eva pushed the pantry door closed and stared at her mother. "For how long?"

Mamm sighed and dropped the tea bags into two mugs. "I guess it's five years now. Ian's been a great support to us. He handles most of the heavy chores."

Eva was stunned, not only because her mother had withheld this information, but because an unwelcome thought came to her. Was Ian looking for a farm to take over? He was the second oldest of four boys, so he would never inherit and run his parents' farm. That privilege would go to his older brother. Yet when they were teenagers, Ian told her he dreamed of owning a farm of his own someday.

How dare he move in on her parents after she left! He wasn't their son, and this wasn't his farm! This farm was supposed to belong to her someday, and then she could pass it on to Junior if he wanted it.

"You recall how Ian used to help your *dat* part-time before you moved away," *Mamm* said. "They worked it out so he could be here full-time and permanently."

Guilt slammed into her as yet another thought came. Did she even deserve the farm? Had she not just left it, but abandoned it?

44

No, that wasn't the point. Ian's betrayal was the point.

The kettle began to whistle, and *Mamm* poured hot water into the mugs. After steeping the tea bags, she dropped them into the trash can and then handed Eva her mug.

"*Danki,*" Eva muttered as she followed *Mamm* out to the back porch.

Eva lowered herself into her favorite rocker and moved it back and forth as she stared out toward the line of barns. Her thoughts spun with resentment toward Ian as she sipped her tea. He'd been her friend. She'd trusted Ian, and she never imagined he'd worm his way into her parents' life this way. This farm had been passed down through three generations of the Bender men, and Ian had no right to it.

"It's a *schee* night. Not too hot yet, but the heat is coming soon." *Mamm* cradled her mug in her hands as she moved her own rocking chair back and forth. "In a couple of weeks, it will be the first day of summer."

"The year is passing quickly." Eva set her mug on the small table beside her and took in the horizon. The sun had begun to set over her father's pasture, painting the sky with vivid splashes of red, pink, yellow, orange, and purple. She'd forgotten just how beautiful her father's land was.

45

"Mamm! Mamm!" Junior called as he exited the fencing around the chicken coop and ran toward the back porch. *Dat* and Ian followed at a slower pace. "Guess what I got to do."

Her anger dissolved, and warmth filled her chest as her son bounded up the back steps. "What did you do, *mei liewe*?"

"*Daadi* and Ian let me help check on the horses and cows." He came to a stop in front of her and worked to catch his breath. "And I also closed up the chicken coop."

"That's *wunderbaar*," Eva said.

"I'm sure you were a great help to your *daadi* and Ian," *Mamm* chimed in.

"Oh *ya*." Eva looked at her mother. "He enjoys helping his *onkel* Nathan with chores back home too."

Something unreadable flickered in *Mamm*'s eyes as her smile faded. Was it jealousy toward the Dienner family because of their relationship with Junior?

Regret came calling again. She could have tried to reconcile with her parents before now, made a separation from Junior less a factor in her relationship with them. But she pushed the regret away.

Eva turned her attention back to Junior and pushed a sweaty strand of blond hair off his brow. "You need a bath."

"I'd love to give him a bath," *Mamm* offered. "If that's all right with you."

"Of course it's all right, and I'd love to take a shower while you do. But I do have to warn you. He likes to splash." Eva laughed as a memory filled her mind. "In fact, he soaked Simeon's *mamm* just last week."

"I don't mind." *Mamm* looked at Junior. "Would it be all right if I gave you a bath?"

Junior nodded, and *Mamm*'s smile returned, brightening her pretty face.

Dat climbed the porch steps. "We finished all our chores with Junior's help, right, Ian?" He pivoted toward Ian, who stood a few feet behind him.

"That's true." Ian smiled at Junior. "*Danki* for your help tonight." Then he turned toward her father. "I'm going to head on home. I'll see you in the morning, Harvey." He looked up at *Mamm*. "*Gut nacht,* Mary. *Danki* for supper. It was *appeditlich.*"

Mamm waved him off. "Don't be *gegisch.* You know you're always welcome."

Eva's back stiffened as she pressed her lips together. Not only was Ian using her parents for their farm, but he was also enjoying free meals.

Ian's eyes met hers. "I'll see you tomorrow, Eva. *Gut nacht.*"

Eva nodded at him.

As *Dat* made his way into the house, *Mamm* stood and took hold of Junior's hand. "Let's get you ready for your bath."

"Bye, Ian." Junior waved at him before walking into the house with *Mamm.*

"*Gut nacht,* buddy," Ian responded with a grin. He took one last look at Eva and then started down the path that led to the small *daadihaus* at the far end of the pasture.

Eva stood and picked up the empty mugs. Leaning forward on the porch railing, she watched as Ian's tall, muscular frame moved down the path. She silently vowed to ask him why he felt entitled to her parents' farm.

As Eva stepped inside, the sounds of giggles filled the house. She washed the mugs and then made her way to the downstairs bathroom. Junior was splashing and giggling as her mother sat on the lid of the commode and laughed. Eva leaned on the doorframe and crossed her arms over her black apron.

Mamm looked up at her and smiled. "He's having a *gut* time."

"Do you want any help?"

"No, no. We're fine here. You can take your shower."

Eva lingered in the doorway as *Mamm*

48

laughed at Junior's antics, her eyes sparkling with something that looked like love infused with joy. Eva tried to swallow the overwhelming guilt that returned and washed over her as she backed into the hall.

As she started toward the stairs, irritation replaced her guilt. If her mother loved Junior so much, why didn't she ask to come to Ronks to see him when he was born?

While she prepared for her shower, that question echoed through her mind. Then her thoughts moved to Ian's place on the farm and in her parents' life. He seemed to be like her parents' second child, the son they never had. Jealousy tightened her chest, and she tried to ignore the sinful emotion as her thoughts moved back to her mother's reaction to Junior's bathtub fun.

She found herself wondering if her parents could love Junior as much as Simeon's parents did. They seemed to have accepted him, yes. And they seemed to enjoy him. But would they be the grandparents Junior deserved in every way? Or in the end, would her mother's underlying resentment affect their relationship with her son?

CHAPTER 4

"I hear you all loud and clear." Ian snickered as the gaggle of chickens clucked and moved around him inside their fenced area. "I know you're hungry, which is why I'm filling your feeder." He crouched before lifting the lid off the metal feeder.

"Ian." Junior ran up to the fence and stuck his fingers through the mesh. Harvey walked up behind him.

"*Gude mariye.* It's about time you got out here to help me," Ian said, teasing.

"What are you doing?" Junior pointed to the feeder. "Can I help you?"

"I'm filling the chicken feeder, and *ya,* you can help me." Ian looked past him at Harvey. "Hi, Harvey."

"*Gude mariye.*" Harvey opened the gate, and he and Junior walked into the fenced area before Harvey closed it behind them. "You're up early."

Ian shrugged. "I was awake, so I thought

I'd get to work." He gestured for Junior to join him at the feeder. "Let me show you how to fill this. Grab that bucket of feed. Now, are you strong enough to lift it and pour it in?"

Ian helped Junior pour the feed into the feeder and then reattach the lid. Once the task was done, Junior rushed off to play with the chickens. Ian stood and followed Harvey out of the pen.

"I'm delighted Eva came back to us." Harvey closed the gate and then looked toward his grandson. "It's a dream come true to meet Junior. For years I've wondered if she'd ever allow us to see him." He turned toward Ian. "He reminds me of Eva at that age. He's so curious and so *schmaert.*"

"And he has her smile." The words slipped past Ian's lips without any warning, and he longed to take them back before Harvey read more into the compliment than he meant to convey.

"You're right. He does." Harvey looked back toward the pen, where Junior giggled as he followed the chickens around.

"How long are they going to stay, Harvey?"

"I'm not sure." His friend's smile faded, and Ian regretted the question. "I'm praying she'll decide to stay indefinitely, but it's difficult to tell what she's planning. Except when she answered our questions about her life in Ronks at supper last night, she's been quiet and standoffish since she arrived. Mary and I had hoped she'd sit in the *schtupp* and talk to us after she put Junior to bed last night, but she went to bed as soon as Junior did. Mary is afraid to ask her how long she'll stay because she's worried Eva will leave if we push too hard and upset her."

"I understand." Ian glanced toward the house, where he assumed Mary and Eva were doing chores.

For years, he'd listened to Harvey lament over the way he and Mary had handled Eva's decision to leave. They regretted not supporting her move to Ronks, and although he didn't know if they ever apologized, he did know they had prayed for the day Eva would forgive them and allow them back into her life. They'd missed her, and Ian had missed her as well. But he'd never imagined she'd come back as both a widow and a single parent.

Memories of Eva filled his mind as he turned back to the chicken pen. They'd known each other ever since he began working part-time on her father's farm at sixteen. She'd always been sweet and friendly to him, and she was a dutiful, respectful daughter. By the time she turned sixteen, she was easily the most beautiful young woman in both her church district and his. With her golden light-brown hair, bright hazel eyes, and sweet laugh, she attracted the attention of many of the young men in her youth group, and she'd dated a few of them.

She and Ian had become good friends, but when he finally asked her to date him, she turned him down. That hurt, but he forgave her. He couldn't blame her if she didn't have the same feelings for him he had for her.

He understood about the conflict between her and her parents when she decided to marry Simeon and move to Ronks, but what had happened to cause her to completely turn her back on her parents?

Ian swallowed a groan as the answer rang through his mind. When Simeon died, she experienced a depth of grief he couldn't begin to fathom. That had changed her.

Junior laughed as he chased another chicken, and Ian smiled. His thoughts turned to Simeon. He'd heard the story of how Simeon died while on duty as a volunteer fireman. Now Junior had to grow up without a father. Did Junior miss his father?

Was it possible to miss someone you never met?

Ian swiveled toward Harvey, who smiled as he continued to watch his grandson play. Ian could feel the love and excitement radiating off Mary and Harvey in waves when they saw Eva and met Junior yesterday. If Eva chose to keep Junior away from them again, it would break their hearts. Harvey and Mary had become like his second set of parents ever since they asked him to move onto the farm and work there fulltime. They'd welcomed him as if he were their son, and he would do anything for them — even help them keep their precious family intact.

Then an idea occurred to him. If he helped to make Eva and Junior feel at home, perhaps Eva would decide to stay, or at least visit often.

Ian turned toward the house again, and his eyes focused on a grassy area near Mary's garden. "Harvey, would it be all right if I put up a swing for Junior?"

"*Ya.* That would be fantastic."

"I could put it there." He pointed to the area he'd already chosen. "I'll attach it to one of the branches on that big oak tree."

"That's perfect."

"Great," Ian said as a plan formed in his

mind. He'd first put up a simple swing, and then if Eva agreed to stay, he would build Junior the perfect swing set.

Eva stepped onto the porch at lunchtime and glanced around the property in search of her father and Junior. When she didn't see them, she headed down the porch steps and toward the largest barn. Voices rang out, alerting her they were inside.

"Hello?" As she stepped into the barn, her shoes crunched on the dry hay, and the aroma of animals filled her senses. "Junior?"

"I'm back here, *Mamm.*" Junior waved as he stood outside a horse stall. "I'm helping Ian muck!" Grinning, he balanced a pitchfork taller than he was.

Alarm shot through her as she rushed to the stall and pointed a finger at Ian. "What are you doing?"

"What?" Ian turned toward her, his dark eyebrows careening toward his hairline. *"Was iss letz?"*

"Why are you allowing him to muck the stalls?" She gestured to Junior. "He's not even four yet. He could get hurt."

Ian leaned the pitchfork against the stall wall and then swiped the back of one hand over his forehead. "I suppose you're right, but he was eager to help. I figured I'd let him give it a try."

"I'm big enough." Junior stood on his tiptoes. "See?"

Eva bit back a smile. "You are big, but I don't want you to get hurt."

"I won't." Junior pointed to Ian. "Ian said I'm a *gut* helper."

"*Ya,* you are." Ian took the pitchfork from him. "But your *mamm* is right. We should be careful."

"Eva." *Dat* stepped into the barn. "Is it lunchtime? My stomach is growling."

"Mine is too." Junior touched his abdomen, and Ian chuckled.

"*Ya,* it is time to eat." Eva touched Junior's straw hat. "After lunch you have to take a nap."

Junior frowned.

"Don't worry, buddy." Ian leaned down to him. "You can help me later if your *mamm* says it's okay."

"Can I, *Mamm*?" Junior's expression was hopeful.

Eva nodded. "*Ya.* Now, go inside and get washed up. *Mammi* put a stool in the downstairs bathroom for you. You're covered in dirt."

Junior rushed out of the barn.

"Don't run!" Eva called after him. With a

sigh, she started toward the exit with Ian in tow.

"We got through more than we'd planned this morning," *Dat* said to Ian as he clapped him on the shoulder.

Ian shook his head. "You say that every day."

Eva glanced at the two men as jealousy once again coiled tight in her belly. It seemed Ian really was like the son her parents never had. Perhaps *Dat* would have preferred a son to a daughter.

Stop feeling sorry for yourself! You're the one who left!

Eva frowned as she continued to walk toward the house.

Junior stopped halfway up the path. "*Daadi!* What kind of bird is that?" He pointed to a tree where a bird sang.

"Which tree are you pointing to?" *Dat* quickened his steps to catch up with Junior.

"Wait a minute." Ian's voice was low and warm in her ear. "Are you all right?"

She halted and looked up at him, surprised by the genuine concern that seemed to emanate from his expression. Did Ian really care about her? Or was he counting the days until she and her son returned to Ronks so he could go back to being her parents' favorite child?

He raised an eyebrow as his lips quirked. "Why are you staring at me?"

"I'm not staring at you." She started walking toward the house. "And I'm just fine."

"Hold on." He grabbed her arm and gently turned her toward him. "I've known you since you were fourteen years old. We used to talk about everything. You can still trust me."

"That was a long time ago." She jammed her thumb toward the house. "I need to go help *mei mamm* serve lunch."

Eva rushed down the path before Ian could stop her again.

Eva moved her dustcloth across the coffee table in the family room later that afternoon. After washing the lunch dishes, she'd put Junior down for a nap and started cleaning. Her mother was in the kitchen, making up menus for the following week.

When Eva shifted to one of the end tables, she spotted movement out the front window and heard the *clip-clop* of horse hooves.

Eva hurried to the kitchen. Her mother was sitting at the table, perusing a cookbook. "Someone just arrived in a buggy. Are you expecting company?"

"No." *Mamm*'s smile seemed to contradict her response. "You should go see who it is."

"What did you do?" Eva asked with suspicion.

"Go on." *Mamm* shooed her away with one hand. "Just trust me."

With apprehension clamping down on her shoulders, Eva tossed the dustcloth onto the counter and hurried through the family room and out the front door.

When her feet hit the front porch steps, Eva gave a little squeal. Her best friend, Miriam Faye Stoltzfoos, was the driver exiting the buggy.

"Eva!" Miriam Faye held out her arms as she climbed the steps. "I'm so *froh* you're here."

Eva hugged her. "I've enjoyed your letters, but it's so much better to see you in person. What a *wunderbaar* surprise!"

"Your *mamm* invited me to come over for tea this afternoon."

Eva touched Miriam Faye's protruding belly. "How are you feeling?"

"Great. I only have a few more months."

"Where's Hannah?" Eva asked about her two-year-old.

"She's at *mei mamm*'s. I thought it would be best if she napped so we can talk." Miriam Faye pointed toward the house. "Is Junior napping?"

Eva nodded. "*Ya.* He's grumpy if he

misses his nap."

"Hannah is the same way."

"Come inside." Eva touched Miriam Faye's slight shoulder. "I'll make that tea *mei mamm* promised, and we can get caught up."

As they started up the steps, Eva glanced toward her mother's garden and spotted Ian. She paused, taking in the breadth of his shoulders as he stood on a ladder and tied the ropes from a swing to a branch of the large oak tree there. She suddenly recalled the compassion in his eyes earlier when he asked what was wrong and reminded her how close they'd been when they were younger.

Even though she'd snapped at him and hurried back to the house instead of answering his question, he'd been pleasant to her at lunch. They talked about the farm, and he made a point of including her son in the conversation. Although it had been six years since she left New Wilmington without saying good-bye to Ian, he was still the same kind and thoughtful man she remembered. Did she even deserve his friendship after the way she treated him?

But she'd allowed her pride and stubbornness to get in her way. Her mother had pressured her to date Ian, assuming Ian would ask her and hoping they'd one day marry. So instead of admitting Ian was a good choice for her, Eva had said no when he finally asked her to be more than a friend. She fled to visit her cousin Mim in Lititz to escape her mother's constant suggestions for her life. Then she met Simeon there, shoving Ian out of her thoughts.

"Eva?" Miriam Faye stood by the front door. "Are you coming?"

Eva turned toward her friend. *"Ya."* She pointed toward Ian. "It looks like Ian is putting up a swing for Junior. I didn't know he was going to do that."

Miriam Faye smiled. "Junior will love it."

"Ya, he will." Eva opened the front door and gestured for Miriam Faye to go inside. "Let's have some tea."

"I'm so glad you invited Miriam Faye over." Eva smiled across the table at her mother as they drank tea and ate homemade oatmeal raisin cookies. "This has been so much fun."

"I'm glad she did too." Miriam Faye swiped another cookie from the platter at the center of the table. "I was excited to hear you'd finally come home. It's been too long."

For nearly two hours they had laughed and talked as they caught each other up on their lives. Miriam Faye had also shared news about their friends from school, church, and their youth group.

"I should get going." Miriam Faye stood and carried her mug and plate to the counter. "I'm sure Hannah will be awake soon, and I need to get started on supper."

"*Danki* so much for coming over," Eva said. "Let me walk you out."

Eva followed Miriam Faye out to her buggy.

"I've really enjoyed your visit." Eva hugged her.

Miriam Faye's brown eyes sparkled in the afternoon sunlight. "How are you really doing since you lost Simeon?"

Eva held her breath as she considered her response. "I'm trying to move on, but it's difficult. Even though I'm expected to remarry, I feel like I need to be with his family as I raise Junior."

Miriam Faye tilted her head. "I know you miss Simeon, but why do you feel that way?"

"Junior is their only link to Simeon. They need him as much as he needs them."

Miriam Faye nodded, but she didn't seem convinced. "Will you be at church tomorrow?"

"*Ya.*"

"*Gut.* I want to meet Junior, and you can

see Joel and Hannah." Miriam Faye opened her buggy door. "See you tomorrow."

Eva waved as the horse and buggy moved down the driveway. Once they were out of sight, she turned and almost walked right into Ian. She jumped with a start and clasped her hand to her chest.

"I'm sorry." Ian held up his hands. "I thought you heard me walk up behind you."

"I didn't." She took a step back.

His handsome face lit up with a grin, and his eyes reminded her of melted chocolate. He seemed to be just slightly shorter than Simeon's six feet. He raised his eyebrows, and she cleared her throat, hoping her thoughts weren't playing out on her face.

"Did you have a nice visit with Miriam Faye?"

"*Ya*, I did. It's been a long time since I've seen her." She folded her arms over her black apron. "I still can't believe she married Joel Stoltzfoos. It seems like only yesterday we were all in school together."

He rubbed his clean-shaven chin. "*Ya*, it does seem like yesterday." Then he grinned. "Do you remember that time the four of us went on a picnic?"

She laughed. "How could I forget? We found the perfect place to enjoy the food Miriam Faye and I made for us — ham sandwiches, potato salad, and brownies. And then it started raining, and we were all wet by the time we got back to your buggy."

"Wet? We were completely soaked."

They both laughed, and then an awkward silence fell between them. She struggled to think of something to say as she looked up into his kind eyes.

"I was wondering if Junior was awake." Ian pointed toward the swing. "I want him to see what I built for him while he was sleeping."

Eva looked toward the swing and admired what Ian had done for her son. "He'll love it."

"Gut." Ian folded his arms over his wide chest. "I'll build him a complete swing set if you and Junior stay."

She pivoted back toward him. "If we stay?"

"Ya, if you stay here permanently, I'll build him a wooden set with a fort and a slide."

Eva studied Ian's expression. Was he using a swing set as some sort of bait to convince her to move back in with her parents? Did Ian truly think all her problems with her parents could be ironed out by a wooden swing set? The notion sent exasperation tumbling through her.

"I'll go get Junior and tell him to come

see you."

As Eva marched into the house, she wondered what her parents had told Ian about her. Did they also believe their issues could be worked out by building something as simple as a wooden swing set? If so, their relationship could never be repaired.

Chapter 5

"Gude mariye."

Ian looked up from his hymnal and echoed the greeting as Will Peachey sat down beside him on a bench. They were seated in the unmarried men's section of the congregation, ready for the service in the Yoder family's largest barn.

"How was your week?" Will picked up the hymnal beside him.

"*Gut.* Busy as usual. How was your week at your harness shop?"

"Very busy." Will set the hymnal on his lap. "An *Englisher* came in and placed an order for two dozen saddles."

"Two dozen? What does he plan to do with so many?"

"Apparently he's opening up a day camp and will offer horseback riding." Will shrugged. "All I know is that it's *gut* for my business."

"It certainly is." Ian glanced across the

barn to where the married women were filing in to sit in their section. His eyes focused on Eva as she sat between her mother and Miriam Faye. When Miriam Faye leaned over to say something to Eva, Eva's beautiful face lit up with happiness, and Ian's insides warmed.

"So Eva is finally back."

Ian swiveled toward his friend. "*Ya,* she arrived on Friday."

"How long is she staying?"

"I don't know."

"Where's her *sohn*?"

"Mary has him." Ian nodded toward where Junior sat on the bench beside his grandmother. He smiled as he recalled how Junior played on the swing nearly all afternoon and evening yesterday. He protested when Eva told him it was time for bed. It seemed the swing meant the world to him, and Ian was overwhelmed by the joy in Mary's and Harvey's eyes as they watched him play.

"She looks *gut.*" Will's observation yanked Ian back to the present.

"*Ya.*" Ian hated the niggling of jealousy that teased him. He had no right to feel any sort of ownership over Eva.

The service began with a hymn, and Ian redirected his thoughts to the present. A young man sitting a few rows behind Ian served as the song leader. He began the first syllable of each line, and then the rest of the congregation joined in to finish the verse.

The ministers met in another room for thirty minutes to choose who would preach that day while the congregation continued to sing. During the last verse of the second hymn, Ian's gaze moved across the barn just as the ministers returned. They placed their hats on two hay bales, indicating the service was about to begin.

When the chosen minister began the first sermon, Ian folded his hands in his lap and studied him, but his thoughts turned to Eva. He tried his best to keep his focus on the message, but his stare shifted to the married women's section across the barn aisle. When his gaze found Eva, she seemed to be concentrating on her lap as if it held all the answers to her deepest questions. Was she praying? Was she thinking of Simeon and drowning in grief?

He longed to help her through whatever emotions she'd struggled with since returning home. If only he could convince her to talk to him, but he didn't want to push her. After all, she'd been home less than forty-eight hours. But although he'd dated other women in the community, his heart had been stuck on Eva since they were teenagers. Not only was she beautiful, but she had a great sense of humor. They'd had fun when they were together. They could always talk to each other, as if they enjoyed a deep connection. Well, at least *he'd* felt the connection. Perhaps he'd only imagined it since she turned him down when he asked to date her, and then she left the community and married someone else.

While the minister continued to talk in German, Ian lost himself in memories of their youth. Some afternoons Eva would eat lunch on the porch with him while they discussed everything from mutual friends to their plans for the future. She talked of getting married and raising several children, and he told her he dreamed of one day owning a farm. What he didn't share was that he'd dreamt of owning that farm with her by his side as his wife.

When she left town six years ago, Ian had been crushed. Not only had she broken his heart by marrying another man, but she also hadn't told him she was leaving. He learned she was gone when her parents told him.

The first sermon ended, and Ian knelt in silent prayer beside Will. He closed his eyes and thanked God for bringing Eva and

Junior home to see Mary and Harvey. He asked him to heal whatever had gone wrong between Eva and her parents, and to help her trust him again as a dear friend.

After the prayers, the deacon read from the Scriptures, and then the hour-long main sermon began. Ian willed himself to concentrate on it, listening to the discussion on the book of Acts. But Ian snuck glances at Eva, taking in her attractive face as she looked at the deacon. As he admired her, he wondered how life could have been if Eva had agreed to date him. Would they have been married? If so, would they have lived on her parents' farm or bought some land of their own? Would they have had children?

More than once, Miriam Faye caught Ian looking at Eva, and she smiled. Ian nodded at her and returned his gaze where it belonged.

After the sermon came the fifteen-minute kneeling prayer. Then the congregation stood for the benediction and sang the closing hymn. Ian's eyes again moved to Eva. He hoped to speak with her when the service ended. Even better, he hoped he could give her a ride back to the farm. Maybe she would finally open up to him so they could rebuild the friendship that had once meant the world to him.

■ ■ ■ ■

Eva smiled as she made her way down the long tables, filling coffee cups for the men. She was thankful a group of teenage girls in the church district had offered to take care of the children so the women could serve the meal. Junior happily went off with the girls when they said they'd feed him in the Yoders' kitchen.

When she came to Ian, she asked, "Would you like some *kaffi*?"

"*Ya, danki.*" Ian smiled up at her as he handed her his cup.

She filled it and then handed it back to him. When her fingers brushed his, electricity zipped up her arm and she swallowed a gasp. Had she imagined it, or had he felt it too?

When his intense eyes locked with hers, her breath stalled in her lungs. She was certain to the depth of her bones that Ian *had* felt it. The attraction that pulled her to him like an invisible magnet years ago was back. Or maybe it had never died. Her mouth dried.

"Could I have some *kaffi*?"

His friend Will's question shook Eva from her daze.

71

"*Ya*, of course." She filled Will's cup and then continued down the table.

When her coffeepot was empty, she exited the barn and started toward the house.

"Eva!" Miriam Faye hurried to catch up with her. "I'll walk with you."

Eva held up her pot. "I ran out of *kaffi* quickly."

"I did too." A smile lifted the corners of Miriam Faye's lips, and she leaned closer to Eva as if to share a juicy secret. "I noticed Ian Miller watching you during the service."

"Oh?" Eva kept her eyes trained on the rock path to avoid Miriam's gaze.

"I think he still cares about you."

"I doubt that." Eva knew it was sinful to lie, but she couldn't admit she might care about him too. She had no room in her life for a relationship, especially when her life was back in Ronks. She was only visiting her parents, and she had no plans to move back here. Besides, Ian was trying to take her place in her parents' life.

"Wait a minute." Miriam Faye stopped walking and grabbed Eva's arm. "I know you loved your husband, and from your letters, I could tell you and Simeon had a *gut* marriage. But before you met him, you told me you cared about Ian and you thought he cared about you too. What happened between you two?"

Eva pressed her lips together as she gathered her muddled thoughts and emotions. "It's complicated. *Mei mamm* started pressuring me to date him. She was convinced Ian would be the perfect husband, and I didn't think it was her place to make that decision for me. Besides, I was young, prideful, and rebellious. I couldn't admit that *mei mamm* might be right. When he did ask me to date him, I said no."

"Huh." Miriam Faye tilted her head. "So that's why you went to visit Mim in Lititz. You wanted to get away from your *mamm,* and meeting and falling in love with Simeon was a bonus."

"*Ya,* that sums it up. I didn't visit Mim with the intention of falling in love. That was God's plan for me." Eva shook her head as her thoughts turned back to Ian's motives for staying with her parents. "I don't understand why Ian moved into the *daadihaus.* I think he's using my parents to get their property since he won't be the son to inherit his parents' farm."

"I don't think that's it at all." Miriam Faye's expression was serious. "Your *dat* isn't getting any younger, and after you left, the part-time help they were getting from

73

Ian wasn't enough anymore. They need him there."

Eva bristled at the insinuation she was at fault. "We'd better get the *kaffi* and go back to the barn before the men start complaining."

Before Miriam Faye could respond, Eva headed up the porch steps and into the kitchen.

"But I want to ride home with Ian," Junior whined as he stood beside Ian's buggy after lunch.

Eva pinched the bridge of her nose as she looked between Junior and Ian. "Junior, we need to ride home with *Mammi* and *Daadi.*" She gestured toward their buggy behind her. "Let's go."

"No." Junior shook his head, and Eva turned to Ian.

Ian's expression showed patience. "You can both ride with me."

Eva hesitated. What would she and Ian discuss for the nearly thirty-minute journey?

"Come on." Ian took a step toward her. "It will be like old times."

That was the problem. She and Ian had made plenty of trips together in his buggy when they ran errands for her parents. She didn't want to open the door to that former friendship. She laced her fingers together and looked back at her parents, who had already climbed into her father's buggy.

"We'll see you at home," *Mamm* called.

Ian waved to them. "All right." Then he opened the passenger-side door and helped Junior hop into the buggy and then climb over the seat to the back. Once Junior was settled, Ian turned to her and made a sweeping gesture.

Eva climbed in, and Ian closed the door before loping around to the driver's side. He settled onto the seat and then began to guide the buggy toward the road.

They rode in silence for a few minutes. Eva kept her hands folded in her lap as she stared out the window at the traffic whizzing by in a blur.

"Did it feel strange to be back in your home church district?" Ian's question broke through the thick silence.

"*Ya,* but it was also a little comforting."

He gave her a sideways glance. "I'm glad you felt comfortable. You seemed to be deep in thought throughout most of the service."

So Miriam Faye was right. He had been watching her.

"I was thinking about how much my life has changed since the last time I went to a service here." She kept her gaze trained out the front window to avoid his eyes. If she looked at him, she risked pouring out her thoughts and opening herself to heartache.

Their conversation died, and the sounds of passing cars, mixed with the *clip-clop* of the horse's hooves, filled the buggy. Eva fingered the door handle and silently willed the mare to move faster to bring an end to the awkward ride.

When a low rumble of snores filled her ears, she turned to the back of the buggy. Junior was curled up, sleeping with his thumb in his mouth. She couldn't stop a smile.

"What's so funny?" Ian grinned at her.

"Junior is snoring."

Ian laughed, and she joined in, the humor seeming to break through the awkwardness. The stiffness in her back loosened as her stress dissipated.

"Now I see why he was so cranky," she offered.

"*Ya,* that does make sense." Ian shrugged. "I'm cranky when I need a nap too."

She smiled, appreciating his patience with her son. "*Danki* for putting up the swing for him. It was all he talked about last night."

"*Gern gschehne.*" He turned his attention back to the road. "My offer of a full swing set still stands if you stay."

"That won't be necessary. We won't be here long."

"Why not?"

She turned toward the road and hoped he would drop the subject. She didn't want to discuss this now. She'd been back in New Wilmington only two days, and she didn't want to be pressured.

They rode in silence for a few moments, and new guilt weighed heavily on her chest. She still had suspicions, but Ian had been nothing but nice to her and Junior while she'd been rude to him.

She shifted toward him and found his focus on the road as he guided the horse. "How's your family?"

His eyes widened for a fraction of a second, as if the question had caught him off guard. Why hadn't she thought to inquire about his family sooner?

"They're fine. *Danki.*" He gave her a sideways glance as he halted the horse at a red light. "My parents are as ornery as ever."

Eva chuckled. "And your *bruders*?"

"They're all married now, and I already have eight *bruderskinner.*"

"Really?"

He nodded.

And why aren't you married?

The question sat on the tip of her tongue

as he guided the horse through the intersection and down the road toward her father's farm. While she longed to learn why Ian had chosen not to marry, she resisted the urge to get too personal with him. She had to keep her distance.

"Tell me about your *bruderskinner*."

"Well, there are five *buwe* and three *maed*. And the *buwe* cause about as many problems for their parents as *mei bruders* and I did for ours." Ian shared stories of his nephews' antics until he halted the horse in front of her parents' house. Then he turned toward the back of the buggy, where Junior continued to snore with his thumb in his mouth. "I'll carry him in for you."

"Oh no." She pushed the door open. "I can carry him."

He met her at the back of the buggy and smirked. "You're still the same stubborn *maedel* who insisted she could carry all the drinks out to the barn at once for a youth gathering. Then you dropped the tray, spilling lemonade all over your *mamm*'s porch."

Eva guffawed and then clapped her hand over her mouth for fear of waking Junior. "You remember that?"

He raised an eyebrow. "How could I forget?" He glanced into the buggy. "I assume he naps upstairs in the room Mary set up for him." When Eva nodded, he said, "Let me carry him for you." She opened her mouth to protest, and he quickly added, "I'd hate for you to fall down the stairs and have you both get hurt."

He had a point.

"Okay," she said, conceding.

He opened the back of the buggy and pulled Junior into his arms. She hurried up the front porch steps, opened the door, and then followed him up the stairs to Junior's room.

Ian set her son on the bed, and Junior snuggled down into the quilt, his thumb never leaving his mouth.

"Do you think he's comfortable?" Ian pushed a lock of Junior's hair off his forehead as a gentle smile turned up the corners of his lips.

A soft lump seemed to form in her chest as Eva watched Ian's tender gesture. He resembled a father. Then a f lash of Simeon filled her mind and tears burned her eyes. Ever since Simeon died, she'd tried to imagine the kind of father he would have been. She was certain to the depth of her soul that Simeon would have been patient and loving. If only he'd escaped that burning farmhouse before the f loor collapsed beneath his feet.

Slamming her eyes shut, Eva held her breath. She couldn't allow herself to fall back into the deep abyss of her grief. Simeon had been gone more than four years, and she'd worked through all the stages of grief with the help of her family and friends in Ronks. She needed to stay strong for Junior.

She opened her eyes and found Ian still focused on her son. He touched Junior's head again, and her heart twisted with admiration. His tenderness for her child was written on his handsome face.

Stop it!

Ian was *not* Simeon. He was *not* Junior's father. Allowing that notion to fill her mind was crazy. What was wrong with her? She was just emotional after attending church in her home district for the first time in six years. She needed rest, but first she had to escort Ian out of the house.

She wiped her eyes before Ian could see her tears and started for the hallway. "We should let him sleep."

"*Ya.*" Ian walked with her into the hall and then quietly pulled the door closed behind them and followed her down the stairs.

"*Danki* for carrying him for me," she said when they reached the front porch.

"*Gern gschehne.*" Ian leaned against the

80

railing. "I want to ask you something."

"Okay." She braced herself.

"Why did you stay away for so long?"

The question echoed through her mind as she struggled to form a coherent answer. While she didn't want to upset Ian, she also couldn't bring herself to lie to him.

"I didn't feel welcome here." She was careful to keep her voice low since she stood near the screen door.

His expression hardened. "What does that mean?"

"My parents made it clear they didn't support my decision to marry Simeon when they didn't come to my wedding. They didn't want me to leave this community, so they acted as if they didn't have a *dochder.*" Her voice trembled as a tear rolled down one cheek. "After the way they treated me when I married him, I knew they wouldn't give me the love and support I needed when he died."

He shook his head as his lips twisted. "You've got it all wrong, Eva."

Her anger flared at his skepticism. "Why are you living here on *mei dat*'s farm?" She pointed toward the *daadihaus.*

"I think that's pretty obvious. Your parents needed my help after you left."

She folded her arms over her chest and

lifted her chin. "Or is it more accurate to say you want their land since you'll never own your parents' farm?"

He flinched as if she'd hit him, and then his brown eyes narrowed. "You think I'm the kind of man who would do that to your parents?" His face crumpled. "Is that why you refused to date me?"

Eva's mouth moved, but no words crossed her lips as guilt grabbed her by the throat.

"Ian." *Mamm* appeared at the screen door and pushed it open. "Would you like to come in and visit for a while?"

"No, *danki.*" Ian kept his cold eyes focused on Eva as he spoke. "I think I've done enough visiting for today." He turned toward her mother. "I'll see you tomorrow." He took a step toward Eva and lowered his head. "Just remember, Eva, you're the one who left."

Guilt, hot and painful, sliced through her chest as Ian stalked down the steps and strode toward the *daadihaus.* Hadn't she said that to herself? *You're the one who left.*

"Is everything all right?" *Mamm* came to stand behind Eva.

"*Ya.*" Eva cleared her throat against another ball of emotion. "Junior's upstairs asleep, and I think I'm going to take a nap until he wakes up."

"You know you can talk to me, right? I'll always listen to you, no matter what you want to tell me." *Mamm*'s voice was small and timid, as if she were afraid of upsetting Eva.

"Ya. Danki." Eva climbed the stairs and tried to erase the image of the hurt in Ian's eyes. As she changed out of her Sunday dress, Ian's words echoed through her mind.

You've got it all wrong, Eva.

But if that was true, why did she feel like a stranger in her childhood home?

CHAPTER 6

White-hot fury boiled through Ian's veins as he walked toward his house after stowing his horse and buggy in Harvey's barn. His hand shook as he unlocked the back door and walked into the small, two-bedroom cottage where Harvey's parents had resided until they passed away.

After hanging his hat on a peg by the back door and removing his shoes, he blew out an irritated sigh as Eva's spiteful words echoed through his mind.

Or is it more accurate to say you want their land since you'll never own your parents' farm?

How could Eva, the woman who had been his dear friend and whom he'd once dreamed about dating and possibly marrying, accuse him of using her parents? He'd always considered her a sweet, kind, caring person, but she seemed more like a self-centered, cynical, pessimistic person now.

Or should he call her misguided, given how grief had surely affected her?

But if Eva was so terrible, why did he still care about her?

Ian swallowed a groan as he entered his small kitchen. After filling a glass with water from the tap, he walked into the family room and sat down in his favorite wing chair. He looked out the front window toward the main house as Eva's biting words swirled through his mind.

I didn't feel welcome here.

He set his half-empty glass on the end table beside him and pushed his hands through his thick hair. How could Eva call her parents unwelcoming? Harvey and Mary had been nothing but kind and generous to him ever since he came to work on their farm. And Eva was wrong to believe they wouldn't have been supportive and loving to her after Simeon died.

Ian rested his ankle on his opposite knee as he again recalled the months after Eva left. Mary and Harvey were never the same. Their smiles were less frequent and their zest for life had dulled.

If Eva truly believed her parents were unaffected by her departure, followed by her almost complete abandonment, then perhaps she never knew them as well as she believed she had.

As Ian picked up his glass, another thought hit him like a bale of hay falling from the loft in one of Harvey's barns. Did Eva accuse her parents of not caring for her to dispel her own guilt over leaving?

Renewed fury filled him at the thought. Perhaps he should enlighten her and tell her how she tore her parents apart by walking away from them and never looking back for six long years. Not only had she crushed their souls, but she had the gall to accuse them of not caring about her or her grief when she lost her husband.

He stood and started for the front door, but then stopped. Marching over to give her a piece of his mind was not how the Lord would want him to spend his Sunday. Giving Eva space to mull over his words was better. He would talk to her after they'd both had time to calm down and think clearly.

Turning toward the sofa, he spotted the devotional he'd begun reading earlier in the week. He retrieved the book and sank down into the wing chair. Once he was settled, he tried to push away his thoughts of Eva and turn his thoughts to the Lord.

Eva moved onto her side as her eyes fluttered open. The green numerals on the digital clock sitting on her nightstand read 12:15.

For three hours she'd tossed and turned, struggling to fall asleep despite the thoughts swirling through her mind. Every time she tried to turn off her brain, Ian's words from earlier in the day would ring through her mind:

You've got it all wrong, Eva.

Remember, Eva, you're the one who left.

She wanted to dismiss his observation, but she couldn't when Miriam Faye had said something similar, also pointing out that she was the one who had left. Maybe it was Eva's fault her parents had rejected her.

But had her parents rejected her? Or had Eva been shortsighted and egotistical? She hadn't even called to tell them Simeon died. She asked Mim to call them, and she instructed her not to invite them to the funeral, not to even tell them when it was. Then she waited more than two weeks to write them. She also hadn't invited them to visit after Junior was born.

Eva swallowed a groan as she rolled onto her back. Yes, she was part of the reason she and her parents had grown so far apart. Everything Ian said was true. Eva was the one who left, and she'd never considered what that might do to them.

Then another thought hit her like a bolt of lightning. How would she feel if Junior left her the same way she'd left her parents? She'd be crushed if he married someone outside of their community and then crippled any meaningful communication, cutting Eva out of his children's lives. She suddenly understood the pain she'd caused her parents.

She had been wrong. She'd hurt both of her parents deeply. And now she realized she'd hurt Ian as well.

Renewed guilt washed over her, stealing her breath. How could she be so selfish and self-absorbed? No wonder Ian had been so angry at her accusation.

But she couldn't blame herself for leaving New Wilmington. When she met Simeon, it was love at first sight. When he introduced himself, she was drawn to his cornflower-blue eyes, his electric smile, and his contagious laugh. She'd never once regretted marrying him, building a life with him.

Yet now, looking back on how she'd handled her departure, she would try harder to keep her parents included in her life. She would never again cut them out the way she had in the past.

She wiped away a tear as she stared up at

the ceiling through the dark. She had to find a way to make amends for the mistakes she'd made — if it wasn't too late.

"Lord," she whispered as a prayer filled her heart. "I'm sorry for not honoring my parents the way I'm supposed to. I want to make things right, but I don't know how. Please forgive my sins and guide my words and my actions to help me earn their forgiveness. And please heal my broken heart. I miss Simeon. And I also miss the relationship I once had with my parents and my friendship with Ian."

Moving onto her side again, Eva blinked back more tears as she waited for sleep to find her.

Eva set a bowl of chicken salad in the center of the table, which had five place settings for lunch. Movement in her peripheral vision drew her attention to the kitchen window that faced the back of the house. She swiveled toward it and found Ian and Junior playing catch in the grass just beyond her mother's garden.

Ian tossed the ball to Junior, who caught it and then beamed as he jumped up and down.

Ian clapped his hands and then said something that looked like, *"Wunderbaar!"*

Eva crossed her arms as she moved to the window. She watched Junior toss the ball to Ian, the ball falling short of Ian by several inches. With a smile, Ian walked over to him and began giving him what looked like instructions on how to throw the ball to make it travel farther.

Ian walked away from Junior and beckoned him to throw the ball again. They volleyed it back and forth several times, and each time Junior's toss improved.

Eva's heart warmed as Ian kept a patient expression on his face while teaching her son how to play catch. Not only that, but he was so handsome as the bright afternoon sun caused his dark eyes to sparkle.

He was a good man to his core, and she had no right to accuse him of using her parents. He had always gone out of his way to be kind to her and her parents. When he was a teenager, he'd work on the farm on his days off and refuse to take extra pay. When a boy in Eva's youth group broke up with her to date her friend, Ian sat on the porch with her for an hour as she cried. He was a true friend, and he deserved her respect, not accusations about his intentions.

Regret nipped at her as she recalled their conversation from Sunday. Somehow, despite her prayer of confession, she'd let four days pass since their heated discussion. And while they'd been cordial to each other in passing, they hadn't worked out their differences. It was hard to know where to begin.

Eva needed to apologize to him. And she needed to thank him for being so kind to Junior.

She also needed to talk with her mother, but it was even harder to know where to begin with her.

"There was a message for you."

Startled, Eva jumped and spun toward her mother as she walked into the kitchen.

"I'm sorry I surprised you." *Mamm* set a pile of letters on the counter and looked past Eva to the window. "What are you doing?"

"Watching Ian teach Junior how to throw a ball." Eva nodded her head toward the window. "Look."

"Oh my goodness!" *Mamm* sidled up to Eva. "Look at him throwing that ball."

"I know." Eva couldn't stop grinning. "Ian is a *gut* teacher."

They stood in silence for a few minutes as Junior and Ian continued to play catch.

"Did you hear what I said earlier?" *Mamm* broke through the quiet.

"What?" Eva pivoted toward her.

"Your mother-in-law called and asked how you and Junior are doing. She asked you to call her when you have time."

"I'll call her later." Eva crossed the kitchen and began pulling drinking glasses out of a cabinet. As she set them on the table, she glanced at her mother, who was placing a napkin under the fork at Ian's spot. "Why does Ian eat every meal here?"

Mamm's forehead furrowed as she looked up. "What do you mean?"

"Why doesn't he buy his own groceries and make his own meals?"

"Because it's part of our deal." *Mamm* shrugged.

"What do you mean?"

"He helps your *dat* run the farm, and in exchange he gets room and board along with a small salary."

"Wait a minute." Eva paused as her mother's words marinated in her mind. "He gets a *small* salary?"

Mamm nodded. "When we all realized we needed his help full-time, Ian asked for only a small salary, insisting he would be *froh* adding room and board and living in the *daadihaus.*"

Eva swallowed as confusion taunted her. She no longer believed Ian was trying to take over her father's farm, but why wouldn't he want to draw a larger salary so he could build a house of his own and have a family?

"Did you see me catch the ball and then throw it to Ian?" Junior asked with a mouthful of chicken salad.

"*Ya,* I did." Eva smiled at her son across the table. "You did fantastic, but please chew and swallow your food before you talk, okay?"

Ian grinned at her and then looked down at Junior. "He's a fast learner."

"*Danki* for teaching him." Eva's words leapt from her lips without any forethought.

"*Gern gschehne.*" Ian's gaze tangled with hers, and the intensity in his eyes caused her breath to stall in her lungs. They studied each other for a long moment, and her cheeks heated as her pulse hammered.

"Do you need anything from the hardware store?"

Dat's question caused Ian to turn toward him, breaking the connection.

"What's that, Harvey?" Ian asked.

Eva looked down at her plate and picked up her chicken salad sandwich as bewilderment raced through her. Where had that connection come from? It was similar to the electricity she'd felt on Sunday when she touched his hand after pouring his coffee. Why were her feelings for Ian so intense after spending such a long time apart?

"I was wondering if you need anything from the hardware store." *Dat* wiped his beard with a paper napkin.

"No, I don't think so," Ian said. "Are you going there this afternoon?"

"*Ya.* Remember? Ted is going to pick us up soon. Mary has some errands, and I'm going with her."

"While you're gone and Junior's taking his nap, I can do a few chores around here," Eva said.

"I'm not tired." Junior rubbed his eyes.

Eva bit back a smile. When she stole a glance at Ian, she found he was watching her. His lips curved into a grin, and her heart jumped. She longed to break this connection between them. She hadn't expected to fall for Ian, but it seemed impossible to ignore her growing affection for him.

"I'll get some supplies to repair the fencing around the chicken coop," *Dat* said.

Ian popped a potato chip into his mouth. "Great. I can get started on that tomorrow."

"Can I help?" Junior asked between bites of his own potato chips.

Eva swallowed a sigh of relief.

Danki, Dat, *for steering Ian's attention*

away from me!

When they were finished eating, Eva helped her mother carry the dishes to the counter as Ian, *Dat,* and Junior disappeared outside.

When *Mamm* began filling the sink with water, Eva rested her hand on her shoulder. "You can get ready to go. I'll clean up."

"Nonsense." *Mamm* shook her head. "I'm not going to leave you with this mess."

"Don't be *gegisch.*" Eva waved off her comment. "Believe me, I've cleaned up worse, and I don't mind doing it. Go get ready."

Mamm hesitated. "Are you sure?"

"Of course I am. I'll get Junior down for a nap and then I'll clean up. You enjoy your errands with *Dat.*"

"Danki." *Mamm* gave her a quick hug, and Eva's heart swelled at the sign of affection. She had a feeling her mother didn't want to let go.

Mamm hurried toward her bedroom, and Eva stepped out onto the back porch, where *Dat* and Ian already stood talking with Ted. Eva waved at him and then turned to her son, who sat on the glider with one elbow on its arm, his head supported by the palm of his hand.

"It's time for your nap."

"No." Junior yawned. "I'm not tired. I want to play catch with Ian."

Eva sank down beside him. "You are tired. And Ian has chores to do."

"No, I'm not tired." Junior's lower lip trembled. "And I want to play with Ian."

Eva rubbed her temple in frustration. Junior was on the edge of a meltdown, and she longed for her mother-in-law to help her distract him.

As if sensing Eva's anxiety, Ian crouched in front of Junior and touched his shoulder. "I have an idea."

Junior looked skeptical. "What?"

"If you promise to take a nap without complaining, I'll play catch with you this afternoon."

"Really?" Junior's eyes sparkled as he sat up straight.

"Only if you promise." Ian held up a finger. "Do you promise?"

"*Ya, ya.*" Junior nodded, his blond hair bobbing up and down.

"*Gut.*" Ian gestured toward the back door. "Go on, now."

Junior stood and rushed into the house.

"*Danki* so much," Eva told Ian after the door clicked shut behind her son. "He was on the verge of a tantrum."

"It's no problem. I like spending time with

him." Ian gestured inside. "You'd better get him in bed before he changes his mind."

"*Gut* idea." Eva went into the house and up the stairs, marveling at Ian's skill with her son.

As Eva turned down Junior's bed, a question filled her mind. Would Ian ever have any children of his own?

CHAPTER 7

The knots in Ian's shoulders were as hard as rocks as he washed a plate, rinsed it, and set it in the drying rack. His mind raced with what he planned to say to Eva when she came back downstairs.

After saying good-bye to Ted, Harvey, and Mary, he had stepped back into the kitchen and started washing the dishes. He couldn't stand the distance between Eva and him any longer, and now was his opportunity to speak to her alone. He prayed she would talk to him while they cleaned the kitchen together. He was going to save their friendship, no matter how long it took them to work it out.

When he felt someone staring at him, he turned to where she stood in the doorway. She was stunning, clad in a mint-colored dress that accentuated the flecks of green in her gorgeous hazel eyes. She seemed somehow more beautiful than she was six years

98

ago. Was he imagining her transformation, or had maturity deepened her beauty?

She crossed the kitchen and folded her arms over her black apron. "What are you doing?"

"The dishes." He held up another clean plate and grinned. "See?"

She rolled her eyes, and he bit the inside of his cheek to keep from laughing. How he enjoyed taunting her!

"I'm perfectly capable of cleaning the kitchen. You can go outside and do your chores." When he didn't move, she added, "Go on, now."

"How about I wash and you dry?" He raised his eyebrows. "Please?"

"No, I'm sure you have things to do."

He eyed her as he dried his hands on a dish towel. "I'll stop washing if you do something for me."

"What?"

He tossed the dish towel onto the counter. "Sit and talk to me." He held his breath when she hesitated.

Then she moved to the counter and opened a cookie jar.

"What are *you* doing?" he asked.

"We can't sit at the table and talk unless we have dessert."

He shook his head. "You're still full of

surprises."

"Pour two glasses of milk to go with the *kichlin,*" she tossed over her shoulder.

Ian followed her instructions, and then they sat down across from each other at the table with a platter of oatmeal raisin and chocolate chip cookies between them. After a silent prayer, they began to eat the cookies and drink the milk, but without speaking.

He gathered his thoughts as he chewed a second chocolate chip cookie. After swallowing, he took a deep breath and gathered his courage. "I need to apologize. I was out of line on Sunday."

"No." She sat up straighter and shook her head, causing the ties of her prayer covering to bounce off her shoulders. "It wasn't your fault. I provoked you. I was wrong, and I'm sorry. I said terrible things to you. Please forgive me."

"Of course I forgive you." He swiped an oatmeal raisin cookie from the platter and broke it in half.

She studied him a moment. "Why don't you allow my parents to pay you a better salary?"

He relaxed back in the chair and blew out a puff of air. "I'm not after your inheritance."

"I know." Her eyes glistened. "I'm sorry for accusing you of that. I'm just trying to understand why you would run this farm for *Dat* and accept only a small salary. Anyone else would expect a larger salary for all the work you do. Why don't you?"

He shrugged. "I care about your parents, and I'm grateful for all they've done for me. They've kept me employed for years, and I like working here."

Soon a single tear traced down her pink cheek, and his heart ached for her. He longed to brush away the tear with the tip of his finger, but touching her that way would be too forward. He handed her a napkin from the holder in the center of the table, and she dabbed her cheek.

"*Danki* for taking such *gut* care of my parents." She sniffed and then wiped the napkin over her nose. "I feel terrible for hurting you."

"Stop." He leaned forward and reached for her hand, but then stopped, pulling his hands away. "It's forgiven." He took a bite of his cookie and then set it on his plate.

"*Danki* for being so nice to Junior. He really enjoys the attention. I think he misses his *onkel.*" She took a sip of milk.

His thoughts moved to Simeon's family and her life in Ronks.

"I'm sorry for all you've been through." He moved his finger over the condensation on his glass. "It has to be tough raising Junior without Simeon."

She stared down at her half-eaten cookie. "It is, but his family has been a tremendous help."

"Does Junior ask about him?"

"*Ya,* he does. We tell him stories about how Simeon fought fires. Now that Simeon's younger *bruder,* Nathan, is a firefighter, Junior seems to understand more."

"Is that what drew you to him?"

"What?" Her eyebrows drew together.

"Were you attracted to Simeon because he was a firefighter?" The words tasted bitter on Ian's tongue.

A faraway look filled Eva's face as if she were recalling the moment she met him. "I suppose that was part of it. It was as if there was this invisible force that drew me to him. It sounds *gegisch,* but when our eyes met, something unspoken happened between us. I couldn't take my eyes off him, and all at once I knew we were supposed to be together." Her cheeks blushed bright red. "I guess it's shallow to say I was drawn to his looks, but it's true. He was so handsome, and his stories about firefighting were exciting."

Ian felt his jaw tighten. He'd known Eva for years, but she took one look at Simeon Dienner and knew she was going to marry him. Somehow that just didn't seem fair. Jealousy was a sin, but he couldn't stop the emotion from sinking its sharp claws into him.

"I was blessed beyond measure when he asked me to marry him," she continued. "We had our tough times like every couple, but we made it work. He was so excited when we found out I was expecting Junior, but he never even got to meet him.

"Sometimes I have nightmares about the night he died. I relive the moment Simeon's fire chief came to the house and told us what happened." Eva paused and took a deep breath, her eyes glimmering with fresh tears.

"In an instant he was gone. I used to wonder what would have happened if he hadn't been on duty that day. Would another firefighter have fallen through the floor and died? But it's a sin to question God's will. There's a reason God took him, and I had to accept that." Her voice quavered, and Ian fought against the urge to rush around the table and pull her into his arms. She grabbed another napkin and wiped her eyes and nose.

"I'm so sorry," Ian whispered. "You must miss him terribly."

"*Ya*, I do." She paused, as if gathering her words. "Simeon's death is a loss that defies words and created an emptiness in my heart that will never be filled." She traced the wood grain in the table with her fingernail. "I miss him every day, and Junior reminds me of him. But having a piece of Simeon makes it easier too. I never imagined I'd lose him that way. I thought we'd grow old together. I thought we'd have more *kinner*." She was silent for a moment once again. "But I try not to let my grief overtake me. I have to be strong for Junior."

"Do you miss Ronks?" Ian braced himself for her response.

"I do." She folded the napkin in half. "I'm very close to my sister-in-law, Kayla, and my mother-in-law, Marilyn. *Mei mamm* said Marilyn left a message for me earlier. I need to call her back and see how everyone is. We all were devastated when we lost Simeon, and we had to be strong for one another. I don't know what I would have done without them."

"You could have come home after Simeon died. Your parents would have supported you. I would have supported you too."

She studied him but remained silent for

several moments. "Why aren't you married?"

He flinched as if she'd struck him, and she laughed at his reaction.

"You look so stunned." She handed him a chocolate chip cookie. "I think you need this."

He smirked before taking a bite.

"Now answer my question. If your *bruders* are married, why aren't you? You're thirty, Ian."

"I guess I haven't found the right *maedel* yet."

"This community has plenty of *maed,* and I'm certain more than one would jump at the chance to marry someone like you." She pointed an oatmeal raisin cookie at him.

He tilted his head as he decided to challenge her with a question. "Why wouldn't you date me when I asked you?"

Her smile faded and her teasing eyes dulled. She sat back in the chair and set the cookie on her plate. "I liked you. But *mei mamm* was pressuring me to date you, even marry you, and I felt trapped."

"Your *mamm* was pressuring you to marry me?" He leaned forward on the table.

She nodded.

"How did she pressure you?"

"She talked about you constantly." Her

gaze fell back to the table, and he longed for her to look him in the eye. "She kept telling me how it was obvious you cared about me. She said I should show you I cared about you as well. Then she talked on and on about how you and I could live on the farm and take it over when she and *Dat* retired. She said we could start out in the *daadihaus* until *Dat* built us a *haus*."

"And you didn't want to build a life with me," Ian surmised, each word stabbing him in the heart.

"It wasn't that, really." She met his gaze and shook her head. "I was frustrated with her because I felt like I couldn't breathe. I wanted to make my own decisions. *Mamm* and I had a huge argument about it. And I guess I wanted to spite her, so I went to visit Mim. Her youth group got together with a few other youth groups in the area, and Simeon came with a few *freinden* he was visiting. We spent a lot of time together, and when I came home, he called me a few times a week and we wrote letters. Then he asked me to marry him. I said yes, and I think they would have been supportive of our marriage — but not if I moved to Ronks. That's when I left."

Ian's stomach churned as jealousy coiled like an angry, venomous snake in his gut.

Why did her mother have to interfere? If Mary had kept her opinions to herself, would he have had a chance with Eva? Could they have built a life together on this farm instead of Ian having to live alone in the *daadihaus*?

But Eva had come back. Maybe God was giving him a second chance with her. He had to tell her how he felt. If he didn't tell her now, he may never have another chance.

"I've always cared about you, Eva." His voice sounded thin to his own ears. "That's why I never married."

Her eyes widened, and then she pushed back her chair and stood.

"I need to get started on my chores. I don't want *mei mamm* to come back to a messy kitchen." She hurried to the sink and began washing a plate.

Ian scowled as he silently berated himself for coming on so strong when they were having their most intimate conversation since she came home. He had to find a way to get her to open up to him again.

He carried their plates and glasses to the counter and set them down. "Let me dry. It will go faster."

"No." She kept her eyes focused on the sink. "You go on outside. I can handle this just fine."

He studied her beautiful profile for a moment and then started toward the mudroom. When he reached the doorway, he turned and looked at her.

"Eva," he began, "your parents have always loved you. You should come home to them. They miss you and they need you."

She closed her eyes for a brief moment and then focused on her task again.

As Ian walked through the mudroom, he was certain he'd ruined his chance to ever win her heart.

As soon as the back door shut, Eva slumped against the sink and released the breath she'd been holding. Ian's admission that he still cared for her had punched her in the chest, knocking the wind out of her. She'd never expected him to say he still had feelings for her.

She turned toward the window and watched him stalk out to the dairy barn. He was still the amazing man she remembered. She didn't regret her life with Simeon, but she still cared for Ian. She had always harbored feelings for him, but she'd been young and prideful when her mother pressured her to date him. Now, with more mature eyes, she saw what a fine, solid Christian man he was. He'd be a wonderful husband and a gentle father.

With a shake of her head, she returned to her dishwashing. She had no business even considering a relationship with a man. She was still emotional after losing Simeon, and her life was complicated because she had to consider Junior's feelings. She was better off living with Simeon's family.

But if she belonged back in Ronks, why did a strong force seem to be pulling her to her father's farm?

CHAPTER 8

"Is this right?" Junior asked as he lifted the fishing line to show Ian the baited hook.

"*Ya,* that's exactly right." Ian pointed toward the pond. "Now, do you remember how to cast your line?"

Junior bit his lower lip, which he always seemed to do when he wasn't sure about something.

"It's okay. I'll show you again." Leaning over, Ian demonstrated how to cast the line.

They'd spent nearly an hour sitting on the edge of the pond at the back of Harvey's property, fishing. The sun was high in the sky, and the humid air smelled fresh and clean. It was the perfect Friday afternoon.

"I can't believe Eva has been here two weeks now," Harvey commented as he sat on the other side of Junior. "I don't want their visit to end." He smiled down at his grandson.

Ian nodded. "I've enjoyed it too."

Junior cast his line and then looked up at Ian. "Did I do it right?"

"*Ya.* You did." Ian mussed his golden hair. "You're *gut* at fishing."

"Really?" Junior's face lit up.

"Really." Ian leaned down and bumped his shoulder against Junior's.

"He has really taken to you." Harvey baited his hook. "And you're a natural with him."

"*Danki.*" Ian cast his line. "He's a great *bu.*"

"I'd love to see Eva and Junior stay with us permanently. We have enough room at the *haus.*" Harvey cast his line and then returned his gaze to his grandson. "Mary and I want to see him grow up, and we don't want to lose Eva again."

"I understand." Ian's chest constricted as he thought of Eva's beautiful smile. If only he could find a way to convince her to stay.

Humming to herself, Eva pulled her father's trousers off the clothesline and folded them before placing them in a large wicker basket. The back door opened and then clicked shut as she pulled down a second pair.

Mamm stepped closer and pulled a shirt off the line. "I guess the men are still fishing?" She folded the garment and set it into the basket.

"*Ya.*" Eva folded the second pair of trousers. "I was surprised when Ian asked to take Junior. He hasn't been fishing before. Nathan has talked about teaching him, but he's been busy volunteering at the fire station and working at the restaurant."

"Ian is so *gut* with Junior." *Mamm* smiled. "He's taught him how to do chores, play catch, and now fish."

"He does have a gift with *kinner.* I guess he's had plenty of practice with his *bruderskinner.*" Happiness buzzed through Eva as she recalled the smile on Junior's face when Ian offered to take him fishing. Ian was like a special uncle to Junior, and it would be difficult to separate them when they left for Ronks.

"I want to apologize to you."

Eva spun toward her mother. "What do you mean?"

"I never meant to push you away when you decided to marry Simeon and move to Ronks." *Mamm*'s hazel eyes misted over.

Eva took a deep breath. It was time to be brave, to clear the air.

"I loved Simeon with all my heart, and it hurt me when you and *Dat* even refused to come to our wedding."

"I know. We behaved badly." *Mamm*'s

expression was grave. "You broke our hearts when you left, but it was your decision." She touched Eva's hand. "I'm sorry."

"I needed you when he died." Eva shuddered as unexpected tears streamed down her face.

"I wanted to be with you, but Mim made it sound as though you didn't want us to come."

"I was still so hurt about the wedding, and I told Mim not to invite you. But looking back now, I realize it was immature and stupid for me to do that. I'm sorry too, *Mamm.*" She sniffed as more tears rained down her cheeks. "I pushed you away too, but I needed you more than I realized."

"Oh, Eva." *Mamm* pulled her into a hug as sobs shook Eva's body. "Shh, *mei liewe.* You're *mei dochder,* and I'll always love you. You never lost your *dat* or me. We prayed God would bring you back to us, and he did. Our prayers are answered."

Eva fought for control of her tears. *"Danki, Mamm."*

"Why were you so angry with me that you went to Mim's in the first place?"

"It was because of how you were pressuring me about Ian. That you didn't seem to understand how your interference was affecting me."

Mamm listened, her expression full of contrition.

"I was immature and naïve, *Mamm.* But I don't regret the life I built with Simeon," Eva said as she carried the laundry basket into the kitchen.

"I know you don't, and I'm sorry I hurt you and made you feel like you had to leave." *Mamm* touched Eva's shoulder. "I only wanted what was best for you. I never meant to push you away. But your future was always your choice, and I should have honored that. Your *dat* and I should have come to your wedding. I understand how much you loved Simeon, and we should have respected your decision to move to Ronks."

"It did hurt that you weren't there, and I wanted you there." Eva wiped at her eyes. "I'm sorry for not including you when Junior was born. I needed you, and you and *Dat* had a right to be a part of his life from the beginning."

"I understand why you did it, but it did hurt us."

"I'm so sorry, *Mamm.* I promise I'll never hurt you like that again. I want you and *Dat* to always be part of Junior's life."

"*Danki.* We want to be a part of both your lives from now on." *Mamm* nodded and

114

wiped her face with a napkin from the table. "Would you consider staying with us permanently? Your *dat* and I would love to have you here. You could still visit Simeon's family."

Eva turned toward the back window and focused her eyes on the *daadihaus.* "I'm not sure about moving here permanently, but I do want to stay awhile. If it's okay with you, we'll stay through the summer."

Mamm hugged Eva again. "We would love that. *Danki.* "

Eva smiled as she relished the feel of her mother's hug.

"I caught three fish, and they were this big!" Junior spread his arms wide as Eva tucked his little body under the bedsheet later that night.

"Really?" Eva chuckled. "So they were the size of dolphins?"

"No." Junior shook his head. "More like whales."

Eva gave a feigned gasp of surprise. "I never knew whales are in *Daadi*'s pond."

"They *are.* " Junior nodded with emphasis.

"You'd better get some sleep, because *Daadi* and Ian will need your help with chores tomorrow."

"I like helping them with chores."

"That's *gut.* They appreciate your help."

"Ian is so nice to me. He teaches me things."

"*Ya,* he does." She touched his nose.

"Can we stay here?"

Eva felt her lips press together in a frown as she brushed back his hair. "I think your *mammi* back in Ronks would miss you, along with *Daadi, Onkel* Nathan, *Aenti* Kayla, and *Onkel* Jamie. Wouldn't you miss them too?"

"Maybe they can come visit us here."

"We'll see." Eva stood. "You need to say your prayers and go to sleep. *Gut nacht.*" She leaned down and kissed his forehead before stepping out into the hallway and quietly closing his door.

As she walked into her bedroom, her heart twisted. Did she and Junior belong in New Wilmington with her family and Ian, or did they belong in Ronks with Simeon's family?

She lowered herself onto the corner of her bed, closed her eyes, and began to pray. "Lord, please show me where *mei sohn* and I belong. I'm grateful you encouraged me to visit my parents and helped me work things out with *mei mamm.* But now I'm confused. Please show me where I should raise Junior."

Eva pushed the ties of her prayer covering over her shoulders as she stepped out of the phone shanty and into the hot August morning sun.

Hugging her arms over her chest, she recalled the conversation she'd just shared with her mother-in-law. She loved hearing about how busy the restaurant was, how Nathan was enjoying both volunteering at the fire department and spending time with his youth group, and how Kayla and Jamie were doing. Marilyn told Eva everyone missed both her and Junior, but she also encouraged her to enjoy her time in New Wilmington and not feel rushed to come back to Ronks.

Eva glanced at the barn and smiled as her thoughts shifted to Junior. They had both fallen into a comfortable routine during the past two months. Junior helped with the farm chores and spent time with *Dat* and Ian, and Eva helped her mother cook, clean, and sew.

She and Junior were happy here, but even after reconciling with her mother and coming to an unspoken agreement with Ian to remain just friends, she couldn't shake the thread of worry that haunted the back of her mind. She still wasn't sure if she and Junior belonged here or back in Ronks. If she decided to move here, it would crush Simeon's parents' hearts. They'd been a part of Junior's life since he was born, and they cherished him as much as she did. How could she rip their grandson from their lives when they craved having a part of Simeon as much as she did? Taking Junior from them would be cruel, and she couldn't fathom hurting them when they meant so much to her.

Ian stepped out of the barn and waved, and Eva picked up her pace as she returned the gesture.

"What brings you out here?" he asked as she approached him.

"I was just on the phone with Marilyn. She updated me on everyone back in Ronks."

"That's great." Ian nodded toward the path that led to the pasture. "Would you please go for a walk with me?"

"*Ya.*" She fell into step with him. "It's a *schee* day for a walk." She glanced up toward the porch, and a memory filled her mind. "Do you remember that time Miriam Faye came over, and we tried making *mei mammi*'s recipe for lemon meringue pie?"

He groaned and shook his head. "It was so bad."

She laughed and smacked his arm. "*Ya,* it was terrible. I didn't cook the pudding enough and it was so runny. You practically needed a straw to drink it instead of a fork to eat it." She smiled up at him. "But you were a trooper. You ate it anyway, and you said it was *gut.*"

He shrugged. "I didn't want to hurt your feelings."

Warmth swelled in her chest as she lost herself in his brown eyes. He always considered her feelings, no matter the circumstance.

He led her to one of the smaller barns, where *Dat* kept his tools and supplies. "I need to show you something."

"All right." Her curiosity piqued as they walked to the back of the barn, where she saw piles of wood and rope. "What's this?"

"It's going to be that swing set. I've been gathering the pieces for more than a month now." He pointed to his collection. "It's going to have three swings, a slide, and a fort. Do you think Junior will like it?"

"He'll love it. But I'm confused." She studied him. "You said you would build it only if Junior and I decided to stay here permanently, and I haven't said we're staying."

"You said you'd stay through the summer, and I don't think a single swing is sufficient for him. He needs a real swing set. Your *dat* and I are going to start building it today."

"Danki." Appreciation mixed with affection wafted over her, and without any forethought, Eva wrapped her arms around his neck and pulled him close for a hug.

Ian pulled her even closer, and she closed her eyes, relishing the feel of being in his strong arms. Her pulse skittered as heat rushed through her from head to toe. For the first time since Simeon died, she felt safe and protected, and she wanted to stay there forever.

Then her spine went rigid. She had no right to enjoy the feel of his touch. She and Ian were treading on dangerous territory, and she needed to put distance between them.

"I'm sorry," she muttered, stepping away from him. "I need to see if *mei mamm* needs my help. Excuse me." She rushed toward the barn exit.

"Eva!" Ian called after her. "Eva, wait!"

She kept moving until his voice faded away.

■ ■ ■ ■

"What's on your mind?" Harvey looked up at Ian as he handed him another screw to hold the slide in place.

"What do you mean?" Ian kept his eyes focused on his work as he added the screw.

"I've known you since you were sixteen years old, and I can tell when something is eating at you. So spill it, *sohn.*"

Ian bit back a grin. He always enjoyed it when Harvey called him that.

Ian reached down for the last screw. "I've just been eager to get this swing set together."

"It's more than that."

"It's nothing." Ian added the last screw to the slide and then tossed the screwdriver onto the ground.

Climbing down the ladder, Ian surveyed their work. The swing set was perfect. He couldn't wait for Junior to wake up from his nap and see it. For the past two days, the boy had begged Ian to allow him to try one of the swings, but Ian explained he had to wait for the full set to be complete. Now that it was, Junior could play on it every day until he and his mother returned to Ronks.

A muscle jumped in Ian's tight jaw. He dreaded the idea of saying good-bye to Eva and Junior. He'd become so attached to them that it crushed his heart to imagine not seeing them every day.

"It's Eva, isn't it?"

Ian's gaze snapped to Harvey's. "What?"

"Your mood." Harvey pointed a finger at him. "You were humming to yourself and smiling a lot. And then you got quiet. You're in love with *mei dochder,* aren't you?"

He'd been caught!

Ian bit back a groan. He couldn't lie to Harvey, especially if the truth was written all over his face.

"It's fine." Harvey rubbed his beard. "In fact, I think it's marvelous. I've always thought you and Eva would make a *gut* couple."

"Really?" Ian hated the thread of desperation in his voice.

Harvey nodded. "Years ago, I had hoped she would marry you so you two could take over the farm. Now that she's back . . . Well, it might be God's plan for you to finally be together."

"It's a *wunderbaar* idea, but I think she's leaving." Ian folded up the ladder and laid it on its side. "I don't think it's in God's plan for us to be together."

"Do you love her?"

Ian nodded without hesitation. "I always have."

"Have you told her how you feel?"

"I told her I've always cared about her, and she went quiet."

"So you didn't say you love her?"

"No, I didn't use the word *love.*"

"Maybe if you told her you love her, and that you want her to stay, she'll stay."

"I don't know." Ian rubbed the back of his head. "I don't think she feels the same way since she turned me down when I asked her to date me years ago."

"She hasn't left yet." Harvey began picking up tools. "Maybe she's waiting for you to declare your love and ask her to stay."

Harvey's words rolled through Ian's mind as he carried the ladder to the barn. As much as he wanted Harvey to be right, he'd seen the shock — and possibly fear — in her eyes when he told her he'd always cared for her.

As he leaned the ladder against the barn wall, hope and possibility lit in his chest. Perhaps it was time for him to tell her exactly how he felt. And maybe, just maybe, Harvey was right. Maybe she would decide to stay.

■ ■ ■ ■

"How was your week?" Miriam Faye asked Eva as she sat down beside her in church.

"It was *gut.*" Eva nodded. "Ian built a swing set for Junior, and he and *mei dat* finished putting it together yesterday. Junior loves it so much. I had to make him get off it last night." She ran her finger over the hymnal as she contemplated Ian. "I can't get over how fantastic Ian is with Junior. Since we've been here, he's taught Ian how to play catch, how to fish, and how to take care of the animals on the farm. He's just a natural with him."

Miriam Faye leaned in closer. "You care about him."

Eva's cheeks felt as if they might burst into flame as she remembered how she'd hugged him a few days ago.

"What is it?" Miriam Faye whispered with a thread of excitement in her voice.

Eva glanced around and then lowered her voice. "I accidentally hugged him on Wednesday."

Miriam Faye grinned. "How do you accidentally hug someone?"

"Shh!" Eva kept her voice low as she explained how she was so overwhelmed with appreciation when Ian showed her the swing set pieces that she hugged him. "I'm so confused. I can't believe I felt comfortable enough to do that. I haven't felt that way about a man other than Simeon. It scared me to let myself go like that. And I just feel so guilty."

"What do you mean?" Miriam Faye's smile faded.

"I have no right to feel that way about any man. I disrespected Simeon's memory and his family by hugging Ian. How could I do that to him?"

"*Ach,* Eva." Miriam Faye touched her arm. "You didn't disrespect Simeon's memory. You have a right to move on with your life. Ian is such a *gut* man, and he obviously cares for you and Junior. I never understood why you turned him down when he asked you to date him, even if your *mamm* was pushing you."

"Really?"

"*Ya.*" Miriam Faye looked across the barn to where Ian spoke to Will. "Just look at him. He's handsome, thoughtful, and kind. The kind of man Simeon would want for you. Why wouldn't you jump at the chance to have a husband like him?"

At that moment, the song leader began to sing the opening hymn, and Eva was thankful the attention was taken away from her. Miriam Faye was wrong to say Eva should allow herself to date and fall in love with Ian. She had to find a way to put a cover over her heart.

But deep in her soul, she knew it was already too late.

CHAPTER 9

Ian's thoughts raced as he rolled over in bed. For the past two hours he'd waited for sleep to come for him, but his thoughts had kept his mind buzzing with images of Eva and Junior.

Harvey's words had haunted him since Saturday, and he couldn't stop wondering if he should tell Eva how he felt about her. He'd almost told her more than once after church yesterday, but each time he was about to say the words, they were inter-rupted.

Now, as he stared at the ceiling, he won-dered if he had the power to keep Eva here on the farm. If he declared his love for her, would she truly stay and possibly consider building a future with him? Or would his declaration put pressure on Eva and cause her to run away again? His chest tightened with the fear of losing her a second time.

Wide awake, he kicked off his sheet and

climbed out of bed. After pulling on a pair of trousers and a short-sleeved blue shirt, Ian slipped on a pair of shoes, grabbed a Coleman lantern from his mudroom, and stepped out onto his front porch.

When he looked toward Harvey's house, he spotted a lantern glowing on the back porch. Curiosity pushed him down the steps and up the path toward the yellow light. His pulse picked up when he saw Eva sitting on the glider, clad in a blue dress and wearing a matching scarf over her hair.

"Ian." She sat up straight, her eyes sparkling in the golden glow of the light. "What are you doing out here?"

He placed his lantern beside hers. "I couldn't sleep."

"I couldn't either." After a slight hesitation he could see in her eyes, she scooted over and patted the seat beside her. "Would you like to join me?"

"*Ya,* I'd love to." He sank down onto the glider, and when his leg brushed hers, heat skittered up it. "Why couldn't you sleep?"

She shrugged as she stared toward his house. Had thoughts of him caused her insomnia?

"Are you feeling okay?" he said, pressing for a response.

"*Ya.* I just have a lot on my mind."

"Would you like to tell me about it?"

She shook her head and then looked toward her mother's garden. "Junior really loves his swing set. It was generous of you to build it for him. *Danki.*"

"I think you've thanked me more than a hundred times now. You don't have to keep thanking me."

"May I pay you for the lumber?"

"No." He rested his elbow on the arm of the glider. "It was a gift. I won't accept payment."

"But you don't draw a very large salary here."

"That doesn't mean I don't have any money. I know how to save, and I received some money when my grandparents sold their farm. I'm not destitute."

Her eyes widened. "I'm so sorry. I didn't mean to imply that."

"Stop." He touched her hand, and she didn't break the connection. Her skin was warm and soft, and his mouth dried as his pulse galloped. "That swing set is just a fraction of what I would like to do for you and Junior. You're both very important to me."

She swallowed.

"You know how I feel about you." He traced his finger down her cheek, and she shivered. Then he quickly brushed his lips over hers, sending heat roaring through every cell in his body.

Leaning away from him, she gasped. "Ian, I-I can't." She popped up from the glider, and he grabbed her hand, holding her in place.

"I can't do this. It's not right," she said.

"Wait." He stood and released her hand. "Don't go."

"It's late." She took a step back. "I should go to bed."

"Just wait. Please." He held up his hands as if to calm her. "I love you, Eva. I want to be with you."

"No." She shook her head and hugged her arms around her waist. "Please don't say that."

"Give me a chance to explain how I feel." His words came in a rush. "I've always loved you. I never stopped caring about you, even after you broke my heart. Start a new life with me. Let me take care of you and Junior."

"I can't leave Ronks."

"Just listen to what I have to say." He pointed toward his house. "We can start out in the *daadihaus.* Then I'll use the money I received from my grandparents to build a bigger *haus* for us. It will be just like your *mamm* said. We can start a life together right here."

"I can't. My life is in Ronks. I can't take Junior away from Simeon's family. Junior is all they have left of their *sohn.*"

"I understand that." He stepped toward her. "But you have to learn how to live again. That's what Simeon would want. That's what God wants."

"How could you know that?" Her voice broke as tears sprinkled down her cheeks, shattering his heart with every drop.

"Simeon would want you to be *froh.* He'd want you to have someone to take care of you and Junior. He'd want Junior to have a *dat* and siblings."

She shook her head. "You don't know what Simeon would want."

"I know you deserve to be *froh.*" He reached for her, and she stepped away from his touch. "You shouldn't spend the rest of your life alone."

"I'm not alone. I have my family back in Ronks."

Disappointment simmered in his gut. "You have family here. And you have me. You should be here. This is your home." He pointed to the floor. "There's no place like home."

"No, I can't stay here, and I can't be with you."

In a flash, she raced into the house, closing and locking the door behind her.

Anguish tightened his muscles as he raised his fist to knock on the door. Then he let his hand drop to his side. He couldn't force Eva to love him, nor could he make her stay.

Had Harvey been wrong? Was this a lost cause? He wanted to believe he and Eva belonged together, but he had to accept she longed to go back to Ronks.

With his heart breaking, he turned off her lantern, picked up his, and started down the path toward his house. Despondency bogged his steps as he made his way.

As he entered his house and walked to his bedroom, he opened his heart to God and whispered a prayer. "Please, God. Help me find a way to convince Eva to stay. Let me take care of her and Junior. Let me love her and make her *froh*."

He stripped down to his boxers and undershirt and climbed into bed. He closed his eyes, and a hollowness filled his gut. Maybe it wasn't God's plan for them to be together. Maybe he had to accept an ugly truth — it was time to give up on Eva and let her go.

■ ■ ■ ■

Tears clouded Eva's vision as she hurried up the stairs to her room. Her thoughts spun as confusion, love, affection, fear, and guilt all warred inside of her. She loved Ian, but she was terrified to allow herself to love a man other than Simeon. She longed to build a life with Ian, but she couldn't bring herself to consider taking Junior away from Simeon's family when he was their last link to their son.

Against her better judgment, she had allowed herself to stay in New Wilmington too long, and she'd become too attached to Ian. It was time to leave. She had to get away from him before she agreed to stay and marry him. She didn't belong here, and she needed to get back home to Ronks.

Pulling her duffel bag out of the closet, Eva began to fill it with the clothes and books she'd brought with her. After she packed it all, she pulled the bus schedule from the drawer in her nightstand and studied it. A bus was scheduled to leave tomorrow morning for Lancaster County. She would call Ted first thing in the morning and ask him to take her to the station. She just had to let Marilyn know she was coming.

She hurried down the stairs and to the back door. Peeking out, she scanned the porch, making sure Ian had gone home instead of waiting to see if she would come back outside. She couldn't face him and tell him she planned to leave.

You're a coward, Eva.

Ignoring her inner voice, she crept out onto the porch and found the lantern where she'd left it. Flipping it on, she hurried down the porch steps and to the phone shanty. She dialed her mother-in-law's number and then waited for voice mail to pick up.

After the beep, she began to speak. "*Mamm,* this is Eva. I'm coming home tomorrow. I've had a *gut* stay here, but it's time to leave. I miss all of you so much, and I think Junior misses you too." She wrapped the phone cord around her fingers as she shared the time she would arrive. "Would you please arrange for a driver to meet me at the bus station? *Danki.*" She held her breath as renewed guilt swamped her. "It's too difficult to be here surrounded by memories. I have to tell you the truth, and I hope you will forgive me."

Her voice sounded foreign to her ears as guilt colored her tone. "You're going to be disappointed in me, but I've fallen in love with an old *freind*. His name is Ian, and he works for my parents. I've known him since I was a teenager. It's tearing me to pieces to be with him. Ian has taught Junior how to play catch and fish. He even built Junior a *schee* swing set. But I know it's wrong to feel this way about him." She paused and sniffed as tears raced down her cheeks.

"Ian asked me to stay and marry him. He wants to build a *haus* for Junior and me, but I can't even think of taking Junior away from you. That's why I need to come home. I have to leave before I tell Ian yes. Please forgive me. I started packing tonight, and I'll finish in the morning. Junior and I will see you tomorrow. *Gut nacht.*"

After she hung up the phone, Eva rushed back into the house. She changed into her nightgown and then climbed into bed. Burying her face in her pillow, she dissolved into sobs.

"Wake up, Junior." Eva gently nudged her son as he slept curled up with his thumb in his mouth. "Come on, *mei liewe.* We have to get to the bus station."

Junior moaned and rolled onto his side, facing the wall.

Eva cupped her hand over her mouth to

stifle a yawn and then began opening dresser drawers and tossing Junior's clothes into the duffel bag.

Junior sat up and rubbed his eyes. "Where are we going?"

"We have to go home to Ronks."

"Why?" he whined.

"Because we have to." Eva's eyes stung as another yawn overtook her. She'd slept less than two hours. Her tears and conflicting thoughts about leaving kept her up most of the night.

"But I don't want to go." Junior's eyes misted as his lower lip trembled. "I want to stay here with *Mammi, Daadi,* and Ian."

"I know, *mei liewe,* but we have to go." She took a deep breath as regret nearly choked back her words. "Now, get up. Go wash your face." She pointed toward the doorway. "You need to eat breakfast, and then we have to go."

"No." He shook his head as tears poured down his cheeks. "I don't want to go."

"We have to." She repeated the words with emphasis. "Junior, I need you to —"

"No!" He yelled the word. "I want to stay here!"

Footfalls echoed in the hallway, and Eva braced herself. She wasn't ready to tell her mother they were leaving. Bitter-tasting guilt swallowed her up as the footsteps came closer.

"I want to stay!" Junior repeated as his shoulders shook. "Don't make me go!"

"What's going on?" *Mamm* appeared in the doorway, her eyes focused on the duffel bag. "What are you doing?"

"We're leaving." Eva winced when she saw her mother's face crumple.

"Why?" *Mamm* grabbed at her chest as if her heart were breaking. "Did I do something to upset you?"

"No, you haven't done anything wrong. It's just better this way." Eva reached for Junior. "Get up now. You have to wash your face and then get dressed." She turned to her mother. "Would you please help him get dressed? I need to call Ted and ask him to take us to the bus station."

Mamm paused for a moment as her hazel eyes glistened. "Tell me the truth, Eva. Did I do something to upset you? If so, please forgive me. I can't lose you again."

"It's not you." Eva's voice trembled as she touched her mother's hand. "It's me. It's too painful for me to stay here surrounded by the memories of what life used to be. Junior and I belong with the Dienners. I promise I will call you every week, and we'll come to visit again soon. Please understand

137

I just can't live here."

"I'll try to understand." *Mamm* nodded, but her face remained wistful. "I'll support you this time."

"*Danki.*" Eva swiveled back to Junior, who was wiping away more tears. "Please get up."

Junior climbed out of bed, rushed across the room, and hugged her mother as he sobbed.

"It's all right, *mei liewe.*" *Mamm* lifted him into her arms and hugged him. "Maybe your *daadi* and I can come visit you. Would you like that?"

Eva wiped away her own tears as she rushed down the stairs, out the front door, and down the path to the phone shanty. When she lifted the receiver to dial Ted's number, she discovered a voice mail message. After she entered the code, Marilyn's voice came through the phone.

"Hello, this is Marilyn Dienner. I'm hoping to reach Eva before she leaves," her mother-in-law began. "Eva, if you're there, please listen to what I have to say. I played your message more than once this morning, and I have to admit it doesn't sound like you really want to come back to Ronks. And that's okay. In fact, I think that's fantastic. When we spoke last week, I could hear how *froh* you were. I haven't heard you sound

138

that *froh* since, well, since we lost Simeon."

Eva gasped.

"Eva," Marilyn continued, "we support you if you want to stay in New Wilmington and build a new life for Junior. We all understand. You deserve happiness, and you're allowed to move on with your life. We all know how much you and Simeon loved each other. You and Simeon had a *gut*, strong marriage, and you shared some *froh* times together. God chose to take Simeon, and we can't question why. But Simeon is gone now, and you and Junior have to find your way without him."

Eva covered her mouth as a sob threatened to escape.

"I believe God put the question in Junior's heart when he asked you to take him to New Wilmington to meet your parents. God is giving you the perfect opportunity to start a new life there with your family. Your parents want to be part of Junior's life and your life. And Ian sounds like the perfect man for you. He loves you and Junior, and Junior needs a *dat* just as you need a husband. Simeon would want you to be *froh*, and he would want a *gut* man to take care of you and his son. Don't miss this opportunity to have the happiness God wants you to find."

Now in tears, Eva nodded in agreement as if Marilyn stood in front of her.

"And don't worry about us here in Ronks," Marilyn said. "We can come visit you and you can come to us. Maybe you, Ian, and Junior can come see us for Thanksgiving. We'd love to meet Ian too." She paused for a moment. "Don't get on that bus today, Eva. Stay there. You can come later for your things or I can have them shipped to you. We'll figure out the details later. We love you, Eva, and we love Junior too. Call me later. Good-bye."

When the line went dead, Eva stared at the phone as Marilyn's words swirled through her mind like a raging tornado.

Tears flowed from her eyes as confusion and regret engulfed her. Covering her face with her hands, Eva began to pray. "God, I don't know what to do. Help me."

Then the answer came to her loud and clear in her mind.

Stay in New Wilmington and build a life with Ian.

Eva gasped again as warmth and happiness flooded her veins. Yes, she did belong here, and she could feel the answer to the very marrow of her bones.

Now she needed to ask Ian if he still wanted to build a life with her after the way she'd rejected him — again.

Wiping the tears from her eyes, she hurried out of the phone shanty, walked around the house, and stopped short when she reached the back porch. Ian sat on the glider talking to Junior, and her father stood nearby, consoling her mother.

Ian met her gaze and stood, his lips twisted into a deep frown. He joined her at the bottom of the porch steps, and when he opened his mouth to speak, she held up her hand, silencing him.

"Before you say anything, I need to clarify something." She took a deep breath. "Were you serious when you said you'd build me a *haus*?" She pointed to the *daadihaus*. "Because I'm not sure two bedrooms are enough room for us."

His mouth worked, but no words escaped for a beat. Then he took his own deep breath and asked, "Do you mean you're staying?"

"*Ya,* but only if the offer is still open for a bigger *haus*. I'm not prideful, but we're going to need more room."

His handsome face broke into a grin and amusement danced in his eyes. "How big are you thinking? I'm not sure I can afford a mansion for you."

She grinned as she tilted her head. "I

won't settle for fewer than four bedrooms."

"Four, huh? I think I can handle that." He rubbed his chin. "But I'm a little confused. Does this mean you'll marry me?"

"*Ya,* I'd be honored to marry you."

He pulled her into a hug. "*Ich liebe dich.* You've just made me the happiest man in all of Pennsylvania."

"I love you too." She touched his cheek. "*Danki* for not giving up on me."

"I could never give up on you." Leaning down, he brushed his lips over her cheek.

She sucked in a breath as heat zinged through her entire body.

"What's going on?" *Dat* demanded as he, *Mamm,* and Junior hurried down the porch steps to join them.

"Junior and I are going to stay," Eva announced as she threaded her fingers with Ian's. "I want to be with my family." She looked up at Ian. "And Ian and I are going to be married."

"Yay!" Junior clapped his hands as *Dat* picked him up and balanced him on his hip.

"I'm so thankful." *Dat* smiled as he looked at Junior.

"What made you change your mind?" *Mamm* touched Eva's arm.

"Marilyn left a message and told me it's okay for me to be with Ian. I realized she's right. Simeon would want me to move on and build a new life."

She looked up at Ian. "And Ian said something I realized is true. Junior and I belong here, because there's no place like home."

DISCUSSION QUESTIONS

1. Eva was devastated when she lost her husband in an accident. Have you ever faced an unexpected death or been severely affected by an accident? What Bible verses would help in a situation like this?
2. When Eva is torn about where she belongs, she turns to prayer for guidance. Think of a time when you found strength through prayer. Share this with the group.
3. Mary feels terrible for alienating Eva. She wants to rebuild her relationship with her daughter, but she's not sure how to do it. Can you relate to Mary and her experience? How so?
4. Ian is devastated when Eva tells him she can't have a relationship with him. Think of a time when you felt lost and alone. Where did you find your strength? What Bible verses would help?
5. Which character do you identify with the most? Which character seemed to carry

the most emotional stake in the story? Was it Eva, Ian, Junior, or someone else?

6. At the end of the story, Marilyn leaves a message that convinces Eva she can move on and start a new life back home in New Wilmington. Do you agree with Marilyn's assessment of the situation? Why or why not?

7. Eva was certain she was supposed to remain a widow and not move on with her life. What do you think caused her to change her point of view throughout the story?

ACKNOWLEDGMENTS

As always, I'm grateful for my loving family, including my mother, Lola Goebelbecker; my husband, Joe; and my sons, Zac and Matt.

Special thanks to my mother and my dear friend Becky Biddy, who graciously proof-read the draft and corrected my hilarious typos.

I'm also grateful for my special Amish friend who patiently answers my endless stream of questions. You're a blessing in my life.

Thank you to my wonderful church family at Morning Star Lutheran in Matthews, North Carolina, for your encouragement, prayers, love, and friendship. You all mean so much to my family and me.

Thank you to Zac Weikal and the fabulous members of my Bakery Bunch! I'm so grateful for your friendship and your excitement about my books. You all are awesome!

To my agent, Natasha Kern — I can't thank you enough for your guidance, advice, and friendship. You are a tremendous blessing in my life.

Thank you to my amazing editor, Jocelyn Bailey, for your friendship and guidance. I'm grateful to each and every person at HarperCollins Christian Publishing who helped make this book a reality.

I'm grateful to editor Jean Bloom, who helped me polish and refine the story. Jean, you are a master at connecting the dots and filling in the gaps. I'm so happy we can continue to work together!

Thank you most of all to God — for giving me the inspiration and the words to glorify you. I'm grateful and humbled you've chosen this path for me.

■ ■ ■ ■

WHEN LOVE
RETURNS

BETH WISEMAN

■ ■ ■ ■

To all of the people impacted by
Hurricane Harvey

CHAPTER 1

Sarah paid the cabdriver and helped Miriam out of the car. They each slung a backpack over their shoulders, Miriam's much smaller than Sarah's. Everything they owned was in those bags.

"Where's the house?" Miriam gazed up at her mother with questioning blue eyes, her dark hair pulled up in a ponytail that Sarah had braided on the ride from the airport to Lancaster County.

Sarah squatted in front of her five-year-old daughter, kissed her on the cheek, and pointed down the dirt road that led to Sarah's parents' house. "It's about half a mile down that road."

"Why didn't the man in the yellow car take us all the way there?" Miriam readjusted the backpack on her tiny body.

"Are you sure that's not too heavy? I can carry it, if it is." Sarah eyed the small brown bag over her daughter's shoulders with *Red*

Cross etched into the mesh-like material.

Miriam shook her head and smiled.

Sarah stood and blew a strand of hair away from her face, wishing she had another rubber band to pull it back. She only found one in her purse among the few things she managed to grab before the water from Hurricane Harvey flooded their apartment.

"Spring is a nice time of year for a walk." And Sarah needed the time to calm her racing heart. She eyed the fields on both sides of them, lush and green, the way she remembered spring in this rural area that felt so foreign now. "When I was a little girl, there were all kinds of animals that ran around this area. You might see a jackrabbit or a wild turkey, ducks, or maybe even a bobcat."

Miriam gasped. "Will they hurt us?"

Sarah put a hand on her daughter's shoulder and coaxed her to start walking. "No, they won't. Don't you know by now, silly girl, that I'm never going to let anything hurt you."

"I know, Mommy. You saved us from the storm."

Sarah took a few steps, memories flooding her mind, as she took in the silo in the distance, orange hues in the background as the sun began its final descent. It was a slightly upward climb for several yards, but when they reached the top of the slope, Sarah's family homestead was visible. She swallowed the emotion that had built over the last few days. She hadn't seen her parents in six years. Or Abram.

"The grace of God saved us from the storm," she said softly as a shiver ran the length of her spine. Sarah had tried to evacuate with Miriam before the hurricane slammed into the Gulf Coast, but the water rose too fast, and her small downstairs apartment in Houston had a foot of water inside before she could pack more than a few necessities and some clothes for her and Miriam. No one in the area was prepared for the epic floodwater.

She'd carried Miriam on her shoulders through waist-deep water until a boat came for them. After a week in a shelter, she finally called Big Jake at the hardware store in Bird-in-Hand and asked if he could get word to her parents to call her, and she left the number for the shelter. Sarah was between paychecks, and she didn't have much in her savings account. The building where she worked had six feet of water inside, and she had no idea when she'd be able to go back. The devastation frightened Miriam.

Sarah's mother had wired her money, even though she hadn't seen or talked to her parents since she ran away from home when she was seventeen and two months pregnant. She'd written them three times over the years, and all the letters returned unopened. Sarah had never been baptized in the Old Order Amish community where she'd grown up. According to the *Ordnung,* she shouldn't have been shunned. But her parents had practiced a shunning of their own. Sarah wondered if they would have sent money if it hadn't been for Miriam, the granddaughter they didn't know they had until the recent phone call.

Sarah would have eventually reached out to her parents again, if only for Miriam's sake. Her daughter deserved to know her heritage. And even amid the complications, Miriam had a right to know her grandparents. But Sarah hadn't had much time to prepare emotionally for this trip. She and her daughter were homeless and broke. She would rather return home without her tail between her legs, which was surely going to give her mother an advantage. She could already hear the scolding that was sure to come — how the *Englisch* world was no place for Sarah and how she'd shamed and disappointed her family and community.

Sarah had friends they could have stayed with, but something deep within beckoned her home to face the people she left behind and those she'd wronged — especially Abram — no matter how much she feared the outcome.

"Is that your mommy and daddy's house?" Miriam pointed at the white two-story home with green shutters in the distance.

"Yep. That's where I grew up." Sarah slowed her pace, tempted to swoop Miriam into her arms and run back.

"What should I call my grandparents?" Miriam scratched her chin as she slowed down too.

Sarah had fielded questions about this subject, and about Miriam's absent father, for the last couple of years. When Miriam's friends in daycare began to talk about their families, Sarah told Miriam that her grandparents lived far away, which was true, and she avoided the father part — a bullet she wouldn't be able to dodge forever.

"What do you want to call them?" Sarah's heart pounded as she wondered how her parents would react to a five-year-old grandchild who had grown up in the city, worlds away from the quiet life here.

Miriam grew up watching cartoons on television, eating food from a microwave, and playing on Sarah's cell phone and iPad, all luxuries the Amish lived without. Grabbing rushed meals from a drive-through was often the norm. Sarah, on the other hand, was raised with three sit-down meals at the table every single day.

She wondered who would be more culture shocked, Miriam or her mother. Even though Sarah had warned Miriam how different things would be at her grandparents' house, her young daughter didn't have much of a filter, and there was no telling what might come out of her mouth. Sarah could imagine her mother's face the first time Miriam asked to heat something in the microwave, or when Miriam said something totally inappropriate. It was bound to happen. And Sarah remembered quite well the expectations her mother had for her only daughter. *Perfection.* Sarah had never demanded that of Miriam.

Miriam shrugged. "Grandma and Grandpa, I guess."

Sarah took in a long, deep breath. "*Mammi* and *Daadi* are the Pennsylvania *Deutsch* names for Grandma and Grandpa. Do you remember I told you that your grandparents speak two languages?"

They walked slowly and quietly for a few moments. Sarah wished she'd had more time to educate her daughter about the Amish ways, but it had been a crash course over the last few days.

"Or you can just call them Barbara and John." Sarah slowed even more, but Miriam took her hand and pulled her forward.

"You said we don't call grown-ups by their first names."

Sarah took another deep breath and blew it out slowly. "That's right. But with Amish people, it's normal for children to call grown-ups by their first name. Things are just different here." *Huge understatement.* She stopped abruptly, causing Miriam to stop too.

"Try to use good manners. Always say 'yes, ma'am' and 'yes, sir.' Remember to say 'please' and 'thank you,' things like that." She squeezed her eyes closed and cringed before she opened them and cupped Miriam's chin, staring into her eyes. "Do you remember what you called Billy Dalton when you got sent to time-out at your school?"

Miriam nodded, then cast her eyes downward. "Yeah. Poo-poo head."

Sarah pressed her lips together and gave Miriam her sternest look. "Right. We never, ever say that. Okay?"

Miriam nodded again.

Sarah trudged forward, squeezing her daughter's hand. This had disaster written all over it. But she wasn't going to find peace if she didn't face her past.

Barbara Zook brought a hand to her chest as she stared out the kitchen window. "John, they're here," she said loud enough for her husband to hear her in the living room.

He joined her at the window. "Why are they walking?" He chuckled. "Did they walk here from Houston?"

Barbara cut her eyes at him. "How can you joke at a time like this? They obviously asked to be dropped off at the end of the road." She refocused on her daughter, whose dark hair was still past her shoulders, but it had obviously been cut over the years, something not allowed according to the *Ordnung.* But then, her daughter clearly had not followed the teachings of their people.

"Practice smiling, Barbara. You will scare the child if you hold on to that expression on your face." John leaned closer to the window, and Barbara saw him smile out of the corner of her eye. "Look at that. Sarah's a *mamm.* And look at that beautiful *maedel* at her side."

Barbara's knees were weak, and despite the cool March temperatures, sweat beaded on her forehead and her hands were clammy as she stuffed them in the pockets of her black apron. The Lord had blessed her with only one child, Sarah. And Barbara's daughter had robbed her of five years of being a grandparent. Worse, she hadn't even known she had a grandchild until a week ago. As she eyed her daughter, a grown woman now, and as she took in the beauty of the little girl who held her mother's hand, Barbara wanted to embrace the situation with all the love she'd stashed away in her heart. But a wall of bitterness and anger had grown over the years, and it wasn't going to crumble overnight. If ever.

John walked alongside her as they crossed through the living room to the front door. Then he reached for her hand and squeezed. She couldn't remember the last time her husband had held her hand. There had been an unspoken distance between them since Sarah left. John had never said so, but Barbara suspected he blamed her.

"Everything is going to be all right, Barbara." John stopped in front of the closed front door and gazed at her for a few long seconds. "But only if you allow it to be okay. Give this a chance."

Barbara bit her trembling lip, not willing to give Sarah the satisfaction of tears. Did she think her mother would welcome her home with open arms, that all would be instantly forgiven? Sarah was only here because she had nowhere else to go.

John opened the wooden door and on the other side of the screen stood Sarah and her child. Barbara's heart hammered against her chest with a built-up vengeance that caused her to feel like she might pass out.

Her husband eased open the screen door, and they stepped aside so Sarah and her daughter could come inside. During their brief phone call, Sarah had referred to the child as Miriam. Barbara put a hand to her chest and tried to will her heart into submission, to stop it from beating so frantically. Instead of looking at Sarah, she gazed down at the child. A beautiful girl with big blue eyes, wavy dark hair, and dimples.

Barbara lifted her eyes to her daughter and forced a smile. "Welcome home." She wasn't sure if the comment sounded as sarcastic as it felt when the words slipped from her mouth, but suddenly two tiny arms wrapped around her legs and squeezed.

"Hi, Barbara," a tiny voice said before the little girl eased away, looked up at her, and smiled. "Mommy said I could call you that, but I don't think it's good manners to call a grown-up by their first name. I'm going to call you *Mammi*, if that's okay."

Barbara brought two fingers to her trembling lips and nodded. A small piece of that wall around her heart chipped loose without warning, allowing a sliver of love to slip out like a traitor latching onto something unknown before: the love of a grandchild.

Barbara forced herself to look at Sarah. Her daughter's eyes were watery, and tiny lines feathered from their corners. Sarah was only twenty-three. What had her daughter been through over the past six years? Sarah's eyes relayed all the fear Barbara felt in her heart.

Another chunk of the wall broke away, but Barbara didn't know what to do with the love that was escaping and filling her up in a way only God could do. But still, her heart needed protection.

"Excuse me." Barbara covered her mouth with her hand, turned, and left them standing barely over the threshold. She closed her bedroom door, sat on the bed, and wept. *God, help me. I can't take any more heartbreak.* Sarah had already said they would be staying only long enough for her to get a job and save some money. Then Barbara's daughter would leave again, taking her grandchild away as well.

She could hear John in the living room

163

making excuses for her. "She's been nervous, and I think it's just going to take some time, and . . ."

Barbara didn't listen to the rest. She took a deep breath, dried her tears, and squeezed her eyes closed, mentally repairing the wall, until she felt it was sturdy enough to contain her emotions. Then she raised her chin and went back to the living room.

CHAPTER 2

Her mother's abrupt exit didn't last long, and when she returned, she motioned for everyone to follow her into the kitchen, saying supper was ready. She hadn't embraced Sarah the way her father had, and she'd avoided looking at her as much as possible, but Sarah caught her sneaking peeks at Miriam. Her daughter had been a jabber box since they arrived, mostly asking Sarah's father questions like, "Where is the TV? How long before I can ride in a buggy? Why is your beard so long — are you secretly Santa Claus? Does everyone dress the way you and *Mammi* do?"

John Zook fielded these questions in the same calm manner Sarah remembered. He was a man who rarely got upset, and Sarah hated herself for what she must have put him through. It was her mother who was the problem back then, and apparently not much had changed. Everything must be

165

done by the rules, according to her mother's way of interpretation. Sarah couldn't imagine what her wrath would have been like six years ago if she'd known Sarah was pregnant. Sarah hadn't stuck around to find out.

"It's nothing fancy." Sarah's mother set a pot of roast in the middle of the table, the same large yellow pot that had cooked many a roast in Sarah's past. There were carrots and potatoes all around the meat, and the aroma filled her senses with memories and regrets all comingled into an emotional whirlwind.

As she glanced around the table, she made note that not much had changed at mealtime either. Jams and jellies were laid out, a tray was filled with pickles and olives, another dish held chow-chow, and a freshly baked loaf of bread was in a basket. Cooking was one thing Sarah couldn't fault her mother for. Everything she prepared was exceptional. Sarah had learned to cook from her mother, but her work schedule often prevented her from making the family recipes she'd grown up with. And the few times she had made some of her mother's recipes, they brought back too many memories, both good and bad.

"It looks great, *Mamm.*" It was the only thing she'd ever called her mother, but when she spun around and narrowed her eyebrows at Sarah, Sarah made a mental note not to call her by the once appreciated endearment again.

Sarah was planning to get a job, save some money, and get back to Houston as soon as possible. She would face and conquer the things she could, and she'd try to make amends with those she'd hurt. But it didn't take a rocket scientist to see that her mother wouldn't be on board the ship of redemption, no matter where it sailed.

Sarah had hoped things would be different. She wanted to reconcile, but her mother wasn't going to make it easy, which seemed unfair to Sarah. Barbara had played a role in all of this too. Maybe if she hadn't always been so hard on Sarah, she could have reached out to her mother for help, instead of fleeing because she was terrified.

After Sarah's mother filled tea glasses for everyone but Miriam, she took a jug of milk from the refrigerator and poured a glass. Sarah hadn't been allowed to have tea until she was twelve years old. *Milk for growing children,* her mother always said. But now, as a mother herself, Sarah didn't see that as such a bad thing.

"We bow our heads to pray silently," Barbara said to Miriam.

"So do we." Miriam placed her palms together, closed her eyes, and lowered her chin to her chest.

Barbara's jaw dropped a little.

"I left *here,* but that doesn't mean I didn't take my faith with me." Sarah regretted the remark and defensive tone immediately when her father sent a warning scowl her way. He was right. This was no longer Sarah's home. She was a guest now. And she didn't want to show disrespect to her parents in front of Miriam. "I'm sorry," she said, then lowered her head.

After the blessing, Miriam reached for her glass of milk and took several big swallows before spewing it all over the roast. "Mommy! What is that?"

Sarah stared at the pot roast now dotted with white spots. "Uh, it's milk, but straight from the cow." She leaned across the table a little. "We don't spit out food or drinks at the table, or ever. Is that clear?"

Miriam crinkled her nose. "It didn't taste like milk."

Sarah glanced at her father, who grinned. "I like roast with a side of milk on top." He carved himself a big slice and transferred it to his plate, along with some potatoes and carrots.

Sarah's *mamm* — or Barbara, as she

would be calling her from now on — pushed back her chair, surely appalled at Miriam's behavior. Sarah sighed before getting herself some milk-splattered meat and vegetables.

"Do you like chocolate?" Barbara asked Miriam as she held out a bottle of Hershey's syrup. *Wow, that's new.* Sarah had never seen her mother with much of anything store-bought, and certainly not chocolate syrup. She tried to picture herself at Miriam's age, spewing milk all over a lovingly prepared meal. She didn't think her mother would have shown such grace the way she just had with Miriam.

Miriam sat taller and smiled. "Yes, ma'am. I like it very much." Barbara squirted a generous amount in the milk, stirred it, then smiled a little as Miriam took a cautious drink, then smiled too. "Yummy. Thank you."

Barbara sat back down, a smug expression on her face. At least she wasn't frowning or scowling. Probably judging Sarah's parenting skills, but she would live with that for now.

"We want to hear all about your life, and praise *Gott* that you and Miriam stayed out of harm's way during the hurricane." *Daed* — who would remain *Daed* in Sarah's mind — was as genuine a man as ever lived. A

169

kind and gentle soul. He was still head of the household, as all Amish believed men to be, but he never ruled with an iron fist. He didn't need to. Sarah had always respected him enough to abide by his rules. Only Barbara's rules had ever been questionable, like the time she made Sarah go out with Jonathan Lapp because she was good friends with his mother. Even though Barbara knew how much Sarah liked Abram.

Sarah became lost in memories as she recalled her time with Abram. He was the person she'd likely hurt the most six years ago. Sarah needed to see him, to try to explain, but she wanted to wait a few days. She needed to plan her words carefully.

"Well, when I first got to Houston, I —" Sarah began in response to her father's inquiry.

"How did you even *get* to Houston?" After the interruption, Barbara stared at Sarah.

"I hired a driver to take me to Veronica's. I had enough babysitting money to take a bus to Houston and rent a small apartment over an older couple's garage for the first month. After that, I cleaned house for the woman, and she got me jobs cleaning some of her friends' houses. After Miriam was born, she became like a . . ." Sarah swallowed hard and decided not to go that route since her mother's eyes reflected an emotion Sarah couldn't quite define. "Anyway, then I got a job working as a legal secretary." She forced a smile.

"How were you able to do that with only an eighth-grade education?" Barbara took a bite of bread but kept her eyes on Sarah. The Amish only went to school through eighth grade, a rule Sarah hadn't liked but had abided by when she still lived here.

"If I'd had the money, I would have furthered my education, but instead, I worked hard, and I had a great boss who took me under her wing." She glanced at Miriam, who was slathering way too much butter on her bread, but one thing motherhood had taught Sarah was that children hear everything, even when you don't think they are paying attention. Sarah didn't want to finish the sentence by saying she couldn't further her education because things like diapers, formula, and daycare ate up every bit of money she made. Miriam was everything Sarah lived for.

She hadn't known how much one human being could love another, which brought her gaze to her mother. Sarah wasn't sure they would ever have a mother-daughter relationship again. Sarah had ruined that.

And her mother would probably punish her the entire time she was here. But Sarah deserved it. She hoped Abram would forgive her. She was less hopeful about her mother. They had been butting heads for over a year before Sarah left. Looking back, she assumed it was her teenage hormones bucking up against her mother's menopausal hormones, which didn't make a good combination.

They were quiet for a while as everyone ate. Sarah wasn't sure she'd ever seen Miriam eat so much, and she was glad her mother had chosen a roast for the meal. Much of what was offered at the shelter, Miriam hadn't been interested in eating.

"Someone is coming up the driveway." *Daed* wiped his mouth before he got up and went to the window. "I recognize that black mare. That old horse should probably be put out to pasture."

Sarah stopped breathing. Surely it wasn't Abram. Surely that wasn't the same horse still carting him around.

Daed turned around. "*Ach,* well, it didn't take that boy much time to come calling. He asked us when you would be here, but you haven't even been home an hour."

"I'm not ready to talk to him." Sarah stood up, walked around the table, and wiped Miriam's mouth with a napkin. "We'll be upstairs."

"*Nee, mei maedel.* Abram has waited a long time for an explanation." *Daed* glanced at Miriam, then back at Sarah. "You owe him that."

"*Daed,* please. Not yet." Sarah begged her father with her eyes, but with age — and six years' absence — her pleading expression wasn't working the way it had when she was a child. She reminded herself that she was a grown woman now and didn't have to talk to Abram if she didn't want to. But she was already on shaky ground with her mother. She didn't want to upset her father.

"Your *mamm* can help Miriam get unpacked and get a bath while you talk to Abram."

Sarah quickly looked at her mother.

"Uh, I need to clean up the kitchen." Her mother hurriedly began stacking plates.

Sarah wanted to tell her mother to go get to know her granddaughter, but under the circumstances, she stayed quiet, hoping to avoid Abram.

"The kitchen can wait." Her father's voice was stern, and her mother sighed as she put the plates in the sink. Then she turned to face them, nodded grimly, and motioned for Miriam to follow her. Miriam looked at her mother, as if she needed to know who was in charge here.

"You go with Barbara, I mean *Mammi,* while I go talk to an old friend, okay?"

"Okay, Mommy." She got up and latched onto her grandmother's hand and smiled. "Mommy sounds a lot like *mammi.*"

Sarah followed them through the living room, waiting for her mother to comment or disengage from the hand holding, but she didn't. Miriam loved bath time. Even at the shelter, she splashed and played like she always had, minus her floating yellow ducks. Sarah wondered how her mother would react when water went sloshing over the side of the tub. Probably with frustration and heavy sighs, like she'd done with Sarah.

As Sarah thought about their small apartment in Houston, she wondered what survived the rising water. She recalled Miriam's yellow plastic ducks floating around the living room when they'd left that day. What about all the pictures she'd taken over the years? A neighbor was supposed to let her know when she'd be able to get back in, which they said could be weeks because of the structural damage. Sarah had grown up without photos being a part of her life, since they were forbidden. But she treasured the pictures she'd taken of Miriam. Everything else could be replaced. Even her car, which had been towed to a parking lot where thousands of other cars waited on insurance adjusters and FEMA.

Sarah paused at the front door and pushed away thoughts of the hurricane's aftermath. She took a deep breath, totally unprepared to see Abram. She'd rather be tucking her daughter in and reflecting on the day's events. As she held her breath in the silence, she strained to hear her mother and Miriam talking, and Sarah hoped Miriam wouldn't divulge every detail of their lives. Not that there was anything really bad to tell, just things Sarah would rather ease into.

"Mommy's old friend is a nice man," Barbara said as she and Miriam walked up the stairs together.

"That's good that he's nice." There was a pause. "And not a poo-poo head like Billy Dalton."

Sarah hung her head and sighed. Then she opened the door to go face the only man she'd ever truly loved. She couldn't help but wonder if God might give them a second chance at happiness. Even though she didn't deserve it. And Abram had surely moved on.

CHAPTER 3

Abram marched across the yard toward Sarah, his chin held high, determined not to let her see the despair he'd carried around since she left. He'd trained himself to never fall in love again after she ripped his heart out and stomped on it, without so much as a phone call or letter.

And now she was back, as beautiful as ever he imagined, and with his child. She'd cheated him out of five years with a daughter he didn't know about. He remembered weeping after Sarah's mother visited and told him Sarah was coming back and that Abram had a daughter. If he wanted a relationship with his daughter, he would have to stow away at least some of the bitterness and anger he felt toward Sarah.

"Abram . . ." She reached out her arms like she was going to hug him, but he snagged her wrists before she could lay a hand on him. The feel of her arms around him might melt the resolve he'd tried so hard to build.

"Where is *mei dochder*?" He struggled to keep his voice steady as he took his hands from her wrists. "I don't need any explanations. I'm sure you had your reasons for running off in the middle of the night without so much as a good-bye note." He looped his thumbs beneath his suspenders, mostly to keep his hands from shaking. Sarah was within reach, and part of him wanted to embrace her, to hold her forever, to take up where they'd left off. But that was a fairy tale, and Abram learned a long time ago that fairy tales rarely come true.

"I don't blame you for being mad." Sarah's bottom lip trembled, which only made him want to hold her that much more. "But you deserved someone better anyway."

He grunted. "Whatever."

She smiled a little. "You sound . . . different . . . more *Englisch*."

He eyed her up and down, purposefully and with disdain. "And you *look* different, definitely *Englisch*." He waved a dismissive hand at her. "In your blue jeans and all that."

Her lip still quivered, but Abram decided not to fault her for that since he couldn't get his hands to quit shaking.

"I hang out with the *Englisch* a lot more since I never got baptized."

Abram and Sarah had been scheduled to be baptized two weeks after Sarah left. Since the baptism was a requirement to get married, Abram had forgone the ceremony, unsure if he would stay in the community since Sarah and God had forsaken him. He'd eventually gotten right with the Lord again, even though he hadn't been able to commit to baptism. He needed to forgive Sarah before he felt worthy of baptism. Abram wasn't sure that was possible.

Sarah took a step forward. Abram ordered his feet to move back, but they disobeyed, and now Sarah's lips were close enough to kiss. So he did. Hard and possessive, until she pushed him away and took a big step back. Then she slapped him. Not hard. But she got her point across.

"What has happened to you?" Her eyes filled with tears. "You never kissed me like that when we were together. And it hurt." She reached up and touched her lips.

"I was just getting something out of my system." *Lies.* He was still as attracted to her as he'd ever been. Even though the Sarah he knew was long gone. And the Abram she'd known had checked out a long time ago too.

"Abram, I'm sorry about everything. But . . . why didn't you get baptized?"

He hung his head, then looked up at her and grinned. "It's none of your business how I've spent the past six years or why I chose not to be baptized into a faith I once cherished."

"Did I do this to you?" She didn't come closer.

"Don't give yourself that much credit, Sarah." Her name slid off his tongue like poison. "I'm only here for one reason, and you know what it is."

She folded her arms across her chest. "I'm assuming you want an explanation for why I left, why I didn't contact you, and why I'm back now."

"I know why you're back. Your *daed* told me. A hurricane. You're broke with nowhere else to go. In all those years, you didn't make any friends? You had to come back here?"

A tear slid down her cheek. "You're not the same Abram I left behind."

He took a step toward her as his nostrils flared. "Did you really think I would be? Did you think I'd ask you to pick up where we left off? Or that I'd profess my undying love?" He pointed a finger at her. "That love has been gone for a long time."

She cried harder, and Abram fought the urge to pull her into his arms. He'd punished her enough.

Spinning on her heels, she ran back to the house.

"Wait!" Abram followed her, and she slowed her pace and turned to face him.

"I can't do this," she said through her tears. "I knew it would be hard to face you, but I didn't know you would be so mean."

Abram's armor was slipping, like melting lava that burned his senses. He couldn't bring himself to say he was sorry, even though her crying was about to unravel him.

He took a deep breath, removed his straw hat, and ran a hand through his hair. After he put his hat back on, he took another cleansing breath, knowing he would have to be civil to Sarah to get what he wanted.

"Even if it doesn't matter anymore, we both know I'll eventually ask. Why did you leave?"

Sarah swiped at her eyes as her long dark hair blew in the breeze, the last of the sun's presence casting a glow on her that left a halo impression around her head. A sign from God? *No.*

"I left because I was pregnant." She looked somewhere over Abram's shoulder.

"And I would have brought shame to my family."

"You brought shame to them by leaving the way you did. If it hadn't been for the driver you hired, we would have wondered if you were snatched from your bed in the middle of the night. But your mother saw you leaving in a car."

"I was seventeen and alone." Her gaze still traveled to a place that seemed far away. "I went to Veronica's house. Remember, my *Englisch* friend? She helped me plan a trip to Houston. She said there were good jobs and she had a friend there." Sniffling, she lowered her head. "I took the bus as far as I could, but none of it worked out the way I planned, which made me feel even more alone. Veronica's friend had a new boyfriend living with her, and sleeping on her couch didn't feel right."

"You weren't alone. How can you say that? Didn't you think I would have married you? We'd planned that anyway. We weren't baptized, so we wouldn't have been permanently condemned for our one pre-marital indiscretion. We could have been a family, but you took away that option by not even telling me you were with child." He walked closer to her, expecting her to back up, but she didn't.

Trying to keep his voice steady, he said, "I know why you're back now, because of the hurricane. Your *mamm* explained all of that, but it has haunted me for years why you left. *Ya,* you denied your parents a grand-daughter, which is terrible, but what about me?" The continued shakiness in his voice surprised him. He'd planned to be strong during this encounter, but his resolve was weakening with each word he spoke.

"I wrote letters to my parents, and they were returned unopened. Since I hadn't been baptized, I didn't deserve to be shunned, but my parents practiced their own shunning, as I knew they would." She paused. "My mother anyway. And I'm sure my father went along with it to keep peace."

Abram's jaw dropped. "You wrote letters to your parents?" He hung his head as he wondered why Sarah's mother hadn't shared that with him. "Why didn't you write to me?"

She covered her face with her hands when she started to cry harder. "I don't know. I was so ashamed."

He took another step toward her and was almost as close now as he was when he kissed her, but her eyes looked beyond him. "Did you love me, Sarah?" He swallowed a lump forming in his throat.

She still wouldn't look at him. "With all of my heart."

He took hold of her arms, gentler this time, but she still wiggled out of his grip, keeping her eyes down.

"If my parents had read the letters, they would have understood why I left."

"Why didn't you write to *me*?" he asked again. "Didn't you think I would want to know I was going to be a father? I would have stood by you, no matter what your parents or anyone else thought."

This wasn't what he'd planned. He'd wanted to keep a civil but uninterested tone with her, to prove that he didn't care or need her explanations, but his emotions had been all over the place since the moment he saw her. He couldn't imagine how he was going to feel when he met his daughter. Sarah's mother had already told Abram that Sarah had never married. Sarah told them that during the phone call she had with them when they called her at the shelter. Even if he couldn't be with Sarah, he at least wanted a relationship with his daughter.

"I want to know my daughter." He blinked back tears, which he definitely hadn't seen coming. He should have. He'd shed plenty of them since he found out Sarah was coming home with a child.

She finally locked eyes with him as tears streamed down her cheeks. "Abram . . ." Her face held little expression as she said, "Miriam is not your daughter." Then she turned and walked away, as if her words would have no effect on him.

Abram's chest tightened and his mouth dropped open.

The front door closed behind her. He stood there for a long time, thinking, letting her words soak in, until he came to a conclusion.

She is lying.

CHAPTER 4

Barbara unzipped Miriam's small backpack and took out two shirts, a pair of jeans, and some underclothes. "Is this all you were able to bring with you?"

Miriam shook her head. "No." She unzipped an exterior compartment. "I have a toothbrush and toothpaste too." Handing the items to Barbara, the child dug deeper into the pouch and pulled out a doll. "She doesn't have a face, but Mommy gave her to me when I was little. I brought her with me so the water wouldn't drown her."

Barbara smiled. *You are still little.* She eased the doll out of Miriam's hands and smelled it, wondering if it still smelled of baby powder, if it still smelled like Sarah. "Did your mother tell you this was her doll when she was your age?" Barbara turned the doll over and eyed the mending she had done on the dress after Sarah tried to run it through the ringer washing machine and ripped the stitching on one side.

"Yes. She said it was her favorite thing."

Barbara handed the doll back to Miriam. "She took that doll everywhere."

"That's why I saved her. I named her Heidi even though Mommy said her name was JoAnne. But there is a girl at my school named JoAnne, and she isn't always nice to people. She's not as mean as Billy Dalton, but —" She slammed her small hand over her mouth, her eyes wide as she lowered it. "I called him a bad name on the way up the stairs, a name I'm not supposed to say."

Barbara stifled a grin and cleared her throat. "I heard you."

"Please don't tell Mommy. She reminded me to use all of my good manners, and I forgot." Miriam crinkled her nose as she scowled. "But when it comes to Billy Dalton, my manners go right out the window." She waved toward the window.

Barbara put a hand over her mouth as she tried to keep from laughing. This child was as dramatic as her mother was at this age. Fond memories of Sarah floated around Barbara's mind, reminders of the good life they'd led — until six years ago. But this little one had no role in her mother's choices, and Barbara didn't know how long it would be until Sarah rushed away with her again. This might be her only chance to get to know her granddaughter. Loving her wasn't an option. Barbara already did.

"Mommy's friend Jack said we should draw a face on Heidi, but Mommy wouldn't let him."

Barbara's ears perked up. "Oh. Was Jack your mother's boyfriend?" She felt a little guilty quizzing Miriam about such a thing, but curiosity had gotten the better of her.

"No. Just her friend. I liked Jack." She gazed up at Barbara. "I wanted him to be my daddy because he was nice, but he moved away. And Mommy said he wasn't the kind of friend who could become a daddy." She paused, sighing. "I don't have a daddy."

Barbara pushed back strands of hair that had come loose from Miriam's ponytail, eyeing her high cheekbones and the shape of her mouth. Just like Sarah's. And there was no denying this was Abram's child. Miriam had his big blue eyes, wavy dark hair, and dimples. Regret washed over Barbara and she wished she'd opened Sarah's letters. Surely she would have mentioned having a child. Barbara fought the knot building in her throat. Things could have been so different.

At the time, she thought if she shunned

Sarah, her daughter would see the error of her ways and return home. That was the purpose of a formal shunning. Barbara had been wrong. And months became years. She'd missed so much. Teething, first steps, the joy of seeing her own daughter hold her child for the first time. If she thought about it any more, she was sure she would burst into tears. She forced herself to focus on what was happening now and the blessing she'd been gifted.

"I don't think we can ever go back to our apartment." Miriam looked down at her doll. "Mommy carried me on her shoulders through the water, and I carried Heidi." She looked up at Barbara. "I was scared, but I think Mommy was more scared. She saved us though. But she said it was the grace of God that saved us."

Barbara tried to imagine what it must have been like for Sarah, Miriam, and the thousands of other people affected by the storm. They didn't have a television, but the newspapers had heavily covered the hurricane and the devastation in Houston. Barbara recalled crying herself to sleep reading about it and wondering if Sarah was safe.

She knew her daughter was in Houston from the postmarks on the letters. *Why didn't I just open them? Could I have convinced*

Sarah to come home? Was Barbara's daughter so afraid of being pregnant that she thought they would want nothing to do with her? Back then, Barbara focused on the importance of appearances. Sarah surely would have brought shame to their family.

Barbara was different now. Losing a child will do that to a mother, and that's what it felt like — the death of a child — when Sarah left. Barbara would do things differently if given a chance. But if everything is according to God's will, then things had happened as they should. But why? And how was Barbara ever going to shed the bitterness she felt toward Sarah? She needed to have a heart-to-heart with her daughter soon, but Barbara was afraid of that conversation. Fearful of things Sarah might say about her that caused her to go away. Maybe she needed to put her focus on the future and leave the past behind.

Easier said than done.

Sarah went straight to the downstairs bathroom in the hall and tried to compose herself by dabbing at her eyes, blowing her nose, and then shaking her head as hard as she could to lose the image of Abram's face when she told him that he wasn't Miriam's father. But she assumed it was a vision that would be with her for a long time.

When she thought about his cruel words, the forceful kiss, and the way she slapped him, she started to cry again. She'd thought about coming home when Miriam was two but abandoned the plan when she was offered a better job at the law firm. A year later, when she had vacation time, she considered the idea again, but it had been too long and she couldn't bring herself to face Abram or her parents.

She stared into the mirror, questioning everything she'd done in her life. The one good and beautiful thing was Miriam. And she had always taken good care of her daughter. She and Miriam didn't have much, but they'd had all they needed. Sarah didn't grow up with fancy things, and she carried that with her when she left. She tried to instill respectfulness, good manners, and all the values her own parents worked so hard to instill in her. But she didn't feel like she'd gone overboard like her mother had at times. Sarah learned early on that parenting didn't come with an instruction manual. Maybe her mother had done the best she could.

Right now, Sarah needed a hug from her daughter. She rounded the corner to go upstairs, but her father cleared his throat from the recliner, the same brown chair he'd always sat in. Sarah slowed her pace and whispered, "Good night," as she started up the stairs. He cleared his throat again, louder this time. Sarah turned around and joined him in the living room. She sat on the couch.

Her father had aged more than her mother over the last six years. Barbara's hair hadn't turned gray, and she didn't have any lines on her face that weren't there before. But her father had considerably more wrinkles and his hair was thinning on top and mostly gray, along with his beard. He was much thinner now too.

Sarah waited for him to ask questions, but that wasn't really his way. He closed the book he was reading and took off a pair of gold-rimmed reading glasses, another thing she didn't remember him needing in the past.

"You've been crying," he said softly.

"I have a lot to cry about." Sarah avoided her father's eyes as long as she could, but when she finally connected with him, he frowned.

"We all have a lot to cry about. It's what you do with the experiences that matters. You can carry the burdens of your past or choose to move forward without the added baggage."

Sarah pulled her hair over one shoulder, twisting it into a rope, then untwisting it, then repeating the process.

"Still twisting your hair, *ya*?"

She tried to smile as she slung it back over her shoulder. "I'm sorry, *Daed.* For everything."

"I know you are."

They were quiet for a while. "*Mamm* hates me, I think."

"I don't know what you've learned out in the *Englisch* world, but we don't hate in this family. Your *mamm* is hurt and bitter."

Sarah looked into her father's wise eyes. "That's carrying the burdens of the past."

"*Ya,* and they are your *mudder*'s burdens to carry and hopefully shed. Not yours."

"But I caused them."

"A person cannot cause another person's burdens. Baggage is the responsibility of the one carrying it, and only they are able to get rid of the weight. God's will is in everything we do, and we can't know His plans for us. Your *mudder* feels cheated out of time with Miriam, and with you." Her father ran his hand the length of his beard. "But let's talk about you."

Sarah let her weight fall back into the couch cushions, tempted to kick her legs up on the coffee table like she did at her apartment in Houston, but that was taboo in her mother's house. "You want to know why I left."

"Do you want to talk about it?"

Sarah felt like she was in a shrink's office. She'd been twice not long after Miriam was born, when she finally had insurance to cover the visits. But she didn't keep going. The woman was getting into her head too much about things she wasn't ready to face — like this. "I was seventeen, pregnant, and scared. I was a different person then."

"Not so different," her father said, then smiled.

"How can you be so calm, *Daed*? I know I hurt you, just like I hurt *Mamm*. Aren't you mad at me too? *Mamm* isn't even trying to hide it."

"I see you as the prodigal daughter who has come home to face the people she loves. That's a hard thing to do. I can hold on to the past or embrace the miracle that you are here. Your *mamm* will find her own miracle in this situation. She just hasn't been able to see clear enough to get past her hurt yet."

Sarah braced herself for the question she knew was coming, the hardest one of all. *Abram.*

193

She heard Miriam giggle upstairs, and a few seconds later, Sarah's mother laughed too. It was a glorious sound, and Sarah wished she could bottle it to listen to over and over again. Maybe she needed to give her mother a chance to forgive her. Sarah wondered if she could ever forgive herself.

More laughter from upstairs, and Sarah smiled. So did her father.

"Perhaps your *mudder* has latched onto the miracle that will bring her joy. I haven't heard her laugh like that in a long time."

Sarah sighed. "We are kind of a package deal, Miriam and me."

Her father stared at her long and hard, his eyebrows narrowing into a frown. "And where does Abram fit into the package?"

"He doesn't." Sarah regretted her quick and harsh response, but she couldn't take it back.

"I see."

CHAPTER 5

Abram walked into his house and was surprised to see his parents on the couch. After he left Sarah, he'd gone to the coffee shop to kill some time, then drove around until he thought his parents would be asleep.

"You're still up." He hung his hat on the rack by the front door, then pulled his suspenders over his shoulders, letting them drop to his sides. "What did the midwife say about Mary?" Abram's younger sister had married a fine man in their community two years ago, and she was due to have their second child any day. It would be his parents' fifth grandchild. His brother and his wife had three of their own. If Abram's daughter was included, that would make six grandchildren for his parents.

"I stopped by Mary and Jacob's today, and the midwife had just been there. She says Mary has a few more days, at least." His mother folded her hands in her lap and sat taller. "Did you finally get to meet your daughter? When will we get to meet her?"

After Sarah's mother told Abram that Sarah was coming home with a five-year-old child named Miriam, he and his parents had quickly done the math and assumed Abram was the child's father. "I didn't see Miriam." It would have felt odd to say "my daughter."

"Why not?" His mother put a hand to her chest. "I thought that's why you went over there."

Abram shrugged as he untucked his blue shirt, then sat in the rocking chair in the corner. "Maybe I should have been nicer to Sarah." He shook his head. "She slapped me."

"What?" His father's eyes widened. "That's not our way."

"Goodness, what did you say to her?"

"Do we have to talk about all of this now? I'm worn out." Abram was sure of the answer, but he figured it was worth a try.

"*Ya,* we absolutely do have to talk about it now." His mother lowered her hands, folding them in her lap again. "We have a grandchild we didn't know about, so we're obviously anxious to meet her."

Abram's parents had avoided a verbal lashing when they found out Sarah had a child. He sensed their disappointment, but it was quickly overshadowed by the revelation that they had another grandchild. Sarah and Abram had gone against God by being together as man and wife before they were married. Abram recalled that day in the barn, the tenderness, the love he felt for Sarah. It hadn't been planned, but they crossed the boundaries they'd set for their relationship. He touched his cheek as he thought about her slapping him today, which he had deserved. Then he cringed when he remembered the way he'd treated her, but Abram had held on to six years of pain and emotions to reach that point. Still, he regretted his actions.

"She said the child isn't mine," he finally said, unable to look either of his parents in the eye.

Silence filled the room. Only the sounds of the outdoors breezed into the house through the open windows. Crickets chirped, an occasional frog made its presence known, and their confused rooster crowed every few minutes.

"Barbara said Sarah left when she was pregnant, too scared to face what the two of you had done." His mother scowled a little. "I can understand her being fearful of her parents, but I don't understand why she didn't let you know. And how could the baby not be yours?"

Abram had had enough time earlier this evening to consider the possibility that Sarah was telling the truth, which made her return to Lancaster County even harder to bear. He didn't believe she could be a cheater, but if the baby wasn't Abram's, who else had she slept with in their community? That thought disturbed him as much as anything else. Was someone walking among them carrying such a secret? And if so, did that person know he was a father? He finally shook his head. "I don't know, *Mamm.* I'm just telling you what she said."

"Do you think she's lying?" His father eyed Abram like he was the one who might be lying.

"I don't know. I did at first. But now I'm not sure."

"*Ach,* that would mean that while you two were promised to be married, Sarah . . ." She brought a hand to her mouth but quickly shook her head. "*Nee,* I don't believe that. Sarah is a *gut* girl. She wouldn't do something like that . . ."

"You mean, she wouldn't do that with someone *else.*"

His mother sighed. "Your *daed* and I aren't proud of the fact that you and Sarah

198

took liberties that aren't right in the eyes of the Lord, but it isn't like you were the first. Lots of times such things are swept under the rug, and there have been a lot of babies come early in this community. I suspect they didn't all arrive prematurely."

"Sarah knew how much I loved her." The more he thought about it, the more Sarah's leaving made sense. She *had* been with someone else. "She knew I would have stuck by her, no matter what, even if she thought we should leave here."

Mamm lowered her eyes to her lap and gripped her apron, frowning.

"I loved her." Abram raised one shoulder and let it drop slowly.

"I know you did." She finally looked up at him with sad eyes. "But you didn't sneak out in the middle of the night, leaving all you've ever known and those you love, without any explanation."

Abram raised an eyebrow. "She didn't give me the choice. Could you have predicted she would do something like that?"

Mamm shook her head. "*Nee,* it was hard to believe when she left."

"I guess it makes sense if the *boppli* isn't mine." Abram stood up and walked toward the stairs. His parents didn't call after him. They realized this was all they could handle.

It was all Abram could handle tonight too.

By the time he bathed and got into bed, he was crying. Again. He hadn't cried this much since he was a little boy. He'd become a master at turning hurt into anger over the past six years. But seeing Sarah today had confused him more than ever and opened a floodgate of tears he'd held back for a long time. *God, help me. I still love her.*

Barbara scooted closer to John in the bed, then lay her head against her husband's shoulder, wrapping an arm around him. Two lanterns lit the room, and she and John were awake much later than normal.

"I heard you talking to Sarah, but I couldn't make out what she was saying."

John was quiet. Barbara sat up and looked into his face to make sure he hadn't fallen asleep. His eyes were wide open.

"What did she say, John?" She nudged him, her bottom lip starting to tremble. "Tell me. Was it about us not opening the letters?" Barbara couldn't shed the regret that was wrapping around her tighter and tighter as she envisioned how different things could have been.

"She's beating herself up for what she did to us by leaving."

Barbara took a deep breath. She picked

up the brush from her nightstand and ran it through her hair a few times before she said anything. "I know. But she will eventually have to forgive herself."

John twisted to face her and propped his head on his elbow. "You will have to forgive her too."

Barbara locked eyes with her husband. "Do you remember our sleepless nights, wondering if she was all right? Until the first letter came, we didn't know if she was dead or alive."

"We should have opened that letter," he was quick to say.

Barbara set the brush in her lap and turned to John, blinking back tears. "*Ya*, I know." She stared into her husband's eyes as she swallowed the knot in her throat. "I should have opened the letters."

"It's my fault too. I should have insisted that we read them."

Barbara sighed. "I wrote her a letter."

John sat up. "What? When? And why didn't you say anything?"

She raised a shoulder and dropped it slowly. "I was afraid she wouldn't write back. And she didn't. So I just didn't mention it. I thought it would hurt you even more to know she was shunning us as well. It was a while before I did, maybe two and a half years." She paused, thinking back. "I never told Abram about the letters we received. He would have resented me for returning them unopened. But at the time, I thought I was protecting him."

They were both quiet for a while.

John ran his hand down his beard. "Somehow we are all going to have to let go of the past and move forward. We can't change the things we did or didn't do back then."

More silence. Barbara was fighting tears. Deep down, she was sure Sarah left mostly because of her, not John, and moving forward was going to be harder on Barbara than her husband. She had much to regret. But if Sarah would just stay, hopefully Barbara and her daughter could make amends. She chose to focus on the miracle that had stepped into their lives.

"Miriam is a beauty, isn't she?"

Her husband smiled. "*Ya,* she is. She looks like Sarah."

Barbara dabbed her eyes with a tissue, then smiled back at her husband. "She looks like Abram too. Did Sarah say anything about her and Abram? They could get baptized and marry, become a family, and at least make things right now."

"She said she and Miriam are a package deal." He cut his eyes at Barbara just enough to let her know he was about to say something important. She'd learned to recognize that expression. "She feels like you will bond with the child, but maybe not with her." He paused, and Barbara had to admit to herself that it was easier to be around Miriam than Sarah. "When I asked her how Abram fit into the package, she said he doesn't."

Barbara resumed brushing her hair, praying she didn't have a full meltdown in front of her husband. "Then they won't stay. I had hoped that her choosing to return had less to do with the lack of a place to stay and no money, and more to do with her wanting Miriam to get to know her father. I thought it would all be a precursor to them getting back together."

John shook his head. "Abram has been an angry man since she left. Maybe any love he had for her is gone. We will have to let Sarah divulge what she's comfortable with over time. If we push her, she might leave again, before we have much time with her and Miriam."

Barbara hung her head. Her husband was right. The past couldn't be undone. She sniffled as a good thought found its way to the forefront of her mind. "It warmed my heart when Miriam told me that her mother said they were saved from the storm by the grace of God."

John propped his pillow, then lay prone and smiled. "I'm happy to see you finding some good in all of this. Sarah held on to her faith. Miriam is our beautiful grand-daughter, and of course we want her in our lives. But we want Sarah in our lives, too, and your daughter needs you. She won't confide in you if you cling to the bitterness. I agree with what Sarah said — they are a package deal."

"I know." Barbara snuffed out the lantern on her side, and John took care of the one on his nightstand. She snuggled into the nook of his arm. "Sarah broke my heart when she left. I'm trying to get past that."

He squeezed her, kissing her on the fore-head. "Pray about it."

"I am. But I hope she is able to reconcile with Abram."

"It's their journey, Barbara. God always has a plan, even when we can't see it."

She sighed. "I'm Sarah's mother. It's only natural for a parent to want to control a child so everything turns out okay." She paused. "Right?"

John kissed her again. "Sarah isn't a child anymore. And she is a mother, too, now. *Control* is a harsh word, but you can bet

Sarah is making decisions based on what is best for her own child. Keep that in mind."

Barbara closed her eyes, knowing sleep wouldn't come for a while. Her daughter was home. She had a granddaughter she longed to know. And as she pulled John's arm around her, she thanked God she was married to a wise man who put up with her during times when maybe he shouldn't have. She recalled throwing kitchen plates across the room about two months after Sarah left, using words she'd only heard the *Englisch* use in fits of anger. John had stood patiently by, then walked to her, scooped her into his arms, and carried her to bed as she cried on his shoulder. When she awoke the next morning, the broken dishes had been cleaned up. John was the love of her life when she was seventeen, and he still was. That was all she'd ever wanted for Sarah.

An hour later, Barbara was still tossing and turning when a loud scream resounded from upstairs. She and John shot out of bed and headed for the stairs. Barbara's heart raced as she took the steps two at a time, wondering what could cause Miriam to scream in terror the way she had. Barbara's motherly instincts kicked in as if they had never left her. "I'm coming, Miriam."

CHAPTER 6

Sarah bolted upright in bed, covered her face, and wept as her daughter wrapped her arms around her.

"Mommy, wake up! It's okay."

Sarah fought to catch her breath as she clung to Miriam, the familiar shame creeping to the surface. A five-year-old should never be woken up from a sound sleep to comfort her screaming mother.

As the door flew open, her parents hurried into the room. Sarah's mother immediately reached for Miriam, touching her on the arm. "What's wrong with Miriam?"

"It's not me, *Mammi.*" Miriam eased out of Sarah's arms and pointed to her mother. "It's her. Mommy gets bad dreams."

Sarah uncovered her eyes but couldn't stop the sobs. If ever she needed a mother, it was now. Would Barbara reach out to her too?

Before Sarah could protest, her father had

picked up Miriam and was leaving the room. "I think we need midnight cookies and milk. How does that sound?" He kissed Miriam on the cheek, but she wiggled out of his arms, almost bringing them both down onto the hardwood floor before she ran back to her mother.

"I'm not leaving Mommy!"

Sarah fought to slow her breathing as she pulled Miriam into a hug. "I'm okay, sweetie. You go eat cookies with *Daadi*. It's not normally allowed, so you'd better take advantage of it." Sarah forced a smile. "Go ahead. It was just another bad dream, and remember how Mommy told you dreams can't hurt you?" Although Sarah was tormented every time she had the nightmare.

"Are you sure?" Miriam blinked teary eyes.

Sarah tried to smile again. "Go, Miriam. I promise. I'm all right."

Miriam slowly got off the bed and went to her grandfather's outstretched hand. Sarah's father closed the door behind them, and she waited for her mother to hug her, to say something, or to show her half the affection she'd shown Miriam since they arrived. But her mother only sat on the bed and stared at her, expressionless.

"I'm fine, Barbara. You don't have to stay."

Sarah swiped at her eyes.

"Barbara? Is that what you're calling me now?"

Sarah hadn't meant for it to slip out. She'd been avoiding calling her mother anything. "I saw the look you gave me when I called you *Mamm* when we first arrived."

"I hadn't heard you call me that in a long time. I was just taken aback for a moment, but I certainly don't want you calling me Barbara. I'm happy for you to call me *Mamm* if you want to."

I do want to. Sarah scooted backward until she was sitting up and leaning against her pillow. "Seriously, you don't have to stay. I had a bad dream, but I'm fine now."

Her mother, dressed in a white nightgown that fell well past her knees, swung her legs up on the bed, fluffed Miriam's pillow, then leaned against it and crossed her ankles, as if she was planning to stay awhile.

Her mother pulled her long dark hair over her shoulder and began braiding it. "What was the dream about?"

"I don't remember." It was a lie, but talking about it was like living it again.

"Does this happen often?"

Sarah wanted to yell for her mother to get out. "No."

"Hmm . . . That's *gut*. Even though it's a lie."

Sarah slowly turned and faced her mother, her chest tightening. But she didn't say a word.

"Miriam has obviously seen this happen before." Barbara — or *Mamm* — finished the braid, left it loose at the end, and put her hands in her lap. "Does Miriam have nightmares?"

"No." Maybe if Sarah kept her answers short, her mother would get the hint.

They were quiet for a while. Sarah folded her arms across her chest.

"How did your meeting with Abram go? Do you think you'll be able to resolve your differences?"

Steam was rising from Sarah's head, she was sure of it. Her mother was still as insensitive as she'd been when Sarah was younger. Why couldn't she just pull her daughter into a hug, instead of marching into her own agenda? Clenching her fists at her sides, Sarah reminded herself that this woman was her mother, but even after taking in a deep breath, she wasn't any calmer.

"I snuck out in the middle of the night and didn't look back." She cut her eyes at her mother. "I'd say there's a little bit more to it than resolving our differences." She rolled her eyes. "I'm sure our coming here will make things awkward for you in the eyes of your friends, and if I would just come to my senses, confess that I made a horrible mistake, get baptized, and marry Abram, your life would be perfect."

Her mother slowly got off the bed, walked to the bedroom door, and gently closed it behind her as she left.

Sarah and her mother fought like feral cats when Sarah was a teenager, but her father always said it was because they were both strong women with strong opinions about things.

The teenager was grown up. Her mother didn't know her anymore. Otherwise, she would have pulled Sarah into a big hug, rubbed her hair, kissed her on the cheek, and told her that everything was going to be all right.

Nothing was ever going to be okay, but Sarah put her best foot forward each day for the one person who mattered. Miriam.

But she didn't feel like the mom right now. She was the child, and as she curled into a fetal position on the bed, she sobbed.

Barbara stood on the other side of the door as her daughter cried, wanting nothing more than to go to her, to hold her, to comfort her. As her own tears poured down her cheeks, she wondered what she'd done wrong as a mother, something she'd pondered for years.

She and Sarah didn't see eye-to-eye when Sarah was a teenager, but there had never been any doubt that they loved each other. At least, not in Barbara's eyes. But the way Sarah spoke to her now made her wonder if Sarah had loved her even half as much as Barbara loved her daughter. Why else would she leave the way she did, pregnant or not? Barbara would have been disappointed, maybe even livid, and surely embarrassed. But they would have gotten through it. And Barbara would have been around to see Miriam grow from a baby into the beautiful and smart little girl she was now. She would have seen her daughter growing into the role of motherhood.

She put her hand on the doorknob and kept it there for a few moments. Then she turned and left to join John and Miriam downstairs, slowing her pace when she reached the landing. She took a tissue from her pocket and wiped her tears. Then she took a deep breath and started walking again. Maybe Miriam would offer more information than Sarah.

"These are the best cookies ever." Miriam

beamed as she talked with her mouth full. Barbara wondered how many chocolate chip cookies she'd had, remembering how sugar late at night used to prevent Sarah from getting to sleep.

"That's my *mammi*'s recipe." Barbara pulled out a chair next to John's, both of them facing Miriam. "Does your mommy have a lot of these bad dreams?"

John cut his eyes at Barbara disapprovingly, as if to discourage her from questioning the girl. But when Miriam nodded, he softened his expression.

"Does she ever say what the dreams are about?" Barbara reached for a cookie. She wouldn't sleep for a while anyway.

"The monster."

Barbara swallowed the bite in her mouth. "A monster?" She glanced at John, who was also listening intently to their granddaughter.

Miriam nodded.

Barbara wasn't sure how hard to push since Miriam hadn't elaborated. "Dreams can be scary, but I'm sure your *mamm* told you that monsters aren't real, *ya*?"

Miriam's cheeks dimpled as she smiled broadly. "I like the way you talk."

Barbara glanced at John, who grinned. Then Barbara spoke to her granddaughter in Pennsylvania *Deutsch,* and Miriam laughed. "What did you say?"

"I said that I have a very pretty grand-daughter."

Miriam smiled, but not quite as much. She put the uneaten half of her cookie on the plate John had gotten for her and lowered her eyes. After a few seconds, she locked eyes with Barbara and blinked a few times. "You know, monsters *are* real. Even though Mommy says they aren't, I know they are."

Barbara tipped her head to one side. "Why do you say that?"

Miriam pinched off a piece of the uneaten cookie but didn't put it in her mouth. She sighed. "Can I go back to bed now?"

Barbara opened her mouth to speak, but John cleared his throat, frowning, and she adhered to the warning not to push Miriam.

"Why don't I go check on Mommy first?" She nodded to John. "And your *daadi* can get you some milk with chocolate in it."

"Okay." Miriam didn't smile. The cookies had been a distraction, and not a very long one.

Barbara walked upstairs, and when she got to Sarah's bedroom, she saw a faint light from under the door, so she tapped lightly.

"Come in."

Barbara stepped over the threshold. Sarah had lit the lantern and was sitting in bed, her knees to her chest. "Is Miriam okay?"

"She's fine." Barbara sat down on the edge of the queen-size bed. Sarah's old bed. The one she was now sharing with her daughter.

"Everything is exactly the same as when I left." Sarah's eyes scanned the room, landing on the bookshelf she'd asked her father to make when she was around ten. "You could have given my books to someone to enjoy."

Barbara glanced at Sarah's collection, six shelves' worth. "I wanted you to have them if you came back."

"And here I am." She smiled slightly.

"And here you are." Barbara swallowed back the lump forming in her throat. After a few awkward moments of silence, she cleared her throat. "Miriam thinks monsters are real. At least, that's what she said."

Sarah sighed. "If you are going to question my parenting skills, you should know that I have told her repeatedly that there are no such things as monsters."

Barbara bit her tongue, recalling the way she and Sarah talked to each other when Sarah was a teenager. She didn't want to go back to that. "I'm not questioning your parenting skills. Miriam is lovely and well-mannered." She planned to keep her promise about not tattling on Miriam for saying "poo-poo head." "It's just that she was so serious when she said that about the monsters being real."

"Miriam is a very smart little girl. All I can do is to keep telling her that the monster is only in Mommy's dream, and it can't hurt us. I regret ever telling her that my nightmares were about a monster, but it seemed easier than telling her the —" She stopped and shook her head. "Never mind."

"Easier than telling her the truth? What is it that wakes you so viciously in the middle of the night?"

Sarah stared at her long and hard. "The monster."

Barbara felt the fear radiating from her daughter, and again she longed to hold and comfort her. But fear of rejection kept her from it. So much armor had chipped from the wall around her heart that she felt totally exposed. Sarah wasn't her enemy, she reminded herself. She was her daughter. Is. And forever would be.

"Does the monster have a name?" Barbara realized she was talking to Sarah as one might talk to a young child. The way she comforted her all those years ago.

Sarah opened her mouth to say something, but then looked away before speaking. "Nope. It's just a silly dream I have over and over again about a monster." She turned to Barbara. "Thank you and *Daed* for entertaining Miriam, but I'm fine now, so you can send her up whenever you want."

Barbara smiled. "Or you could come eat midnight cookies. We certainly didn't allow that when you were that age."

Sarah smiled a little too. "I think I'd just like to cuddle up with Miriam and go back to sleep."

"*Ya.* Okay." Barbara stood and was almost out the door when she turned around. "Do you need anything?"

Sarah sighed. "To face the monster, I guess."

The monster. Barbara's heart raced. She was sure they were no longer talking about a child's version of a monster. This was something real.

CHAPTER 7

Sarah flicked the reins until the horse settled into a slow trot. Her father had been right, it was like riding a bike. The drive to Abram's house wasn't far, and she wanted to see if the Abram she remembered was still in there somewhere. Sarah was sure he wouldn't be ugly to her in front of Miriam. And Miriam had been begging for a buggy ride. Sarah heard her parents say Abram's sister was having a baby, so she hoped his parents wouldn't be at home. She wasn't ready to face them.

"I wish I could ride in a buggy everywhere!" Miriam clapped her hands together, grinning from ear to ear, her blue eyes wide with excitement.

"You might feel differently in the wintertime." Sarah could still remember the blustery, cold rides.

Miriam leaned closer to the dash. "Where's the heat button?"

Sarah chuckled. "There isn't a heat button. Sometimes people use battery-operated heaters, but trust me, it's still cold."

Memories flooded Sarah each time they passed a homestead, but regret also swam with the wonderful recollections. She'd grown up playing in those yards, barefoot and carefree. How she would love for Miriam to have grown up that way.

"Is that your friend's farm?" Miriam pointed to a large white house on the right when Sarah slowed down. Abram's mother planted petunias in the flower beds at this time every year, and the pink flowers were in full bloom. Sarah recalled the many gardens she and her mother had created. There was nothing like tilling the land in preparation for God's blessed harvest. Something else Miriam had missed out on living in the city.

Sarah wondered if this trip was a mistake, but Abram must have felt like he'd been sucker punched when Sarah told him Miriam wasn't his child. She'd given him a couple of days to let that soak in before she chose to visit.

Abram was in the yard wearing ear buds when they pulled in. She couldn't help but smile. By the way he was tapping his foot as he milked the cow, he was enjoying an uplifting Christian song. Abram had always loved music, and even though he was still in his *rumschpringe,* maybe he only indulged when his parents weren't around, like he did years ago. Sarah didn't see his parents' buggy, so she pulled to a stop and tethered the horse — again, like riding a bike. Miriam didn't wait for her, even though she asked her to, but her daughter was fixated on the cow and the person doing the milking.

Sarah ran to catch up to her daughter just about the time Abram pulled out his ear buds. "Sorry. She ran ahead before I could get the horse tethered."

Abram glanced up at Sarah and pushed back the rim of his straw hat, his eyes wide for a few seconds. After their last conversation, she hoped he didn't send them away. But he smiled a little and turned his focus quickly to Miriam. He extended his hand. "I'm Abram, and you must be Miriam."

Miriam squeezed her eyes closed, as if she was trying to remember something, then opened them. "Yes, sir. I am Miriam."

Manners. Good girl.

"Doesn't that hurt the cow?" Miriam pointed to the bucket partially filled with freshly squeezed milk.

Abram laughed, which took Sarah all the

way back to the day he proposed. A red wasp had circled him, landed on his shoulder, and stung him in the middle of the proposal, and he'd hopped around like a jackrabbit on the verge of cursing. When the pain finally lessened, he'd taken a deep breath and tried to finish asking Sarah to marry him. But she burst into laughter at his wild display. Then he laughed, and Sarah had jumped into his arms and whispered, "Yes," in his ear.

"*Nee,* it doesn't hurt the cow." Abram looked long and hard and lovingly at Miriam.

If only he knew the truth.

"If you stand right here in front of me, I can show you how to do it."

Miriam looked at Sarah for permission and Sarah nodded as she edged closer. Abram was gentle as he instructed Miriam, folding his hands over hers, helping her stroke the teat. Miriam jumped, giggling when milk began to squirt into the bucket. Sarah had always known Abram would be a good father.

As she watched, Sarah fought the knot building in her throat as she thought of what could have been. She'd spent a long time being angry at God, wondering why He sent her down a path so different from the one she'd envisioned for her life. But over time, she began to soften. Every time she looked at her daughter, there was no denying what a blessing Miriam was, and God had gifted Sarah this precious child. Eventually, she reclaimed her relationship with the Lord, knowing He would be there waiting for her. She wanted Miriam to know God, and she'd made sure she did, as much as a five-year-old could.

"You're *gut* at this," Abram said to Miriam before he looked over his shoulder at Sarah and smiled.

You are still in there. His smile was the same. He just hadn't revealed it to her during their last visit.

"Mommy, look, I'm doing it!" Miriam didn't turn around, but the excitement in her voice warmed Sarah's heart. But then came more regret as she thought about all the firsts she could have experienced with Miriam out on a farm — first time collecting eggs, seeing a calf born, driving a buggy, learning Pennsylvania *Deutsch,* and then watching her master English when she would have started school at five. Even now, she could picture Miriam in the traditional Amish clothes Sarah had grown up wearing.

"You're doing a great job." Sarah's voice

cracked a little. Her daughter didn't seem to notice, but when Abram slowly turned to look at her, his eyes were softer than they were two days ago.

Sarah turned around when she heard the *clip-clop* of horse hooves, a sound she still heard in her sleep sometimes. Her heart flipped in her chest when she recognized Abram's parents, and she wondered what kind of reception to expect from Elizabeth and Lloyd. Surely they believed Miriam to be Abram's child too. And, like her parents and Abram, Sarah was sure they had suffered from her leaving. They'd always treated Sarah like a daughter.

Miriam walked back to her mother when Abram said they were done. Then he moved the milking stool and picked up the bucket of fresh milk. He set it down beside him, then knelt in front of Miriam, not saying anything for a few moments, just eyeing the most beautiful child alive, his expression filled with tenderness and kindness as he lightly touched her cheek. It was impossible not to notice that Miriam and Abram had the same dimples.

"*Danki* for helping me," Abram said softly before he lowered his hand.

Miriam glanced at Sarah.

"*Danki* means thank you." Sarah coughed,

hoping to clear the itch in her throat. But the knot continued to grow as she fought tears, and she could see out of the corner of her eye that Elizabeth and Lloyd were walking toward her. She braced herself for a cool reception, then silently prayed that things would be civil in front of Miriam. But by the time Elizabeth reached her, civility wasn't a concern. Elizabeth's eyes were filled with tears as she pulled Sarah into a hug and held her tightly.

"Welcome home," Elizabeth whispered, and Sarah wept openly as Abram's mother rubbed her back. "There, there. Everything is all right, *mei maedel.*" Sarah cried harder, wondering why her own mother couldn't have welcomed her home in a similar way. Sarah had hurt Elizabeth's son deeply. She'd hurt all of them. But aside from her father, Elizabeth was the only one who seemed to accept her return as a blessing and not a cruel reminder of all she had denied them. At that thought she eased away from Elizabeth and found Lloyd's eyes, but they weren't on her. Lloyd was looking at Miriam and smiling.

Sarah wondered if Abram and his parents had made a pact to embrace her as family since they so desperately wanted to believe that Miriam was Abram's daughter. But when Elizabeth pushed back a strand of Sarah's hair, the woman's eyes reflected genuine love, and Sarah wondered how she would ever forgive herself for hurting them all. If anyone was to blame, it was Sarah's mother. If she had only opened the letters — maybe things would have turned out differently. In truth, though, she had to admit that it wasn't her mother who was to blame at all. Sometimes it was just easier to lay blame there than to shoulder all of it on her own. Sometimes the burden was just too heavy.

Miriam talked loudly with excitement as she told Elizabeth and Lloyd about milking the cow, and with all the wonderment and discovery of grandparents, they showered her with laughter, hugs, and love. Surely Abram had told his parents Miriam wasn't his daughter. Although it was hard to deny the resemblance.

Lloyd eventually turned his attention to Sarah as he stroked his beard. She waited to see if Abram's father would welcome her home with the same enthusiasm as his wife. After a few moments, he nodded at her. " 'Tis *gut* to see you, Sarah." He glanced at Miriam. "She is a beautiful girl."

"Danki." The word eased off her tongue as if she'd never stopped speaking the dialect.

"Maybe your mommy and your . . ." Elizabeth paused as she realized what she'd almost said. "Maybe your mommy and Abram would like to talk, and perhaps you would like to come inside for some apple pie?"

"Can I, Mommy?" Miriam bounced up and down on her toes.

Sarah nodded. Then Elizabeth offered her hand to Miriam. They'd only taken a few steps, Lloyd walking beside them, when Miriam said, "We had midnight cookies at my grandparents' house last night."

"Oh my. That's late to be having cookies," Elizabeth said, her voice fading the farther away they got.

"Yeah. My mommy had a bad dream about the monster, and it made her scream, and . . ."

Sarah didn't hear the rest, but she could only imagine what Miriam might tell the people who had almost been her in-laws. She finally turned to Abram, but his eyes looked past her and didn't meet hers until the front door closed and Miriam was out of sight.

"We don't have to talk," Sarah said. "I can wait on the porch, or maybe join them, or . . ." She shrugged when the words caught in her throat.

Abram walked closer to her, as close as he'd been when he kissed her the day before, and Sarah took an instinctive step backward.

"Don't worry. I'm not going to kiss you again." He said it as if doing so would make him sick, even though Sarah longed for him to kiss her the way he used to, back when she could feel all the love he had to give. "But you cannot tell me that Miriam isn't *mei dochder*. She looks exactly like me."

But I can't tell you she is either. "You both have dimples." That was the most noticeable feature Miriam and Abram shared, but they also had the same-shaped blue eyes. Some days, Sarah convinced herself that Miriam was Abram's child and that she could see how much Miriam looked like him.

"It's more than the dimples," Abram said softly, his expression reflective of a man who had been wronged, but who might be on the verge of softening his position for the sake of a child he believed to be his. "Do you think I'd try to steal her away from you now that you're back? You know that isn't our way. But why can't you just admit that she is *mei dochder*? I know you're lying when you tell me she's not."

Sarah longed to fall into his arms, to press

226

her cheek against his firm chest, and to hold on to him forever. She wanted to tell him that Miriam *was* his daughter and that she wished more than anything they could be a family. But Sarah wasn't the same girl who left this place, and there were questions that needed answers. Had she lived in the *Englisch* world too long to ever reclaim her life here, the life she'd thought she was destined for? *Help me, Lord. What do I say?*

She listened for God's guidance. When she didn't hear anything, she deflected the situation by slowly moving toward Abram, then searching his eyes before she kissed him lightly on the mouth. As he cupped the back of her head and pulled her into the kind of kiss she remembered, it was as if no time had passed. They were Sarah and Abram, engaged to be married and looking forward to a lifetime of blessings together.

Abram wasn't just bitter and angry. He was wounded and had allowed his hurt to consume him. But with each kiss he shared with Sarah, the spark that had been extinguished a long time ago came alive again and grew into an inferno of hope. But years had passed, and they were both so different. Even though Abram had wanted to punish Sarah for the hurt she'd caused him, an eye for an eye just wasn't going to work. He still loved her as much as he ever had. This was his Sarah, the only woman he'd ever loved. And inside with his parents was his daughter. No matter what Sarah said.

He eased her away, brushed back a strand of her dark hair, and gazed into her eyes as a tear rolled down her cheek.

"I'm sorry about yesterday, about the way I kissed you." He'd lost sleep last night over that.

"I'm sorry I slapped you. You deserve to be angry."

Abram gently wiped away her tear with his thumb. "I had planned to be angry at you for the rest of my life."

She lowered her head, her shoulders shaking as she cried. He pulled her to his chest. She trembled as if it were twenty degrees outside, and he wondered what hardships she'd faced on her own in the *Englisch* world.

"But you can't be angry at someone for the rest of your life when you still love that person." Abram held her tighter as fear crept up on him. He was so scared she would leave him again. Even if there was hope for them, would he always worry that she'd leave?

"I love you too. I always have, and I always

will." Her voice was frail. "But something happened, and it had nothing to do with me not loving you."

Desperation for answers made his blood pump so fast, he thought a vein might burst. Whatever had happened to Sarah was eating her up from the inside out. And pushing her now wasn't in either of their best interests. They loved each other. But would it be enough to put the past behind them?

Then Miriam stepped out onto the porch and waved. And Abram decided love would have to be enough. Love, and a heavy dose of patience until Sarah was ready to talk to him. For today, he'd take her gift of love and visit from his daughter as a wonderful first step toward putting the past behind him. He hoped she would be able to do the same.

CHAPTER 8

Miriam skipped to the bathroom, and once she was out of earshot, Barbara moved to the far end of the couch to be closer to John's recliner. "I wonder how long Sarah will be job hunting. She's been gone two or three hours." Barbara felt guilty but hoped it would be most of the day so she and John could have Miriam all to themselves. Maybe if Miriam grew close to them, Sarah wouldn't want to snatch her away.

"I won't be able to bear it if Sarah leaves here with Miriam and doesn't allow us to see her." She folded her hands in her lap as she shook her head.

John put down the *Die Botschaft* he was reading and looked at her over the rims of his reading glasses. Her husband sighed. John enjoyed reading the weekly correspondence from Amish folks around the nation. She wasn't sure if the sigh was due to the interruption of his reading or the context of what she'd just said. "Barbara, embrace the joy. I don't think that will happen."

"But Sarah . . ." She blinked a few times, fending off tears. "Sarah is so angry with me. Beyond that, I feel like she doesn't even like me."

"And you haven't liked her very much." He grinned. "Sometimes you and I don't like each other. But we always love each other. Same with you and Sarah. Give it time."

Miriam walked back into the room but skipped past Barbara when the front door opened and Sarah came in. Miriam ran to her mother's outstretched arms, and Sarah smothered her with kisses, telling her how much she loved and missed her. *Just like I used to do with Sarah.*

"*Mammi* and *Daadi* took me in the buggy to a farm down the road, and do you know how many kids that family had?" Miriam's eyes were as round as golf balls.

Sarah gasped. "I don't know. How many?"

"Fourteen!" Miriam leaned closer to her mother. "I didn't know mommies could have that many babies. I thought only cats could."

John chuckled, and Barbara smiled as Sarah answered her daughter. "I'm not sure cats can have that many babies. Maybe, I guess."

"They had big kids that looked like grown-ups, and they had babies too. And I've decided I want thirteen brothers and sisters too."

"Oh my," Sarah said, glancing briefly at Barbara, who had wanted as many children as possible. The Lord had blessed her with only one. If Sarah remained in the *Englisch* world, she would never give Barbara that many grandchildren. "That's a lot of kids."

Miriam turned to Barbara. "Why doesn't my mommy have a lot of brothers and sisters?"

"I think it is time to collect eggs. What do you think, Miriam?" John to the rescue. He knew it was a hard subject for her.

"I can take her, *Daed,*" Sarah said. "It's the woman's job to collect eggs, and I want to help out while I'm here."

Barbara wasn't sure if that was a jab at her or not. Ever since she'd been attacked by one of their roosters, John insisted on collecting the eggs. Even after they ate that unruly bird for supper. Barbara had scars on the back of her calf still. She tried to talk her husband out of doing that particular chore since it was woman's work, but Sarah didn't know any of that because it happened

232

two years ago. She fought the bitterness building again.

"*Nee,* you stay and visit with your mother. This is a job for me and Miriam."

Perhaps John's timing was intentional, to force a conversation between Barbara and her daughter, but she suspected he also wanted some bonding time with Miriam. Barbara had certainly hogged their granddaughter today. John also knew that sometimes Barbara and Sarah just needed to battle it out by themselves before they could get past whatever problem they were facing. Barbara wasn't sure they'd be able to do that this time, but she was going to try to communicate with Sarah, and maybe their time apart would spare them a screaming match. Even if she and Sarah were beyond hope, she wanted a relationship with Miriam.

"Did you have any luck job hunting?" Barbara sat on the couch next to Sarah. It felt strange and awkward, and her stomach churned.

"*Ya,* I did."

It was also odd seeing Sarah wearing jeans, with makeup on and her hair down, and speaking in her native dialect, a language she hadn't used in six years. But Barbara loved hearing her use it, and she recalled her husband's words. *Embrace the joy.* "That's *gut*. What kind of work did you apply for?"

"Two administrative positions. One at the hospital in Lancaster and another one at the Stoltzfus Clinic in Paradise. That one would be much more convenient while I'm living here."

"Your *daed* said you went to see Abram yesterday." Barbara reminded herself not to push too hard.

"*Ya*, I did. I saw his parents too." Sarah scrunched up her nose, frowning like she'd always done when she was put out about something. "They were very happy to see me, and Elizabeth welcomed me with open arms."

Barbara's chest tightened. She was determined not to let Sarah pick a fight with her. "I'm glad they got to meet their granddaughter."

Sarah slowly put her feet on the coffee table, which they'd never allowed. But Barbara didn't say a word. Sarah folded her arms across her chest and stared at her shoes. "I never said Miriam was Abram's daughter."

Barbara's jaw dropped, and it was a few seconds before she could speak. "But — you left almost six years ago, and Miriam is five,

234

and . . ." Was Sarah saying this because she didn't want anyone to assume she wanted to get back together with Abram?

"The math works. I know." Sarah turned and glared at her mother. "If you had opened my letters, you would know the truth."

Barbara hung her head, shaking it. "At the time, I thought I was doing the right thing. I thought you'd come back, realize you'd made a terrible mistake."

Sarah dropped her hands to her lap, took her feet off the table, and looked away. "Do you think I didn't want to come back? I was in trouble! But you shunned me even though I hadn't been baptized."

Barbara's breath caught in her throat. "If you were in trouble, why didn't you come to me before you left?"

Sarah sighed. "Because I knew what you would say. And I was scared to talk to you, and even more afraid to talk to Abram. Running away felt like the only thing to do." She rubbed her throbbing temples for a few seconds. "We didn't exactly get along very well back then, and trust me, my news would have taken your shame to a whole new level."

The front door opened and John stuck his head inside. "Okay for me to take *mei mae-*

del on a buggy ride?"

"Please, Mommy." Miriam's blue eyes pleaded with her mother.

"Sure, sweetie. That's fine."

After they left, Barbara searched her mind for a way to somehow get things right between her and Sarah. Whatever bitterness she had carried over the years, it seemed that her daughter was also toting a heavy load of it. Before she could come up with anything, Sarah got off the couch and headed upstairs. Barbara wanted to call after her, not caring if she was being pushy. But then she heard footsteps coming back down the stairs. Sarah came into the living room carrying something. She tossed some envelopes on the table.

"It's been four years since I mailed the first letter, but maybe now you'll have more interest in reading them." She raised a shoulder, smirking, before she said, "Or maybe you still don't care."

Barbara stood up. "It was never that I didn't care. Your *daed* and I made the decision together, to see if our lack of communication would bring you back to us."

"You talked *Daed* into it. I'm sure of that." Sarah clenched her fists at her sides, directing all her anger at Barbara like a knife to her gut. Because she was right. Barbara had talked John into returning the letters unopened, despite his begging her to reconsider, saying they should at least read them, even if they didn't respond. Barbara hung her head.

"Well, now's your chance if you're interested." She nodded to the letters. "I'm going to the market in Bird-in-Hand to pick up a few things." She took her purse from the rack by the door. "I don't feel about certain things in those letters the way I did then, but you'll understand more if you read them. And I'm sure they are reflective of my eighth-grade education at the time." Shrugging again, she said, "Up to you." She opened the front door.

"Wait." Barbara took a step toward her. "I mailed you a letter."

Sarah pulled her purse up on her shoulder as she shifted her weight. "When?"

"A couple years ago. I'd kept the return address from your first letter."

Sarah humphed, then shook her head. "You returned all my letters unopened, but then decided to write to me?" She scratched her forehead. "I never got a letter from you."

"It was never returned to me." Barbara had always wondered if Sarah had received it and tossed it in the trash unopened.

"I didn't live at that address anymore."

Sarah's voice had softened, but only a little. "Just for curiosity's sake, what did the letter say?"

"That we loved and missed you."

Sarah looked at her mother for a while with a blank expression before she turned and left, gently closing the door behind her.

Barbara watched through the window as Sarah walked to her car, the one she'd just purchased with the FEMA check she received. It was old, but Sarah said it was all she could afford and that it would help with her job search. As the engine started, Sarah lay her forehead against the steering wheel. When she lifted her head, Barbara saw tears streaming down her cheeks. She wasn't sure how much more her heart could take, but she walked to the door. By the time she opened it and stepped onto the porch, Sarah was backing out of the driveway. They locked eyes for a few seconds, but Sarah left.

When Barbara walked back into the house, she stared at the letters before she picked them up. She thumbed through the postmark dates and picked the one Sarah sent first. She stared at it, knowing that after she knew the truth, she couldn't un-know it.

But she'd waited too long for answers, so she slid her finger along the seam and pulled out a piece of yellow ruled paper folded in thirds. She opened it and noticed the date at the top of the page. Sarah would have been gone about a week when she'd written it.

Dear *Mamm* and *Daed*,

CHAPTER 9

Barbara brought a trembling hand to her chest as she read.

I'm sorry for the way I ran away, but I was scared. Me and Abram went against God and were together as *mann* and *fraa* before marriage. We knew it was wrong and prayed for forgiveness. I didn't think you could make a *boppli* the first time. But then something terrible happened.

Barbara's heart hammered against her chest so hard she was almost afraid to keep reading, but she took a deep breath and continued.

That same week, I told you I was going out to eat with my friend Veronica, but we didn't go eat. We went to a party.

Barbara hadn't liked Sarah's *Englisch* friend, Veronica, but she and John had allowed Sarah to go to supper with her a few times since Sarah was in her *rumschpringe*. The girl had been gracious enough to drive family members to doctor appointments when it was too far to travel by buggy. Barbara braced herself with a deep breath.

A boy at the party gave me a drink that had alcohol in it. I'm not sure, but it might have had something else in it, too, because when I woke up the next morning, I didn't remember anything that had happened. But two buttons on my blouse were undone, and my shirt was untucked. I think we did what me and Abram did.

And then I missed my monthly so I bought an *Englisch* baby testing kit. I'm going to have a baby, *Mamm* and *Daed,* and I don't know who the father is. This would bring even more shame to our family. It must have been my fault the boy did that to me because I was wearing *Englisch* clothes, showing more of myself than a respectable girl would. I think God is punishing me for what me and Abram did.

I'm scared. Please write me back and tell me what to do.

Love,
Sarah

Barbara covered her face with her hands and sobbed. She took several moments to allow her emotions to go full circle. What had she been thinking to return the letters unopened? Sarah had been so testy back then, and Barbara truly thought that by not reading her daughter's excuses for running away, she'd come home. But if anyone was to blame for her running away, it was Barbara.

Her hands shook even more as she reached for the next letter. She remembered how much John had wanted to open it, even more than the first one. In Barbara's mind, Sarah was okay, since she was writing to them. To return them unopened felt like the best way to get her to come home at the time.

She opened the second letter, the postmark dated a few weeks later. Her daughter basically repeated what she'd said in the first letter, and it wasn't any easier to read the words a second time. She held the letter to her chest as another tear slid down her cheek. Then she reached for the third letter, only to find a more desperate plea that ended with, *This is my last try to talk to you. I lieb you. I'm sorry. God has forsaken me. And I guess you have too.*

Sobs racked Barbara so violently that she

began to gasp for air, her chest tightening. Why didn't God speak to her back then? Maybe He did, and she just wasn't listening.

Sarah knocked on Veronica's door. She'd gotten the address from Veronica's mother. It was a small house outside Bird-in-Hand, and after wandering around the market, she forced herself to make the visit. Hopefully through Veronica she could face the monster wearing a cowboy hat who haunted her dreams. Veronica might know if he was still in the area or what had become of him. Sarah never told her friend what happened that night. Veronica had been in a bedroom with some other guy, and Sarah's shame kept her silent on the ride back to Veronica's house the next morning.

Veronica opened the door, and her mouth fell open as her false dark lashes flew up. Gasping, she threw her arms around Sarah's neck and squeezed. Sarah slowly put her arms around her former friend. She'd never blamed her for what happened, but the association between Veronica and that horrible night had been enough that Sarah hadn't contacted her since she left.

"I always wondered what happened to you." Veronica held her at arm's length, studying her, looking her up and down.

"You look great."

Sarah forced a smile. "So do you." Veronica's long blonde hair was now cut in a short and stylish bob, and as Veronica lowered her arms, she placed a hand on her stomach, a small pooch showing beneath a yellow T-shirt. "You're pregnant."

Veronica held up her left hand, sporting a small diamond ring. "And married." She rolled her eyes. "Not exactly in that order, but we're very happy. This is actually our second baby on the way. We got married before Haley was born. She's almost two now." She motioned for Sarah to follow her over the threshold into a small living room. It wasn't fancy, but it was clean and smelled like cookies baking. "Haley is napping, but I hope she wakes up before you leave. She's our everything."

"I'm so happy for you." Veronica had made a good life for herself, and Sarah was glad. They'd grown up in different worlds, but Veronica had always been good to her, and if she'd known what happened that night, she would have comforted her.

Sarah shivered when she recalled the woozy way she'd felt that night and how she'd vomited most of the next day. In her dreams, the monster always said, "I actually did it with an Amish chick." She had no idea if that was said in real life, but the words had hung in her mind for six years and haunted her sleep, which only solidified to her that the worst had happened.

Jayden Meyers. The monster in the cowboy hat. She could still see his face and the way he chuckled the next morning as he left her sitting on an unmade bed, not knowing how she'd gotten there in the first place.

Veronica sat on a green-and-white couch, motioning for Sarah to do the same. "So, I have to know. Why did you disappear the way you did? I made your mom promise to tell me if she heard anything, and I gave her my phone number, but I never got any news. Where have you been? And what are you doing back?"

Sarah hadn't planned what she would say, and she wanted to be careful how she explained the situation to Veronica. She didn't want her to feel responsible in any way. All her friend had done was invite Sarah to the party, which was mostly *Englisch* kids, but a few Amish teenagers in their *rumschpringe* had been there too.

"Well, I left because, um . . ." Sarah cleared her throat. "I, uh . . ."

Veronica held up a finger. "Hold that thought because I want to hear everything. But I hear Haley waking up." She left the room and walked down a small hallway, so Sarah took a deep breath and tried to think of what to say. But when Veronica came back, she was beaming with a smile stretched across her face. She kissed the little girl on the cheek, then set her on the couch between them. The toddler promptly buried her head in her mother's lap.

"Haley, this is my friend Sarah. Don't be shy." Veronica gently tickled the little girl. "Look up, sleepyhead."

Sarah smiled, remembering when Miriam was that age. Haley looked briefly at her. "She's adorable."

"We love her so much." She lifted Haley onto her lap as the girl burrowed against her mother's chest.

"Motherhood suits you." Sarah was glad to see Veronica so happy. Back then, she'd worried about her. Veronica had partied too much, done a few drugs, and was even arrested once for shoplifting a pair of earrings. But she'd always been a good friend to Sarah. Trustworthy and kind. Sarah's mother hadn't liked her, but Barbara didn't care for most of the *Englisch.* There were a lot of times Veronica had driven Sarah, her mother, and her grandmother to doctor's appointments, and even once to the hospital when her grandmother had broken her hip.

Veronica was always willing to pick up prescriptions too. Sarah used to remind her mother of that when she questioned Sarah's friendship with Veronica. But it wasn't just about the rides. Veronica was a nice person, deserving of this life she'd made for herself. Simplistic, but real, it seemed.

"So, where have you been?" Veronica reached for a pacifier on the coffee table and handed it to the child, who quickly put it in her mouth. "She's too old for it, and we're trying to wean her off, but . . ." She smiled. "So, go on."

"I was pregnant, and back then I was terrified to face my parents."

Veronica pressed her lips together as lines formed across her forehead. "Did you, uh . . . keep the baby?"

Sarah brought a hand to her chest. "Yes, of course. Yes. Her name is Miriam."

Then Sarah gave Veronica a brief rundown of the past six years. "I lost everything when Hurricane Harvey hit. I could have stayed with friends, but it seemed like an opportunity to come home, to test the waters. I'm not the same as I was then. I'd like to think I'm stronger now."

"Wow." Veronica breathed a clear sigh of relief. "I'm so glad you're here now, but you should have written me or called or something."

"I know. And I'm sorry. There were weird circumstances." Sarah was fumbling and wondering if she should even tell her friend what happened. But Veronica was her only link to Jayden, and he might even be long gone.

"You know, I'm not the same as I was back then." Veronica lowered her head. "After you left, I was partying way too hard. And I started dating this horrible guy." She cringed. "I mean, he was really bad news. He had a horrible temper, and every time I tried to break it off, he got violent." A slow smile filled her face. "But then a knight in shining armor rode into my life and swept me off my feet. He was handsome, chivalrous, and we fell in love. That was over three years ago, and not a day goes by that I don't thank the Lord for him. He is a wonderful provider, a great father, and I'm blessed to have snagged such a man."

Sarah smiled at her friend. "You deserve all of this, Veronica, and I am so happy for you."

Veronica kissed Haley on the cheek when she lifted her head. "I don't know about deserving, but we're blissfully happy." She smiled. "You might even know my husband.

He was around back in the day. His name is Jayden Meyers."

Sarah felt the color leave her face.

CHAPTER 10

Abram discreetly pulled his cell phone from his pocket and checked the time, then quickly stowed it when two *Englisch* women walked into Dienner's Country Restaurant. Non-Amish folks were always shocked to see an Amish person with a phone, even though it was allowed for business purposes and emergencies. And when you were in your *rumschpringe* and hadn't been baptized. He'd even had an *Englisch* woman reprimand him once, reminding him that cell phones were not allowed among his people. The tourists sometimes expected anyone Amish to act a certain way, like they weren't getting their money's worth for the experience if Abram's people didn't act the part.

He finally sat on the bench in the waiting area. Sarah said to meet him here at three, that it was important that she talk to him. Hopefully she'd decided to give them another chance and to admit that Miriam was his daughter. At first, he was sure Miriam was his. But now he was beginning to wonder if it had just been wishful thinking. She was a precious little girl, and Abram had always wanted children — children with Sarah. They couldn't go backward, but with love in their hearts, anything was possible. Abram had to consider the possibility that the resemblance between him and Miriam was coincidence, which would mean Sarah had been with someone else within a week or two of being with Abram. That part was hard to come to terms with.

Glancing around, he checked his phone again. The restaurant only had a few patrons this time of day. Abram had taken Sarah here for their first date, so he was hopeful there was a connection in her wanting to meet here.

He stood when he saw her and rushed toward her. "What's wrong?" His heart pounded, and he wondered if she knew how red her eyes were. "What's wrong, Sarah?" he asked again.

"Can we go somewhere?" Her desperate eyes and shaky voice caused Abram's stomach to churn. "Please, can we just go somewhere more private?"

He instinctively put an arm around her

and led her toward the door, but paused at the booth to leave three dollars for his soda. He pulled her to him the moment they were in the parking lot. "Whatever it is, I'm still here for you, Sarah."

She eased away from him, shaking from head to toe as she stared into his eyes for a long time.

Abram glanced at the car she'd purchased recently, then looked back at her. "I don't think you should drive being this upset. I can't leave the horse here anyway, so I can take us somewhere nearby and private."

Sarah nodded, and after Abram readied the animal for travel, he climbed into the buggy beside Sarah, who was struggling to catch her breath. "Is it about your parents? Are you and your *mudder* fighting?" Abram remembered how much Sarah and Barbara had fought, but Sarah shook her head.

"Nee, it's not about *mei mudder."*

Abram wondered if she even realized she was using *Deutsch.* Then his adrenaline spiked. "Is it Miriam? Is she okay?"

Sarah nodded. *"Ya,* she's fine."

Abram crossed Lincoln Highway and headed down a less traveled gravel road. Up the way was an abandoned sawmill. He could pull in there and hopefully find out what was troubling Sarah. He still couldn't believe how much he'd wanted to hurt her when she first arrived. Now he wished he could take all her pain away and chided himself for the terrible thoughts he'd had about her over the years. He remembered at times squeezing his eyes together and trying to will her to come home. He hadn't understood why God allowed this to happen. But Sarah was home now. It had to be God's perfect timing, but why was this the plan? Maybe Abram would never know.

He turned into the dirt driveway that led to the sawmill, then wound around to the back of the building so they were out of sight. Facing her, he was selfishly scared to hear what she had to say. Was she leaving again? Was she taking Miriam with her?

Sarah was surely too young to have a heart attack, but her chest was so tight that she considered the possibility. She didn't look at Abram once as she relived what had happened six years ago. She left out the part about Veronica being married to Jayden. Squeezing her eyes closed, she couldn't hold back her tears. But she couldn't hear Abram breathing, so she slowly lifted her gaze. His face was as red as a barn and his nostrils flared.

"It sounds like this guy drugged you with

alcohol and pills."

"It must have been my fault, though, right?" Sarah was wise enough to know better, but that was part of the nightmare, always questioning what she could have done to prevent whatever happened.

Abram latched onto both her arms and looked in her eyes. "*Nee.* It was not your fault. I want to kill that guy."

Sarah gasped through her tears. "Don't say that." Not only was it not their way, but Jayden was a husband and father now. Sarah wondered if he ever thought about that night, if he felt remorse. But his feelings were not her burden to carry. She had enough shouldering her own.

Abram let go of her arms, faced forward, and leaned his head back. "You should have told me." He turned his head toward her. "Did you think I would leave you? If something did happen that night, you were not a willing participant because I know you never would have cheated on me."

Sarah blinked her eyes a few times, sniffling. "*Nee,* I wouldn't have. But I still don't know who the father of my child is." The statement came out louder than she meant it to, but it was the truth.

Abram ran a hand through his hair and clenched his jaw. She'd seen him angry before, but not like this. Sarah was glad she didn't tell him she knew where the monster lived.

Monster. A far cry from the knight in shining armor Veronica had described. In her heart, Sarah knew she had to face Jayden before she could truly move on, but what would that do to Veronica? Would it ruin her friend's life? Would Veronica even believe her? What about Haley and the baby on the way? All worries for another day, she decided. Right now, she was going to try to keep the focus on Abram and his emotions.

"I'm sorry," she said through more tears. "I've decided to have a DNA test." It was a terrifying thought, considering Miriam could be Haley's half sister. What then? Would Sarah tell Veronica and Jayden?

Abram lifted an eyebrow.

"It's a test to see who the father is."

Abram narrowed his eyebrows. "But you don't know where the other . . . *guy* . . . is." He spewed venom as he said "guy."

"It doesn't matter. The test will show if you are the father, and I know how badly you want to believe you are." Sarah wanted to believe that, too, and she was terrified to learn the truth. If Abram wasn't Miriam's father, she would lose the ability to even fantasize that he was.

"She's my daughter." Abram said it with such conviction that Sarah was sure he'd be devastated if she wasn't.

"We won't know without the test."

Abram faced forward and was quiet for a few minutes before he turned back to her. "If you and I are being gifted a second chance at happiness, I will raise Miriam as my own, no matter what any test reveals." He paused. "Don't even have the test, Sarah. A home and a family are built on love, not DNA."

"I have to know." She sniffled and dabbed at her eyes with a tissue. "I must look a mess."

"You look beautiful."

"*Danki* for saying so." She paused as she worked the tissue below her eyes. "I'll have to save the money. I think it's around five hundred dollars, but I'm not sure."

Abram shook his head. "*Nee,* I will pay for the test if you are sure this is something you have to do." Before Sarah could argue, he looked her way again. "Do your parents know?"

Sarah thought about the letters she'd left her mother. "They do now." She explained and Abram's face turned red again.

"We would have had answers if your mother had just opened the letters."

Sarah wondered what her mother's re-action had been, and she regretted tossing the letters at her. In hindsight it seemed like a mean thing to do, especially after her mother said she had written to Sarah. "*Mamm* did what she thought was best at the time. She thought if they shunned me I'd return home." When Abram didn't say anything, she said, "What's done is done."

If things had played out any differently, it could have altered the Lord's plan for all of them. If Sarah had told Veronica what happened that night, she probably wouldn't have had anything to do with Jayden or married him. There wouldn't be a Haley or another baby on the way. What if Haley was meant to grow up and cure cancer or do some other amazing thing that wouldn't come to pass if things had gone any differently?

But what about me? She wished she could put that night behind her and never think about it again. But that was never going to happen. She'd spent six years wondering exactly what had happened that night and who the father of her child was. It was a chapter she wanted to close, and when Miriam was old enough, she deserved to know her biological father, even if it wasn't Abram.

"Are you hungry? Do you want to go back to the restaurant and eat?" Abram asked after a lengthy silence. It was after the supper hour now, so they'd both likely missed a meal at home.

Sarah shook her head. "*Nee.* I'm not hungry, and I should go home." She was suddenly very worried about her mother, and even though her stomach growled, she didn't think she could eat a bite of food.

"What will I need to do for this DNA test?"

"I think they just swab the inside of your mouth, but I'll find out for sure."

They agreed they would make arrangements to pick up Sarah's car from the restaurant when she wasn't so upset. When they arrived at her parents' house, Sarah opened the door to get out of the buggy but instead just sat there for a few seconds. Somehow her hand found Abram's. "I'm not the same, you know."

"I'm not either."

Sarah hung her head for a few seconds before she locked eyes with Abram. "I know we've both grown up, but I lived a very different life in Texas. I wore *Englisch* clothes. I worked. I owned a car. I had electricity, and Miriam grew up watching television. We went to movies and did a lot of other things that aren't acceptable here."

Abram stared at her for a while. "I know. But if you held on to the most important thing of all, your faith, then nothing is impossible."

Sarah nodded. "I took my faith with me when I left. I was mad at God for a while, but I worked through it knowing He would stay close to me." She longed for a way for she, Abram, and Miriam to be a family.

She squeezed his hand, but when she made a move to get out of the buggy, Abram pulled her back in, gently cupped her cheeks with both hands, and kissed her. "I might not be the same. But I love you today as much as I did back then."

She gazed into his eyes, kissed him back, and said, "But is love enough?"

Abram smiled. "I believe it is."

CHAPTER 11

Barbara had shown John the letters when he and Miriam returned from their ride. His expression might as well have screamed, "See what you did!" but he remained calm and was quick to offer Miriam another buggy ride, so they hopefully wouldn't be home when Sarah returned. Barbara waited until they left before allowing herself another good cry.

When Abram's buggy turned in the driveway, Barbara dabbed at her eyes with a tissue, the letters in her other hand, as she wondered if Sarah's car had already broken down. She'd tried to plan what to say to her daughter, but her thoughts were jumbled. How would Sarah ever forgive her if she couldn't forgive herself?

Sarah walked in with swollen eyes and red cheeks. Barbara ran to her and embraced her. "I'm sorry! I'm so sorry!" She was yelling and shaking and so sad she wanted to go to sleep to ease the pain. She eased out of the hug.

"I'm the monster in the dream, aren't I?" Barbara covered her face as shame wrapped around her like a cocoon of regret.

Sarah shook her head. "*Nee, Mamm,* you aren't the monster. My monster wears a cowboy hat."

Barbara sat on the couch, fearful she might fall otherwise. She looked up. "Lord, what did I do?" Then she turned to Sarah, who was still standing just inside the doorway. "What have I done?" Grief pounded against her temples and her stomach roiled.

Sarah sat beside her. "*Mamm,* it's okay."

Barbara shook her head and loose strands of hair spilled across her face from underneath her *kapp.* "You needed me, and I wasn't there."

Sarah's eyes darted around the room. "Where is Miriam?"

"With your *daed.*" Barbara sniffed. "She loves riding in the buggy. She's her mother's daughter. Remember how much you loved to ride in the buggy?"

Sarah smiled a little. "I still do."

"Where is your car?"

"It's at Dienner's. Abram met me there, and we decided to leave it there for now."

"I'm sorry," Barbara said again. "I will be

261

sorry for the rest of my life."

A tear rolled down her daughter's cheek. "*Mamm.* It's okay. I wasn't the easiest person to get along with when I was a teenager. And I know you were only trying to force me to come home. I forgive you, so please don't be sorry for the rest of your life."

She took Barbara's hand in hers, which only made Barbara cry harder. Her heart was shattered seeing her daughter like this, knowing what she'd had to endure alone.

"I want to get a DNA test to determine who Miriam's father is."

Barbara nodded and tried to still her shaking hands by folding them in her lap. "I suppose Abram and his folks have a right to know if she is their grandchild. I'll give you whatever you need to have the test."

"I don't want you to do that. Abram wants to pay for it."

Barbara sighed. "Child, I'd give you my soul if I thought it would make things right."

Sarah tucked her chin as tears spilled into her lap. Barbara had been so caught up in her own emotions that she hadn't even asked why her daughter was so upset when she first came in.

"Sarah, what's wrong? Has something else happened?" She raised a finger. "I'm not prying. You don't have to tell me." She remembered all the times Sarah had told her that she was meddling in her business.

Sarah lifted her eyes to Barbara's. "A lot has happened. And I need time to process some things. I had a long talk with Abram, and I'm just very emotional right now."

Barbara stood when Sarah did. "Of course. I understand." She bit her bottom lip, hoping to gain control of her emotions. Sarah had enough on her plate and didn't need to be consoling Barbara.

Sarah wrapped her arms around her. "I love you, *Mamm*."

"I love you, too, sweet *maedel* of mine."

They stood in the middle of the living room holding each other for a long time. It would never be long enough for Barbara.

Sarah waited until the following Saturday before she went back to Veronica's house. The house she lived in with the man who had possibly drugged and impregnated Sarah. The more Sarah thought about it, the more she knew the monster would stay in her nightmares unless she faced Jayden.

Her father had taken her in his buggy to pick up her car the day after she'd left it at Dienner's, so she could continue to look for work. She'd landed a job that she would start on Monday as the receptionist at the Stoltzfus Clinic, and the DNA test results should be ready by the end of the week. She wanted this behind her as she rebuilt her life. But to do that, she needed to know what actually happened. Perhaps she could have already done so, if Miriam's paternity hadn't hinged on that night.

She knocked on the door, and Veronica answered with Haley on her hip. "Hi! What a great surprise. Jayden is cooking us a late breakfast, so you're just in time to eat."

The thought of sitting down at the table with that man caused bile to rise in her throat until she felt like she might vomit. "*Nee, nee.* I don't want to interrupt your meal." She had been working on a way to talk to Jayden by herself, but she didn't really have a plan. She might not need one when Jayden saw her. He'd probably throw her out before there was time to say too much. Sarah was surely the last person in the world Jayden would want showing up at his house.

Veronica giggled. "You still have the accent, like you're Amish. And you still talk like you're Amish." She pushed the door open, and the aroma of bacon wafted up Sarah's nose. She loved bacon. But she might never eat it again now. Would she think of this moment every time she smelled bacon? "Do you think you'll ever be Amish again?" Veronica eyed Sarah up and down. She was wearing blue jeans and a white T-shirt with *Houston Astros World Series 2017* etched into the logo.

Sarah couldn't think that far ahead. She couldn't think past the next few seconds when she saw Jayden over Veronica's shoulder, heading their way. He swung the door wider so he could see who was on their porch. When he locked eyes with Sarah, he smiled. The smile that had melted her resolve all those years ago. He'd said they were going to the bedroom to talk.

"Sarah, this is my man." She boosted Haley up on her hip. "Jayden, this is an old friend of mine, Sarah. She lived here until about six years ago when she moved to Houston, but she's back with her parents now. She lost everything in the hurricane."

Sarah couldn't move or breathe. She waited, but Jayden turned to his wife and took Haley out of her arms. "I told you, sweetie, don't carry her around so much. You have another one to think about now."

"He's a bit overprotective of this unborn child." Veronica rolled her eyes. "I was just telling Sarah that she's in time for breakfast."

Jayden kissed Haley on the cheek and put her down when she started to squirm. The toddler rushed to an open red suitcase stuffed with toys in the living room. "Absolutely. I made plenty. Veronica eats a lot these days."

Veronica playfully poked him in the arm. "Oh, hush."

Jayden stuck his hand out, and Sarah jumped. Then she took two steps backward. "You know what? I-I just remembered something. I'll stop by another time."

Veronica scrunched her nose. "Well, okay. But don't be too long. We have more catching up to do."

Jayden yelled, "Nice to meet you," just before Sarah opened the car door. Once inside, she gripped the steering wheel. What had she almost done? She would have ruined their lives. It was six years ago. But how was she ever going to find peace if Jayden didn't tell her what happened that night?

She jumped when someone knocked on the window, and when she looked up to see Jayden, she hit the lock, then realized how silly she must look, no matter the circumstances. She slowly rolled down the window.

The monster wasn't smiling now, and Sarah braced herself for what might be coming. An apology, perhaps? A threat to never come back? She had no plans to visit Veronica again. This was the moment, and Sarah had no words.

"Listen," he said before blowing out a heavy sigh. "Do we know each other?"

Is this guy for real?

"I mean, it's impossible not to see that I startled you or something. Veronica knows about my past. I did some pretty awful things before I got into NA, Narcotics Anonymous. I don't remember a lot of the year before that. Did we date or hang out or something? You look familiar."

Sarah swallowed hard. *Help me, God.*

"Anyway, I'd been clean for a while when I met Veronica, and I could tell she was headed down the same path I'd been on." He hung his head, then locked eyes with Sarah again. "We have a good life, but I'm trying to make amends with anyone I hurt back then. So if I did something to you, or offended you, or anything at all, I'm sorry. God has led me onto a good path, but I'll take total responsibility if I hurt you in any way."

Sarah finally swallowed. "Uh, no. No. I'm happy for you and Veronica."

Jayden smiled and walked away, and she

wondered if the monster would be gone from her dreams.

CHAPTER 12

It was Friday when the lab called Sarah at work to let her know the DNA test results were in. It took everything she had to wait until five o'clock to go pick up the envelope that would tell her if Abram was Miriam's father. She'd prayed for it to be true. And she was sure her parents and Abram's had as well. Everyone had fallen in love with Miriam, and she with them. It was the family she'd always been meant to have, and Sarah didn't see herself leaving this place again. She wasn't sure about her and Abram, especially if Miriam turned out to be Jayden's. Did she owe it to him to let him know he had another child, if that turned out to be the case?

As she drove her car to the hospital where the test results were, she prayed again to forgive Jayden. It wasn't going to happen overnight, and she knew God had already forgiven him. But upsetting his and Veronica's life didn't seem like a good plan, and there was nothing to gain by it. That could all change if Jayden was Miriam's father, but for right now, Sarah could only take one step at a time. Jayden had turned his life around, and apparently he'd turned Veronica's around too. Sarah hadn't had a nightmare since the visit.

At the hospital, she walked to the lab, and the receptionist handed her an envelope with the results inside. Sarah's hand shook as she took it, then put it in her purse.

Back in her car, she took the envelope out and stared at it. She thought she would have ripped into it by now. But whatever the results were, lives were going to change. She ran it all through her head again. If Jayden was the father, she probably wouldn't tell him. She wasn't sure. She'd have to pray hard about it. If Abram was the father, could they put the past behind them and be the family they were meant to be? It seemed they could. And if Abram wasn't the father, would she and Abram still have a shot at happiness? Could he really raise another man's child as his own? The questions bounced around in her mind like a ping pong ball that had been hit too hard. She took a deep breath.

■ ■ ■ ■

Abram jumped from the plow when Sarah's car turned into the driveway, and he saw his father slow the mules until they stopped. His parents knew today was the day. He looked toward the house, and his mother was peering out the window. They all loved Miriam, whether Abram was her father or not. But his nerves had been on edge all week waiting for the results. He'd seen Sarah twice for lunch, and there were so many uncertainties in the air, they decided to wait until the test results before they tried to get too far ahead of themselves. But Abram already knew what he wanted, and a piece of paper wasn't going to make any difference.

He ran to where Sarah was leaning against her car, an envelope in her hand. They stared at each other. Abram had assumed he would be able to read the results in Sarah's expression, but he had no idea one way or the other by the blank look on her face.

"I need to tell you something," he said, breathless. "I love you. I love Miriam. I want us to be a family. And I know we have to start over in some ways and get to know each other again. But as far as I'm concerned, you can tear up the results, whatever they are. It doesn't matter. I'd raise Miriam as my own no matter what."

Sarah didn't flinch.

"Say something."

She glanced at the envelope.

Abram meant what he'd said. He would raise Miriam as his own no matter what, but his insides were spinning.

"I haven't opened it," she said in a whisper. "I've spent the last six years fantasizing that you were Miriam's father. I'm scared to find out now."

Abram swallowed hard. "Just tear it up. It doesn't matter."

Sarah barely smiled. "We both know it does."

He leaned down and kissed her on the mouth, even though both his parents had eyes on them. "I'll love Miriam no matter what."

She stared at him, then smiled again. "I believe you."

Sarah waved to Abram's father when she saw him staring from the field. If she had to guess, Abram's mother was probably watching from the window. Everyone had a vested interest in Miriam's paternity. But if the results weren't what they'd all hoped for, would Abram and his parents truly embrace Miriam as their own?

"You'd really be okay if we just tear it up and don't look?" Sarah looked at the envelope, then back at Abram as the color drained from his face. "We've come this far. I think we have to know."

"It won't change anything." Abram wiped sweat from his forehead. It was a pleasant and cool spring day, but sweat was pooling at Sarah's temples as well.

She stuck her finger in the same place on the envelope as she had in the car. She'd only slit it open a couple of inches when she decided to wait. But now, the moment was upon them. She looked at Abram.

"Breathe," he said as she slid the paper from the envelope. She read the results, then fell to her knees and wept.

"I love you, Sarah. I'll love Miriam. I promise. Please don't cry." Abram was on the ground with her, his voice shaking as he spoke, tears in his eyes. "It's fine. I love you both. I'll spend the rest of my life loving you if you'll have me. I know it will take time, but —"

"She's yours," Sarah said through her tears. "You are her father."

They fell into each other's arms, and

Sarah smothered him with kisses. Then she looked to her Father above. *Thank You.*

They sat in the grass for a while. Abram hadn't been able to hold back his own tears, and as they cried, they also rejoiced. It hadn't been either's plan, but only God's plan was perfect. She thought again about Veronica and how differently her life might have turned out if she hadn't met Jayden. Would she have overdosed or been under the influence while driving, or any other horrible thing that her partying could have led to?

"I think there are reasons everything happened the way it did." She cupped Abram's cheeks in her hands. "I'm sorry you missed out on so much." She hung her head. "Her birth, her first steps." She looked back at him. "And I don't know if any pictures survived the floodwater in Houston."

Abram kissed her hand. "We are going to take things one day at a time." He kissed her on the mouth, gently, the way she remembered. "But I have a *gut* feeling about us, that we'll be a family."

"I want that." Sarah looked around at the pastures, at the flowers in full bloom. "There's no place I'd rather be, and I want Miriam to experience this life." She paused. "Abram, we can't predict how things will turn out for us. I know we are both hopeful, and I know we love each other. But I am willing to walk beside you as we take things one day at a time."

He kissed her again, then chuckled. "I can see *mei mudder* in the window. She's probably bitten off all of her fingernails wondering if our tears are happy or sad." He nodded to the field where his father was. "And *Daed* hasn't moved an inch since you got here."

Sarah smiled. "I should probably go home. I feel like *mei mamm* and I are ready to have some hard talks, but that *gut* things are on the horizon there too."

They shared one final kiss before Sarah headed home. Joy filled her heart, and she thanked God repeatedly for His grace along her route.

When she came to a stop at her house, her stomach did a somersault, and all the joy that had just filled her heart met with her churning insides. She stepped out of her car and walked slowly across the yard to where Jayden was standing.

"I told your folks I wanted to wait out here for you for a while, that I was an old friend and needed to talk to you." He glanced at his white truck. "Your parents didn't know how long you'd be gone. I was just getting ready to leave, so I'm glad you showed up."

Friend? Hardly.

"I remember you," he said before he looked down and stuffed his hands in the pockets of his jeans. Slowly, he lifted his eyes to hers. "We were at a party together. I think you came with Veronica, but I didn't really know her back then." He paused, shifting his weight. "Maybe you don't remember."

"I remember being there." Sarah swallowed hard, wanting to believe that she never would have cheated on Abram, no matter what, but now as she faced off with Jayden, she was afraid to know. "I don't remember what happened."

Jayden took his hands out of his pockets, still shifting his weight and nervously kicking at the ground with one of his running shoes. "I put something in your drink that night. Back then, I thought it would be cool to, um . . ." He sighed. "To do it with an Amish girl."

Sarah felt her cheeks turning red as she held her breath.

"Anyway, I knew I wasn't just imagining the way you were looking at me when you came to our house. I was sure you looked familiar." Pausing, he looked past Sarah. "I don't want any secrets between Veronica and me. Granted, I don't think she needs to know every single thing I did before we got together, but since you two are old friends, I think I need to tell her what happened."

Sarah was already shaking her head. "Obviously, you've changed. It's in the past, so just keep it there." She surprised herself when she spoke. After years of seeing Jayden's face, the way he laughed at her, the monster in her dreams, she was sure she would want to slug him. She'd spent years wondering if he could be Miriam's father. But everyone deserved redemption, and it sounded like Jayden had saved Veronica by applying what he'd learned.

"At the very least, I'm sorry. I'm really sorry." Jayden locked eyes with her, then looked away again. "I'd better go. I just wanted to tell you that." He turned to leave.

"Jayden."

He slowed his nervous stride, then faced her again. "Yeah?"

"What *did* happen?" Sarah held her breath.

"Nothing. You kinda passed out, and then I did too."

Sarah let go of the breath she was holding. "Nothing happened?"

He shook his head. "No. Nothing at all."

She waited until he got in his car, until he rounded the corner and was out of sight, before she looked up again. *Thank you, God.*

As she walked across the yard to the house, she saw her mother watching her out the window, a hand to her chest, something she did when she worried. But the time for worrying, regrets, and heavy burdens had passed. Instead of rolling her eyes like she might have in the past, Sarah smiled and waved, which was enough for her mother to rush to the front door.

Sarah fell into her arms. "Miriam is Abram's daughter, and we are hoping to work things out."

Her mother's embrace tightened. "So, you're staying?"

"*Ya*, I am." She eased away. "I love you, *Mamm.*"

Her mother wept. "I love you, too, *mei* sweet *maedel.*"

Sarah looked forward to a bright future with the family she'd always dreamed of.

EPILOGUE

Twelve years later

Sarah waddled to the kitchen when she smelled bacon cooking. It was her job to cook the family meals, but she'd been mostly on bed rest the past few weeks. Her little bundle was trying to come early.

Abram raised an eyebrow from his place at the head of the table, the same seat Sarah's father had occupied for years. But her parents had moved to the *daadi haus* not long after Abram and Sarah married. Sarah couldn't believe she and Abram were approaching their eleventh anniversary. *Where has the time gone?*

"You're supposed to be in bed," Abram said, trying to sound stern, but when Sarah waved him off, he returned to his meal.

"*Mamm, Daed*'s right." Miriam pulled a second pan of biscuits from the oven. At seventeen, she'd taken over Sarah's responsibilities until after the baby was born.

"I can't stay in that bed all day long. I've read every weekly edition of the *Die Botschaft* and the two gardening magazines you bought for me, and I've knitted two blankets for the new *boppli*."

"*Ya,* I know." Miriam eased the biscuits from the pan and set them on a platter. "But it's not for much longer."

Three knocks sounded at the front door. That was Sarah's mother. She still knocked, even though Sarah had told her years ago to just come on in.

"Come in!" Miriam yelled from the kitchen over the noise.

"Why aren't you in bed?" Sarah's mother slapped her hands to her hips. "I came to help Miriam this morning."

Sarah's mother had settled into the role of grandmother with ease, and with each child Sarah had given birth to, her mother took on a motherly glow as if she'd birthed each and every grandchild herself. Barbara was a mother, a grandmother, and Sarah's best friend. Once they realized how much alike they truly were, the friendship role came easily, and the Lord had blessed their relationship abundantly.

Sarah grunted. "If one more person asks me why I'm out of bed, I'm going to scream." She walked around the table and kissed each of her *kinner* on the cheek and thanked the Lord for His many blessings.

Miriam was still at work, slathering butter on the biscuits with her right hand and stirring the eggs with her left. Sarah's mother took over that duty, but Sarah edged her way in between them.

"Do either of you remember when Miriam told us that she wanted thirteen brothers and sisters?" Sarah smiled.

Her mother laughed. "I remember."

Miriam stopped what she was doing, grinned, and said, "I must have been five when I said that. We hadn't been here long."

All three women turned around. Abram wiped jam from Anna's mouth. Elizabeth banged her biscuit on the tray of her high-chair, giggling. The twins, the oldest after Miriam at ten, were shoveling down bacon as if there were a shortage of pigs in the world.

Sarah let her eyes drift to each of her children. All nine of them. She looked at Miriam and winked as she patted her stomach. "You just might get your wish."

Sarah and her mother and daughter smiled, each one surely remembering a time when life had been challenging. But God had taken those challenges and blessed Sarah and her family in more ways than they could have imagined. She thanked Him every day for the gift of family.

DISCUSSION QUESTIONS

1. Barbara and Sarah bickered even before Sarah fled the community. Even though they were apart for six years, do you think the bond they have forged at the end would have been possible if they hadn't been separated for so long? Would they have continued to argue and not get along? Was this part of God's plan in the big picture, for the women to realize how important the mother/ daughter relationship is?

2. As readers, I think we were all rooting for Abram to be Miriam's father. Was there a point in the story where you doubted this and believed Jayden would be the father of Sarah's child? If that had been the case, how do you think the situation would have played out? Would Abram have still raised Miriam as his own daughter? Would Sarah have told Jayden about Miriam?

3. Barbara returned Sarah's letters un-

opened in an effort to force Sarah back home. At the end of the story, Sarah's mother regrets that decision. What do you think would have happened if Barbara had opened Sarah's letters when they first arrived in her mailbox?

4. If Abram hadn't confessed his love for Sarah and didn't want to give them a second chance, do you think Sarah would have still stayed in her Amish community?

5. Out of all of the characters in the story, who could you relate to the most and why?

ACKNOWLEDGMENTS

My continued thanks to my family and friends for walking alongside me on this amazing journey. Who could have imagined there would be this many books, lol?

I'm so appreciative of my publishing team at HarperCollins Christian Fiction. Thanks for all you do to make my books the best they can be.

To my assistant and dear friend, Janet Murphy, you're always in the background, handling things that would likely not get done otherwise. You rock, and I love and appreciate you!☺

A big thank you to my awesome agent and friend, Natasha Kern. Glad we're in this together!☺

And, as always, my heartfelt thanks to God for allowing me to create stories that I hope glorify Him as well as entertain readers.

■ ■ ■ ■

THE COURAGE TO LOVE

SHELLEY SHEPARD GRAY

■ ■ ■ ■

To Annie Sturt. Thank you for all of your kindness and support. Irene's story is for you!

This is my command — be strong and courageous! Do not be afraid or discouraged. For the LORD your God is with you wherever you go.

— JOSHUA 1:9 NLT

Experience is a different teacher, giving you the test first and the lesson later.

— AMISH PROVERB

CHAPTER 1

When was the last time she'd laughed so much? Irene Keim couldn't remember.

But maybe it didn't matter anyway. Not really. All that mattered was that she was sitting at Mary Ruth and Henry Wengerd's kitchen table playing Clue by candlelight. She was sipping hot spiced cider, listening to a roaring fire in the stone hearth, and enjoying a large platter of Rice Krispies treats she'd made herself. She made them even more special by adding creamy peanut butter to the marshmallow mixture and a layer of chocolate coating on top.

So far, Henry had eaten four.

He was also grinning from ear to ear. "Irene, you really don't think that shady Mr. Green did it with the rope?"

"*Nee,* Henry," she said around another giggle. "Mary Ruth already told us she had Mr. Green's card."

"Huh."

293

Mary Ruth, Henry's wife of forty years, leaned back with a sigh. "No matter how much I try to get him to think like a detective, he doesn't seem to make any progress."

Henry didn't look fazed by the criticism one bit. "It's *gut* that murder and mayhem ain't in your life, then. Ain't so?"

Mary Ruth's expression softened, and her pale skin turned a pretty peach color in the flickering glow of the fire. "Indeed."

When she rolled the dice again, then took her sweet time trying to decide which room to investigate next, Irene sipped her cider and took a moment to give thanks that murder and mayhem weren't in her life either.

However, the fact that they once had been still made her insides raw. Less than a year ago she was involved in a terrible situation with her best friend Alice. The father of one of Alice's preschool students had threatened to shoot both Alice and Irene while they stood on a frozen pond. She'd never been so scared in her life.

But even though that moment had been terrible, what kept Irene up at night was what had happened next. Her unexpected hero, West, an *Englisher* and most unsavory, had run onto the ice to save them. And he did indeed save them. But he lost his own life in the process.

Irene didn't think she'd ever be able to erase the image of him falling through the ice. She still woke up at least once a night gasping from the horror of it.

After she recovered from the traumatic experience, she took a leave of absence from her waitressing job and went on a month-long Pioneer Trails bus trip out west. Mary Ruth and Henry were two of the many senior citizens on the trip. When they returned to Hart County, the couple asked Irene to move in with them in exchange for her help around their big farmhouse.

Just ten days ago she'd moved in, very happy to have the opportunity to help them. But what she soon discovered was that they were helping her. It was evenings like this, playing a simple board game at the kitchen table, that soothed her like few things ever had. For the first time in her life, she felt like she was part of a family. And though she knew she would never actually be part of the Wengerd family, Irene was grateful for the chance to experience something other people had known since childhood.

As memories of the hurt and neglect that had filled her life threatened to overtake her, she flinched. Her parents were dead now. They couldn't hurt her anymore.

"Your turn, Irene," Henry prodded.

"What? Oh, sorry." She rolled the dice and moved three spaces.

"You ain't going to get very far with rolls like that," Henry chided.

"I'll try to roll those dice better," she replied with a smile.

"Don't worry about getting better. I've taken a shine to this game." Henry got up and trotted to the counter. "And your cereal bars too."

"Henry, you put that down! Five Rice Krispies bars is four too many," Mary Ruth said just as the kitchen door opened with a squeak and a burst of cool air.

Irene froze . . . until she noticed that both of her landlords sent the newcomer happy smiles.

"Marcus!" Mary Ruth exclaimed. "You've returned!"

Irene watched as a man about her age enfolded Mary Ruth in a hug. "I was only gone two weeks, *Mamm.*"

"It felt like a year. I missed your voice and your face too."

"Your *mamm* says that even when you're gone for a day, Marcus." Henry grasped his son's hand. "She can't help herself."

"I missed you both too." He slipped off his jacket and hung it on a peg by the door.

"Did you get a new horse?" Henry asked.

"I did. A healthy, brawny Percheron." Marcus looked as if he was going to share the details when he noticed her. "Ah. I see you have company."

Irene stood and felt the weight of the newcomer's stare. Ill at ease, she forced herself to step forward and smile. "Hello. I'm Irene."

He smiled slightly. "Just Irene?"

Mary Ruth playfully slapped a hand on his arm. "She's Irene Keim, son."

"Irene Keim." A line formed between his brows as he stared at her more intently. "I'm sorry. Have we met before?"

"Nee."

Mary Ruth chuckled. "I know why the name sounds familiar. She's the young woman *Daed* and I told you was on the bus trip. Don'tcha remember me telling you about our new friend?"

He nodded, still gazing at Irene. "Ah. Of course. That must be it." He sounded doubtful, though. "Sorry. I guess I assumed the woman was older."

Henry laughed. "You mean old like us."

He shook his head like he was used to his parents' antics as he strode forward. "Nice to meet you. I'm Marcus Wengerd, these two old codgers' son."

She shook his hand and was pleased when hers didn't tremble. "Welcome home."

"Danke." He dropped her hand, but he was now gazing at her with a warm expression. One that was more appreciative.

At one time, she would have found a look like that exciting. It was always nice to know that a member of the opposite sex found her pretty. But now? It only made her uneasy. Would she ever trust herself again?

"Where is your buggy?" Marcus asked. "I didn't see one outside." Before she could speak, he continued. "Or did you ride a bike? Do you live close by?"

"Marcus, stop interrogating Irene and come sit down in the living room," Mary Ruth said over her shoulder as she bustled around the kitchen. "Would you like some cider or a marshmallow treat?"

"Jah. Sure." He sat in the big, down-filled chair that was his father's favorite. Henry often said the chair fit him like a glove and eased his old bones like little else.

Irene never would have considered sitting in it. In fact, she found herself watching Henry warily, sure he would ask Marcus to move. But he didn't. Instead he sat in the chair to the left, as if his son deserved to sit in his place of honor.

After Marcus propped his feet on the ottoman, he gestured to the game that was still set out on the table. "Are you all playing a board game?"

"It looks like it, don't it?" Henry said dryly.

"What game is it?"

"Clue," Irene answered. "Have you played it before?"

"Nee."

"It's great fun," Mary Ruth said as she returned to the living room with a large stoneware mug filled with cider. She handed it to Marcus, then carefully took the biggest dessert bar, set it on a plate, and placed it on the table next to the easy chair.

Looking eager, he took a big bite of the bar. After he swallowed, he smiled at her. "This is real *gut, Mamm.*"

"Don't compliment me. Compliment Irene. She made them."

"It's tasty, Irene," he said dutifully, though a spark of amusement lingered in his eyes.

"Danke." Irene smiled, a bit annoyed with him, though she couldn't exactly say why. Well, other than he seemed to take his wonderful parents for granted.

"Do you need a ride home?" he asked. "I'd be happy to drive you. It ain't safe to walk anywhere in the dark."

When Irene looked at Mary Ruth, she

cleared her throat. "Actually, son, something happened recently that we need to let you know about."

"Oh? What is that?"

Not wanting to simply sit and be talked over, Irene said, "Your parents invited me to move in. I'm living here now."

"You're what?"

"She's our boarder," Mary Ruth said. "Isn't that wonderful?"

He stared at her more intently and asked, "What was your last name again?"

"It's Keim. My *nohma* is Irene Keim." She was irritated with him enough to pronounce it extremely slowly, like he didn't understand English.

Marcus stopped in mid-nod as a shocked expression settled on his face. "Wait a minute. Now I know where I've seen that name before. I read about you in *The Budget.*" Before she could respond, his voice turned more incredulous. "You were one of the women involved with that shooting, weren't you?" Before she could respond, he added, "Some people said you were friends with that man who died."

Now feeling all three pairs of eyes on her, Irene swallowed hard. "You're right, Marcus. I was there. And I was friends with the man who died." She lifted her chin and practically dared him to back down. "West Powers saved my life before he drowned."

Marcus got to his feet. "*Mamm, Daed,* did you know about this?"

Henry nodded. "We did. And now you do too. Sit back down."

He didn't move an inch. "But don't you think we ought to discuss this?"

"There is nothing to talk about," Mary Ruth said, her voice crisp. "Now, please. Sit back down and relax. You're making Irene upset."

At last Marcus did what his mother asked, but it was obvious he wanted to discuss things further.

Irene looked at her feet and tried to calm down. It was difficult, though, because she could feel the tension in the room.

"You are letting your past taint the present, son," Henry said.

"This has nothing to do with Beth," Marcus blurted before closing his eyes. After exhaling, he looked at Irene again. "I'm sorry for my outburst. I . . . well, I must be more tired than I thought."

"It's all right," Irene murmured, though she knew she was lying.

She hadn't appreciated his outburst at all. Honestly, it was as if all the joy she'd felt only thirty minutes earlier had evaporated and left the air in the room feeling almost brittle.

Though it was selfish, she felt like glaring at Marcus. Why had he decided to visit his parents this very night? They'd been having such a good time.

Then she remembered something West had once told her: Nobody's past could remain a secret forever. It always came back to call.

It seemed hers had picked that very evening to do so.

CHAPTER 2

As the flames continued to cast a soft glow through the room, Marcus covertly studied their newcomer. Irene Keim was pretty. She was slim and had blonde hair, blue eyes, and an adorable dimple in one of her cheeks.

But she was more than that.

She had the type of angelic features Marcus had always favored in a woman. Maybe because he farmed all day and was accustomed to hard work, he'd always dreamed of having a woman who was more delicate. She would be someone he could care for, who would soothe his mind and body with her sweet softness.

Maybe even heal him.

But, of course, he now knew that such fantasies were for fools. Angelic sweetness and delicacy were useless in the real world. A man needed a partner, not someone to coddle.

Looks weren't what was important either. He'd certainly learned that from Beth. She'd been lovely, but that loveliness had covered a deceitful character.

No, what really mattered was a good heart. Qualities like honesty and compassion.

As he recalled the rumors and the gossip that surrounded Irene after the incident at Floyd's Pond, he feared she wasn't nearly as sweet as his parents were making her out to be.

He thought he remembered something about her coming from a broken home. She'd been a little wild during her *rumspringa*. Maybe she still was. After all, the newspaper had reported that her friend who died was the leader of some kind of illegal gang from the big city.

Even if she was on the straight and narrow now, she didn't seem like the best person to be living with his parents. They had always been far too trusting of others.

He became even more worried and turned to them. "So you two are really okay with Irene's past?"

"Did we know that Irene here has been through a terrible tragedy and needed some comfort and kindness?" *Daed* asked, a new, disapproving tone tingeing his voice. "*Jah,* son. We did."

He loved that his parents were so giving, but he feared that made them vulnerable too. They were getting older. Maybe even a bit forgetful. "*Daed.* You should have talked to me before —"

"Let's all sit down and clear the air," *Mamm* interrupted in that voice she'd perfected when he was young and sometimes argued.

No longer wanting to sit in the living room, Marcus walked over to the table, pulled back the unoccupied chair, and sat. His parents sat too.

But Irene stayed where she was, her hands now gripping the back of the rocking chair by the fireplace. Almost like it was a lifeline. "I think maybe it would be best if I went up to my room, Mary Ruth. That is, if you don't mind."

"But we didn't finish our game," *Mamm* said.

Irene darted a look his way before she faced his mother again. "I'm afraid it would be rude to finish it in front of your son. Plus, I think you all have some things to talk about."

His father's expression softened. "You're part of the family now, Irene. We can include you in the conversation."

Part of the family? Marcus barely stifled a groan.

Irene heard. "*Danke,* but I don't think that would be best," she replied in a strained tone of voice. "I have to work early in the morning. I should probably get some sleep."

"You work?" he blurted. Inwardly, he winced. Even he could tell he sounded like a jerk.

"*Jah.* I'm a waitress at Bill's Diner," Irene replied, her voice as strained as her posture. She didn't add anything else, just looked as if she would rather eat nails than stay in his company another minute.

"I'll see you in the morning, dear," his mother said.

"*Jah.* Sleep well, Irene," *Daed* added.

Irene opened her mouth but didn't speak. Just nodded before she walked toward the staircase.

The three of them stayed silent as she made her way up the stairs.

For a moment, Marcus felt a twinge of regret. He knew he'd been unforgivably rude, but he also knew he'd had no choice. Someone had to look out for his parents' well-being, and that person was him. There was no one else.

When she was safely out of earshot, he spoke. "You all really should have talked to me before you invited her into your home. I'll do my best to see that she leaves as soon as possible."

His mother closed her eyes. "Oh, Marcus."

"You will do no such thing," his father bit out. "In fact, the only thing you should have on your mind is how to make amends to our guest."

His father's tone stung. "I know I was harsh with her, but you two don't know her reputation. It's worse than bad, *Daed.* I'm sure she's been taking advantage of your kindness. Getting her out of your lives is for the best."

"What exactly is your problem with Irene?" *Mamm* asked. "And you need to keep your voice down. I don't want you to hurt her feelings any more than you already have."

"My problem is that you've invited a woman you don't know much about into your home to live with you. A woman who doesn't have the best reputation." He lowered his voice. "And I think you knew I would be concerned about her living here. It isn't like you not to tell me about a new guest in your home, *Mamm.*"

"Perhaps we were hoping to avoid this very situation." His mother stood and started cleaning up the coffee cups that were sitting on the table.

Marcus picked up a plate and placed it in the sink. "I know you think I'm being judgmental, but the man she admitted to being friends with wasn't just an *Englisher.* He was a known criminal."

Daed folded his arms across his chest. "You sure know a lot about an incident that wasn't any of your business."

"That incident was all anyone talked about for days," Marcus retorted, unable to keep from raising his voice. "It was on the front page of *The Budget.* Television crews came to town too. Surely you both remember how awful it was."

"We know how awful an experience it was for Irene, Marcus," *Mamm* corrected.

"We know her friend that you don't think she should have known saved her life. He took a bullet for her. He drowned because the ice broke. Because of his sacrifice, Irene and her friend Alice survived. He was a hero."

"But he shouldn't have been in Hart County in the first place. He was the leader of a gang. After that all happened, Alice Yoder left the faith and moved to Cincinnati."

"Alice didn't simply leave the faith, Marcus. She married the other man who helped save them," his mother corrected. "Nothing is ever as simple as it might seem."

"All I'm saying is that trouble seems to follow her around. I don't want any of it to touch you."

To his surprise, instead of looking shamed or even reflective, both of his parents laughed.

"I'm a little too old to worry about getting a new reputation," his father said. "And truth be told, if people started thinking I was a bit dangerous, I might even like that."

"I'm being serious."

"I know you are, son. And I appreciate your concern, but it's time you settled down. Right now you seem to have forgotten everything we taught you about forgiveness and compassion."

Forgiveness. Compassion. Marcus felt his cheeks heat with embarrassment. His *mamm* and *daed* were right. Even sheltered women with fine reputations like his ex-girlfriend Beth could do hurtful things. He knew that better than anyone. He shouldn't have lashed out about Irene's past.

No, he shouldn't have been so quick to judge her. "I'm sorry, *Mamm*."

"I am too." Eyeing the staircase, his mother sighed. "Lord only knows how I'm going to get poor Irene to feel comfortable here again. I hope she doesn't decide to leave."

"She won't, Mary Ruth. She knows we need her here."

Maybe that was what had really bothered him. "Why do you need Irene here, *Daed*? I try to visit you several times a week. Is something going on with you both that I don't know about?" Studying them carefully, he swallowed. "Is one of you sick?"

"Nee," *Mamm* said quickly. "Nothing like that. It's more that she's been helping us with the cooking and cleaning. It's been wonderful having her help."

"Are you sure you're both all right?" Guilt flooded him as he realized just how much he'd taken their steadiness for granted. He'd always adored them and never imagined that they wouldn't be there for each other.

Daed patted his shoulder. "We're fine, Marcus. Don't worry about us."

His father's brown eyes looked clear and direct. He wasn't hiding anything. Feeling a little better, Marcus exhaled. "I'll try not to worry. But I have a feeling I still will."

"Instead of worrying about us, I'd rather you concentrate on how you are going to mend things with Irene."

"Yes, sir."

Looking pleased with him at last, his father reached for the small brown envelope on the table and carefully pulled out the three cards hidden in it.

"Professor Plum. Rope. Dining room. Huh. Never would have imagined killing someone with a rope in the dining room. You'd think a candlestick would be a better option."

His mother yawned. "All this excitement has made me tired. You'd best be on your way, son."

Still feeling like things weren't settled, he hesitated. "All right. But I'll be back tomorrow morning to apologize to Irene."

"She won't be here. She'll be working. You can talk to her at Bill's."

"And then?"

"And then? We'll look forward to seeing you soon." *Mamm* smiled at him softly before she walked toward her bedroom.

There it was again. His mother illustrated how to behave with grace and forgiveness.

Marcus told his father good night, then grabbed his jacket and walked out the door. The night air cooled his face, and he realized that was the first time he'd left his parents without feeling like everything was right in the world.

Once he climbed into his buggy, he let up

the brake and clicked his tongue. "Let's go, Sue," he said as he gently motioned the mare forward.

For the majority of the drive, he reviewed everything he'd said to Irene. Then he thought about all the things his parents had said.

Then, to his dismay, by the time he unhitched Sue and gave her fresh water, Marcus was thinking about Beth Vance again. He remembered how sure he'd been that everything between them would always be picture-postcard perfect.

He remembered how hurt he'd been when he realized she'd been cheating on him.

At last, he forced himself to face the fact that he'd never dealt with her betrayal. Instead, he'd pretended that he wasn't hurt and that he hadn't really loved her.

He realized now that all that covering up hadn't helped him recover from Beth's rejection at all. Instead, the pain had festered inside of him, never reaching the surface but tainting his future relationships.

"You hurt me, Beth, but I'm going to move on," he said to the empty barn. "It's time. *Nee,* it's past time."

CHAPTER 3

"Irene, what the devil are pumpkin pancakes?" old Mr. Graves asked. He was staring at the breakfast special written on the new chalkboard hanging by the diner's kitchen.

For some reason known only to him, Bill had decided to start serving breakfast and dinner specials that were out of the ordinary. The pumpkin pancakes had shown up for the first time that morning, and already they'd created quite a stir. Bill's regular customers looked on any new food concoctions with suspicion.

Those pancakes had also given Irene the beginnings of a headache. She was starting to wish Bill would stick to the same menu and leave his need to experiment in the kitchen at home.

"Mr. Graves, they are exactly what they sound like," she said with a trace of exasperation. "Pumpkin pancakes are made with canned pumpkin. They're tasty."

"Truly?"

"*Jah.* You should try them."

Looking at her skeptically, he barked, "What kind of syrup?"

"Regular syrup. Bill puts powdered sugar on them too."

"Well now, I don't know if I want sugar all over my pancakes. That don't seem like the right way to start a day."

"Try 'em or don't, Ernie, I don't care!" Bill called out. "But make up your mind and let Irene get on her way."

Irene fought back a laugh as Mr. Graves scowled. "Do you want to think about it for a bit?"

As she expected, Mr. Graves's bushy gray eyebrows shot up. "No, Miss Impertinent. I'll have two fried eggs, bacon, and wheat toast."

In other words, what he had every single time he came in. "Yes, sir. I'll get that right out to you." She smiled before turning around in relief.

She gave Bill the order, then grabbed a coffee carafe and headed over to the booth where May had just seated their newest arrival. "Sorry it took me a minute," she said with a smile. "Would you like some . . ." Her voice trailed off as she realized who she was talking to.

Marcus Wengerd. The last person on earth she wanted to see.

"Kaffi?" she finished at last.

Looking as uncomfortable as she felt, Marcus turned over his cup and slid it her way. *"Jah. Danke."*

Hardly looking at him, Irene poured the brew carefully. "Do you know what you want to eat? Or do you need a few minutes?"

"I know I don't want any pumpkin pancakes."

Startled by his teasing tone, she met his gaze . . . and realized he was looking at her with an almost warm expression.

Now what was she supposed to do with that?

"It looks like you need some time." She nearly sighed in relief. She would be able to take a few minutes to gather herself. "I'll let you look."

"Nee. Wait. I want to talk to you." He lowered his voice. "Can we talk?"

She chose to deliberately misunderstand him. "You want to talk about the menu?"

"Nee. About what happened last night at my parents' *haus."*

Oh *nee.* No way was she revisiting that incident mere steps away from her boss and a good portion of the town's population.

"I'm working now. I don't have time to chat."

His brown eyes searched her face. "When do you get off? Maybe I could wait."

Irene was torn between telling him to leave and lecturing him about his overbearing nature with his parents. Then there was the additional selfish part of her that wanted to sit across from him and plead her case so she could continue living with Mary Ruth and Henry. If she couldn't mend things between herself and Marcus, his parents would be upset. And if that continued, they'd eventually ask her to leave. They would never side with her over their son, nor would she ask them to.

In the past, she would have done any of those things. But over the last year, she'd learned that it was better to keep her emotions reined in. The less she shared, the less of a chance that someone could hurt her in the future.

His expression softened. "Irene, please?"

It was the "please" that did it. How could she ignore that one word, so filled with desperation? She'd certainly felt that a time or two.

"Marcus, I promise I'm not trying to be difficult. I simply can't stop to chat. I need to do my job."

"What time do you get off?"

"Three."

A line formed in the center of his forehead. "But it's only eight in the morning. You're putting in a lot of hours."

"Yes." She smiled tightly, thinking he might have suddenly realized there was more to her than a difficult past.

"Irene?" Bill called out. "Do you have a problem?"

She glanced over her shoulder at her boss and shook her head before facing Marcus again. "I really canna talk right now, Marcus. I need to see to my other customers. Would you like to order now or wait?"

He exhaled. "I'll wait."

"Then I'll come back for your order in a few minutes."

She could practically feel his gaze on her back as she retrieved an order from Bill for a table of four, chatted with a mother and son who'd come for blueberry pancakes, and took care of the ticket for one of her regulars, Mr. Nolan.

At last she returned to Marcus. "Have you decided what you want?"

"I'll have the western omelet and some hash browns."

"I'll get that out for you as soon as I can."

Right as she turned away, he said, "Irene,

I'm just going to say it now. I want to apologize."

"All right. *Danke.*"

"Please listen to me. I really am sorry. I . . . well, I shouldn't have been so rude to you last night."

His heartfelt apology melted her insides — and made her want to forgive him far more quickly than she'd intended. "They're your parents. Of course you want to be protective of them."

He visibly relaxed. "You do understand."

"I understand wanting to protect the people you love." Could she understand his being so rude to her? Not so much.

He smiled tentatively. "I'm sure you would've done the same with your parents."

Her parents were dead. But even if they were alive, she doubted she would've tried to do too much to shield them from anyone. Remembering their years of abuse, she mentally shivered. "I need to put in your order."

By the time she crossed the diner and handed Marcus's ticket to Bill, she felt like she'd been through the wringer.

"You all right there, Irene?" May asked.

"Jah."

"I didn't know you knew Marcus Wengerd so well."

318

"I don't." Since May knew all about her past, her bus trip out West, and her efforts to settle in again, Irene added, "He's been out of town and just found out I moved into his parents' house. I guess they didn't tell him."

"That was their choice, not yours. Remember that."

Irene nodded. That was something she certainly did need to remember. She couldn't take responsibility for other people's actions.

Her life hadn't been easy. She was born to a pair of people who were dissatisfied with their lives and angry at the world. They'd taken out most of their frustrations on her in private.

After her father died, life at home was even harder. Irene had tried to avoid her mother as much as possible — and find comfort from other people.

She had a laundry list of mistakes and regrets, but the important thing was that she had learned to never push her problems on anyone else.

She was in charge of her life now. It might not be perfect and it might not be a life that a man like Marcus could appreciate, but it was hers and hers alone.

It was something she could be proud of.

CHAPTER 4

Only Alice Fisher could brighten Irene's day with just a smile. She gave her best friend in the world a warm hug, then drew her over to one of the back booths next to the kitchen. "Have a seat. I'm almost done," she said as she took in her friend's neatly pinned red hair and plain-looking blue dress that accented her eyes.

Alice looked as lovely as ever . . . and like she had made the adjustment into the English world with ease. "Would you like some coffee? It's chilly outside."

Alice smiled. "Could I have some hot chocolate instead?"

"Of course. I'll be right back."

"Bill, I'm going to take a ten-minute break," Irene said as she hurried into the kitchen.

"It's quiet here and I see who you're sitting with. How about you make it at least twenty?"

She grinned at him, knowing that if the dining room stayed fairly empty he would let her take as long as she needed to reconnect with Alice.

Irene quickly prepared two hot chocolates, both topped with generous dollops of whipped cream, and returned to her friend. "Here you go. I decided to have some too." She slid into the booth across from her friend.

"This looks *wunderbaar*." Alice smiled as she took the first sip. *"Danke."*

"It's a treat for me too. I don't remember the last time I had hot chocolate. Probably the last time I saw you."

"If that's the case, it's been far too long. I haven't been back in seven months."

"Now, tell me what's been going on with you. How is married life with Calvin?" Last year, around the time Irene had gotten to know West Powers, Alice had fallen in love with Calvin Fisher. He was staying with his brother Mark, who lived across the street from Alice's brother's house.

Irene hadn't trusted Calvin one bit. His family had a dark history and there were rumors that he was involved in a dangerous gang. It turned out that Irene's new friend West was the head of that organization and Calvin had only pretended to be associated with West in order to help the police.

Alice leaned back with a contented smile on her face. "I love being married to Calvin. He's attentive and sweet. Fun too. It's *wunderbaar.*"

"How is living among the English?"

"Some things are challenging, of course, but it helps that Calvin is from Hart County. He understands when I'm feeling overwhelmed."

"And he brings you back here to visit."

"That he does. We both wanted to see our families for a spell, so we're here for a full week." Smiling broadly, Alice continued. "We're sleeping at Mark's house for half the time and at my brother Edward's for the other half. Calvin thought moving from house to house was silly, but everyone wants to see us." She shrugged. "This way we won't be a burden on anyone for too long either. You know what they say about houseguests and fish. Three days is enough."

Irene smiled at the old joke. "I'm mighty glad you made time to see me too."

Alice pushed her cup to the side. "What are you talking about? I didn't just make time, silly. I wanted to see you. I even told Calvin that I want to spend a couple of hours together one evening with you at your apartment."

"I would like that . . . except I'm not living in that basement apartment anymore." She thought of Marcus. She should probably find out if her old place was available.

"Why did you move?"

"It's a long story, but one of the couples I met on my bus trip invited me to live with them. They've given me a room in exchange for my help with cooking and cleaning."

Alice raised her eyebrows. "Are you happy with that arrangement? It seems you already do your share of cooking and cleaning here at the diner."

"Helping Henry and Mary Ruth is no trouble. I like living with them." Well, she did, but she doubted she was going to be happy there anymore, thanks to Marcus. There was no way she was going to share that burden with Alice though.

"I know you're working now, but we need to make plans. I want to spend more time with you."

"I would love that. I'd love to see your parents too. How about I come over on Sunday?"

"My parents are hosting church, you know."

"I know. I'll come over in the morning and help you prepare, and help clean up after the service."

Alice frowned. "I want to see you, and my parents will, too, but you don't have to come over to work. My brothers and sisters-in-law will be there to help."

"I'll still want to help out as much as I can."

"All right then. I'll see you Sunday morning. I can't wait to let *Mamm* and *Daed* know you'll be there. They'll be so happy." Alice smiled. Then, as she studied Irene, she said, "Are you sure you're all right? You seem a little bothered by something."

"Oh, I'm just working. You know how that goes."

Alice nodded. "Of course." She looked like she wanted to say something else, but her husband, Calvin, walked in. With his dark hair and bright blue eyes, he was handsome enough to take one's breath away.

But what caught Irene's attention was the way he didn't seem to notice anyone else in the entire diner except Alice. He stopped at the front, scanned the surroundings, and seemed to focus only on her.

Irene watched him approach and took in his faded jeans, black shoes, and hunter-green sweater. She thought he looked as dangerous as he had when he was working undercover a year ago.

But when he bent down and kissed his

wife lightly on the lips, Irene saw that Calvin had changed. It was as if Alice had smoothed out his hard edges.

"You all right?" he murmured to Alice before straightening.

"Of course. Except that you walked right by Irene without saying a word."

Scrambling out of the booth, Irene laughed. "Don't worry about me, Alice. I'm glad Calvin only has eyes for you."

Looking a little sheepish, Calvin turned to her. "I'm sorry, Irene. Hello," he said before giving her a light hug.

The hug was surprising, but his kindness was not. "Hello, back. Your wife and I have been catching up and making plans."

"Oh?"

"Irene's coming over to help my parents set up for church," Alice said as she stood up too.

"I had forgotten about church. Will we be able to stay for church?"

Alice ran her fingers over her plain-looking chambray dress. It wasn't Plain, but it was modest and looked comfortable. She nodded. "I talked to my family about it before we came. They reminded me that our services are open to anyone, and that includes you and me."

"Perfect. But you mustn't do too much.

Let everyone else do the heavy lifting."

Irene watched as a blush bathed Alice's features. "I will, Calvin."

Irene was confused. She couldn't understand why Calvin was treating Alice so tenderly, as if she was fragile. Surely he knew Alice was used to hard work.

Then, like a lightning bolt from the heavens, it hit her.

"Alice, are you . . . ?" She let her voice drift off. Amazing how even at this age, and after everything she'd been through, she still hesitated to mention some things in mixed company.

But it didn't matter. Alice smiled and nodded. "I am. Four months now." Her eyes softened as she gazed up at her husband. "We're mighty happy about it, aren't we?"

Calvin grinned. "Ecstatic."

"I'm ecstatic too," Irene said as she gave her a gentle hug. "Congratulations."

Danke," Calvin said as he guided his wife back into the booth and sat by her side.

"How have you been feeling?" Irene asked as she sat down again. "Have you been sick? Are you going to find out the baby's gender?"

Looking like a kid in a candy store, Alice began telling Irene all about her pregnancy, their plans, their families' reactions, their decision to eventually learn whether they were having a boy or a girl, and the foods she'd been craving.

It was adorable, and Irene was genuinely excited and happy for her friend. But in another way, it seemed to highlight just how far apart their lives had become. Here Alice was married and starting her family and not Amish anymore.

And Irene? Well, she was still attempting to figure out life. She was renting a room in an older couple's house, and even that wasn't secure. She didn't have anything else to look forward to either, other than waiting tables at a diner.

By the time Alice and Calvin said goodbye — Alice giving Irene a hug and promising to see her again at church on Sunday — Irene was fighting a sudden bout of melancholy.

All these events emphasized that she needed to do something different with her life, or at least move forward. Worrying and fretting about the past wasn't doing her any favors.

And it was becoming more and more apparent that she only had herself to depend on. That made her kind of sad, but she tried to think of it in a positive light. At least she wouldn't feel abandoned again.

CHAPTER 5

"Irene, this is perfect timing," Agnes Weatherbee said as she opened and closed drawers and shifted things around on her desk. "I was just thinking I might have to put an ad in *The Budget* to find a suitable renter."

"I'm glad I stopped by," Irene replied with a smile. She'd gone to bed thinking about Alice and Calvin and their new life together. Their happiness reminded her that she needed to get back on her own feet again. When she overheard two customers talking about Agnes's apartment, Irene decided to visit as soon as she got off work. "Thank you for letting me see the apartment right away."

"Oh, the store is always slow at this time of day. It's no problem to put a note on the door and tell everybody I'll be right back." At last the bookstore owner pulled a worn-out sign from the side drawer and set it on the counter.

"I can never find half the things I need right away," Agnes said. "My Jeff used to say I'd lose my head if it wasn't attached to my body!" She laughed to herself as she led Irene to the small apartment above the bookshop. She huffed and clambered up the stairs.

As Irene followed, Agnes continued to talk. "Every time I climb these steep stairs, I get to thinking that they get about five times longer than they were the day before. Oh well, climbing stairs is supposed to be real good for the heart. If that's the case, I'm gonna keep mine strong and fit."

The spry widow laughed again, and Irene grinned, privately thinking it might be a good thing her new landlord didn't like climbing the stairs too much. Otherwise she would never get a moment's peace.

Agnes reached in a pocket on her dress for a ring of keys, then opened the door. "Well, here it is. And here are the keys. You take your time looking."

"You're not coming in?"

"Nope. I learned some time ago that it's better to give people space from time to time. My Jeff used to say that I could talk a mule's ear off, whatever that means."

Irene wasn't sure what it meant either, but she couldn't fault Jeff's meaning. Agnes really was a chatty one. "I'll take a look around and be down soon."

"Take your time. Just be sure to lock up when you're done," she said before going back down the stairs.

After her footsteps faded, Irene walked into the apartment and closed the door behind her. Then, unable to help herself, she gave a little gasp.

It was far nicer and bigger than she imagined. The floors were polished wood, and one of the walls was made up almost entirely of windows. The molding around the ceiling was ornate and white. The walls were painted a light grayish-blue. It was also spotlessly clean.

Earlier Agnes told her the apartment was sparsely furnished and that Irene could either keep the furniture or move in her own. Since she didn't have any furniture, she'd asked to keep it, but she had worried a bit about the condition it would be in.

Like the floor and the walls, the furniture was in good repair and clean. The living room had a tan love seat, chair, and two side tables. They were next to a little galley kitchen, which had two barstools under the counter. Already she could imagine baking cookies in the cozy kitchen, then curling up on the love seat with a book and a cup of hot tea.

She might even find the quiet relaxing after a long day on her feet at the diner.

The bedroom had the same floor and walls, with a double bed, a small white dresser, and a white wicker bedside table. The bathroom had white tile.

It was all very comforting and perfect for her. She wouldn't have to do too much — if anything — to get situated. Truly, it was a blessing.

So why did she feel like crying?

The answer was obvious, of course. Though this place gave her privacy and comfort, it didn't give her any of the things she'd come to love about the Wengerds' home. It felt barren, while the Wengerds' home felt lived-in and comfortable. Cool, while the couple's house was warm.

Most of all, it served to emphasize the very things she'd been feeling while talking to Calvin and Alice. She was alone while everyone else in her life seemed to have more relatives and close relationships than they knew what to do with.

Because of all that, it was so very tempting to go back downstairs and tell Agnes she would have to pass on the apartment.

But of course, she couldn't do that. The

apartment had the one thing that trumped everything else — the lack of a judgmental son.

Marcus had apologized, but he hadn't exactly said he was comfortable with her living with his parents. It would be better for everyone if she moved before she was asked to leave.

When she returned to the bookshop, Agnes was opening a carton of books. "What did you think, dear?"

"I think it will do just fine." She opened her purse and pulled out her wallet. "How much do I owe you for the first month's rent?"

After Agnes named her price, a customer came in. "Just put it in the cash drawer. I'll get to it later." She walked away to help the man.

Irene froze. Something suddenly didn't seem right, especially now that Agnes had disappeared down one of the shop's crowded aisles.

Was it Agnes's breezy way of handling her business that bothered her so much? Or was it that Irene now knew that anyone could wander over and help themselves to the money in that drawer?

Either way, she felt uncomfortable simply putting her money in the drawer and walking away. And even more so about having Agnes as her landlady, especially since she just remembered that some customers she'd overheard in the diner said that doing business with Agnes was difficult and frustrating.

But she really didn't have a choice. She needed to move.

She and Marcus were at least talking now, but Irene wasn't going to fool herself into thinking he would ever accept her living with his parents. She needed to move out so she wouldn't create any more tension between him and his parents.

She owed Mary Ruth and Henry too much for that.

CHAPTER 6

Every fall, Marcus shared a cow with his parents and two other families. It wasn't a live cow, of course. He butchered one of his steers and split the meat. Usually when he brought his parents' share to them, he felt a source of pride. They'd given him so much, and he enjoyed giving back to them.

Usually they eyed the white paper packages, each one neatly labeled, like Christmas had come early. But today? Well, it seemed they weren't too enthusiastic about the meat's arrival. After greeting him with a smile and a hug, his mother claimed she had laundry to see to.

He watched her scurry away as if she were rushing to a chat with her best girlfriends. Never could he recall her being so enthused about clothes to wash.

Thinking that maybe he should've given her some warning that he was going to stop by, Marcus shrugged and carried the heavy

Styrofoam cooler down the narrow basement stairs, his father on his heels.

"I put in a little bit of everything, *Daed.* But if you want something more, just let me know. I still have plenty of meat in the big freezer on the farm."

"I'm sure this will be more than enough," Henry replied as he opened the lid to the giant freezer and started neatly stacking the one-pound packages. "All this meat is most generous of you. *Danke,* son. This cow will come in handy during the winter."

The gratitude seemed a little excessive, and not exactly needed either, given that he was farming the land he inherited from them. "You're welcome," he said, feeling awkward. "But you know I've got my reasons for bringing it over. I know *Mamm* will make some wonderful-*gut* meals out of it that I hope to enjoy."

"No doubt." *Daed* leaned farther down and pulled up a brisket.

It might have been his imagination, but Marcus thought his father was straining a bit from the weight of the cooler. "I can put the rest away. Why don't you sit down?"

Rubbing his shoulder, Henry straightened. "That's a *gut* idea. I guess I ain't as young as I used to be."

"None of us are," Marcus teased. He

privately thought his father wasn't as old as he was acting either. What was going on with him? Marcus recalled his earlier worries and rested a hand on his father's arm. "Hey, *Daed,* are you all right? Are you getting enough sleep?"

"I'm sleeping well enough."

"No offense, but you seem a little more tired than usual."

"That's probably because I am."

"You're doing too much." He thought of Irene and her deal for living with them. "Where is Irene? Is she working at the diner? I was surprised when I didn't see her helping *Mamm* with the laundry."

"It would be fairly hard for her to do the laundry since she ain't here anymore."

Suddenly the three-pound roast in his hands felt too heavy. He hastily placed it in the freezer. "Where did Irene go?"

"She found another place to rent. She left two days ago."

He was stunned. And, truth be told, feeling more than a little guilt-ridden. He meant to go back to the diner and apologize better, but things had gotten busy at the farm. "Is that why you're feeling tired? Did she have a lot of boxes to move out of here?"

"There weren't much for her to move." He looked grim and continued. "Irene didn't have much. Only a suitcase and a laundry basket of items."

One suitcase and a basket. The sum of everything in her life. He felt a lump form in his throat. "Where did she move to?"

His father ran a hand down his beard. "Why are you so interested in her whereabouts? You thinking of running her out of her new apartment too?"

"That's hardly fair."

"*Nee,* son. What is hardly fair is you making her feel bad about living here with us. And since we're on the subject, your mother and I told you to fix things with her. You were supposed to apologize, not make her leave our *haus* at the first opportunity."

"I did apologize to her. I went over to the diner and spoke to her the next morning. I promise I did."

"You must not have been very convincing," he retorted as he stood back up. "She rented a room that very same evening. Nothing we said would convince her to stay."

Now he felt even worse. "I'm sorry, *Daed.* But, um, maybe her reasons were more personal? Perhaps she simply wanted to be someplace else."

"She liked living here with us. She liked being a part of a family, and we liked hav-

337

ing her here." Looking disappointed again, his father spoke softly. "I love you, but you really hurt a vulnerable girl's feelings."

"I'll try to make things better."

"I don't see how you can, son. What's done is done." His father eyed the Styrofoam container that was still half-full and sighed. "You'd best get the rest of that meat put away before it starts to thaw. I'm going upstairs."

"*Daed,* I promise I'll talk to her again. Where is Irene staying? I'll go there and apologize."

"You'll have to find her at Bill's and ask her yourself where she's living."

Stung, Marcus said quickly, "I'll explain to her that she acted too rashly. I'll tell her how much you and *Mamm* miss her. Maybe then she'll want to move back here. And if she does, I'll even help her bring her things."

"Son, do you hear what you are saying? You canna simply ask her to come and go as you see fit. This is her life we're talking about."

While Marcus stood there gaping, his father turned and walked back upstairs.

When he was out of sight, Marcus reviewed his brief conversation with Irene. Tried to think how she could have misconstrued what he said. But no matter how

338

many times he reconfigured it in his head, he couldn't see how he could have done things differently. She'd seemed to accept his apology. But maybe she'd only been trying to end their conversation.

He finished emptying the container, closed the freezer case up tight, then trudged back upstairs. They seemed steeper than usual, but maybe it was his mood. He'd gone from feeling like he was his parents' savior to their problem in the space of ten minutes.

"Marcus, did you get the meat all put away?" *Mamm* asked from the kitchen.

"I did."

"Did you close the lid up tight?"

"*Jah.* Everything is secure." He joined her. "But I did forget to ask if you wanted something left out. Would you like me to take out some steaks or a roast and bring it up to you?"

"*Nee, danke.*"

"Are you sure? It's no trouble —"

"If I need something, I can get it later." Her voice was noticeably cool. Just like his father's had been.

He realized then that he'd taken his parents' love and support for granted. They'd always rooted for him, championed his wishes, and taken his side no matter what.

Until now.

Frustrated with both himself and the situation, he said, "*Mamm,* I already told *Daed* that I tried to fix things with Irene. I'm going to talk to her again. Maybe she'll change her mind about moving away."

His mother nodded. "Having her back here would be nice, but I'd rather hear that the two of you are getting along. She needs all the friends she can get."

"Is she still mourning her friend who died?"

"I think so. But it's more than that, Marcus. I have a feeling that there haven't been many people in her life who have stayed by her side and supported her. I hate the thought of her thinking she has to be all alone again."

Swallowing the lump that had just formed in his throat, he murmured, "I'll try to make things better, *Mamm.*"

"*Danke,* Marcus. I have always felt that it took a lot of courage for Irene to reach out to your father and me. It pains me to think she might regret it."

Afraid to say anything else, he took a step back. "I'd best get on my way. I've got more meat to deliver."

"*Danke* for bringing us the meat, Marcus. It was kind of you."

Feeling empty, he leaned down and kissed his mother's cheek. Then, without a word, he grabbed his coat and hat as he walked out the door. When he finished his deliveries, he was going to sit down someplace and take some time to pray and ask for the Lord's help. This was definitely not something he could handle on his own any longer.

CHAPTER 7

Irene wasn't exactly hiding in the kitchen of Bill's Diner. It was just easier to fill pitchers of water from the sink in the back than the faucet near the counter.

Unfortunately, she didn't think a single person who worked there believed that for a minute.

"He's back," Lora sang as she rushed into the kitchen. "And that handsome Marcus Wengerd doesn't want me to wait on him either. He asked for you," she said with a smirk.

Irene didn't think she could be any more embarrassed. "I'm sorry. He shouldn't do that."

"Sure he should," Lora said. "Watching his 'diner courting' is the highlight of each day."

May chuckled. "You'd best get out there and give him his daily glass of water, Irene."

"At least you have his pitcher all ready to

go," Bill teased as he pointed to the plastic container she'd filled and set off to the side. "That man drinks more water than a deer with a salt lick."

Irene didn't think much of the comparison, but she couldn't disagree with the gist of it. It was true. Marcus Wengerd really did drink a lot of water. Gallons of it.

She knew because she continually poured it into his glass every time he came to eat.

And in the past week, he came into the diner a lot.

Just as she was getting ready to serve Marcus and ignore his attempts at conversation, Lora continued. "Irene, you must have bewitched that man. He only comes here when you are working, he only sits at your station, and he doesn't look at anyone but you the whole time he's here."

She was good and embarrassed now. "Hardly."

"Pretty close to it."

"She doesn't lie, dear." May fanned a menu across her face. "It's almost the most romantic thing that's ever happened here."

Bill, who had been concentrating on the three hamburger patties on his griddle, looked up. "Almost? I thought you thought I was plenty romantic."

While Irene giggled, May winked at Lora.

"Though you are mighty handsome, Bill, there was something about watching our handsome deputy court Lora here. Eddie Beck used to watch Lora like the sun couldn't rise or fall without her."

"Marcus is real handsome too," Lora said. "Maybe Irene will finally give in and start smiling back at him."

"I doubt it," Irene said airily as she walked back into the dining room.

However, she didn't think she was fooling anyone for a second, least of all herself. Lora hadn't been exaggerating. For days now, Marcus had entered the diner and sat down at her station, never allowing anyone to wait on him but her.

She picked up a glass and carried it in one hand with the pitcher in her other.

"Good afternoon," she said, attempting to keep her voice as calm and cool as she could. "Would you care for something to drink?"

His lips twitched, though his tone was just as formal and cool as hers. "I would. I was starting to think you weren't coming out."

"Sorry. It was busy in the kitchen."

"It's a shame Bill makes you work so hard in both the kitchen and in the dining room."

She was flustered. None too gently, she set the plastic pitcher on his table. "You're in luck. I decided to give you a pitcher all to yourself today."

"That is *gut* news. But I'd rather you talk to me more often. It's why I'm here. I guess you've figured that out by now."

"I did." Of course she did. But what she didn't understand was why. "Marcus, I already told you I've forgiven you."

"Though I'm glad to be forgiven, I want something more."

A shiver ran through her before she tamped it down hard. "More?"

"*Jah.* I want to be friends. Real friends."

It was time for some drastic measures. After glancing around the dining room and seeing that it was still fairly empty, she scooted into the booth on the other side of him. "Why?"

"Because I think there's more about you than I've seen. I think there's more of you that I want to know."

Those words. Who said such things? Feeling even more confused, she cleared her throat. "I'm sure we will get to know each other better over time. After all, I'm still friends with your parents." At least, she hoped she was. She hadn't seen them since she moved out.

"Maybe I want to be part of that close-knit group."

Maybe he really was sincere. Maybe . . . maybe they really could form their own bond. "If you're sure . . ."

He smiled. "Mighty sure." Just as Irene's heart melted a little, he said, "*Mamm* and *Daed* miss you terribly. They're not going to be pleased with me until things are better between us."

"So you want to be friends so your parents will be happy with you again."

"That is true," he said slowly. "But that's not the only reason." He lowered his voice. "I'm being honest, Irene. I want to know you better."

Feeling like she was walking on an emotional tightrope, she cleared her throat. "Actually, I realize now that living with your parents probably wasn't the best situation. I'm getting settled in my new place above the bookstore and it's fine."

"That's where you're living? Above the Printed Page?"

"*Jah.*"

"Isn't the owner Agnes Weatherbee?"

She didn't care for the way he was scowling. "It is."

"Is she nice to you?"

"She's nice enough, I suppose. Why do you ask?"

Looking like he was carefully weighing his

answer, he said, "She doesn't have the best reputation, Irene."

Frustrated, she glared at him. "So we're back to that again? Worrying about reputations?"

He held up a hand. "*Nee.* Please listen." Just as she was about to get up, he blurted, "What I'm trying to say is that I've heard she doesn't have a good reputation as a businesswoman. I know someone she hired to build bookshelves and never paid. Then when he tried to press her about it, she refused and spread lies about his character. That's what I meant about her reputation."

"Oh." A part of her wanted to prove Marcus wrong, but Irene didn't know if she would be able to do that. In truth, Irene wasn't sure if Agnes was nice or not. She'd been kind of scatterbrained and had even knocked on Irene's door and asked her to watch over the shop for an hour while she ate supper. It was kind of an odd arrangement.

He studied her for a moment, concern in his eyes as he took another sip of water. "Let's talk about something else."

"All right."

His brown eyes warmed. "You know, there's a fall festival on Saturday. Are you working?"

"*Nee.* I mean, I'm not scheduled."

"*Gut.* Since you're free, why don't you come with me?"

He was asking her out. Almost like it was a date. But she was still too afraid to get her hopes up. "Marcus, you don't have to take me around for us to be friends."

"Maybe I just want to spend time with you."

Before she realized she was doing it, she smiled.

He smiled right back. "Does that mean what I think it does? Will you say yes and go with me to the fall festival?"

"*Jah.* I will."

He grinned. "*Danke,* Irene. You've made me happy."

She felt her cheeks heat and scooted out of the booth. "What do you want to order?"

"Well, about that . . . I think I'm going to sip on my water and then be on my way. I've eaten here a lot lately, you know. I'll come to your apartment at ten on Saturday."

"I guess I'll see you then."

"You surely will, Irene."

Turning away from him, she felt a little tingling in her spine. At first it was so faint she could hardly recognize it for what it was. But then she knew. It was attraction. And hope.

Against her will, against her better judgment, she was attracted to Marcus. Surely it was a mistake.

He might be flirting with her a little bit, but maybe he was simply being nice. Or maybe he really was reaching out to her because of his parents. He loved his parents and they loved her. He wanted to make them happy.

She truly wasn't sure what to think. She wanted to believe him. Wanted to believe that a positive and healthy relationship was in her future. But a lifetime of bad decisions and painful memories of being forgotten and hurt by her parents made it hard to believe such a thing could be possible.

But still . . . Maybe it was time she tried.

CHAPTER 8

Marcus had been to the fall festival many times, but as he walked by Irene's side, he took in every detail as if for the first time. The air smelled of popcorn, baked apples, freshly fallen leaves, and honeysuckle. Vendors were sharing samples of their wares, everything from fresh apple pastries to bags of roasted peanuts to Irene's favorite, caramel corn nestled in brown paper cones.

The scents of pumpkin and cinnamon were strong too. They were surrounded on one side by a field ready for harvest and on the other by dozens of trees dressed up in their fall finery, a kaleidoscope of orange and gold, red and yellow.

Everything suddenly seemed more vibrant, more interesting, more tantalizing.

Especially Irene.

When he knocked on her door a few hours earlier, he was struck by two things — her beauty and her scent. For once, her expression was open instead of guarded. She'd been smiling big enough for her dimple to show. She also smelled faintly of lavender. It must be her shampoo or lotion. Who knew what girly thing it was. All he did know was that there was a reason bees enjoyed buzzing around flowers in the springtime. He didn't want to stay far away from that scent either.

Irene popped one last caramel-coated kernel in her mouth and smiled up at him. "I'm beginning to get embarrassed."

"Why is that?"

"We've been here two hours and so far I've eaten a whole cone of caramel corn and a bag of roasted peanuts, I've drunk a mug of hot cider, and I even considered eating a hot dog. You, on the other hand, have only had some water."

"I had some of your popcorn."

"Not much."

Unable to resist teasing her a bit, he said, "I happen to like water."

She giggled. "Oh, I know. I've never met a man as thirsty as you."

"Now I'm the one who's getting embarrassed. I guess I drink more than most."

"I'm not complaining about you. I just don't want you to think I'm being a pig. Or taking advantage of you. You haven't let me pay for a thing."

"Don't worry about it. I'm having a good time seeing you enjoy yourself."

Irene was slim, bordering on skinny. Until that moment, he'd always assumed it was by choice. But now, as he recalled just how much pleasure she took in every little treat, he wondered if she was used to not having the means to eat as much as she liked. "All I want is for you to have a good time. If you're enjoying the food, then that makes me happy."

She looked away. *"Danke."*

"What did I say?" When she only shrugged in reply, he pressed. "Irene, talk to me."

"You are just a lot different than I thought," she said hesitantly. "Not too many people have talked to me like that before. I guess it still catches me off guard."

Irene was acting like he'd bought her expensive gifts and given her flowery compliments. Remembering Beth and the way she complained that he never did enough for her, he was confused. "Like how? And I'm not pressing for compliments — I truly don't know what I said."

She looked at her feet before she raised her eyes to his. "Like you want me to be happy."

"No one's ever wanted that for you?"

"People have been nice, of course. I mean, your parents couldn't be more giving. And my friend Alice has always been close. But no one has gone to so much trouble just for me before. You've stayed by my side, waited when I wanted to look at some of the crafts, and even pulled me to the side when that group of teenagers ran by. It feels like you are putting my needs before yours."

"Those kids weren't watching where they were going. Of course I was going to look out for you. Anyone would."

She shook her head impatiently. "I'm afraid I don't think that's true."

"Who didn't look out for you? Are you thinking of that *Englisher*?"

"West?" She looked surprised. "Oh *nee*. West was kind to me." She smiled softly. "He had a different personality, though. Kind of gruff. Kind of bossy."

"Ah." A stab of jealousy hit him hard, catching him off guard.

Realizing she was looking embarrassed again because he hadn't responded with much of an answer, he tried to bring the conversation back around to them. Okay, to him. "Your wishes matter to me, Irene." Actually, he was coming to realize that she mattered to him.

How had that happened? He'd courted Beth for years. His love for her had grown slowly over time, aided by his head reminding him of how suitable they were. But now it seemed like his heart was in charge instead of his mind. He kind of felt like he was on a runaway horse and simply along for the ride.

Looking over at the corn maze in the distance, he pointed to it. "Would you like to give the maze a try?" He'd never been a big fan of them — probably because he had plenty of corn rows on his own farm — but he knew a lot of people loved to walk around in them.

But instead of looking intrigued, she quickly shook her head. *"Nee."*

"You sound so certain. What happened?" he teased. "Did you get lost in one when you were little?"

"*Nee*, but I did get lost once at a flea market when I was a little girl." She darted a glance at him.

"What happened?"

"I was probably only five or six. My parents took me, but they had other things on their minds." A shadow passed over her face. "They usually had a lot of other things on their minds besides me." She cleared her throat. "Um, anyway, when I stopped to look at some dolls, I guess they thought I was behind and kept going. By the time I realized I'd stopped too long, I couldn't find either of them anywhere."

He was horrified. "How long were you alone?"

She shrugged. "It felt like all day, but maybe it was only two or three hours."

"Two or three hours? Irene, that's terrible. I bet you were frightened half to death."

"It really was terrible." Her voice turned faint. "I was so small, and everyone and everything looked so big. I was only knee-high and everyone's knees looked the same." She smiled, obviously trying to make light of the situation. "Then, of course, I got hungry and tired, but I didn't have any food or anyplace to sit. It was a long day."

He couldn't find it in him to smile. "How did they find you? Did your mother start calling your name or something?"

She shook her head. "*Nee.* Nothing like that. I ran into Alice and her family. They helped me."

"Thank goodness you saw them."

"It was a blessing, but they've always been a blessing to me. I don't know what my life would have been like without them, Marcus. They're the ones who taught me what a family was supposed to look like."

Yet again, her words humbled him, and he was reminded of how much he'd taken for granted, especially when he was a little boy.

Needing to know the rest of the story, he said, "Did Alice's *mamm* help you find your parents?"

She pressed her lips together, as if what she was about to tell him was hard to speak of. "*Jah.* They'd been having lunch and weren't happy to be bothered by Alice's mother. They got really mad at me later."

Feeling like he was about to choke on the lump in his throat, he said, "We'll stay away from corn mazes."

"If you really want to go, I could give it a try."

"I'm not a fan of them either, Irene. I grow corn on my farm. I'm in no hurry to wander around even more cornstalks."

"Oh! There's Alice and her husband, Calvin," Irene said, pointing to a man wearing jeans and a zip-up navy hoodie and a redheaded woman dressed in a modest calf-length dress. "Would you like to meet them?"

"Of course. I can't wait to meet them."

The smile she gave him was so luminous he felt like he'd just given her the moon.

It was humbling to realize that only a few

weeks ago he probably would've avoided them because he knew they both left the Amish faith. Now he realized he would probably do anything so Irene could see her friend Alice. After all, Alice had been there for her when no one else was.

Looking animated, Irene waved at Alice and increased her pace. Marcus stayed behind her a bit so she could have a moment to give her friend a hug.

By the time he joined them, Calvin was looking at him with interest. "Calvin Fisher," he said quietly.

"Marcus Wengerd." After they shook hands, he smiled at Alice. "And you must be the woman Irene has told me so much about."

Alice laughed. "If you still want to meet me, then I know Irene hasn't told you everything."

"She told me enough. I'm glad to know you."

After darting a look at Irene, Alice smiled warmly. "*Danke.* If you are putting this smile on my best friend's face, I'm glad to know you too."

Seeing that Irene looked self-conscious, he said, "I would take the credit, but I think it's all the snacks we've been eating. We were just about to grab some lunch. Would you like to join us?"

Irene put her hand on his arm. "Marcus, are you sure?"

That gesture — and the expression in her eyes — was so sweet. "*Jah.* Remember, all I've had is water."

"And let me guess, you've already eaten a mountain of caramel corn," Calvin said.

"How did you know?"

"Because *mei frau* has eaten almost a tub of it," he teased. Looking back at Marcus, Calvin said, "We'd love to join you. Alice needs to get off her feet for a little bit and eat something a little healthier."

"*Ack,* Calvin. I'm fine."

Irene frowned. "I was going to eat a hot dog. That isn't too healthy. Maybe we could find —"

Alice interrupted. "I want one of those, Cal. Please?"

He laughed, making it obvious to Marcus that he didn't like to deny his wife anything. "I guess we'll eat a bunch of vegetables for supper, hmm?"

They all walked toward the food vendors, and Irene remained at his side. "You didn't have to invite them to join us, but I'm glad you did."

"I'm glad too. I'm looking forward to getting to know them."

"Do you like them so far?"

"Of course. Calvin is sure protective of her. I didn't expect that."

"Oh." She lowered her voice. "Alice is expecting a baby. That's the reason for him worrying about her vegetables."

"Ah. That's *wunderbaar.*"

She sighed. "It really is. I'm happy for them."

He smiled back at her, but Marcus wished he could take Irene in his arms instead. Right then and there, she had so much longing in her eyes, it just about broke his heart.

CHAPTER 9

Another week had passed. Another week of Agnes knocking on Irene's door early in the morning on her days off to ask for help in the bookstore. Another week of putting in forty hours at the diner.

And another week of seeing Marcus almost every day. Sometimes he came to the diner for a meal. Twice he walked her home at the end of a shift.

Though the girls at work teased her, Irene loved his attention. Little by little, she was starting to trust him . . . and to realize she was becoming close to him.

Now they were at his parents' house. It felt familiar but different too. There were four of them at the table instead of only three.

They enjoyed a simple supper of roast chicken, squash casserole, and rice with Mary Ruth and Henry. After eating, she and Marcus were sitting in the back of his parents' house in something called a three-season room. She hadn't really understood what that meant until Marcus pointed out that the night was cool but they were cozy sitting in the wicker chairs and looking out at the backyard in a room made up almost entirely of windows.

He'd brought big stoneware mugs filled to the brim with hot chocolate and Mary Ruth's homemade marshmallows. The concoction was tasty and as decadent as sitting in a glass room and looking out at the stars.

After taking a couple sips of his own drink, Marcus put his mug down. "You look content. Like a cat with a large bowl of cream."

She smiled, liking the description. "I feel like that cat. I was thinking that it feels almost sinful to sit in this beautiful space. Sometimes I canna believe that you grew up like this."

A shadow filled his eyes. "When you say things like that, I never know how to respond."

"There's no need for you to respond. I was simply telling you how I felt."

"I know you didn't grow up this way."

Thinking of the small rooms, of the many evenings she'd gone to bed hungry, she smiled tightly. "You're right. I didn't. But

361

you know that." Feeling a little queasy, she picked up the mug again and took another sip.

She realized with a start that her body had been reacting to those memories as much as her head. It seemed she would always have that survival instinct. She remembered her mother's disappearance when she was eight or nine. Her father had just died, and her mother was gone for two days. Irene closed her eyes. Before her mother left, she tried to make Irene eat a plate of pork and sauerkraut. Irene had refused, finding the spices too strong. Her mother yelled at her and told her she'd learn her lesson, one way or another.

And she had.

Ever since then, Irene was too afraid to refuse anything in case it was never offered again.

Marcus leaned forward and rested his elbows on his knees. "Any chance you're willing to tell me what it was like?"

"I'm not sure why you want to know."

"Because I want to know more about you."

Wariness took hold of her. "I'd rather not talk about it."

"Is it because you don't trust me?"

Maybe. "It's because I get no joy revisiting my childhood, Marcus. That's all."

"Maybe you could tell me about Calvin and West." When she still hesitated, he reached across the small gap separating them and squeezed her knee. "Let me in, Irene," he coaxed, his tone thick with emotion. "I know you're still worried about trusting me, but I've been trying to change your mind. Let me show you that I won't hurt you again."

Marcus was right. She was never going to have a real, loving relationship like Alice did with Calvin if she didn't start letting down at least some of her walls.

Plus, if she shared, she could find out more about him, too, and she really wanted to do that.

Before she could back down, she said, "I first met West at Bill's Diner. I didn't even realize he knew Calvin. That he, um, thought Calvin worked for him."

"Thought?"

"Alice's husband was undercover in the gang. West was the leader."

Marcus blinked. "Boy, I had no idea about Calvin being secretly undercover."

She smiled slightly, not missing the irony of his statement. "You weren't supposed to." She shrugged. "Anyway, I waited on West and one of the other members of the Kings.

But then some men I didn't really like came in and I had to wait on them."

"Why didn't you like them?"

"They, uh, used to make fun of me when I was little." Oh, this was so hard. She took a cleansing breath and reminded herself that having fewer secrets with Marcus would be a good thing. "West heard them and saw me run outside when I got upset."

"They made you cry?"

"Almost." She was still happy the bullies hadn't brought her to tears. "He came out and we talked and he gave me a card with his private phone number on it."

"Why?"

"He told me he didn't like how I was all alone in the world. He wanted me to have his number in case I ever needed anything. That's when he told me he had a lot of power. Um, a lot of influence. That if I ever needed anything or was in trouble, all I had to do was let him know and he'd take care of it."

"And you took the card?"

"*Jah.* I don't know if I ever would have called him or not. But you don't know what his words meant to me."

"I'm trying to understand, but he was so different. And a stranger."

"That's because you have your parents

364

and the farm you inherited from them, Marcus. They've never knowingly hurt you and you've never gone hungry. You've never gone to sleep at night knowing that you were completely alone."

"You're right. I'm sorry."

"It's nothing to apologize about." She smiled at him softly. "After all, if your parents weren't so kind and giving, I wouldn't have become friends with them."

"Or me."

Realizing that they were now truly friends, she nodded.

"Irene, I'd be happy to tell you more about myself, but it ain't mighty interesting. I grew up with loving parents, and now I farm."

"How about you tell me something I don't know, then?"

"Like what?"

It would be so easy to move into a lighter conversation. They could talk about their mutual interests and likes — maybe even his horses or the animals on his farm.

But that wasn't enough. She wanted to know something about him that mattered. "How about like Beth?"

All the warmth that had been shining in his eyes disappeared. "She was my old girlfriend. That's all."

"Why did you break up?"

"She, ah, she started seeing someone else."

"While you were still courting?"

"Jah." He opened his mouth, looked ready to say more, but then, just as quickly, he shook his head. "I'm sorry, Irene. I can talk to you about a lot of things, but not that. Not yet."

Not that. Not yet.

He stood. "I know we just had hot chocolate, but would you like something else?" His voice brightened. "Maybe some peppermint tea? It's a little chilly in here."

She searched his face. He looked stressed, like he needed a break from their conversation. "Tea sounds *gut,*" she murmured. *"Danke."*

He gave her a strained smile, then turned and walked down the hall.

Irene was glad she'd worn a green wool sweater over her dress. She curved her arms around herself. He was right. It had become a little chilly. Unfortunately, she wasn't sure if it was from the cold breeze outside or the realization that she felt very alone all over again.

CHAPTER 10

He was Marcus Wengerd. Only son of Mary Ruth and Henry. He was Old Order Amish. A farmer and a landowner.

These titles and descriptors fit him. Now Marcus realized he'd been wearing them like a well-fitted shirt.

As he wandered down the halls of the sprawling one-story farmhouse where both he and his father grew up, Marcus realized he'd also begun to feel as if his blessings were his rights. He'd begun to act as if he was better than other people, simply because he was born to the best parents in the world.

To his shame, he realized he used to think he was better than people like Irene Keim.

That wasn't the case now. She was the one who was impressive. He'd received so much while she had so little, but instead of letting that stop her, she'd used her hardships to propel her forward.

He had a life of security and comfort. In

many ways, his only real source of heartache had been Beth's betrayal.

He'd acted like it was a terrible crisis. And while her duplicity hurt and being rejected was hard, it wasn't a matter of being homeless or hungry.

Marcus poured himself a glass of water, then walked outside to the back porch. He always thought it was the best part of the house — private and peaceful, looking out on the ten acres of cornfields he now farmed.

Of course, the cornfields reminded him of Irene walking by his side at the fall festival and the story she shared. Now that he was alone, he allowed his dismay and anger to boil to the surface. Anything could have happened to her. She could have tripped and fallen. Gotten too close to a horse or buggy or car. Or someone could have hurt her, taken her.

"Marcus, you around?"

Startled, he sprang to his feet. He relaxed when he saw his neighbor Jesse Lauder. "*Jah.* I'm in the back, Jesse."

"I thought you might be." His English neighbor walked around the perimeter of the house and joined him. "It's too nice to be inside, isn't it?"

"It is a *gut* night, for sure." He shook

Jesse's hand. "I was thinking I might burn some wood in the fire pit. You want to stay awhile?"

Jesse lifted a can of beer. "Yeah, I even brought sustenance."

Marcus grinned. Jesse was about his age, a farmer, and a newlywed. About once a week he stopped by for what he called male bonding. It usually involved his one nightly beer and a lot of conversation about their trade, his cows, or whatever confusing thing his bride recently said or did.

"If you brought your beer, I guess I'd better light that match."

"I've got a story for you too. You might even need to top off that glass of water."

"Sounds serious."

"Just you wait."

Marcus grinned as he arranged the wood and kindling in the metal fire pit, then struck a match. The second one caught, and after a few seconds of poking and prodding with a stick, the men had a real nice fire going. It cast a soothing glow and warmed up the chilly night air. It was the perfect accompaniment to the sunset.

"What's your story about?" Marcus asked as he took a fortifying sip of water and Jesse popped open his beer. "Does it have to do with cows or Samantha?"

"Sam." Jesse, wearing jeans, a pair of worn tennis shoes, and a long-sleeve T-shirt emblazoned with some country singer on it, sighed. "She's pregnant."

Marcus just about choked on his water. After he set the glass down, he grasped Jesse's hand again. "Congratulations!"

"Thanks." Jesse smiled, but it was strained.

"What's wrong? Is she not feeling good?" Marcus pulled two chairs close to the fire pit and they sat.

"It's nothing like that. It's . . . Well, it was an accident. We hadn't planned on having a baby yet. We were going to wait two years." He frowned. "Instead, we only made it seven months."

"Ah."

Jesse looked him in the eye. "Ah? Marcus, you always have good advice. That isn't cutting it."

"If you were talking corn or heifers or a leak in your roof, I could offer you some advice. I don't know much about babies, though. Nothing other than them being a blessing, *jah*?"

Jesse leaned back in his chair, holding his can in both hands, and stared at the fire. "When Sam told me, I made her cry."

"What happened?"

"Yesterday morning, right as I was getting out of the shower, she came running at me holding one of those pregnancy sticks." He cast a sideways look at Marcus. "You know the ones I'm talking about — they actually say 'pregnant' or 'not pregnant'?"

"I'm a bachelor, Jesse. I had no idea such things existed."

"Oh, just you wait. You'll find out one day. Anyway, there I was, wrapping a towel around my waist, and she shoves that thing in front of my face." He lifted his hands, obviously illustrating Samantha's movement. "Next thing I know, I'm blinking and staring at the word 'pregnant' clear as day."

"Uh-oh. What did you say?"

"About what you would expect me to say." Looking sheepish, he mumbled, "Something like, 'What the heck is that?' But, uh, I didn't actually say 'heck.' "

"Uh-oh."

"Yeah. It was bad. Samantha's smile turned to tears, she dropped that stick on the floor, and then she ran into the bedroom. So there I was, half naked with a crying wife and a pregnancy wand thingy staring up at me."

"Wow. What did you do next?"

"First I got on some clothes, because I figured a pretty big moment like that de-

371

served pants, you know?"

Marcus's lips twitched. "Uh-huh."

"Then I did what I knew I should've done in the first place. I picked up that blasted stick, set it on the counter, and went to the bedroom to try to calm Samantha down."

"Did you?"

"I guess." Jesse wasn't smiling. "I think I really messed up, Marcus. This was one of the most important moments of our lives and I ruined it. Don't know how to make it better."

"Did you apologize? Say you were happy?"

"Yeah." After taking another sip, he continued. "And the thing of it is, I *am* happy. I mean, once I got my head around that we have a baby coming? It's awesome."

"Samantha loves you, Jesse. She'll know you were being stupid."

He exhaled. "You know what gets me is that I focused on all the wrong things. Instead of realizing what a gift a baby was, I was focused on the stupid idea that this wasn't what we planned. That starting a family right away wasn't what we talked about."

Jesse turned away from the fire's glow and stared hard at Marcus. "What does that even matter, anyway? Why was I so sure that my plans were the best? I mean, obviously

God decided this is the right time."

Marcus felt like every word Jesse said was directed at him. He'd done the very same thing with Irene. She wasn't the kind of woman he thought he'd be attracted to. Her appearance in his life had felt too soon — he hadn't wanted to be in a relationship again for at least a year.

But like Jesse said, what did that even matter if the Lord bestowed such a blessing on him in the first place?

"You were focused on the wrong things," Marcus said at last.

Jesse blinked. "Yeah, man. That's what I just said."

"Sorry. You reminded me that I've been doing the same thing with a woman I know."

A slow smile spread across his friend's face. "Wait a minute. Do you have a girlfriend now, buddy?"

"*Nee.* I mean, no. We're just talking." One trip to a harvest festival meant one date, not a courtship. "Actually, we only just started. But I got things off on the wrong foot." And now he'd been afraid to be honest with her, fearing that if he allowed her to see him as someone to be rejected, she might reject him too.

"What did you do?"

"I made some judgments about her based

on things I didn't really know about." He also kind of forced her to move from his parents' house. Then, after begging her to trust him, he couldn't even tell her how hurt he was when he discovered Beth had cheated on him.

Jesse's eyebrows rose. "That's too bad, but people do that from time to time."

"I've also made some other mistakes." He swallowed. "I'm trying to make amends, though."

"How's that going for you?"

"Slow."

"And you're sitting home alone tonight."

A little defensive, he said, "If I wasn't home, you wouldn't have anybody to talk to."

"You're right." Looking marginally better, Jesse said, "So when are you going to see her again?"

"My parents invited her over to their house for supper. I'm going to join them in a little bit."

"Were you invited?"

"Not really. But they won't care."

"Will she? What's her name?"

"Irene. And I hope she won't. But I need to see her. I never told her how torn up I was about Beth. I think I need to."

Jesse chuckled. "I wish Samantha was

here. She's always telling me the Amish have quiet, thoughtful, organized lives."

"Sorry, but we're all just as confused as you English."

"I'll pass that on."

"And I'll pass on my advice."

"Which is?" Jesse leaned forward.

"You need to go on home, neighbor, and see to your wife."

"She knew I was coming over. I think she was going to call her mother."

Marcus grinned. "Then you really need to get on home. You don't want her mother giving her ideas. Go on and talk about that baby some more."

Jesse got to his feet. "You know what? I think I will. Thanks, Marcus. Talking to you helped a lot."

"You helped me too. *Danke.*"

"Let us know when you bring Irene over for supper or something. Samantha and I would be glad to join you. She'll be okay with that, won't she?"

Irene would be very okay with that because she was so accepting of everyone. Marcus smiled tightly. "She would like that a lot, actually. I'll let you know what happens."

"Good."

As Jesse started walking across the field,

his empty can in one hand, Marcus called out to him, "Hey, Jesse!"

He turned. "Yeah?"

"Congratulations! You're going to be a father!"

Jesse grinned broadly. "And so I am!"

When he turned back around, there was a new energy to his pace. Marcus realize he needed to get moving too. He'd found a girl who just might be the woman he needed in his life. Now all he had to do was figure out how to make her see that he was someone she needed too.

CHAPTER 11

"You are going to be my lifesaver this week, Irene," Agnes said as she concluded the tour of the back rooms of the bookstore.

Irene chuckled. Agnes said over-the-top things like that all the time. "I'm glad you asked me to start working twenty hours a week."

"I'm glad you said you would."

"It's a great fit since I'm just upstairs." The extra money would come in handy too.

"I was just telling my grandchildren that I wished I could see them more. Now I can tell them that we can make plans." She frowned. "But of course, I don't want to take up all of your free time. You're a young lady. I'm sure you have lots of things to do."

It had been two weeks since the harvest festival. Other than Marcus visiting her at work and the supper at his parents' house, he hadn't asked her out again.

All her old doubts about being able to stay

in a relationship settled in again. Maybe she'd revealed too much. Or maybe she'd pushed too hard. She'd known he didn't want to talk about Beth, but she'd pushed him anyway.

"Anytime I'm available is fine. Just not tonight. I do have plans for supper."

Agnes looked at the antique grandfather clock that proudly stood in the center of the shop. "Since it's almost that time, I'd best let you go. I'll put some dates and times on an index card and slip it under your door later tonight."

"That will be fine. *Danke.*"

Irene went upstairs to her apartment and added a sweater to her dark burgundy dress. She picked up the box of cookies she'd made earlier that day–cranberry, oatmeal, and white chocolate. Not too sweet but terribly addicting. She hoped Mary Ruth and Henry would enjoy them.

After locking up, she rode Agnes's bike to the Wengerds'. It was red with a tan wicker basket that made her smile. She hadn't actually seen Agnes ride it, but from the way her face lit up when she talked about her bicycle rides, Irene suspected it kept her young at heart.

Forty minutes later she parked the bike off to the side of the house and rang the front doorbell.

"Irene, you're right on time!" Mary Ruth said as she opened the door. "Come on in. What do you have there?"

"Cookies for you and Henry."

"Well, that's perfect, because I was just wondering when I was gonna have time to bake."

"Oh? Have you been busy?"

"Busy as a bee, child. Look who else came for supper!"

Irene's smile froze as she turned. Then she felt confused at the sight of Marcus standing right in front of her. "Hi."

He walked right up to her and pulled the box out of her hand. "Hiya, Irene," he said, standing a little closer than was necessary. He was smiling at her in a way that made her feel special.

"I didn't know you were going to be here."

"I wanted to surprise you."

His mother clucked in the background. "Marcus, go make yourself useful. Put the cookies in the kitchen and help me get supper on the table."

He dutifully followed her into the kitchen, and Irene glanced at Henry.

He winked. "They've been like this since Marcus arrived. Mary Ruth is trying to give him tips about courting you, but so far it ain't working too good."

Could her cheeks be any redder? "Why would she be doing that?"

"Oh, no reason. Just something Marcus might have told us the other day."

"What did he say?"

"Don't you worry about that." Looking suddenly stricken, he groaned. "I bet I said too much. Have I made ya uncomfortable?"

Yes, he had. But instead of allowing herself to feel awkward, she forced herself to think about how happy she was that Marcus had been talking about her. Maybe things between them weren't over after all.

She was just about to offer to help Mary Ruth with supper when Marcus walked back into the room.

"*Daed,* I know we're about to eat, but can I speak to Irene alone for a moment?"

"*Jah.* Sure."

Marcus smiled at her. "Will you speak with me for a minute?"

She nodded before she followed him to the three-season room. When they were alone, he closed the door.

"Marcus? What's going on?"

He exhaled and turned around. "Ever since you asked me about Beth and I didn't really answer, I've felt bad. I should have been more forthcoming."

She was stunned and felt a little embarrassed too. "I was hurt," she admitted, "but I should have remembered that people only share secrets when they are ready. One day you'll be ready to tell me about Beth." She placed a hand on his arm, ready to lead him back to the kitchen.

He covered her hand with his, but he didn't budge. "Irene, Beth cheated on me with one of my best friends. I discovered her over at his house one afternoon."

"Oh, Marcus."

After a pause, he spoke again. "I realized they'd both been lying to me. I don't know why one of them didn't just come forward. It would have been easier."

"It would have been the right thing to do."

He nodded. "When I stood in front of them and the truth came out, Beth started crying and my friend looked embarrassed. I wanted to yell at them."

"Did you?"

"*Nee.* I knew it wouldn't change anything." A muscle in his jaw twitched. "I ended up just turning around and leaving."

"You were hurt."

He nodded. "*Jah.* I was very hurt. And embarrassed." He looked down at their hands and shifted so their fingers were linked. Finally he met her gaze again. "Since then, I've been pretending I wasn't as hurt as I was. I thought if I did that, the pain would ease."

"But it didn't."

"It didn't . . . until I allowed myself to be hurt and angry."

"And now?"

"Now that I've shared my story with you?"

"Yes."

He squeezed her hand. "I feel better. At last."

Smiling at him, their hands linked, Irene finally allowed herself to believe in them. To believe in what they could be.

After they all sat down in the kitchen and prayed silently, Irene looked at the huge meal spread out on the table. "Roast, potatoes, carrots, peas, and fresh rolls. It's a feast."

"We know it's your favorite meal," Mary Ruth replied. "Have you been eating? I need to go see your little room above the bookstore."

"I've been eating just fine. Don't forget that I work at a diner."

"I don't know if you do eat enough," Marcus said. "You need to splurge from time to time."

"I only ever see you drink water," she

teased. "I'd like to see you take your own advice."

"Point taken." He grinned at her.

When they were almost done with the meal, Irene said, "I have news. Agnes asked me to help out at the bookstore part-time. Twenty hours a week."

Instead of congratulating her, all three Wengerds looked concerned.

"Irene, are you sure that's a *gut* idea?" Henry asked, his expression full of concern.

"Why wouldn't it be?"

"Well, first of all, you already work one job. Most folks would think that is enough," he said.

"I have some extra time. I don't think it will be a problem." She didn't have the heart to remind them that she'd been planning to do chores around their house in exchange for room and board.

Mary Ruth looked pained. "Please be careful. She has a reputation for taking advantage of people."

"Marcus already told me about her not wanting to pay one of his friends for some bookshelves he built."

"*Jah,* I heard about that," Mary Ruth said. "But I've heard other things too."

Irene appreciated their concern, but she had already told Agnes she would work for her. "I appreciate your concern, but I think I'm going to make my own opinions about her."

Mary Ruth nodded. "Oh. Of course."

"I like to read and I'm happy to help her." She lifted her chin. "She didn't have to rent me that room so quickly, but she did."

Marcus looked down at his plate. "You know I feel bad about that."

"I didn't say that to make you feel bad. I'm just saying I think this is a good opportunity for me. I wasn't much of a student in school. I . . . well, I missed too much, so I struggled a lot. Helping people look for books feels like a step in the right direction. A step up, if you will."

"You were already doing a good job that a lot of people wouldn't do well," Marcus said. "You don't have to prove anything to anyone."

She gaped at him. "*Danke*. That's kind of you to say."

"It's the truth."

Embarrassed by the look being exchanged between Mary Ruth and Henry, Irene sipped her water.

The conversation turned to other topics. Mary Ruth was volunteering for a quilt auction and Henry had just made plans with two other men to go hunting around

Thanksgiving.

"I have news, too, though it ain't exactly about me," Marcus said.

"What is it?"

"My English neighbor Jesse came to see me earlier tonight to tell me his wife, Samantha, is pregnant."

Mary Ruth clapped her hands. "That is wonderful-*gut* news. I bet their parents are so happy."

Marcus laughed. "I imagine so. I know he and his wife are, though it was kind of a shock."

"Babies always are," Henry said. "Even when they are planned."

As the talk continued about babies and Samantha and Jesse, Irene tried to push back the surge of melancholy that took hold of her.

Every time she heard about parents being excited or anticipating a baby, it made her realize just how different her own parents must have reacted. Her father had died when she was seven. On her best days her mother had treated her like an unwanted burden.

For the first time in years, Irene wished her mother were still alive. Then she could ask if she'd ever looked forward to Irene's birth. But did she really want to know the answer? What if her mother was completely honest and told her she hadn't?

"Irene, would you like a second helping?"

"Hmm?" To her surprise, she'd cleaned her whole plate. "*Nee.* I'm fine, thank you."

"Then let's play Clue," Henry said.

Irene glanced at Marcus. "Are you going to stick around?"

He winked. "Of course. It's one of the reasons I came."

"It's his first time, so we'll have to go easy on him," Irene said.

"No, we won't," Henry said. "Marcus can hunt for clues just like the rest of us. Nobody gets special treatment here. We're all just the same. Ain't so, Mary Ruth?"

She winked at Irene. "For sure and for certain."

Although Irene knew Henry and Mary Ruth were only joking, she felt her heart swell. They were giving her what she'd always wanted — a chance to feel like she belonged. A chance to feel like she was really part of a family.

CHAPTER 12

Two days had passed since Marcus sat across from Irene at his parents' old oak kitchen table and realized what he wanted his future to be like. Everything about those two hours had been so perfect. The conversation was easy with each person adding to the discussion like a needed leg to a treasured piece of furniture. They'd teased and joked, supported and enhanced each conversational tangent.

For the first time in his memory, Marcus felt like he had his own identity, independent from his parents. He wasn't just the link between them. He was his own person. It felt freeing, new, and gratifying. Almost like it had taken two dozen years, but he'd finally become Marcus Wengerd.

The reason was Irene, of course. Not only had she fit in so perfectly at his mother's table, but she'd also become a vital member of their small group.

It shouldn't have been a surprise. After all, Irene had a spark and a wit that shone brightly. She was the reason they laughed so much, and his father played off her quips, joking with her in a way he did with few others.

Irene's vulnerability drew his mother to her as well. *Mamm* fussed over Irene like she was a wayward filly, just trying out her first steps and in need of a steady hand. It was obvious to him that his mother missed fussing over other people. She needed Irene to feel needed.

Marcus was pleased his parents got along so well with Irene, but he needed her unique personality even more. She was strong and complex, kind and easygoing.

She was so much more than he deserved.

The night before, when he was falling asleep, Marcus imagined the Lord himself had found Irene for him. She was such a perfect fit.

Marcus also couldn't help but admire her beauty. With her golden hair, light-blue eyes, slim build, and pretty smile, she drew his eyes like no other woman had.

Well, not since Beth.

Now it was obvious he and Beth were never meant to be. There had been an attraction between them — a shared interest in their religion and family — but that was where their similarities ended. No matter what was at hand, Beth always wanted more. More land, more attention, more of him. She needed to be the focus of every conversation, of his whole day. When she wasn't, she was crushed, and he felt like he'd let her down.

He now saw that Beth had been toxic to both him and his parents. Looking back, he realized his mother had always been nervous around Beth because she could never seem to do enough for his girlfriend.

And his father? Well, he'd just avoided her. The idea of the four of them playing Clue at the kitchen table was so outlandish he might as well have tried to imagine them playing poker. It simply wouldn't have happened.

Marcus was busy at the farm this week and was only able to say hello to Irene for a few minutes at the diner before returning to his corn and the upcoming harvest.

He was glad she was working that afternoon at the Printed Page because he had a surprise for her. After the shop closed, he was going to walk her down the street to the new pizza place on the corner.

Everyone said it was awfully good. He liked the idea of taking her someplace where neither of them had to cook, his parents weren't right next to them, and she didn't have to serve anyone.

He entered the shop and the door chimed, signaling his entrance. Irene, who knelt on the floor as she shelved a stack of books, looked over and treated him to a smile. "This is a surprise."

"I hope it's a *gut* one." He grinned as he strode inside and took a moment to appreciate how the forest-green dress she wore made her golden hair and blue eyes even more striking.

When she moved to her feet, he shook his head. "*Nee,* don't get up. Finish what you're doing."

The dimple he'd become so fond of punched her cheek. "All right. I'm almost done," she said as she clasped another hardcover and slipped it on the shelf. "The store closes soon."

"I know," he said as he crouched next to her. "I thought I'd take you out for pizza afterward. What do you say?"

Her eyes lit up. "Since I'm starving, I think it sounds wonderful-*gut. Danke.*"

"Miss?" a woman with a stack of children's picture books in her arms called out from the front of the store. "Can you check me out?"

Irene jumped to her feet. "Of course," she called out in a bright voice. After she placed the last book on a shelf, Irene walked to the cash register and rang up the woman's purchase, running her fingers along each book like it was a treasure. "I hope you will enjoy the books."

The woman smiled. "I know my son Jeremy will love them. We read books together every night before bed."

"That is a lovely tradition, ain't so?"

The woman beamed. "I hope one day he'll think so. Thanks for your help, Irene."

"You're mighty welcome."

She gave them both a smile and left with a canvas bag of books in her hand.

Marcus noticed that Irene was smiling as she watched the woman leave. It was obvious she enjoyed helping the woman. "You do a good job with the customers," he said. "I can tell that you're already making an impression on them."

"I don't know about that," she murmured. "But working here feels easy, almost like I'm working with friends. I like reading and talking about books with everyone."

Marcus leaned against the side of a wooden bookshelf and watched as Irene straightened the stack of receipts on the counter. "Are you about ready to get out of here?"

"I am. I hope you like everything on your pizza."

He laughed. "I should have known that was your favorite."

"Why?"

"Because when it comes to food, you enjoy everything. It's adorable." He laughed, liking the way she looked mildly embarrassed.

Agnes appeared from the back, looking like a frazzled hen. "Irene, are you all done?"

"Yes, ma'am," she said quickly. "I was just about to close out the register."

Marcus noticed that some of Irene's lighthearted demeanor faded. He knew now that while she truly enjoyed the bookstore, she wasn't always as fond of her employer and landlady as she'd hoped.

"I'll do that. There's a few things I want to check. You walk around the shop and make sure everything is spick-and-span. Especially the children's section."

"All right." Irene cast an apologetic look his way. "I'll just be a minute."

"How about I walk with you? I can pick up books as easily as you."

She smiled at him but fussed with the apron on her dress a bit. It was obvious she was becoming distressed. That worried him. Just minutes before, she seemed to love the job.

When they walked down one of the aisles and were partly concealed, he pressed his hand to her back. "Hey, are you okay?"

"I'm fine."

"You don't seem like it."

She lowered her voice. "I love working with the customers. But sometimes . . . Well, let's just say Agnes has been especially hard to please today."

Since he'd already shared his worries about her boss, he tried to keep things light. "Everyone has a bad day now and then. Maybe it's her turn."

Still looking uneasy, she nodded. "I hope that's it."

"From what I saw with that customer, you are doing a fine job here, Irene." Unable to help himself, he leaned down and kissed her cheek lightly. "Please don't worry so much."

Her eyes widened at his gesture, but she didn't seem upset. "You're right," she said with a little smile. "I need to relax and be more confident."

"There you go," he said as he continued to walk by her side. Every few feet Irene stopped to straighten books or knelt to pick up a stray piece of trash on the floor. He helped when he could, placing books on the high shelves when she asked.

Every time they made a turn, Marcus glanced over at Agnes. She stood at the front desk punching numbers in her calculator with a frown on her face. He could almost feel animosity radiating from the older woman.

Marcus decided right then and there that he would encourage Irene to quit sooner rather than later. Though he knew she loved being around books, he thought his parents were right. She already worked so hard at the diner. She didn't need to be stressed out at the bookshop too.

"Almost done," she whispered.

He reached for her hand and squeezed it gently. "*Gut.* I'm starving."

As if she couldn't help herself, Irene smiled and giggled. Then slapped a hand over her mouth.

"Irene, come here."

Irene flinched but dutifully walked to the front of the store. "*Jah,* Agnes?"

When they got to the desk, Marcus saw that Agnes had several checks and credit card receipts on the countertop . . . and a business-size envelope. She was also glaring at Irene like she'd done something awful.

"I just tried to close out the register. Unfortunately, I wasn't able to do it because we're missing cash."

Irene's eyes widened. "Are you sure?"

Agnes pulled out a sheet of paper. "This is yesterday's report. I know I had a hundred and twenty dollars in this envelope this morning. Now there's only sixty. Half is gone."

Irene stepped closer. She looked from the envelope to the notations, and finally to Agnes's angry expression. "I don't know what to say."

"You handled most of the sales today. It looks like you made a mistake."

Paling, Irene shook her head. "*Nee.* I am careful when I check people out." Pointing to a light-pink notepad, she said, "See? I always write everything down so I remember to tell you what books were bought."

Marcus approached and saw Irene's list of each item sold and the amount of each sale. It was obvious she put a lot of effort and care into it.

"Well, I certainly didn't take my own money. So either you made some very big mistakes or you have some explaining to do."

"I don't know where your missing money went." She glanced at Marcus and looked even more agitated.

He wondered why.

Seeing that Irene looked near tears, Marcus said, "Maybe other people know the envelope is there. Maybe someone took the money out while Irene was helping other customers?"

Irene bit her lip and nodded. "*Jah.* I don't like to think of anyone doing that, but it might have happened."

"I don't know what else could have happened. It was there last night and now it ain't."

"M-maybe you miscounted the money?" Irene said, her voice quivering.

"Or maybe you took advantage of my generosity." She jabbed a finger on the counter. "I think it's high time you told me the truth."

"I did."

"If you insist on lying, I'm going to have to call the sheriff and file a report."

Irene wiped away a tear. "If you want to file a report, you should. But you mustn't blame me. I haven't done anything wrong."

Marcus had had enough. He pulled out his wallet and placed three twenty-dollar bills on the counter. "Here is your missing money."

"Marcus, no."

"You don't have to stand here and take this, Irene. It's not worth it. And neither is this job."

The expression on her face was filled with pain. "Do you believe me?"

Not caring that Agnes was watching them, he stepped closer and lifted her chin with his thumb. "Of course I do. You wouldn't steal money any more than I would."

"I don't know what happened."

"Agnes will figure it out. Or she won't," he soothed. "I don't really care because we won't have to worry about you being here any longer."

"But —"

"And we're going to move you out of that apartment tonight."

Agnes shook her head. "She can't do that. Irene, you said you'd give me two months' notice."

Irene turned to her, her expression slack. Then it hardened. "You said you didn't want to write a contract, so we don't have anything that says that. Marcus is right. I'm leaving tonight. I don't want to sleep any-place I don't feel safe."

Marcus was so proud of her. "*Gut* job, Irene."

Agnes glared. "You are making a big mis-take."

"You are too," Marcus bit out. "I just hope you will be humble enough to admit your mistakes when you realize you were completely wrong and misjudged Irene."

He watched as Agnes picked up his money without the slightest hesitation. "I appreciate you paying this, but I feel like it is my duty to warn you that you should probably stay away from her, Marcus."

Marcus wrapped an arm around Irene and pulled her close to his side. "I don't want to hear that you're making up tales about Irene. If you do that, I'll make sure no one comes to this store."

While Agnes gaped at them, he linked his fingers through Irene's and pulled her toward the stairs leading up to her room.

"Come on," he said softly. "We've got to pack you up."

CHAPTER 13

As soon as her door closed behind them, Irene started crying. Big, noisy tears. Marcus wrapped her in his arms.

"Hey now," he soothed as he rubbed her back. "Shh . . . shh, now. Don't fret. It's going to be all right."

She rested her head against his strong chest for another moment, then raised her head so she could look him in the eye. "I'm not crying because of her."

Still rubbing her back, he said, "Why, then?"

"Because of you." When he blinked in confusion, she pressed her palm to his cheek. "You really did believe me."

"Of course I did." He stepped away slightly and tilted his head down to meet her gaze. "I know you would never steal from anyone."

Irene shook her head. "*Nee,* you don't understand. Marcus, for my whole life, I've felt like no one ever really believed in me. My parents never acted like yours. I never felt safe or happy or loved at home."

She braced herself, then continued, wanting to be completely honest with him. "I've made plenty of mistakes. More than you can imagine."

"We all have."

"Maybe so." Maybe she'd been so hard on herself for so long that she'd forgotten she wasn't any different from everyone else. People made mistakes and sometimes said things they didn't mean. But they could also apologize for their actions, make amends, and forgive each other.

Just like she'd done with Marcus. Just like God's grace did for all of them.

"What I'm trying to say is that even though I've made some mistakes, getting to know you isn't one of them. You've been a blessing to me. A good friend."

"Only just a friend?" he asked, his voice suddenly soft.

She smiled. "*Nee.* Something more than that."

Pleasure entered his eyes. "Good. I want to be more. I want to mean so much to you that you won't ever be afraid to tell me the truth or to let me see anything bad about you. Or ever worry that I won't take your side."

Had anyone ever given her a better gift? "Your trust in me means so much."

"I hope so, because I feel the same way about you." He placed his palm against her cheek and lowered his voice. "I want to mean a lot to you too. I want you to trust me. I want you to believe in me. Because . . ." His voice drifted off.

"Because?"

"Because I love you, Irene."

Her breath hitched. "Truly?"

He nodded. Looking a little worried, he pressed two fingers against her lips. "Irene, hush. You don't have to say a thing. You don't have to say the words back."

"But what if I want to? What if all this time I've been trying to find the courage to give my heart to someone? Trying to find the courage to give it without worrying that it's going to get hurt?"

"Your heart is safe with me. I can promise you that."

What more did she need?

She gathered her courage. "I love you too."

His gaze heated. "Promise?"

"Oh yes."

As they smiled at each other, Irene realized that nothing else mattered.

Nothing to her, at least. What mattered was that they loved each other and that he was going to handle her heart with care, just as she was determined to protect his.

So thankful for that knowledge, Irene closed her eyes as she relaxed against his chest. It had been such a horrible afternoon, but it was followed by the sweetest moments ever.

He loved her. Marcus Wengerd loved her. At that moment, she couldn't think of another time when so few words had meant so much.

CHAPTER 14

One month later

"Rats!" Henry shouted when Marcus held up the small envelope and announced that the murderer had been Professor Plum with the wrench in the ballroom. "I was going to say wrench but it didn't make sense. No man is going to be carrying around a wrench in a ballroom."

Sitting on the floor in a cranberry-colored dress with one of Marcus's hoodies over it, Irene giggled. "Henry, when are you ever going to learn that you aren't supposed to make sense of the crime, just look for clues?"

"Next game, hopefully." He looked sheepish as he started cleaning up the cards and plastic pieces. "Does anyone want to play again?"

"Nee!" Marcus, Irene, and Mary Ruth all said at the same time.

"We already played an extra game because

you whined and complained, Henry," his wife said. "We need to get some sleep."

Henry got to his feet and groaned as his knees popped with the effort. "That's probably a *gut* idea. I am suddenly feeling tired. Let's go up to bed, Mary Ruth, and let the kids clean up the rest of the mess."

Mary Ruth raised her eyebrows at them. "Would you like some help cleaning up?"

"Go on up to bed, *Mamm.* We've got this," Marcus said.

"I won't argue with you. I really am tired," she said as she covered a yawn. *"Gut naut."*

"*Gut naut,* Mary Ruth," Irene said to her future mother-in-law. "Sleep well."

"You too, dear." After squeezing Marcus's shoulder, Mary Ruth followed her husband up the stairs to bed.

"Alone at last," Marcus said with a grin. "I was beginning to think my parents would never leave the room."

"Oh, stop. I had fun with them."

"I had fun with them too. But that doesn't mean I don't like being alone with you."

Smiling at Marcus fondly, Irene felt the same way. So much had happened in the month since Agnes accused her of stealing and Marcus came to her defense. And admitted his love for her.

She moved out of her room above the

store and back into her room at his parents' home. When Henry and Mary Ruth heard about Agnes's accusations, they were vocal about her defense. So much so that Bill and May from the diner had gone over to the bookstore and demanded to help Agnes organize her financial books — and soon discovered that Agnes might know a lot about books but next to nothing about accounting.

It soon became apparent that she'd simply miscounted the cash and the previous day's receipts and instead of taking the blame for her mistakes had decided to blame Irene.

When Alice and her husband, Calvin, heard about it, they gave Agnes a piece of their minds too. Calvin acted very official and told Agnes that legally she had to hire someone to manage the store's finances.

No doubt stung by all the negative reactions, Agnes eventually did apologize to Irene, but it was grudgingly.

As far as Irene was concerned, she realized she didn't need Agnes's apology — heartfelt or not. She now had people in her life who were willing to have her back and stand up for her. Those people were important to her. Not Agnes.

She and Marcus were planning a Christmas wedding. It was going to be small and simple. Irene thought it sounded perfect.

Walking up to her side, Marcus pulled the game board out of her hands. "Put that down," he whispered. "We can finish cleaning up in the morning."

"But we promised your mother —"

He kissed her quickly, shutting off her protest.

His lips were warm, and the way he wrapped his arms around her made any further protest quickly fade away.

"Our wedding day can't come soon enough," he said with a heated gaze.

Irene smiled, though she wasn't sure she agreed.

"What?" he said. "Aren't you as anxious as me to be living together at the farm?"

"I am excited for that . . . but I also have to admit that I kind of like this time. There's so much to look forward to." It was a relatively new feeling and one she planned to savor as much as she could.

Marcus's gaze softened. "You're exactly right, Irene. I have you. I have your love and your promise to be my future. That is something to savor indeed."

She rested her head on his chest.

Irene breathed deep, enjoying the scent of the fire, the cinnamon candles, and the faint scent of soap on Marcus's skin.

She was more than happy knowing the best was yet to come.

DISCUSSION QUESTIONS

1. Both Irene and Marcus were afraid to reveal parts of their pasts. Why do you think it's so hard to be vulnerable with other people — even people you love and trust?

2. God placed Mary Ruth and Henry in Irene's life at just the right time. In what ways did they help her heal?

3. I used the scripture verse from Joshua as my guide for this story. "This is my command — be strong and courageous! Do not be afraid or discouraged. For the lord your God is with you wherever you go." What part of this verse resonates with you?

4. I thought the following Amish proverb, "Experience is a different teacher, giving you the test first and the lesson later," went especially well with Irene's and Marcus's story. In what ways did their past experiences give both Irene and Marcus the courage to love?

ACKNOWLEDGMENTS

I was so excited to be asked to be a part of *An Amish Homecoming*! I've known Amy, Beth, and Kathleen for quite a few years, so having the opportunity to publish a story alongside them felt like writing with friends. I also am indebted to Erika Tsang, my editor over at Avon Inspire, for first allowing me to introduce Irene's story in *His Risk*. She gave me the freedom to bring a real variety of characters together and run with it. I'm also indebted to editor Kimberly Carlton for helping me fine tune Irene's story so it would actually make sense to new readers! She also was instrumental in helping me make Marcus into a hero worthy of Irene. Yay for that! Finally, I'm grateful for my readers, who loved Irene as much as I did and asked me to give Irene her own happily ever after.

■ ■ ■ ■

WHAT LOVE BUILT

KATHLEEN FULLER

■ ■ ■ ■

To James. I love you.

CHAPTER 1

I said I would never leave you.

Atlee Shetler knelt in front of his wife's grave and touched the small, plain stone that marked her resting place. May had lain here for twelve years, and he'd mourned her death every single day — something he would do for the rest of his life. He'd also intended never to leave Fredericktown, not even to visit somewhere else.

Funny how intentions could change.

No, it wasn't funny at all. But with the prodding of his English friend Derek, along with an invitation from Jesse Bontrager — or rather Thomas, as he preferred to be called now — Atlee found himself leaving his beloved wife to visit Birch Creek.

Resisting the urge to stay with her longer, he slung his duffel bag over his shoulder and headed back to his house to wait for Derek, who was going to pick him up and take him to the bus station. He would be

417

gone for only a few days. And if he was completely honest, he'd have to admit a small part of him wanted to go. Leaving May was hard, of course, but taking a break from the suffocating community his small district had become wasn't a bad idea.

When he reached the driveway of his small house, Derek's truck was just pulling in. Atlee opened the passenger-side door, the air-conditioned cab cooling his face from the effects of the hot morning sun.

"Atlee." Derek nodded from beneath a frayed Cleveland Browns baseball cap. "Looks like a nice day for a trip."

Atlee tossed his duffel bag on the floorboard, then shut the door and clicked his seat belt in place. "I guess."

With a smirk, Derek backed out of the driveway. "You're not having second thoughts, are you?"

"No." A lie, but he wasn't in the mood for another pep talk from Derek. He'd known the man for about five years, since he first called him for a ride to Mansfield. Although he was fifteen years younger than Atlee, Derek was wise — which was why Atlee had given his suggestion of a change of scenery some serious thought.

"How long have you known Thomas?" Derek turned off Atlee's road and onto

Main Street.

"A long time. Since when May and I were courting."

"It's good timing he invited you to come see him now."

"I suppose."

Derek paused. "Atlee, I don't mean to pry into your business."

"You're always prying into my business," he said with a mild chuckle as he turned to look at his friend. But he didn't mind too much. It was nice to know someone cared. Yes, his community made sure he wasn't left out. A few of the married ladies occasionally gave him a casserole or a dessert, and he was never without a place to go on Christmas Day. Derek's family invited him over regularly too. But that didn't mean he wasn't lonely at times. Lately, he'd been lonely a lot.

"That's true," Derek said. "And I'm glad you took my advice and decided to get away. You've seemed restless over the last year."

"You know work has been slow."

"That it has. But I don't think that's the whole reason."

Atlee suspected his friend wanted further explanation from him, but he remained silent. *Restless* was a good word for how he was feeling, but he wasn't sure why. Besides, he didn't have to explain himself to Derek, friend or not.

"How long are you planning to stay?" Derek asked.

"A week, maybe."

Derek clicked on his turn signal. "Only a week?"

"That's long enough."

Derek didn't press him, and they made small talk the rest of the way to the bus station. Atlee was glad for the reprieve. When he received Thomas's letter, he hesitated to answer it, much less accept the invitation. Now that he was on his way, he wasn't sure what he was going to do when he got there. Help Thomas with the farm, he guessed, even though he didn't know much about farming. He was a cabinetmaker by trade, and he mostly worked freelance. But he didn't have any jobs lined up for a while, which freed him to go to Birch Creek. Another fortuitous happenstance, he supposed. *Or God's plan.*

Derek stopped the truck in front of the bus terminal. "Atlee, enjoy yourself, and don't think about things here."

Atlee knew he meant May. Not thinking about her would be impossible, but he nodded anyway. "Will do."

As Derek drove away, Atlee paused and

looked in the direction of his Amish community. "I'll be back, May," he whispered. "I won't be gone for long."

For the first time since she returned to Birch Creek, Carolyn Yoder wondered if she'd made a mistake.

She glanced around the bakery — or what was supposed to be a bakery. *Her* bakery. The dream that had kept her going while she spent years doing upholstery work in an RV factory in Nappanee, Indiana. The dream she'd held on to while she built up her bank account, being miserly with her spending while still fulfilling God's will for her to be generous with others. The dream that was inexplicably turning into a nightmare.

Why had she listened to Freemont in the first place? She'd fully planned to stay in Nappanee and open her new business there. She'd even had the building picked out for purchase. So when she received her brother's letter four months ago, not so subtly telling her she should return home, she had initially balked at the idea. But Freemont could be convincing, and she knew if he had to he'd write to her every day until she agreed.

So she prayed about it. The reason she

left Birch Creek in the first place had disappeared, and she had missed her brother and sister-in-law, as well as her nieces and nephews.

The clincher had been another dream, this time a real one, two nights before she packed and left Nappanee. The details were fuzzy, but she'd awakened with a start in the middle of the night, feeling an urgency to return to her former hometown. That had propelled her here, to buy a property that in hindsight might not have been a good deal, and to make the foolish announcement to her family that she would have the bakery up and running in less than two months. She now realized that would take a miracle.

She drew in a deep breath and then marched to the long stainless-steel table behind one of two display counters in the store. If she couldn't open the bakery on time, it wouldn't be from lack of trying. Just because a thunderstorm two weeks ago had blown shingles off the roof, and one of her large gas ovens had broken after one use, and the yeast she'd purchased from a supposedly reputable company had failed, didn't mean she was going to have to give up her dream or her deadline. These were only a few minor setbacks. At least that's what she was telling herself.

The front door opened, and her nieces Ivy and Karen walked in. She pushed her thoughts away and smiled at the sisters. She still couldn't believe how fast the years had flown, and that her little nieces were married and living on their own. Carolyn had met their husbands, Noah and Adam, and she was impressed with both men. Then again, her nieces were special. They deserved to be happy.

Don't I deserve to be happy too?

"We stopped by to see if you need any help," Ivy said.

"But we have a feeling you'll say *nee*," Karen added.

Ivy was a tiny woman, less than five feet tall and several inches shorter than her ginger-haired sister. They had grown into lovely, strong women, and Carolyn had to keep reminding herself not to regret how much time she'd missed with them and their three brothers over the past eighteen years. Letters and the few rare visits her brother's family made to Nappanee hadn't been enough.

But she also wasn't going to impose on them. Her bakery, her problem, and she was used to handling everything in her life alone. "I'm fine," she said, tightening the ties on her apron and turning back toward the kitchen. "I'm just going to bake a few rolls and try out the oven I had repaired." It had taken nearly a week to get the oven repaired because the technician had to special-order a part.

"Then we'll help you," Ivy said as she and Karen followed her.

"*Nee.* It won't take any time to whip up these rolls." Carolyn opened the oven door and waved her hand, testing the heat. She still didn't trust the oven or its indicators. The only way to truly know if it was hot enough was to feel the heat for herself. "It's 365," she mumbled, closing the door.

"It's set to 350," Karen said, peering over her shoulder.

"But it's running at 365." Carolyn sighed and turned down the temperature. She'd have to call the repairman back out here tomorrow. She turned around and said, "Now, I appreciate the offer, but you two have *yer* own *familyes* to take care of. It's almost suppertime."

"They'll be fine," Ivy said.

Karen nodded. "It won't hurt our husbands to eat leftovers for one night."

Carolyn shook her head. That wouldn't do. "Every *mann* deserves a hot meal after a long day's work."

"*Aenti,*" Ivy said, looking up at her. "Noah

and Adam know we're here. We want to help you."

"We all do," Karen added.

Carolyn knew they were referring to the rest of the Yoder family and possibly even the community. But she couldn't expect everyone to put aside their lives because of her tight timetable.

"I know," she said, shooing them toward the front door. "But as you can see, everything is going according to plan."

Karen and Ivy exchanged a confused look, and Carolyn pretended not to notice. She grabbed two packages of donuts she'd made the night before off the counter. At least her deep fryer worked.

"Here," she said, thrusting one package at each of them. "Take these home to *yer mann.*"

They took the bags and looked at them. Six donuts sat at the bottom of each huge, clear-plastic bag.

"Sorry," she said, feeling sheepish. "The company sent the wrong size bags."

"It's fine," Ivy said. "Oh, and *Mamm* said anytime you want her to make donuts for *yer* customers after you open, she's ready and willing."

Oh dear. Mary was an excellent cook and a decent baker, but she was notorious for making bad donuts. "I'll, uh, keep that in mind."

Karen and Ivy chuckled. "You do that," they said in unison.

The three women laughed again, and Carolyn took the opportunity to send them on their way. When they reached the screen door in the front area, she opened it and smiled. "Don't eat all those donuts at once."

"Aenti," Ivy said with another chuckle, "we're grown women, not *kinner.*"

"I know that," Carolyn said quickly. "Just as I know neither of you can resist *mei* lemon cookies. And plenty of those will be available when I open."

Karen frowned as Ivy looked away. "Are you still planning to open so soon?"

"In two weeks." She lifted her chin. "Just like I promised."

"I don't think anyone would mind if you opened later," Ivy said.

Carolyn would mind. Word about her bakery had already spread, and the news had been met with enthusiasm. Birch Creek had gone from the small, insular community of her childhood to a growing and thriving district, with new Amish families moving in every month. She couldn't let them down. She had made a promise, and she intended to keep it.

"You'll have those fresh lemon cookies in two weeks," she repeated. "Not a day later."

"All right." Karen nodded. "But at least let us —"

"Bye!" Carolyn put her hands on her nieces' shoulders, gently pushed them outside, and shut both doors behind them. Then she pulled out a small pad of paper and a pencil stub and added the words *call repairman* to her ever-growing list.

After wiping down a worktable in the kitchen, she removed the damp towel over a bowl of rising dough. Satisfied, she formed the rolls and put them in the oven. Sweat pooled on her brow. The two screened windows and inside door in the kitchen were open, but she should have left the solid front door open after Ivy and Karen left so she could get a cross breeze through both screen doors.

Then again, it was the middle of June and not much cooler outside. Why hadn't she waited until winter to do this? Or at least fall? Baking was hot business, especially with an oven that ran at a higher temperature than it was supposed to.

"Please let this oven work, Lord." She shut the door, turned on the timer, and then faced the unfinished bakery again. Her hand went to her pocket, overwhelmed by the list inside. Where to start? This wasn't how she anticipated spending the rest of her life, back in the community she left for good reason. Yet she sensed a different atmosphere here. The people seemed happier, more at peace. Even her brother — who, she knew, never wanted to be a bishop — was content. And she had to admit, when she wasn't fretting about the bakery, she had sensed a calm in her soul.

But she had also been settled in her adopted hometown of Nappanee. It had taken time and adjustment, but she'd been happy living there. Well, maybe not happy, but life in Indiana was acceptable. So why had God brought her back here?

Carolyn sighed. She might not know why, but she did have faith that God would reveal all in his time. If there was anything she'd learned in her forty-five years, it was that God did things on his own schedule. Definitely not on hers.

She was organizing some supplies in the pantry when the timer dinged. She pulled the rolls out of the oven. They were golden brown on top, and she quickly ran a brush dipped in melted butter on top of them.

After they cooled she would take them back to her brother's house and let his family try them. She lived with Freemont, at least temporarily. He was almost finished with the small *dawdi haus* he was adding to his property. Once that was completed, she would move in. She loved him and his family, but she was used to having a home of her own.

She put the hot, buttery rolls on a large plate to finish cooling so she could wrap aluminum foil over them. She washed the dishes and gave the floor another quick sweep. Her shop might not be finished, but at least it was tidy.

After locking the back door and closing the windows, she was about to leave when she saw an open bag of flour pushed to the back corner of the kitchen counter. Not wanting to dip into her large bags of flour too soon, she'd bought it yesterday to make the rolls, and it was still three-quarters full. She went to put it away in the pantry, but then thought a better use for it would be to make fresh bread at home for her nieces. Although she had rejected their help, she was touched by their offer. She crimped the very top edge of the flour bag, grabbed her purse, and walked to the front of the shop.

She opened the screen door, then yanked on the inside door. She was shocked when it opened freely, and with such force that she tumbled backward, tripping over the edge of the large welcome mat on the floor.

"Oh *nee!*" a deep voice rang out.

Did something — or someone — brush against her? She lost her balance and hit the wood plank floor . . . and the bag of flour landed on her head.

CHAPTER 2

Atlee knelt next to the woman covered in flour. "Are you okay?" He didn't think she'd hit the floor that hard, but he liked to err on the side of caution. "Did you break anything?"

Flour sputtered out of her mouth. "Only *mei* dignity." She started to get to her feet. He held out his hand to help her up, but she ignored it. "I'm fine," she mumbled as she stood. She shook her head, and flour floated to the floor like powdery snow.

He grimaced. Not exactly the best way to make a first impression in Birch Creek. He'd called a taxi to take him from the bus station in Barton to Thomas's address. The driver, who looked to be barely old enough to drive, said he knew how to find where Thomas lived. After getting lost for nearly half an hour, Atlee asked the kid to drop him off in front of this house. When he saw a small business sign in the window, he decided to break down and ask for directions or he'd end up roaming around the county all night.

What he hadn't counted on was knocking over the very first person he met.

"I'm sorry," he said. "I didn't realize you were on the other side of the door."

She brushed her hands over her face, pale with white flour. Some of it had settled into the wrinkles at the corners of her blue eyes, which, along with the streaks of gray running through the brown hair peeking out from underneath the top of her *kapp,* hinted that her age might be close to his. Without thinking, he reached out and brushed off one of her shoulders, then jerked his hand back. "Sorry," he said again.

The woman sighed as she shook more flour off her dress. Then she looked up with a half-smile. "It's all right." Her tone was softer now. "Can't help that it was an accident. That seems to be the way of things around here lately."

Atlee found himself smiling back. He was glad she wasn't that upset. "I'll replace the flour."

She waved him off. "I've got plenty more in the pantry. You probably saved me from spilling it on the way home." A shadow passed over her eyes, but only for a second.

With a bright smile she said, "Welcome to Yoder's Bakery."

He looked around, noticing the gas ovens in the back of the house, which appeared to be stripped down to two large rooms. The one in the back was obviously the kitchen. It housed appliances and two large stainless-steel worktables. The room they were standing in was expansive, as if walls had been removed to create the space. Near the front door was another counter and what he assumed were two display cases, with plenty of room for lots of baked goods. Yet there wasn't a pie or cake to be seen.

"As you can see, we're not open for business yet. But we will be soon. Sorry I don't have anything to sell you."

"I'm not looking to buy anything. I'm a little . . . lost." Not something he could easily admit, but since he'd already embarrassed himself, there was no turning back now. "I'm looking for Thomas Bontrager's *haus.*"

"Oh, then you're not that lost." She licked her floury lips, then made a disgusted face before wiping the back of her hand over her mouth. "He's three houses down."

Figures. "I should have kept walking. Then I wouldn't have —"

"Turned me into a lump of flour?" She

looked at her hands, which were spotted white. After she brushed her palms together, she held out one slightly cleaner hand. "I'm Carolyn Yoder."

Atlee shook her hand, surprised by her firm handshake. He wasn't used to a forth-right woman. The women in his district were more subdued, and May had been the most subdued of all. She'd been petite. Soft. Quiet. Even timid at times. "Atlee Shetler," he said. "I'm a friend of Thomas's."

She gestured for him to follow her, walked to the sink in the kitchen, turned on the water, and started washing her hands. "Nice to meet you." Then she splashed water on her face. Eyes closed, she turned off the tap and reached for the towel hanging on a hook nearby. When she kept missing it, he moved to hand it to her. *"Danki,"* she said, patting her face dry. "I can show you the way to Thomas's if you'd like. I live near the Bontragers', and I was on *mei* way home when . . ."

"I knocked you over." Now that her face was clean, he could see she was a rather striking woman. Possibly downright beauti-ful in her younger years. He blinked. He hadn't noticed a woman's looks since May died. "I can help you clean up this mess."

"I won't take long," she said as she lifted

the broom leaning against a wall of the kitchen and a dustpan from a peg beside it. She moved to the front area of the store.

"Allow me," he said as he caught up with her. Sweeping up the flour was the least he could do. He took the broom and went to work.

"You don't have to do that."

He ignored her and kept sweeping. "Dustpan?"

She gave it to him, and he made quick work of the pile of flour before dumping it into a trash can in the kitchen. He handed the broom and dustpan back to her.

Instead of looking grateful, she seemed annoyed. "As I said before, you didn't have to help me. I'm capable of cleaning up *mei* own bakery."

"I'm sure you are." He frowned. He hadn't meant to offend her. He also noticed a smudge of flour on her left cheek, but considering he'd irritated her, he didn't think it was a good idea to point it out.

She hung the broom and dustpan on the pegs and then turned to him. "I'll show you how to get to Thomas's."

"I'd appreciate that."

As she locked the front door, against his better judgment he asked, "Are you putting in a glass door?"

"What do you mean?"

"Usually businesses have glass doors instead of solid wooden ones. More inviting that way."

"Oh. I hadn't thought about that." She whipped a small pad and pencil out of her apron pocket, scribbled something down, and then tucked it back in the pocket. "*Danki* for the idea."

"You're welcome."

He followed her to the end of the driveway. "The Bontragers are on the left," she said, pointing south. You'll probably see a pack of *buwe* playing in the front yard."

Atlee nodded. "Thomas does have a large *familye*."

"Do you know him well?"

"He and I were friends when his *familye* lived in Fredericktown. He asked me if I wanted to come out here for a visit. I finally took him up on his offer."

Carolyn nodded. "And *yer* wife?"

His head dipped as he touched his beard. He couldn't bring himself to shave it off. "Passed. A long time ago."

"Oh." Her features softened. "I'm sorry."

He was used to hearing such sentiments. "*Danki,*" was all he could say.

"I'd better get home." She put her hands on her hips. "*Mei bruder* and his *familye* are expecting me for supper. I keep telling them I can fend for myself when it comes to meals. Been doing it for a long time now."

He nodded, a bit curious. Was she widowed too?

"Oh *nee.*" She scowled. "I forgot my purse." She reached in the pocket of her apron for the keys. "Don't wait for me. *Geh* on and see *yer* friends." She started to head back to the bakery.

"*Danki* for showing me the way," he called out to her.

She waved and went back to the house.

Atlee paused, watching as she unlocked and opened the door, then disappeared inside the small bakery. Nice woman, and unlike him, she'd made a good first impression. For some reason, that made him smile.

Carolyn cringed at her reflection in her brother's bathroom mirror. She thought she'd removed all the flour from her face back at the bakery, but there was still a smudge on her cheek. She leaned over and washed her whole face. As she patted it dry with a hand towel that smelled like it had just come off the clothesline, she looked in the mirror again.

She didn't usually take much time to focus on herself, especially now that she was older. Mostly she used a mirror to make sure she looked halfway presentable. But lately she'd noticed the years creep up in the wrinkles and creases on her skin. She wasn't a vain woman, but a pink hue formed on her cheeks as she suddenly thought of Atlee.

He seemed like a nice man. Handsome too, and from the patches of gray in his beard, she could tell he was near her age. Since he had a beard, she'd assumed he was married. And perhaps he thought he was, even in his wife's death. He wouldn't be the first person to lose a spouse and stay loyal to the memory of their marriage.

What was she doing, thinking so much about Atlee? That wasn't like her. She'd come to terms with her singleness a long time ago, much like Cevilla Schlabach, the elderly but spry woman who moved here while Carolyn was away. Although she'd kept her distance from most of the women in the community so far, she'd gotten to know Cevilla a little bit. They were two single women in a town filled with married women and an overflow of young bachelors. Like Cevilla seemed to be, she was content with her life. Except for the bakery right now. But once that was launched and successful, she would be happy, truly happy, for the first time in her life.

She hung up the towel and went downstairs. Supper smelled heavenly, and her stomach started to growl. "Meat loaf?" she asked, going to Mary, who was pulling fresh rolls from the oven. She'd forgotten the ones she intended to bring home! But these looked good enough to sell in the bakery. She'd have to mention that to Mary. Her sister-in-law was welcome to sell anything she'd like — except donuts. Those were off-limits. "What do you need me to do?"

Mary set the cookie sheet on top of the stove. "*Nix.* Judah made the salad a little while ago, and the potatoes are already whipped." Mary turned and looked at the table. "Oh. You could pour the drinks."

"Sure thing." Carolyn went to the gas-powered fridge and got out the milk and iced tea. Judah, the youngest Yoder, was the only one who still drank milk. The older boys, Seth and Ira, drank tea like the rest of them. All three boys were outside with their father, helping him finish up the day's farm work.

"How was *yer* day?" Mary asked as she put the rolls in a tea towel–lined basket.

Carolyn set down Judah's glass of milk. "Every time I turn around, something's wrong with the building." *Oops.* She hadn't meant to say that out loud.

"Maybe you shouldn't have bought such an old *haus*," Mary said, giving her an overly sweet smile.

Carolyn blanched, mentally reminding herself to keep her mouth shut about her problems. But she had to acknowledge that Mary was right, and Mary had tried to warn her about purchasing the property too. So had Freemont. But she'd been so excited to find a place within walking distance of her home. The allure of a short commute, not to mention the eagerness of the seller — who had wanted to get rid of the house, given her a good deal, and told her converting it to anything she wanted would be "easy-peasy" — had clouded her decision a bit. Okay, a lot.

Also, she hadn't thought about how the road in front didn't get much traffic. Some families like the Chupps and the Bontragers, who at least had a passel of kids, lived on this road, but unless word of mouth alone could make her business successful, she'd have to figure out how to attract other customers. And now Atlee had pointed out the need for a new door. There was another hit to her dwindling bank account.

"It will be okay, though," she said, injecting as much confidence into her words as possible. Not only for Mary's benefit, but for her own. She wouldn't admit defeat.

"Carolyn," Mary said, her tone a little sharp. "I don't understand why you won't accept any help."

She turned Judah's milk glass, pretending to be concerned with how it sat on the table.

Mary sighed, walked over, and put one hand on her shoulder. "You moved back to the community, but you refuse to be a part of it."

Carolyn stiffened. Yes, she held herself at a distance from everyone here. But she had her reasons. Although Birch Creek had plenty of new residents, and some of the former ones had left, enough people here remembered the past to make her uncomfortable. She didn't want them to see the old Carolyn, who had been rebellious and petulant, at least according to Emmanuel Troyer, the former bishop. She would prove to them, and herself, that she had changed. Making her bakery a success would go a long way in doing that.

And if she asked for help now, everyone would know about all her problems. Just thinking about her failures being public made her chest tighten.

Her brother and nephews came in, and she let out a breath as Mary went back to the stove. As Carolyn had thought with her nieces, she couldn't believe how much her nephews had grown, and not just physically. Seth, who was eighteen, had taken on more of the farm's responsibilities. Ira, sixteen, was quiet, but had a sweet personality. Judah, eight, was more rambunctious and adventurous, but he pitched in without complaint. Yes, her brother had a great family, and she was grateful he'd made her a part of it.

After everyone had washed up and taken their seats, they bowed their heads in silent prayer. Carolyn didn't focus on asking God to bless the food. *Please make* mei *bakery a success* had been her prayer ever since she'd come back. So far God seemed to be doing the exact opposite.

"Something wrong?"

She opened her eyes to see Freemont looking at her. *"Nee,"* she said, forcing a smile. "Everything's wonderful."

He raised a skeptical brow but didn't say anything further.

Carolyn focused on her supper, listening to the chatter of the boys as they inhaled the meat loaf, potatoes, stewed tomatoes, homemade pickles, and fresh rolls with butter, then asked for seconds. When she looked up, she saw Mary and Freemont exchange a soft glance. She felt a tiny pinch in her heart, but it wasn't envy. Longing, perhaps. But that was quickly replaced with peace at being surrounded by family.

After helping Mary clean up, she went outside and sat on the patio, looking at the stars and sipping a cool glass of lemonade. She enjoyed this time of night when she usually settled in and had personal time with the Lord, something she'd been too busy to do much of lately. Her days and evenings had been filled with working, thinking, and, yes, worrying about the bakery. *"Do not be anxious about anything . . ."* She knew the verse from Philippians well, but she couldn't seem to apply it lately. She also missed having time to take long walks and commune with nature, which had always been one of her favorite things to do. Instead she felt like she was balled up in a knot most of the time.

"Am I intruding?"

She turned and saw Freemont standing behind her, what looked like a mug of steaming coffee in his hand even though it was still hot outside. *"Nee,"* she said, gesturing to the seat next to her. "Of course not."

He sat down and took a sip. From his side profile she could see he was pensive. *Uh-oh.* When her brother looked like this, she knew he had something weighing on his mind. "Are you all right?" she asked.

He looked startled at the question. "*Ya.* I was about to ask you the same thing."

"Again?" She looked out into the yard. "I already told you everything is fine."

"Then why are you so worried?"

He could be so annoying, especially when it came to recognizing her moods so easily. She wanted to tell him to mind his own business. But she couldn't do that. She couldn't lie to him either. "I'm just going through a rough patch. That's all."

"About being back home?"

She paused. Home. Nappanee had been her home for eighteen years, and she had expected to miss it. But she didn't, despite the reminders of the past still here in Birch Creek that should make her want to go back to Indiana. "*Nee.* I'm . . . glad to be home." Another honest answer, but she wasn't going to elaborate.

"*Gut.*" He tapped on the side of his mug. After a long silence he said, "If you ever want to talk about what's bothering you, I'm here."

She chuckled. "You're offering to have a meaningful discussion with *yer* little *schwester*?" She gave him a side look. "How things have changed."

He grinned, although he looked a little uncomfortable. "I've changed because I've had to. Being responsible for the community does that to a person."

That made her sober immediately. "I can see that. You're doing well, Freemont."

He didn't look at her. "I appreciate you saying that. It's only because of the Lord's help."

"The Lord knows *gut* character. And a *gut* heart."

He drained the rest of his coffee and stood. She could see he was pleased, and she knew he was too humble not to change the subject. "Better get to bed," he said. "Sunrise comes early in the summer."

She nodded, grateful for his company and his decision not to bring up the past. She wasn't ready to talk to him about it, and he seemed to accept that. *"Gute nacht."*

Carolyn lingered outside after Freemont left. Despite her brother's discretion, her memories came to the surface. She gripped her glass and pushed them down. But she knew from experience that no matter what she did, they were never far from her mind.

CHAPTER 3

"I have to say, I'm surprised you took me up on *mei* invitation."

Atlee settled back in a comfortable hickory rocker on the front porch and took a bite of an oatmeal butterscotch cookie Thomas's wife had baked. Inside she was wrangling several young boys, making sure they washed up and said their prayers before climbing into bed. The activity of the house made him tired, but it also infused him with a little joy. He and May couldn't have children, and although he had come to terms with that, sometimes he wondered how he would have been as a father. He knew without a doubt May would have been a wonderful mother. "I'm more surprised you wanted to see me," he said, focusing on the conversation.

"Why? Because the bishop took advantage of you when you were in a low spot?" Thomas shook his head. "That *mann* has *nee* business being a bishop."

Atlee agreed, but there was nothing anyone could do about it. And it felt a little wrong to criticize someone who had been chosen by God to lead the community. But why would a man led by God think it was a good idea for Atlee to marry Thomas's daughter, Phoebe, who was nearly thirty years younger than him? "I'm glad you don't hold that against me," he said.

"Phoebe doesn't either, because it wasn't *yer* doing. When Joseph Weaver proposed that nonsense and then tried to force the marriage, I knew we had to leave. The Lord brought me and *mei familye* to the right place, and Phoebe is married to a *gut mann.*"

"I'm glad to hear it." After the Bontragers left, there had been whispers throughout the community that Thomas had defied God and that was why his farm had struggled for so long. But Atlee had never believed them. He'd known Thomas for a long time. The man had been there for him when May died, and he had understood why Atlee couldn't move on as fast as everyone expected him to. Thomas's faith was as strong as that of anyone he knew. Atlee had missed his friendship over the past two years. "I've been wondering. Why are you going by

447

Thomas now?"

"Thomas was *mei vatter*'s name." He paused. "I'm not sure this will make sense, but I started a new life here. The old Jesse is gone. When I moved here, I decided to make a completely fresh start."

It did make sense to Atlee, even though he'd never heard of someone doing such a thing. He knew there were God-ordained name changes in the Bible, like Abram to Abraham and Jacob to Israel. He didn't see anything wrong with what Thomas had done. It was his name, after all. "You're happy here, then, *ya?*"

"Happy and thriving. I'll admit, I used to wonder if God was punishing me and *mei familye,* like Joseph said."

When May died, the bishop had alluded to a lack of faith — not on Atlee's part, but on May's. "Perhaps she should have prayed harder for healing," Joseph had said. His comment had angered Atlee so much he almost left the community right then. But he couldn't leave May, and there was always the niggling thought in the back of his mind that maybe *he* hadn't prayed hard enough for his wife. If his faith had been stronger, maybe she would still be here. God was in the business of doing miracles, after all. *Yet he didn't do one for May.*

"But I realized I was wrong. Trials will come *nee* matter what. That's what happens in a fallen world." Thomas paused. "I know how hard May's death has been on you," he said, as if the man could read Atlee's thoughts. "But I'm glad you decided to come visit."

"I'm not sure what I'm going to do while I'm here," he said. "I can't say that I know much about farming, but I'm glad to help you any way I can."

"Help is one thing we have plenty of." He explained to Atlee about his role in his son-in-law Jalon's farming business. "The *kinner* are taking right to it, much more than they did back in Fredericktown. But you're welcome to pitch in if you want." He pressed his palms on the arms of the rocker. "How long you planning to stay?"

"A few days, tops."

"You can extend that, you know."

Although he'd been here for only a few hours, he was already feeling more relaxed. Yet the Bontragers' house was full, and he felt like an intruder. He'd also lived alone for so many years that he wasn't used to so many people and so much activity. "I appreciate the offer."

After a long moment of silence, Thomas stood. "I'm heading inside. Early day tomorrow, like all of them. See you in the morning."

Atlee nodded his good-bye, then stared off into the distance at the beautiful farmland surrounding him. According to Thomas, it hadn't always been so nice here, but Jalon Chupp and his cousin, along with help from their combined families, had turned this stretch of land into something prosperous. He had to admit it was encouraging to see. He had felt stuck in a deep rut for so long. And lately, even the community around him wasn't just suffocating to him, but also stagnant. Seeing progress and success was invigorating.

He got up from his chair and headed down the road. He wasn't ready for bed just yet. Maybe a walk would tire him out. A brisk walk was also a habit he'd gotten into the past couple of years. The exercise helped him clear his head while filling his soul.

Along the way, he stopped in front of Carolyn's bakery. Nothing about the outside of the house made it look inviting, or even like a place of business. He still felt a little guilty about knocking her over. Maybe he could do some landscaping for her, or help her replace the front door. Although he was a cabinetmaker, he was pretty good at most repair jobs — much better than he was at farming.

Then again, he should probably mind his own business. She was a capable woman, something she didn't hesitate to point out. She probably wouldn't accept his help even if he offered it. He shoved his hands into his pockets and headed farther down the road, putting Carolyn and her bakery out of his mind.

But the next morning Atlee made the short trek to Carolyn's bakery. He'd fought with himself during his walk last night, then while he was falling asleep, and again this morning. Finally, he made the decision to come here. He could at least offer to help her with something, if only to ease his conscience.

As he walked to the front door, he again noticed the small handwritten sign in the corner of the picture window. Yoder's Bakery. She'd need something bigger than that to get folks' attention. Unlike last night, the solid front door was open, though the screen door was shut. He was about to knock when he heard something that sounded like a screeching cat.

"Just a closer walk with theeeeeeee . . ."

Atlee froze. Was that singing? He recognized the English hymn, but not the tune.

"Grant it, Jesus, is my pleeeeeeeea . . ."

He didn't think it was possible, but the singing was getting worse as it went along. He peeked through the screen and saw Carolyn back in the kitchen, her hands deep inside a metal bowl as the squalling words came out of her mouth.

"Daily walking close to theeeeeeee . . ."

He stuck his finger in his ear and gave it a twist. Hopefully she didn't sing that loud in church services. God wasn't deaf. He knocked on the doorframe. When she didn't respond, he knocked louder.

"Let it be, Lord, let it —" She stilled, her hands in the bowl, then looked toward the front door. She cleared her throat. "We're not open to the public yet," she called in English.

Opening the screen door, he said, "Can I come in?"

Carolyn nodded. She cleared her throat again as he came into the kitchen. "Hello, Mr. Shetler. What brings you by?" she said as she resumed mixing the contents in the bowl.

He gripped the tool belt he'd borrowed from Thomas. "I came to see if you need any help."

She looked at him, her eyebrows raised. "You're offering to help me bake?"

He shook his head. "I wouldn't want to

452

chase *yer* customers away."

"*Nee* worries about that right now." She sighed and took her hands out of the bowl. Thick clumps of floury dough stuck to her fingers. She pulled off each one, then wiped her hands on a nearby towel. "I'm not sure how you could help me. I'm sorry you brought *yer* tool belt for nothing."

"I could rehang that screen door."

"What's wrong with it?"

"It's crooked. Off by half an inch, I suspect."

Her brows raised again. "You can tell that just by looking?"

She stepped from behind the table when he nodded, and he turned and went back to the front. The doorframe, like the rest of the house, he thought, had good bones. He put on his tool belt.

"You don't have to —"

"Won't take me but a minute." He started taking off the door's hinges.

"But . . ."

He glanced over his shoulder as she went back to the kitchen. He saw the frown on her face. Not that he was surprised, but at least she was letting him fix the door for her.

When he finished, he turned around and saw that she was rolling out the dough on the table, now covered in flour. "What are you making?" he asked as he walked back into the kitchen.

"Chocolate-and-orange bread twists." When he arched his brow, she smiled and added, "It's one of *mei* specialties."

She had a pretty smile, he had to admit, and he was glad she wasn't frowning anymore. He was also impressed with how efficiently and quickly she worked. Clearly, she was an expert baker. The only thing that seemed to be holding her back was the state of her bakery. "I don't believe I've ever heard of chocolate-and-orange bread."

"Then you can be *mei* first taste tester. I need to give one of my ovens one more trial run before I call the repairman back out here."

There was something wrong with her oven too? "Since I'm here with *mei* tool belt, is there anything else that needs repairing?"

"What doesn't need fixing?" he thought he heard her mumble. She wiped her hand across her cheek, then shook her head. "*Nee,* I'm fine."

"So everything else is in working order?"

She bit the corner of her bottom lip. "Well, the pantry shelves are crooked, but I'm going to fix those while the bread twists rise. *Mei* nephews, Judah and Ira, hung them for me. Bless them, they're *gut* at farming, but not at hanging shelves. *Mei bruder* insisted they do it, though." She lifted her chin. "Not that I needed them to."

Wow, she was a stubborn woman. But he could be stubborn too. "I'll take a look at them."

"I can rehang them myself."

But he was already walking to the back of the kitchen. "I pretty much expected you to say that. I assume the pantry is over here?"

She hurried to him. "I don't need *yer* help, Mr. Shetler."

"Atlee. And I heard you the first time." He turned and faced her, noticing another spot of flour on her cheek. "But since I don't make knocking over women a habit, fixing *yer* door and shelves is the least I can do."

Her face twisted into a scowl. "I'm capable of doing it myself."

"Did you hang the screen door *yerself?*"

Her cheeks reddened as her scowl deepened. *"Ya."*

"You did a pretty *gut* job." The door hadn't been that crooked. He lowered his voice. "To be honest, I could use something to do while I'm in Birch Creek."

"Why? You came here to visit Thomas."

"*Ya,* but he's busy with the farm during the day, and he's got plenty of help there. He doesn't need me."

"Neither do I."

Ouch. Fine. She didn't need him, so he wouldn't bother her anymore. "Got it," he said, brushing past her so fast he was surprised he hadn't knocked her down again. Even if he had, he would have helped her up — or tried — and nothing more. She'd made her point loud and clear.

"Atlee, wait."

He paused at the front door. He should walk out and leave her to her own devices. She and the bakery weren't his problem. But he couldn't do that. Not without hearing her out first. He turned. "What?"

She rushed to him and hung her head. "I'm sorry." She looked up at him. "You're right. I'm just not . . ." She blew out a breath. "I'm just not used to letting people help me."

He found that odd, considering one of the most important commandments in the Bible was to love and care for your neighbor, and the Amish took that seriously. Then again, he understood pushing people away. He'd done enough of that over the years.

"I shouldn't have been so rude to you," she added. "If you still want to fix the

456

shelves, I would appreciate it."

He relaxed and smiled. "I'll be happy to do it."

"But only if I pay you."

He held up his hand. "Now, wait a minute, I didn't say anything about paying me —"

"You could be *mei* employee. *Mei* first one. Although come to think of it, I should be interviewing potential clerks by now." She took out her small pad of paper and wrote something on it with the pencil stub.

"Carolyn, I . . ." She was smiling, and there was a sparkle in her eyes. He had the urge to brush the flour dust off her cheek.

His face heated. Was he blushing? He hadn't blushed since he was a youth. Nah, it had to be the heat from the oven and the hot summer morning.

"The pantry is where you were headed." She flashed him another smile as she pointed. "The two battery-powered sensor lights on the ceiling should come on when you walk in."

His mind was whirling a bit, and not only because, somehow, he'd managed to become a hired hand for Carolyn Yoder. He was still taken by her smile, and the warm feeling stirring inside him couldn't be blamed on the kitchen or the season. He hadn't felt anything like this since he first met May.

May. This was the first time he'd thought of her since waking up this morning. That jolted him back to his senses. "I, uh, better get to work, then."

"Me too. Those bread twists aren't going to bake themselves." She headed for the kitchen, and he caught himself watching her walk away. He shook his head. She had thrown him for a loop, that was all. He'd fix the shelves, accept whatever payment she offered, and be on his way.

Yet he couldn't help but notice that one of the planks in the center of the floor was loose. When he happened to glance at the ceiling, he saw a stain on the drywall. Why hadn't the community helped her fix everything? She seemed to be alone in trying to get her business off the ground. But from what she said, and how she reacted to him earlier, it had to be her own fault.

CHAPTER 4

Carolyn leaned against the table, tempted to break out in song again. But she decided against it. She knew Atlee had heard her singing — or caterwauling, as Freemont called it when they were growing up. She also could tell he was trying to hide his stunned expression. He was a polite man, after all. But even though she couldn't carry a tune if someone handed her a bucket, she loved to sing church hymns, and she often did when she was alone. They comforted her, much like baking did. They also made her happy.

She paused, guilt washing over her because of the way she'd treated Atlee, remembering the shocked look on his face when she said she didn't need him. And she didn't. But she also didn't want to hurt his feelings, and she knew she had. The only way to make it right was to let him fix the shelves. And when she came up with the idea to pay him, she felt much better about him working on the repairs.

She went back to making the bread twists. She shouldn't be baking right now. The Lord knew she had plenty of other things to do. But she needed to make sure the oven wasn't functioning properly before she forked out money for another repair visit.

Quickly, she twisted the soft dough that held flecks of dried orange zest. Once they were baked, she would drizzle chocolate on top of them. At Christmas she made them extra special by adding small pieces of candied orange peel on top, but she didn't have time for that level of detail right now.

By the time she was ready to check the oven temperature, Atlee had reappeared. "That was a quick job," he said. "The shelves weren't in bad shape. *Yer* nephews did *gut* work."

"They'll be happy to hear that. *Mei bruder* will too." She felt the heat from the oven. This time it was close enough to 350 degrees. She relaxed her tensed shoulders. Maybe it wouldn't need to be repaired after all. She reached for the twists, her arm brushing Atlee's. "Sorry," she said, grabbing the tray. She looked up at him and was surprised to find him gazing at her.

"*Nee* problem."

He didn't move, and neither did she. She couldn't stop looking at him. Deep-set blue eyes that resembled slate. Average height, but several inches taller than her. His hair was a little on the long side, and she could see the salt-and-pepper strands threaded through the dark brown waves coming from under his hat.

Suddenly he grabbed the other end of the tray. "Looked like you might drop it."

She glanced down and saw she *was* losing her grip. *Not to mention* mei *senses.* Carolyn nodded her thanks and hurried to put the twists in the oven. Heat blasted her already hot cheeks.

"I noticed a few more things that need some attention," he said.

She shut the oven door, set the timer, and took a calming breath. She didn't need to pay any mind to Atlee's nice hair or blue eyes. She needed to get her focus back on track. She turned around, squaring her shoulders and giving him what she hoped was her most businesslike expression. "Such as?"

"There's a stain on the ceiling for starters."

"Oh."

"Then there's the uneven floorboard and the exterior trim to be painted. Also, you need some decent landscaping in the front. A bigger sign too. You have to make this place inviting to *yer* customers both inside and out."

All those things were on her list, except for the landscaping. And the sign. She resisted the urge to dig her pad out of her pocket. "I suppose you can fix all that too?"

"It will take a couple of days, but *ya*. I can take care of it."

"You seem to know about running a business."

"Used to have *mei* own cabinetry shop. I also did retail for a couple of years. But that was a long time ago. Before . . . before May, *mei* wife, and I got married."

She saw a shadow of grief pass in front of his eyes. She took a step toward him. "She must have been a wonderful woman."

"She was." He glanced away, his mouth tugging into a sad frown. Then he looked at her again. "When are you planning to open up shop?"

"In two weeks." She steeled herself for his questioning look.

He remained impassive. "All right. What do you want me to start on first?"

Carolyn was relieved he didn't interrogate her further about her deadline. But his next question gave her pause. It was bad enough

462

that he was discovering all the problems she was dealing with. Now she had to admit her financial situation. "I can't afford to pay you for all that work." Maybe for one or two jobs, but definitely not the landscaping. That would take extra money she didn't have to spare. She was learning the hard way how difficult it was to open a bakery, and she felt foolish for not planning better.

"Then don't pay me," he said. "Problem solved."

"But you're *mei* employee."

"Okay, I quit."

That made her laugh, and it felt good. "I still can't let you do all that work without compensation."

"Hmm." He sniffed the air. "The bread twists smell *gut.*"

"You want me to pay you in baked goods?"

"That would be great for *mei* taste buds, but not *mei* waistline." He patted his flat abdomen.

Carolyn snapped her fingers. "I know. I could teach you how to bake."

His brow went up. "A baking lesson?"

"*Ya,*" she said, warming up to the idea. "You don't know how to bake, do you?"

"I can barely cook."

"Everyone needs to learn how to make cookies, at least. Or fry pies."

He scratched his chin through his beard. "I do like a *gut* fry pie."

She smiled. "I'll teach you how to make them in exchange for repairing the ceiling and floorboard."

"Don't forget the landscaping and painting."

She shook her head. "One baking lesson isn't going to cover all that."

He looked thoughtful. "All right, how about this? I'll do it all" — he held up his hand when she started to protest — "and after *yer* bakery is open and you've made a little money, you can pay me."

"But you won't be here."

"I'll give you *mei* address and you can send me a check."

She leaned against the table. "You trust me to do that?"

He tilted his head and looked at her. "Of course."

Carolyn put out her hand. "Then we have a deal."

He shook her hand. "I'll get started on the floorboard."

She watched as he went to the broken floorboard and pulled a claw hammer from his tool belt. She blew out a long breath. He was right. A building free of problems, spruced up, and with nice landscaping would entice customers — who would then, hopefully, enjoy her baked goods enough to spread the word around the area. As far as the community — well, their coming would be hit or miss, especially the long-term residents. She was certain Emmanuel Troyer had poisoned some of them against her.

Emmanuel. She didn't want to think about him. He'd disappeared from Birch Creek, and from all accounts no one knew where he was. She did feel sorry for his wife, Rhoda, a nice woman who didn't deserve such a cruel husband. Mary mentioned that Rhoda still held hope for Emmanuel's return. It might not be Christian of her, but Carolyn hoped she'd never see the man again.

She'd tried to forget the harsh words he'd flung at her before she left the community, but even in Nappanee they were never far from her mind. *Rebellious. Useless. Stupid. Homely.* She was none of those, and she knew that. Although she wasn't exactly a looker. But those words had wounded her so deeply that although some had become merely scars, others had never fully healed.

Opening the bakery and making it a success would give her the confidence and respectability she was missing. She wasn't that odd, misfit young woman anymore. The time had come for everyone to see that.

After Atlee finished fixing the floorboard, he found a few others in the bakery that needed nailing down. Several times while he worked, he glanced at Carolyn as she finished making the bread twists. She seemed to be in a better mood now — humming, even, as she drizzled melted chocolate over the twists, which smelled amazing. At least she wasn't singing. But remembering her enthusiasm as she sang that hymn made him smile. God didn't care about pitch accuracy. It was the heart behind the singing that mattered.

Even though they'd agreed he would do only certain jobs, he decided to make a thorough inspection of the property while Carolyn worked in the pantry. Fortunately, the plumbing was okay, but the sink in the small bathroom had a long crack in it, and it would eventually have to be replaced or it would leak. After making a mental note of a few repair jobs on the inside, he went outside to inspect the landscaping — or lack thereof. It would take a while for him to thoroughly weed out the front flower beds.

At one time this house must have been a great place to live, and he could envision it being a nice bakery. But he was skeptical of

Carolyn's two-week deadline. Even with his help, he wasn't sure how this place could open for business in that amount of time — unless she had other people pitching in to finish the rest of the work. He didn't even know if she had a business license, although with a bakery this small, she might not need one.

The screen door squeaked as she stepped outside from the back of the house. He'd have to remember to oil that later. "The floor looks terrific," she said.

He nodded his thanks. "Nothing a few nails couldn't fix." He took a step toward her. "Everything else will take longer, obviously."

Her shoulders slumped a little. "I know."

"Got anyone else helping you out?"

She crossed her arms as she lifted her chin. "*Nee.* Like I said, I can —"

"Do this *yerself.* Right." Amazing how she could switch from relaxed to defensive in a split second. She wasn't going to like his next question either. "Did you have an inspection before you bought this place?"

She bit her bottom lip. "Um, *nee.*"

"Has anyone looked at the roof or the foundation?"

Her cheeks turned light pink, and she shook her head. "Inspections cost money."

The morning sun beat down on the back of his neck. It was going to be a hot one today. "They can also save you money in the long run."

"Fine," she said. "I'll get an inspection. I'm not stupid, you know."

"I never said you were." He approached her, wanting to extinguish the defensive spark in her eyes. "I'm sorry if I made it seem that way."

She looked away. "It's not *yer* fault. And I haven't been as smart as I should have been with *mei* business venture." Then she looked up at him. "But that doesn't mean I'm a failure. I bought this place on *mei* own. I painted both the interior and exterior walls, refinished the floors, purchased and brought in the tables, had the ovens installed, cleaned the windows —"

"I get the picture." Where was all this defensive defiance coming from? "Carolyn, you're not a failure. There's always a learning curve when it comes to running a business. I made plenty of mistakes with mine." He was glad to see the strain at the corners of her mouth ease.

"I'm sorry." Her voice was soft as she uncrossed her arms. "I keep snapping at you, and that's not right. *Mei bruder* did check the plumbing and took out the wiring, but he also told me I should have gotten an inspection. I should have listened."

"You'll know next time."

"There won't be a next time." She looked up at him, her eyes a beautiful shade of light blue. "This is *mei* only chance."

Only chance? What did that mean? And why couldn't he stop looking at her? She was completely different from May, not only in temperament but in appearance too. May had been slight, while Carolyn was plump. May was close to his height, Carolyn a few inches shorter. May would be forever young in his memories, while Carolyn's round face showed her age. But in that moment, the past didn't matter. It barely grazed his mind.

"I promised you some bread twists," she said, her gaze still holding his.

"*Ya.* You did."

She rubbed her lips together. "They're probably still warm."

"It is hot out today." He kept his eyes on her.

The pink hue on her cheeks deepened. "Then we should *geh* inside." She turned and walked into the bakery's kitchen.

The screen door squeaked shut and he blinked. What just happened? He touched his own face, feeling the heat there. Yes, it was hot outside. But that wasn't why his face felt like it was on fire, or why his pulse was only now starting to slow back to normal. None of this made sense. It was as if he were attracted to Carolyn Yoder. That couldn't be possible, because he had always been sure May was the only woman for him. He went inside, tamping down his confused emotions.

Carolyn was placing a bread twist on a paper plate as he approached her, and he put whatever happened outside out of his mind. "Here you *geh,*" she said as she handed it to him. Atlee took a bite as she walked over to an orange watercooler on a small table in the back corner of the kitchen. She took a paper cup from the stack next to it and filled it. Then she handed it to him.

He took a drink. Fresh water and a delicious bread twist that practically melted in his mouth. What more could he ask for? "This is *appeditlich,*" he said. "There's a hint of both orange and chocolate, but nothing overpowering. It's a great combination." When she smiled at his compliment, his heart lurched. So much for pretending.

"I'm glad you like it," she said, taking a cloth and wiping crumbs off the table.

"Aren't you having one?"

She shook her head. "I'm not hungry. Besides, I could stand to lose a few pounds."

Her comment drew his gaze to her figure, which he thought was just fine.

"I did have to check the oven again, but maybe I shouldn't have spent so much time testing recipes the last few days." She straightened her apron. "I just want everything to be perfect."

He set down the twist. "It will be, Carolyn." He didn't know why he was compelled to make the promise, but right now he would do anything to erase the defeat on her face.

"Do you know how to do inspections?" She rubbed her finger across the edge of the stainless-steel table, not looking at him.

"I'm not licensed. But I could check the roof and foundation. I can spot major problems, but you'll still want to have a professional do a thorough walk-through at some point."

Carolyn looked at him. "I will, once I have some money coming in."

He was about to tell her that it would be a while before she'd make a profit, but now wasn't the time to point that out.

"How much for the inspection?" she asked.

"It will cost you another baking lesson."

She chuckled. "I haven't given you the first one. You might not like baking."

471

"Or I might love it."

That made her laugh, which brought a grin to her face. Which made him notice her smile, which then amped up his heart rate. This time he didn't bother fighting it. This was the most alive he'd felt since May's death. Being able to help Carolyn achieve her goal and making her smile took the edge off his loneliness. He wasn't ready to let go of that great feeling just yet.

CHAPTER 5

I've never met a mann *like him.*

Carolyn stood in the backyard while Atlee inspected the roof. He'd already looked at the foundation and hadn't seen any problems there, which was a huge relief. She'd told him about the fallen shingles before he climbed up on the roof, and hopefully he wouldn't find anything else wrong with it.

She should be in the phone shanty calling the local paper and putting out an ad for bakery help. Karen and Ivy had offered to work for her for free, but she'd turned them down. Probably a dumb decision, like a lot of the other decisions she'd made lately, but she couldn't ask them to change their minds now. Besides, she'd set aside some money to hire and pay two people for at least a month.

But instead of calling the paper, she was watching Atlee, praying silently he wouldn't fall. He was in good shape, but neither of them were spring chickens, and it would take only one slip for him to fall off the roof. She couldn't live with herself if that happened. This man had planned to be on vacation, and now he was doing all this work for her — which not only touched her but confused her. Why was he so eager to help her? She was a stranger to him, and they had only their Amish faith in common.

He was also attractive, something she couldn't stop focusing on while he was inspecting the roof.

He was up there only a few minutes, but it felt longer. Finally, he descended the ladder. When his feet touched the ground, she went to him, thankful he wasn't injured. "Are you okay?" The question flew out of her mouth before she realized it.

"I'm fine." He pushed his hat from his forehead, and she saw the perspiration on his skin. Today was the hottest one yet, and a twinge of guilt hit her.

"I'll get you a drink," she said, rushing inside. She filled another cup with water and was prepared to take it outside when she heard the squeak of the screen door. She'd meant to oil that last week.

When she gave him the drink, he downed it, then smiled.

Such a warm smile. Her palms grew damp,

and she thrust her hands behind her.

"Other than the missing shingles, the roof looks *gut*. And since I didn't see any problems with the foundation, it probably won't take me more than a week to finish up here."

"Really?" Hope filled her heart.

"Really." He grinned again.

"But I don't want to take up all *yer* time here in Birch Creek. What about Thomas and his *familye*?"

"I can extend *mei* stay."

"Isn't there someone waiting for you back home?"

His gaze met hers. The same shadow that passed over his eyes when he mentioned his late wife had returned.

He tilted his head. "What about you?"

She looked at the hardwood floor and the tip of her shoe, realizing he didn't answer her question. She was prudent enough not to pry. "What about me?"

"Anyone . . . special?"

An incomplete question, but she caught his meaning. "Oh yeah," she said, looking up at him and laughing. "I've got men lined up at the door for me." Her laugh faded at his serious look. Her choice to laugh off her nervousness had been the wrong one. "*Nee*. There's *nee* one special."

The corner of his lips lifted, but she wasn't

sure what that meant. Was he glad to hear she wasn't married or dating? But that didn't make any sense. He still had his beard, and he was clearly devoted to his late wife. She had been a blessed woman to have that kind of loyalty. No, he wasn't interested in her. He was a kind man who lived out his faith. She shouldn't read anything else into it.

"I'll need to get some supplies," he said. "Landscaping material, something to patch the ceiling, some paint, that kind of stuff. If you tell me where I can get those things, I'll pick them up this afternoon and bring them over tomorrow."

"There's a hardware store and a nursery in Barton. You'll need to hire a taxi to get there." The bill was adding up, and he hadn't even started working.

"*Nee* problem. Can you recommend a driver?"

She bit her bottom lip. "Actually, I haven't used too many taxis since I've been here."

"How long is that?"

"Two months."

"Ah." He adjusted his hat again. "Now it's all making sense."

She frowned. "What is?"

"Why the community isn't helping you, other than *yer bruder* and nephews. I'm sure

476

it's hard moving to a new place, much less getting a business started."

"Uh . . ." She could let him think she was new to the community, but if he was staying here for more than a couple of days, he would probably find out the truth. She tried never to lie. "I'm from Birch Creek. I moved back here from Nappanee."

"Oh."

She started placing bread twists on a paper plate. "You can take these to the Bontragers," she said, hoping he'd get the hint that she wasn't going to tell him anything else.

"I'm sure they'll enjoy them."

Only when she finished covering the plate with plastic wrap did she look at him. "I'll get you a check for the supplies."

"I'll cover them. You can pay me back later."

She didn't answer him as she handed him the plate, and then she went to the small room next to the pantry. It had been a mudroom, but she converted most of it to a tiny office, leaving only the back door intact. She sat down at her desk and pulled out her checkbook. When she looked at the balance, she cringed. She'd have to make do with one employee to start, because she wasn't going to be any further indebted to

Atlee than she already was.

When she returned to the kitchen, she opened the checkbook. "How much do you need?"

"I'm not sure." He set the plate of twists on the table. "Seriously, you can pay me later."

She gave him a direct look. "How much?"

He paused, then told her an amount. She held back a wince and wrote out the check. "Here."

Atlee took it, his frown deepening. "Are you sure?"

"*Ya*. I'm sure."

"All right. I'll be back in the morning, then." He picked up the twists, gave her one last look, then walked into the outer room and through the front door.

She put her hands on the table and sighed. She had just enough money in her account to finish what was necessary to open the bakery — as long as nothing else went wrong. According to Atlee, she was so close to making her dream a reality. That lifted her spirits enough to allow her to set her worry to the side, at least for the time being.

At the end of the day, Carolyn was locking the front door when she saw Atlee walking up the driveway. What was he doing back? "Did something happen?" she said, going to him. She should have known something would go wrong.

He shook his head. "Everything's fine. I just came by to give you these." He handed her several door catalogs.

She wanted to sag against him with relief. She was so sure disaster would strike just as she was gaining hope. *I should have more faith than that.* "*Danki,* but you could have given these to me tomorrow morning."

"I thought you might want to look at them tonight." He swatted at a fly between them. "They have a lot of choices. How was *yer* afternoon?"

"*Gut.* I put an ad in the local paper for a cashier —"

"You're hiring outside the community?"

"*Ya.*" His question annoyed her. "Now, if you'll excuse me, I need to get home."

"Since you're walking today, mind if I walk with you? We're going in the same direction."

She looked up at him. Only one man had walked her home, and he had been a seventeen-year-old boy. Micah Hostetler. She'd had a crush on him for six months, even though she was almost twenty, and when he offered to walk her home from a singing, she couldn't believe it. That was shortly after she moved to Birch Creek with Freemont and Mary when they had newly married. None of them had known what they were getting into with Emmanuel Troyer.

"Carolyn?"

"Uh, sure. It's a free country." What was wrong with her? She sounded like a surly teenager. "I mean, *ya*. I'd appreciate the company."

The sun was low in the sky, but the temperature was still warm. Birds fluttered in the trees and chirped as they walked along the side of the road.

"Not too much traffic around here," Atlee said.

"Did you get the supplies you need?" She wasn't in the mood for him to point out her mistake in choosing this location.

"*Ya*. But I had to order the materials to fix the ceiling, and they're delivering a load of mulch here tomorrow. I picked out a few plants, but I wasn't sure what you wanted."

"I'm sure anything you choose will be fine. I've never been *gut* with plants."

Atlee slipped one hand into his pants pocket. "But *yer bruder* is a farmer."

"He has ten green fingers. Mine are all black."

"Doesn't affect *yer* baking skills."

She chuckled. "*Nee,* it doesn't."

They walked a little while longer, and she thought that would be the end of their conversation. Thomas's house wasn't that far, and she didn't expect him to walk with her to Freemont's. But when they were a few yards from the Bontragers', he said, "Why did you move back to Birch Creek?"

She gripped the catalogs in her hand. "To open a bakery."

"You didn't want to open one in Nappanee?"

Why was he being so nosy? But he was also helping her, so she felt she owed him some explanation. "I worked in the RV industry when I moved there. I needed a job, and even though the economy was difficult at the time, there was an opening, and I had to take the work I could get. The area has several bakeries, but they never hire outside their *familye* and friends." She tasted the bitterness of her words, and she wished she hadn't said anything.

"That's usually how it works, which is why I'm surprised you're hiring outside the community."

She'd had enough of his interrogation. "I can walk by myself from here," she said, quickening her steps.

"Carolyn, I'm . . ."

But she didn't answer him or turn around. He was getting too close, too personal, and they barely knew each other. But that wasn't the only reason she was rushing off. She had to get away from him before she told him everything. She could easily find herself doing that.

CHAPTER 6

Atlee whipped off his hat and batted at a horsefly, missing it completely. Why hadn't he kept his mouth shut? He was prying. He knew what it was like when people asked personal questions. He'd heard enough of those since May died. Everyone had expected him to move on, at least eventually, and when he didn't, they wanted to know why. They were concerned about him, yet that didn't make him any less resentful.

But he couldn't stop himself, and now he'd done the same thing to Carolyn. No wonder she took off the way she did. She'd probably fire him tomorrow.

He headed for Thomas's. If she did fire him, she'd be doing him a favor. Somehow, he'd become too involved with her and her bakery problems. It wasn't the work he minded, but he couldn't get her out of his thoughts while he was in Barton. Why did she seem so isolated? So defensive?

More puzzling, why did he care?

When he reached Thomas's driveway, he paused. He had to apologize to her, something he seemed to be doing often. But he had no one else to blame. She hadn't asked him for a single thing, other than the inspection, and that was after he inserted himself into her business. *Why, Lord? I spent twelve years keeping* mei *distance. Why can't I do that with Carolyn Yoder?*

He turned, and a few minutes later he was on the Yoders' front porch, wondering what he was going to say. Before he could knock on the door, it opened. A boy — around ten years old, he guessed — stepped onto the porch and looked at him. "Hi," he said.

"Hi." Atlee shifted on his feet. "Is, uh, Carolyn home?"

The boy poked his head inside. "*Aenti!* Some *mann* is here to see you." Then he ran past Atlee and down the porch steps.

Through the screen he heard footsteps. He swallowed, still unsure what to say. Carolyn appeared, and after hesitating she opened the door. "Judah could have at least invited you in."

"That's okay. I just wanted to apologize." Once he started talking, the words came tumbling out. "I should have minded *mei* own business. I usually do. Actually, I always do. I don't know why I kept on talking . . . or why I'm still talking now."

She stepped outside. "It's okay. I'm sure from the outside looking in, *mei* decisions seem nonsensical. And some of them are."

He didn't respond. He'd already made a big enough mess as it was.

She walked over to a small two-seater porch swing. She gave it a small push before she turned around. "I guess I should clear up a few things. You are *mei* employee, after all."

"Right." Although this was the strangest working relationship he'd ever been in.

"I left Birch Creek when I was twenty-seven." Her voice was low, and he had to move closer to hear her. "I planned to live here all *mei* life, but the bishop at the time . . ." She looked up at him. "He made it impossible."

He nodded. He knew all too well how difficult bishops could be, how they brought out helpless and conflicting emotions when they acted contrarily to God's Word. Carolyn hadn't said as much, but Atlee could read between the lines.

"He wanted me to marry a man of his choosing. All I wanted was to run a bakery."

"He tried to arrange a marriage for you?"

"He didn't get that far. Anyway, that's in

485

the past. When Freemont became bishop, he asked me to come back. I thought I could make a fresh start here, but I have to do it on *mei* own terms. And I hope you can accept the way I'm doing things, even if you don't agree with them."

"Carolyn." Atlee saw the pain in her eyes. Whatever went on between her and the former bishop hurt her deeply. "It doesn't matter what I think."

She didn't say anything as she went to the front door.

"I'll see you in the morning, then," he said, wishing he could go after her, knowing he couldn't, not understanding why he continued to be drawn to her.

"Ya," she said in a quiet tone. She opened the screen door. Unlike the one at the bakery, this one didn't squeak. She looked at him through the gray mesh. "It matters, Atlee."

"What does?"

"What you think. It matters to me." She went inside, the screen door shutting behind her.

Atlee had arrived in Birch Creek on Monday, and by Saturday morning he was ready to finish the landscaping. It wasn't an expert job by any stretch, since May had always done the gardening, but it was much better than it used to be. He'd even added a couple of hanging baskets from the eave, a big pot filled with impatiens for the large front stoop, and two window planters with more colorful annuals. They had cost a little more than what he quoted Carolyn, but he made up the difference, a little fact she didn't need to know.

As he worked on the repairs, painting, and landscaping, Carolyn had spent most of her time in the bakery, except when she was visiting the phone shanty to make calls. A couple of young English women had stopped by, and he assumed they were applying for the cashier job. But he didn't confirm that with Carolyn, and she didn't volunteer any information.

The only time they really talked was at lunchtime. Carolyn always brought enough packed lunch for them both, even though he said she didn't have to. Yet he looked forward to her delicious sandwiches made with fresh bread she baked herself. There was always a treat for dessert too — chocolate chip cookies, lemon meringue pie, banana bread — all of which she made in her bakery in the mornings. "I have to test all the recipes," she said, but he wondered about that. Not only had she admitted earlier in the week that she shouldn't be spending so much time testing recipes, but her baked goods were perfect. She worked so quickly and efficiently he thought she could bake in her sleep.

Then he realized baking was more than a job to her. It was a passion. Her customers would be happy to enjoy the fruits of her labor. He enjoyed her company during their lunches, and he'd also taken to walking her home after the workday.

When he arrived at the shop on Saturday morning, he was surprised Carolyn wasn't there. She was always there before him, even though he arrived early, eager to get started on the day.

He inserted the key she'd given him into the front door lock, and when he walked inside, he gave the bakery a quick survey. While the outside showed the most progress, he and Carolyn knew what he had done to get the inside ready for opening day next Saturday. The store was spotless, since Carolyn insisted on cleaning every evening before they left. Two empty glass cake stands stood on top of the larger display case, and a stack of small, handmade cards lay in the middle. He thumbed through them. Chocolate Whoopie Pies. Apple Cinnamon Muffins. Sugared Date Rolls. Orange Bliss Cake. He'd had breakfast with Thomas's family, but the cards were making his mouth water.

He set the cards back on the display case. Carolyn's tidiness and attention to detail reminded him of May.

A burst of guilt ran through him. He hadn't thought about May much this week, or the fact that he'd promised her he wouldn't be gone long. Now he found himself reluctant to leave Birch Creek, at least not until after Carolyn's opening day. *I'm sorry, May.*

The front door flew open, and Carolyn rushed inside. "I'm so sorry I'm late. I'm never late. But I overslept — I have *nee* idea why. I can't let this happen when I open the bakery —"

"It's okay." Atlee went to her, concerned that she was so frazzled. "Carolyn, you've been working hard, and you're tired. *Nee* one's going to blame you for oversleeping one time."

"You don't understand." Her chest heaved as she gasped for breath, walked to the worktable, and set her purse on it. She bent her head for a moment, as if she were praying, and then she looked at him, her harried expression replaced with a smile.

He couldn't help but smile back, even

though he was still concerned. There was something about Carolyn Yoder when she was happy. Her face shone, like the sun on a bright summer day. Her plump cheeks always turned a tiny bit rosy, which made her even prettier. But he knew her well enough to realize her positive disposition wasn't completely genuine — whether enhanced for him or for her own benefit, he wasn't sure. Yet he didn't hesitate to play along, especially if it made her feel better.

He stood by the table. "I have only a few things to finish up today," he said. "It shouldn't take more than an hour or so."

"Everything's done?" At his nod she let out a low whistle, which was as out of tune as her singing. He almost smiled again, but caught himself. "Even the landscaping?" she asked.

"*Ya.* You didn't see it when you came in?"

"*Nee.*" She moved past him and headed toward the door. "I was in too much of a hurry."

He followed her outside. When she stopped in front of the bakery and turned around, her hand went to her mouth. "Oh, Atlee."

Pleased by her reaction, he practically skipped toward her. "You like it?"

"*Ya.* It's beautiful."

"I've got a surprise for you." He grabbed the sign he'd left leaning against the side of the building. Holding it in both hands, he went to her, unable to contain his grin.

"Yoder's Bakery," she said, her pretty eyes growing wide.

"I ordered it while I was in Barton. I didn't think it would be here until next week, but they finished it early."

She touched the wooden sign. It was simple, but the name of the bakery was prominently displayed. There would be no doubt about this building's purpose now. "I . . . I don't know what to say." She looked up at him, her eyes shining.

He swallowed, surprised by the depth of his own emotion. It was as if the place was part his, too, in a way. "Do you want me to hang it up?"

"*Ya,*" she said with a laugh. "Please do!"

Atlee gathered the hardware he'd purchased for the sign and hung it from the eave to the right of the front door. "How does it look?" he said, turning around.

"Perfect." She pressed her knuckles under her chin. "Absolutely perfect."

When he finished the last of his work two hours later, he found Carolyn in her usual spot, behind the kitchen table, going through a box of index cards. From the food stains on them, he could tell they had recipes on them. "Find anything *gut*?"

"These were *mei grossmutter*'s, so they're all *gut.*" She shut the box and beamed at him.

"That's nice." For some reason he couldn't find the words to tell her he was finished. There was no reason for him to stop by now. For them to have lunch together. For him to walk her home. His job here was done, and nothing was keeping him from leaving right that minute. Yet not only wouldn't his mouth work, but his feet seemed stuck to the floor.

Her smile disappeared. "You're finished, then?"

He nodded. *"Ya."*

"Oh." She ran her finger across the table, something he noticed she did when she had something on her mind. "I didn't realize you'd be done so soon."

"There wasn't much left to do."

She looked up at him. "So I'm ready to open?"

"*Ya.* I think so." He looked toward the empty display cases in the front area. "Although you might want to put out some desserts to sell before you do."

"Already on the list." She patted her apron pocket. "That's for next week, though. I want *mei* customers to have the freshest baked goods possible."

"I know they'll be delicious." He looked down at the shiny table, and he found himself mimicking her earlier movement. He ran his finger across the edge of the cool steel.

"What are *yer* plans now?" Carolyn asked.

"I guess I'll go back to Fredericktown on Monday."

"I mean right now."

With a shrug he said, "I'll head back to Thomas's. He and the *buwe* are planting the fall vegetables today. I might give them a hand if they need it."

"Or . . ."

He glanced up and saw her sly grin.

"I could give you that baking lesson." She opened the recipe box and flipped through a few cards before pulling out one that was well-worn. "Peach fry pies happened to be *mei grossmutter*'s favorite."

"Interesting." He smiled back, glad for the chance to stay a little longer. "They happen to be mine too."

CHAPTER 7

"I have some lovely canned peaches from Benton's Orchard — they're a few miles outside of Birch Creek," Carolyn called to him as she headed for the pantry. She couldn't stop smiling. For the first time since she'd returned home, she had confidence that everything would turn out fine. Other than hiring an employee — the two English girls she interviewed for the cashier job weren't interested when she told them the pay — and baking what she needed for opening day and the week following, there wasn't anything to do. Thanks to Atlee. She hadn't expected the landscaping to be so perfect. And the sign . . . She let out a long sigh.

"Need some help?" she heard him call out from the kitchen.

"*Nee,* I'll be right there." She grabbed two cans of peaches and hurried out of the pantry. She turned on the deep fryer, and as she passed the oven, she turned it on, too, knowing she'd be baking something in the afternoon. It had behaved for her all week, and now she was certain she wouldn't have to worry about it.

She set the peaches on the counter and looked at Atlee. He was thin and wiry, something she noticed when he was inspecting her roof a few days ago. She also noticed he eagerly ate the lunches she prepared, which made her think about him spending his evenings alone, eating supper for one. The thought saddened her. She wanted him to have delicious hot meals every night.

"I already washed up." Atlee rubbed his hands together, but there was doubt in his eyes. "What do I do first?"

"You put this on." She handed him one of her aprons that had the least stains.

He eyed it dubiously. "I have to wear that?"

"*Ya.* You don't want to mess up *yer* clothes."

"In all *mei* years of working, I've never been worried about *mei* clothes."

"Well, you should, because food can stain." She held it out further. "Step number one."

After a moment's hesitation he took it and wrapped it around his slim body, circling the ties around his waist twice and then tying the top of the apron around his neck. "There," he muttered. "Now what?"

"I'll teach you how to make the dough."

Half an hour later, Carolyn wondered what she'd gotten herself into. For someone who was so nimble with his hands, Atlee was a disaster in the kitchen. Flour was everywhere, and he was attempting to roll out the dough for the fifth time. He mashed the rolling pin on the dough as if in battle, as if it were an enemy to be conquered.

"Nee, nee." She sighed and scooted in front of him, putting her hands over his. "Be gentle with it. If you overwork the dough, it will be tough." She didn't add that he'd already overworked the dough and then some, but she'd set a bit aside just in case. "See?" She moved the rolling pin back and forth. "Like this."

Carolyn was so focused on making sure the dough was rolled out correctly that she was surprised to hear Atlee clear his throat, then see him pull back his hands and move away.

"What's wrong?" When she looked up at him, her breath caught. He seemed different to her. They weren't as close as they'd been when they were rolling the dough together, but he also didn't move any farther away from her. His blue eyes took on an even darker hue, which made her stomach flutter.

"Carolyn," he said, his voice low and husky. That made not only her stomach but her heart seem to flip. "I think I've got the hang of it."

"Oh. Of course." She stepped away. "*Geh* ahead and finish." She put her hand on her chest, feeling the racing rhythm of her heart. Why was her pulse racing? Why couldn't she stop looking at him? Why didn't she care that he ripped another hole in the dough?

He set the pin aside. "I'm hopeless."

"*Nee*. You just need to practice." She moved past him, her pulse skipping again as her shoulder brushed against his chest. "I'll finish this up. Hand me the peaches, please."

"Sure thing."

She blew out a breath and pulled up the ruined dough. Setting it aside, she took her spare ball of dough and quickly rolled it out. Her pulse was slowing, but she could still remember the look in Atlee's eyes when their gazes met.

"Here you *geh*." He set the peaches next to her.

She nodded, unable to look at him, afraid he could hear her heart pounding. "I think you can handle this part," she said, taking a round cookie cutter and cutting the flattened dough into circles. "Just put a spoonful of peaches in the center of each circle."

"Got it."

To her relief, he managed that fine. Then she showed him how to fold each pie and crimp the edges. By the time the pies were ready to be dipped into the hot frying oil, she was back to her normal self. Thank goodness. She felt like a fool for even experiencing what had to be a lapse in . . . in something. What that was exactly, she didn't know.

"The oil must be at 400 degrees," she said, now sounding professional as she carried the plate of raw pies to the stove. She dropped a tiny piece of leftover dough into the oil. It immediately sizzled. "Perfect." She picked up the basket strainer by its long handle and put one of the pies in the oil. "Lay it in gently," she said before handing him the strainer.

"Gently," he repeated.

To her delight he managed to put three more pies into the fryer without mishap. "After a little while you'll turn them," she said.

"When?"

"When they're ready to be turned."

"And when is that?"

"Three or four minutes. I usually know by looking." She frowned. He might have thought he was failing as a student, but maybe she was failing as a teacher.

"All right."

They stood there, watching the fry pies float in the oil. Carolyn thought she should say something, but Atlee kept his concentration on the fryer. "Now?" he said after what seemed an eternity.

"*Ya.* Flip one over and see if it's brown on the other side."

He did, and it was perfect. He turned to her and grinned. "They smell delicious."

Again, her heartbeat accelerated. Oh, this wasn't good. She was out of her depth here. She didn't want to feel like this with a man who was still grieving his late wife. He'd mentioned May only in passing, but she had seen the love in his eyes and heard the tenderness in his voice when he did. Besides, he was going back to Fredericktown on Monday. She wouldn't see him again.

That brought her to her senses. She focused on the pies, and when they were all done and draining on a wire rack, she showed him how to sprinkle them with powdered sugar. "There. Now they're ready."

"That wasn't so bad." He turned to her.

"Actually, it was kind of fun."

She thought so, too, but she wouldn't dwell on that. She grabbed some wax paper, wrapped a hot pie in it, and handed it to him. "Here. Enjoy. Just don't burn *yer* tongue."

"I appreciate the warning." He took a small bite, and his eyes grew wide.

"Best ones you ever had?"

"Definitely. I'm glad I didn't ruin them."

She picked off the corner of a pie and put it in her mouth. The crust was flaky, which wouldn't have been the case if she hadn't used fresh dough.

"I'll help you clean up," he said.

The thought of standing close to him while they washed dishes had her shaking her head. She couldn't do that, not when she was finally on an even keel. "I'll get it. I'm going to make another mess anyway."

"You sure?"

"Ya."

"Then I guess I'll head to Thomas's. Unless you need something else."

Surely he wasn't stalling. "*Nee.* You've done enough for me."

"I haven't done that much."

He was understating his contribution, and she wasn't surprised. *I'm going to miss him.* Quickly, she grabbed another pie and wrapped it in wax paper. "One for the road."

He looked at the pie in his hand. *"Danki."* He lifted his gaze to hers. "I know we'll see each other at church tomorrow, but in case we don't get a chance to talk . . ." He glanced down at his shoes before looking at her again. "It was a pleasure to meet you, Carolyn."

"Same here," she said softly.

He nodded, then turned and left.

When he was gone, the bakery — and her heart — seemed emptier than it ever had.

CHAPTER 8

Carolyn traveled with Freemont and his family to church the next morning. They took two buggies, the adults in one and the three boys in the other. Once they arrived, she still held back, politely greeting everyone but not being too open or friendly. Yet for the first time she wished things were different. She wished she hadn't disappointed the people she left behind. She wanted to feel a part of this town that had changed so much. Maybe she would after her bakery opened and she proved Emmanuel wrong.

She went inside the barn and took a seat right before the service started. She looked over at the other side of the church where the men sat and saw Thomas Bontrager. Thomas's sons surrounded him. They ranged from preschool to teenager, and they had become good friends with her nephews. Then she saw Atlee. Her heart warmed again, but her mind splashed cold water on

502

it as she reminded herself he was leaving tomorrow. She pulled her gaze from him and focused on the service.

When church was over, she tried not to look for Atlee and stayed to the side as everyone visited. They had said their good-byes yesterday, in the privacy of the bakery. She would rather have done it there than here among the rest of the community. Yet she couldn't help sneaking a few glances around to see where he was.

"I hear you're opening *yer* bakery next week." Cevilla Schlabach approached her, leaning on her cane as she walked. She was more than eighty years old, but she had a youthful soul. "I can't wait to taste *yer* bread twists. Mary says they're the first treats I should try."

Carolyn smiled. "I'll make sure to save you some."

Leaning closer, Cevilla said, "I also heard you've been spending some time with Atlee Shetler."

Her cheeks grew hot. Was she the subject of gossip now?

"Oh, don't worry. *Nee* one's talking about it. Not like you think." She nodded and gestured behind Carolyn. "There's that charming young *mann* now."

Carolyn had to resist turning around. She

also had to resist chuckling. Atlee wasn't exactly young, but in Cevilla's eyes, she guessed, everyone was.

"Ignoring him, I see." Cevilla gave her a crafty smile.

"I'm not ignoring anyone," she snapped. Then she apologized. "That was uncalled for."

Cevilla's expression turned from crafty to serious. "It's difficult to do things all by *yerself.* Makes a person tired and lonely. *Gut* thing you've at least had Atlee and *yer bruder* to help you."

"*Ya,*" she said softly. "*Gut* thing."

Cevilla put her hand on Carolyn's arm. "Don't fight it too long." She patted her sleeve, then said, "Oh, there's Joanna Byler. She's another excellent cook. The two of you should swap recipes." With steps slowed by age, she started toward the woman.

Carolyn saw Joanna talking with her sisters, Abigail and Sadie. The three of them had been young girls when Carolyn left, and now they were all married and had children.

She set those thoughts aside as she pondered Cevilla's words. What had the woman meant? What was she fighting? Nothing, as far as she could tell. Everything was finally on track.

■ ■ ■ ■

Atlee took a walk after an early supper. His mind was troubled, and it hadn't been focused on the service today, which also bothered him. No, he'd been thinking about Carolyn. It had taken everything in his power to keep from seeking her out at church, even though they had parted ways at the bakery. Still, he wanted to see her again, and that was a problem.

He was so confused. Inside he was warring with guilt over his attraction to Carolyn and his devotion to May's memory. He'd never been so conflicted. Everything in his life had been straightforward — except when May died. And even then, after he settled into his grief, his life was uncomplicated. But the past year he'd changed. Something had shifted inside him, and that shift was continuing, although this time he knew the catalyst.

He had to ignore those feelings. That would be easy enough once he was back in Fredericktown. Then he could return to his normal life — a life that, though he'd been restless and lonely, unexpectedly didn't appeal to him at all anymore.

He found himself in front of Freemont's

home. That wasn't surprising considering the short distance between the houses. The fact that he stopped was. Even more so, the fact that he was considering paying Carolyn another visit, although he didn't have a reason to, befuddled him. *See how confused I am, Lord?* Mei *thoughts are more jumbled than a thousand-piece jigsaw puzzle.*

He should just go back to the Bontragers'. He could take a nap. Or even better, pray for clarity. He could do a number of things on a Sunday evening besides visit Carolyn Yoder.

But none of them appealed to him more.

Atlee's palms grew damp as he approached the front door. He wiped them on the thighs of his broadfall pants. He also took off his hat and smoothed his hair before replacing the hat on his head and knocking on the door.

Freemont answered. They'd met at church that morning, and Atlee had immediately liked him. "Hello, Atlee. What brings you by?"

"Uh . . ." He cleared his throat. "I was wondering, if, um . . ."

"Carolyn is home?"

Atlee nodded, wondering how Freemont knew he was going to ask about her. Had Carolyn said something to her brother about him? The idea that she might be mentioning him to her family made him feel warm inside.

"She went for a walk. She usually does on Sunday afternoons, and she's not back yet."

"Ah. Sorry I missed her, then."

Freemont's expression remained blank. "Should I tell her you stopped by?"

He paused. "*Nee,* that's fine."

"All right. We'll see you around, then."

"Actually, I'm leaving tomorrow."

"I see. Traveling mercies, then. Hopefully you'll come back and visit soon."

Atlee nodded and left. Would he be back? Other than visiting the Bontragers, he wouldn't have a reason. *Except for Carolyn.*

He went back to Thomas's, but then he decided to keep going. He knew Carolyn wasn't at the bakery since it was Sunday, but he had to look at it again. Sear it in his memory. Remember the place and the woman who had brought him back to life.

When he arrived, though, the front door was open. Odd. His heartbeat sped up. Maybe she had stopped by too. He could see her for the last time. He went to the closed screen door. "Carolyn?" he said, opening the door and walking inside, expecting to see her in the kitchen where she always was.

But what he saw froze his blood.

CHAPTER 9

Ruined. It's all ruined.

Carolyn knelt in the middle of her bakery's outer room, too shocked to move.

Devastation surrounded her. She'd decided to take her usual Sunday afternoon walk, knowing the exercise combined with nature always fed her soul. But as she passed by the bakery, she couldn't keep herself from stopping in front of it. She marveled at Atlee's handiwork, still touched by the sign. That's when she noticed the inside door was open. Panicked, she went in, and what she found turned her dream to dust.

Graffiti had been sprayed on every wall. The glass display cases were smashed. The counter was also covered in graffiti, some of it vile. The adding machine was broken, pieces strewn on the floor. The stainless-steel table was upended, and someone had marked up all the counters with a knife.

Even the small label cards she'd carefully written by hand were torn and scattered. She didn't dare go into the kitchen. She knew she would find much of the same, and she couldn't face that right now.

"Carolyn."

She didn't turn around at the deep, gentle voice coming from behind her. Atlee. What was he doing here? The question sat in the back of her mind, but she couldn't bring herself to care why. She was numb. She had failed. There was no coming back from this, no proving herself to the community. No showing Emmanuel Troyer, even though he wasn't here, that she had made something of herself. That he hadn't broken her. She'd ended up broken anyway.

She sensed Atlee kneeling beside her. Felt his hand on her shoulder. Strong. Stable. Just like him. Still, she couldn't look at him.

"What happened?" he asked.

"I don't know." Her throat felt thick, as if she had a bread twist stuck in it.

"Did you call the police?"

She shrugged. *"Nee."*

"You need to do that, Carolyn."

"Doesn't matter." She pushed away his hand and stood. *"Nix* matters anymore."

"You're wrong about that." He stood as well and stepped in front of her. She looked up at him. "This" — he gestured to the devastation around them — "matters very much. You put *yer* heart and soul into this place. We're not going to let all that effort *geh* to waste."

"We? There is *nee* we, Atlee." She poured her frustration out on him. "I've always said that. I will succeed . . . and fail" — she choked on the last word — "on *mei* own. I don't need anyone . . . especially you."

He regarded her for a moment, and she expected a flash of anger in his eyes. Instead he said, "I know you're upset, so I'm not taking those words to heart. I know what it's like to lose something important to you. Something you love."

His words brought her out of her fury, her heart pinching with guilt. "Atlee, this doesn't compare to May —"

"*Nee,* it doesn't. You can bring *yer* business back. May . . ." He swallowed, his Adam's apple bobbing. "The point is you're hurting. This is a loss to you. I'm just letting you know I understand how you feel. That you don't need anyone, or want anyone. You believe you must exist on *yer* own, because you can't be hurt again. You wouldn't survive it. But that only works for a little while, and if you're not careful, you'll end up empty inside. You'll wake up every morning wondering why you're still here."

Somehow the conversation had taken an unexpected turn. "Atlee, I'm sorry."

"You can't keep pushing people away, Carolyn. Especially when you're grieving. We're not meant to get through this life alone. I think I'm finally understanding that." He took a step back. "I'll be here when you need me, Carolyn. That's a promise."

She watched him leave the bakery — or what used to be the bakery. She tried to absorb his words, to understand what he had realized, but for herself. She didn't have to be alone.

Dread pooled inside as she went into the kitchen. As she'd suspected, it was in even worse shape. In a daze, she went to the phone shanty. Her fingers shook as she dialed nine-one-one. "Hello," she said when dispatch answered. She gripped the receiver. "I need your help."

Atlee realized he'd walked past Thomas's house, almost to Freemont's. Should he tell Carolyn's brother what happened? Of course, he would find out soon enough, and Carolyn said she wanted to be left alone. But he couldn't walk away. Not from this. Not from Carolyn.

He looked up at the sky. *I want to be true to May's memory. But I can't keep living this way.* He closed his eyes. *Show me what to do, Lord.*

After she called the police, Carolyn went back inside and started sweeping up broken glass. She was working on Sunday, but surely God would understand that she needed to get all the shards of glass off the floor before someone was hurt. She let out a bitter sound. No one would be here to hurt themselves. She wasn't opening the bakery next week . . . or ever.

She got a dustpan. When she came back, she saw her brother standing in the front doorway. Of course. She should have known Atlee would tell him. She turned her back to him as she swept the glass pieces into the dustpan.

Freemont let out a long whistle, and unlike hers, his was on key. "*Gut* grief. What a mess."

She whirled around. "Is that all you have to say?"

He put his hands into his pockets. "What else do you want me to say?"

Sometimes she didn't understand her brother. He could be as emotionless as a stone, but she knew his heart was made of pure gold. "You don't have to be here. The police are on their way."

"You called them?"

"*Ya,* I did."

"Well, that's a surprise. I figured you would try to find the people who did this *yerself.*"

"I'm not a detective, and you don't have to be sarcastic."

Freemont went to her. "Carolyn, I'm sorry."

The tenderness in his voice made her look at him. She and her brother usually got along well, and as they were growing up they were good friends, even though they had the usual sibling spats. Since it was just the two of them, they were kind of a team too. Then he got married and they moved to Birch Creek. That's when her life fell apart. The years of distance were keenly felt now that she was standing in the middle of her destroyed bakery. "*Danki* for *yer* concern."

"I mean it. Why are you being so stubborn about accepting help? About being a part of this community again?" He paused. "Is this about Emmanuel?"

Her jaw dropped. "What do you know about Emmanuel?"

Storm clouds gathered in Freemont's

514

eyes. "I learned a lot about that *mann,* especially after he left the district. And I also know he was the reason you left."

Carolyn stared at him. "Who told you that?"

"I saw you going into his *haus* that day. I was driving past, by coincidence. I knew you would only *geh* see him under duress since you two didn't see eye-to-eye on a lot of things. I was concerned, and Rhoda let me in. I waited in the living room while you were in his office. When Rhoda went to get *kaffee,* I got up and listened near the doorway to hear what you were talking about."

"You eavesdropped?"

"I was worried." He swallowed. "I couldn't make out anything, but I knew when something had happened. You were so angry you stormed out of his office and didn't even see me — or recognize my horse and buggy. You left for Nappanee the next morning."

Carolyn thought back to that day. She'd been doing more of that this week than she had in the past eighteen years. All she saw that day was red fury at Emmanuel's threat and insults. "If you knew something was wrong, why didn't you say anything?"

"Believe me, I've asked myself that same question over the years." He looked at the glass-strewn floor, then back at her. "But I also thought it might be for the best. You were chafing under him, Carolyn. We all knew that, just like we knew you were destined for something different." He took a step toward her. "Things here have changed now. You had to have noticed that since you came back."

She had, but it didn't change anything for her. She'd failed.

He put his hand on her shoulder and gently turned her to face him. "Carolyn, you don't have to prove anything to anyone here. I'm sure whatever Emmanuel said to you that day wasn't true. And maybe I should have gone after you, but I think you did the right thing by leaving. You escaped some bad things happening here. But when you said you would finally come back, I was so happy. I've missed *mei schwester.*" His eyes turned glassy. "You have to let me in. You have to let other people care about you. *Nee* one will ever hurt you like that again."

"How do you know that?" she said, her voice trembling.

"Because we care about you. Some of us even love you, believe it or not. I wish you could see that. I know how much you love this bakery and want to see it succeed. I want to help you succeed. So does *mei fami-*

lye and the rest of the *familyes* here in Birch Creek, even the ones you don't know very well yet. We need to do this together. Please let us."

Carolyn's heart started to break, the ice around it thawing. Tears flowed down her cheeks. "I don't know how to accept help," she said. "I've done everything on *mei* own for so long."

"Then we'll show you. I'll send out word, and everyone who's available to help this week will come and get this place back in shape so you'll be able to open for business. I'll also talk to the elders about using some money from the community fund to help you replace what can't be repaired."

"It can't be done," she whispered. "It's too much."

"Not for us. And not for God." He looked at her. "Now, I'll stay with you until the police have come and gone. Then come home with me. Let's figure all this out together."

CHAPTER 10

Carolyn dragged herself to the bakery Monday morning. When a tall, serious policeman arrived the evening before, he explained there had been a rash of vandalism in Barton and that the culprits were expanding to the small communities around the city. "We'll be on the lookout, but make sure your doors are locked," the officer said.

"I lock the bakery every time I leave," she told him.

He gave her a sympathetic look. "I don't know what to tell you, other than we're on the trail of these people. Since their aim is to destroy and not steal, we think they're a group of high school kids. As soon as we catch them, you can bet you'll get restitution."

"That doesn't matter," Freemont said.

Carolyn agreed. She didn't want revenge or restitution. And now she wasn't sure she even wanted the bakery anymore. Getting it ready seemed like too much work to do over, and even though she'd agreed to accept help, she didn't expect everyone to drop what they were doing — especially with the way she'd been so distant since she came back.

Then there was Atlee. He said he'd be there for her, but how could he when he was leaving today? Her heart sank. She'd lost everything in the span of one day. Not that she ever had Atlee. But she was missing him already.

She opened the front door, and to her surprise her nephews and brother were already at work. Freemont had a key too. "I thought you were out on the farm," she said.

"The animals are fine," Seth said.

"We fed them," Judah added.

"*Daed* says we can work in the fields this afternoon," Ira explained.

She looked at Freemont, who gave her one of his rare smiles before he went back to dismantling the ruined display cases. In the kitchen, she set her lunch cooler on a worktable, then picked up a rag and filled a bucket with water and dish soap to start wiping the graffiti off the walls. Fortunately, whatever the vandals used was water soluble and came off with a little scrubbing.

The bell above her front door rang, and

to her shock people from the community came pouring in with buckets, rags, brooms, and mops. Several men had tool belts slung around their waists. Without a word other than hello, they set to work.

As she looked at her family and community busy fixing what someone else had destroyed, she realized Emmanuel hadn't broken her spirit. Neither had the vandals. She hadn't lost everything, because even if she couldn't get the bakery up and running, she had this — her family and the people of this community. Even Cevilla had come. She was sitting in the corner directing people at various jobs.

Most important, she realized her faith had been misplaced. She'd wanted God to do her bidding — to make her bakery a success. But that was for her own pride, the pride that had let Emmanuel's hateful words sink deep into her soul. Instead of giving her what she wanted, God was giving her what she needed. Community. Humility. Cooperation. She'd been too self-absorbed to see it sooner. It was so overwhelming that Carolyn had to get some fresh air.

She walked out the back door of the bakery. Without warning, her thoughts turned to the last day she'd seen Emmanuel.

He had summoned her for another talking-to, although she had no idea which picky *Ordnung* rule she'd violated this time.

"Do you really think I can let you continue in yer *rebellious ways?"*

Carolyn threaded her fingers together, her mouth and throat feeling like cotton. "I said I was sorry."

"A weak apology." Emmanuel sat down in his chair and looked up at her. Even though he was seated and she was standing, she still felt like he was looming over her. "If you were truly sorry, you wouldn't continue to disobey God's rules."

*"*Yer *rules, you mean."*

His right brow lifted, the only visible sign that he had heard her. "They are one and the same."

They weren't, but she was already in enough trouble. She didn't need to dig herself into a deeper hole. She gritted her teeth as she looked down at her black tennis shoes.

Emmanuel folded his hands over his abdomen. "You were told not to work for non-Amish businesses."

She glanced up. "But how else am I going to learn how to run mei *own bakery?"*

He scoffed. "You won't. Birch Creek doesn't need a bakery. It will invite outsiders to our community."

"I don't see the problem with that. Birch Creek has to grow eventually."

His eyes turned dark. "The future of mei community is none of yer concern."

Carolyn didn't miss the use of the word mei. "Yer community?"

Emmanuel rose from his chair. "You will quit yer job in Barton. You will stay at home, learning how to care for a haus and familye, until you marry."

She lifted her chin. "What if I don't want to marry?"

"Oh. You will get married. I will make sure of it."

"And I'm sure I will have mei own business." Although she was shaking inside, she was angry enough to lash out at him. "And if I marry, it will be to a mann I love."

To her surprise he laughed. "Do you really think you'll be successful in any endeavor after yer disrespect today? Everyone already knows you're full of trouble. You'll be lucky to have a friend, much less anything else."

"Is that a threat?"

"Nee, Carolyn." He moved closer to her and said in a low voice, "It's a promise."

She'd always blamed Emmanuel for everything, and she'd harbored a grudge against him for so long. But while she knew in her heart he'd been wrong, she hadn't handled herself well either. She'd been prideful even then, more worried about her own goals and dreams than anything or anybody else. It had taken her a long time to understand what God had been trying to show her. Emmanuel hadn't been standing in her way. She had.

"Oh, Lord, forgive me." She looked up at the sky, the clouds hazy through the sheen of her tears. "Forgive *mei* pride and *mei* hardened heart. Even though I thought I lost everything . . . you are still merciful to me." She hung her head, tears slipping down her cheeks.

"He has a way of surprising us, doesn't he?"

She looked up to see Atlee walking toward her. She wiped her cheeks. "I thought you went back to Fredericktown."

"I was going to." He moved closer and looked down at her. "But someone needed me. Yesterday I said I'd be here when you needed me, Carolyn. Remember? That was a promise."

She lifted her trembling chin. "I never said I needed you." But her words were weak. She was weak, and from now on she would turn to God for strength.

He gave her a half-grin. "You didn't have to."

Without thinking, she fell into his arms and breathed out a sigh when he held her close. When she realized what she'd done, she pulled away. "I'm sorry." She could barely look at him. "I shouldn't have done that."

"It's okay. I didn't mind."

"Still, it wasn't right. I'm not in *mei* right mind, obviously." The words started spilling out, as they did when she was embarrassed. "So much has happened, I'm just over-whelmed and not thinking straight —"

"Carolyn. It's okay."

She looked up at him, nearly drowning in the kindness she saw in his eyes. There was also something else, something that gave her heart hope. "What about May?" she whispered.

He grew serious. "I'll always love her."

The hope deflated a bit. "I know." His response wasn't a surprise. And although she understood, and respected him all the more for his loyalty, she felt like a fool for wishing he also felt something else. Some-thing for her.

"But I have to move on." He glanced at the ground before facing her. "I've known it for a long time. What I didn't understand was how I was going to do it. I think I'm starting to figure it out, though."

She shivered, but she forced herself not to jump to any conclusions. "You have?"

He nodded. "I can't keep living in the past, even if it's easier in some ways. And I'll admit I'm a little scared of the future. But you've inspired me, Carolyn. You took *yer* dream and made it a reality."

"Look how that turned out."

"But you're here today. And you did what you had to do — you accepted help." His expression grew soft. "I have to take that first step to living the rest of *mei* life too. When you asked me if someone was waiting for me back home, I realized there's nothing there for me except May's memory." He put his hand over his heart. "And I can keep her close to me here."

"That's . . . nice." And it was. Beautiful, actually. "She was a lucky woman."

"I was a lucky man." He tilted his head. "Still am, I hope." He moved closer to her. "I like you, Carolyn. It feels rusty to say that. But it also feels right."

"I . . . like you." It didn't feel rusty to her at all. It felt new and exciting.

"But I'm asking for patience. I'm struggling with guilt over May. I have to admit that. I need to work out some feelings before I can come back for *mei* next baking lesson."

She couldn't believe he was bringing up baking at a time like this. Yet it was the perfect thing for him to say. "I guess you're holding me to *mei* word, then?"

He nodded. "And you can hold me to mine. As soon as I can, I'll be back. By then you'll have the bakery up and running, and you can teach me all *yer* baking secrets."

She laughed, the tension from the last few months finally releasing. She held out her hand to him. "Consider it done."

He gathered her in his arms and leaned his chin on the top of her white *kapp.* "Consider it done."

EPILOGUE

Six months later

Carolyn turned the sign on the clear bakery door from Open to Closed. Another great day. She had sold out of her bread twists and wheat rolls, and she had only grape jelly fry pies left. She made a note to bake more twists, rolls, and fry pies tomorrow morning and let Mandy and Leah, her two employees — a mother and daughter — handle sales.

Several women had offered to help her run the store, but as the bakery was being repaired, Mandy and her daughter answered the ad. They weren't put off by the low pay. "We need the work," they said. "We'll do anything." Carolyn had been happy to hire them.

Normally she would tidy up the store and head home to her house behind Freemont's. But not today. She left the back door unlocked and went to the pantry. The police had caught the vandals several months ago, and as the officer had predicted, they paid her restitution, which she promptly gave to Freemont for the community fund. Her business had thrived so well that she didn't need the money.

"Carolyn?"

She smiled as she took the cinnamon off the shelves. Tonight's lesson would be cinnamon rolls, at Atlee's request. He was waiting for her by the worktable, an easy smile on his face. She could tell he'd showered, which she would have expected him to do at the end of his workday as a cabinetmaker in Barton. He'd secured his job shortly after he returned to Birch Creek — to stay. He was also building a home down the road from Freemont. He kept busy, but he always had time for their lessons.

Carolyn set the cinnamon next to the other ingredients. "Ready?"

"In a minute." He took her hand and led her back into the pantry, where the sensor lights came back on, and closed the door.

"What are you doing?" she asked.

"This." He took her face in his hands and gently kissed her. When he pulled away, he had the biggest smile she'd ever seen.

"What was that for?" She pressed her hand against her heart, feeling it thrum beneath her fingers.

"I've been waiting to do that for a long time." His grin faded. "And you've been very patient with me."

"You've made it easy." And he had. Lately she'd felt a kind of sizzle between them, but they had taken their friendship very slow. They'd been getting to know each other and their histories. He learned about her time in Nappanee, and she learned about May. Two months ago, he surprised her by shaving off his beard.

"I don't want to wait anymore," he said.

"For what?"

"Let's get married. Right after Christmas."

"But that's two weeks away!"

He laughed. *"Yer bruder* is the bishop. I'm sure he'll find time to marry off his *schwester."*

"Humph." But she couldn't stop smiling. She leaned against him, sighing as he put his arms around her.

"I love you, Carolyn," he whispered. "I never thought I'd love anyone again."

"I love you too." Months ago, she couldn't imagine why she'd come back to Birch Creek. The community had been filled with painful memories. But she had let those go. She was ready to build something new — not just her bakery, but with Atlee. With *love.*

529

DISCUSSION QUESTIONS

1. Carolyn let her past get in the way of letting others help her. Has there ever been a time in your life when you've rejected help? What would you do differently now?
2. Like Carolyn, Atlee had difficulty moving beyond his past. What advice would you give him to help him move past his grief?
3. Carolyn had to learn to surrender her pride, and it took losing the most important things in her life in order to get to that point. Why is pride so difficult to overcome? What are some ways we can surrender our pride to God?
4. Carolyn found love when she least expected. Has God ever surprised you with something you didn't expect, but discovered you needed?

ACKNOWLEDGMENTS

I'm blessed to have the best team of editors in the business helping me shape and refine my stories. Thank you to Becky Monds and Jean Bloom for their hard work on this novella. And as always, thank you, dear reader friend, for visiting Birch Creek with me.

ABOUT THE AUTHORS

Amy Clipston is the award-winning and bestselling author of the Kauffman Amish Bakery, Hearts of Lancaster Grand Hotel, Amish Heirloom, and Amish Homestead series. Her novels have hit multiple bestseller lists including CBD, CBA, and ECPA. Amy holds a degree in communications from Virginia Wesleyan University and works full-time for the City of Charlotte, North Carolina. Amy lives in North Carolina with her husband, mother, two sons, and three spoiled rotten cats.

Visit her online at AmyClipston.com
Facebook: AmyClipstonBooks
Twitter: @AmyClipston

Beth Wiseman is the award-winning and bestselling author of the Daughters of the Promise, Land of Canaan, and Amish Secrets series, as well as novellas that have been included in many bestselling collections such as *An Amish Year* and *An Amish Garden.*

Visit her online at BethWiseman.com
Facebook: AuthorBethWiseman
Twitter: @BethWiseman

Shelley Shepard Gray is a *New York Times* and *USA Today* bestselling author, a finalist for the American Christian Fiction Writers prestigious Carol Award, and a two-time HOLT Medallion winner. She lives in southern Ohio, where she writes full-time, bakes too much, and can often be found walking her dachshunds on her town's bike trail.

Visit her online at ShelleyShepardGray.com
Facebook: ShelleyShepardGray
Twitter: @ShelleySGray

Kathleen Fuller is the author of several bestselling novels, including the Hearts of Middlefield novels, the Middlefield Family novels, the Amish of Birch Creek series, and the Amish Letters series as well as a middle-grade Amish series, the Mysteries of Middlefield.

Visit her online at KathleenFuller.com
Twitter: @TheKatJam
Facebook: Kathleen Fuller